About the Authors

Sharon Kendrick started story-telling at the age of eleven and has never stopped. She likes to write fast-paced, feel-good romances with heroes who are so sexy they'll make your toes curl! She lives in the beautiful city of Winchester – where she can see the cathedral from her window (when standing on tip-toe!). She has two children, Celia and Patrick and her passions include music, books, cooking and eating – and drifting into daydreams while working out new plots.

Cathy Williams is a great believer in the power of perseverance as she had never written anything before her writing career, and from the starting point of zero has now fulfilled her ambition to pursue this most enjoyable of careers. She would encourage any would-be writer to have faith and go for it! She derives inspiration from the tropical island of Trinidad and from the peaceful countryside of middle England. Cathy lives in Warwickshire her family.

Sarah M. Anderson won RT Reviewer's Choice 2012 Desire of the Year for *A Man of Privilege*. *The Nanny Plan* was a 2016 *RITA®* winner for Contemporary Romance: Short. Find out more about Sarah's love of cowboys at www.sarahmanderson.com

Secrets and Seduction

For three fabulous writers who helped with the
Australian detail in my 100th book,
A Royal Vow of Convenience.
Helene Young and Margareta Young,
for the inspiration and the insight—
and Rachael Johns, for the Tim-Tams!

SECRETS OF A BILLIONAIRE'S MISTRESS

SHARON KENDRICK

MILLS & BOON
HEROES
At Your Service

Experience all the excitement of a gripping thriller, with an intense romance at its heart. Resourceful, true-to-life women and strong, fearless men face danger and desire – a killer combination!

MILLS & BOON

MODERN

Power and Passion

Prepare to be swept off your feet by sophisticated, sexy and seductive heroes, in some of the world's most glamourous and romantic locations, where power and passion collide.

JOIN US ON SOCIAL MEDIA!

Stay up to date with our latest releases, author
news and gossip, special offers and discounts, and
all the behind-the-scenes action
from Mills & Boon...

 millsandboon

 millsandboonuk

 millsandboon

might just be true love...

MILLS & BOON

THE HEART OF ROMANCE

A ROMANCE FOR EVERY READER

MODERN

Prepare to be swept off your feet by sophisticated, sexy and seductive heroes, in some of the world's most glamourous and romantic locations, where power and passion collide.

HISTORICAL

Escape with historical heroes from time gone by. Whether your passion is for wicked Regency Rakes, muscled Vikings or rugged Highlanders, awake the romance of the past.

MEDICAL

Set your pulse racing with dedicated, delectable doctors in the high-pressure world of medicine, where emotions run high and passion, comfort an love are the best medicine.

True Love

Celebrate true love with tender stories of heartfelt romance, from the rush of falling in love to the joy a new baby can bring, and a focus on the emotional heart of a relationship.

Desire

Indulge in secrets and scandal, intense drama and plenty of sizzling hot action with powerful and passionate heroes who have it all: wealth, status, good looks...everything but the right woman.

HEROES

Experience all the excitement of a gripping thriller, with an intense romance at its heart. Resourceful, true-to-life women and strong, fearless men face danger and desire - a killer combination!

To see which titles are coming soon, please visit

millsandboon.co.uk/nextmonth

Secrets and Seduction:
All or Nothing

SHARON KENDRICK

CATHY WILLIAMS

SARAH M. ANDERSON

MILLS & BOON

First Published in Great Britain 2022
By Mills & Boon, an imprint of HarperCollins*Publishers*, Ltd
1 London Bridge Street, London, SE1 9GF

www.harpercollins.co.uk

HarperCollins*Publishers*
1st Floor, Watermarque Building,
Ringsend Road, Dublin 4, Ireland

SECRETS AND SEDUCTION: ALL OR NOTHING © 2022 Harlequin Books S.A.

Secrets of a Billionaire's Mistress © 2017 Sharon Kendrick
A Pawn in the Playboy's Game © 2015 Cathy Williams
Seduction on His Terms © 2019 Sarah M. Anderson

ISBN: 978-0-263-30442-8

MIX
Paper from
responsible sources
FSC™ C007454

This book is produced from independently certified FSC™ paper
to ensure responsible forest management.

For more information visit: www.harpercollins.co.uk/green

Printed and Bound in Spain using 100% Renewable electricity at
CPI Black Print, Barcelona

CHAPTER ONE

RENZO SABATINI WAS unbuttoning his shirt when the doorbell rang. He felt the beat of expectation. The familiar tug of heat to his groin. He was half-tempted to pull the shirt from his shoulders so Darcy could slide her fingers over his skin, closely followed by those inventive lips of hers. The soft lick of her tongue could help him forget what lay ahead. He thought about Tuscany and the closing of a chapter. About the way some memories could still be raw even when so many years had passed and maybe that was why he never really stopped to think about them.

But why concentrate on darkness when Darcy was all sunshine and light? And why rush at sex when they had the whole night ahead—a smorgasbord of sensuality which he could enjoy at his leisure with his latest and most unexpected lover? A woman who demanded nothing other than that he satisfy her—something which was easy since he had only to touch her pale skin to grow so hard that it hurt. His mouth dried. Four months in and he was as bewitched by her as he had been from the start.

In many ways he was astonished it had continued this long when their two worlds were so different. She was not his usual type of woman and he was very definitely not her type of man. He was into clean lines and minimalism, while Darcy was all voluptuous curves and lingerie which could barely contain her abundant flesh. His mouth curved into a hard smile. In reality it should never have lasted beyond one night but her tight body had been difficult to walk away from. It still was.

The doorbell rang again and the glance he shot at his wristwatch was touched with irritation. Was she daring to be *impatient* when she wasn't supposed to be here for another half hour? Surely she knew the rules by now...that she was expected to fit around his schedule, rather than the other way round?

Barefooted, he walked through the spacious rooms of his Belgravia apartment, pulling open the front door to see Darcy Denton standing there—small of stature and impossible to ignore—her magnificent curls misted with rain and tugged back into a ponytail so that only the bright red colour was on show. She wore a light raincoat, tightly belted to emphasise her tiny waist, but underneath she was still in her waitress's uniform because she lived on the other side of London, an area Renzo had never visited—and he was perfectly content for it to stay that way. They'd established very quickly that if she went home after her shift to change, it wasted several hours—even if he sent his car to collect her. And Renzo was a busy man with an architectural practice which spanned several continents. His time was too precious to waste, which was why she always came straight from work with her overnight bag—though that was a largely unnecessary detail since she was rarely anything other than naked when she was with him.

He stared down into her green eyes, which glittered like emeralds in porcelain-pale skin and, as always, his blood began to fizz with expectation and lust. 'You're early,' he observed softly. 'Did you time your visit especially because you knew I'd be undressing?'

Darcy answered him with a tight smile as he opened the door to let her in. She was cold and she was wet and it had been the most awful day. A customer had spilt tea over her uniform. Then a child had been sick. She'd looked out the window at the end of her shift to discover that the rain had started and someone must have taken her umbrella. And Renzo Sabatini was standing there in the warmth of his palatial apartment, looking glowing and delectable— making the assumption that she had nothing better to do than to time her visits just so she would find him half-naked. Could she ever have met a man more arrogant?

Yet she'd known what she was letting herself in for when she'd started this crazy affair. When she'd fought a silent battle against everything she'd known to be wrong. Because powerful men who dallied with waitresses only wanted one thing, didn't they?

She'd lost that particular battle and ended up in Renzo's king-size bed—but nobody could say that her eyes hadn't been open at the time. Well, some of the time at least—the rest of the time they'd fluttered to a quivering close as he had thrust deeply inside her until she was sobbing with pleasure. After resisting him as hard as she could, she'd decided to resist no more. Or maybe the truth was that she hadn't been able to stop herself from falling into his arms. He'd kissed her and that had been it. She hadn't known that a kiss could make you feel that way. She hadn't realised that desire could make you feel as if you were floating. Or flying. She'd surrendered her virginity to him and, after his shocked reaction to discovering he was her first lover, he had introduced her to more pleasure than she'd thought possible, though in a life spectacularly short on the pleasure front that wouldn't have been difficult, would it?

For a while things had been fine. More than fine. She spent the night with him whenever he was in the country and had a space in his diary—and sometimes she spent the following day there, too. He cooked her eggs and played her music she'd never heard before— dreamy stuff featuring lots of violins—while he pored over the fabulously intricate drawings which would one day be transformed into the glittering and iconic skyscrapers for which he was famous.

But lately something had started to niggle away inside her. Was it her conscience? Her sense that her already precarious self-worth was being eroded by him hiding her away in his palatial apartment, like a guilty secret? She wasn't sure. All she knew was that she'd started to analyse what she'd become and hadn't liked the answer she'd come up with.

She was a wealthy man's plaything. A woman who dropped her panties whenever he clicked those elegant olive fingers.

But she was here now and it was stupid to let her reservations spoil the evening ahead, so she changed her tight smile into a bright smile as she dumped her overnight bag on the floor and tugged the elastic band from her hair. Shaking her damp curls free, she couldn't deny the satisfaction it gave her to see the way Renzo's eyes had darkened in response—although her physical appeal to him had never been in any question. He couldn't seem to get enough of her and she suspected she knew why. Because she was different. Working class, for a start. She hadn't been to college—in fact, she'd missed out on more schooling than she should have done and nearly everything she knew had been self-taught. She was curvy and red-headed, when usually he went for slender brunettes—that was if all the photos in the newspapers were to be believed. They were certainly mismatched on just about every level, except when it came to bed.

Because the sex was amazing—it always had been—but it couldn't continue like this, taking her on an aimless path which was leading nowhere. Darcy knew what she had to do. She knew you could only fool yourself for so long before reality started hurting and forced you to change. She'd noticed Renzo was starting to take her for granted and knew that, if it continued, all the magic they'd shared would just wither away. And she didn't want that, because memories were powerful things. The bad ones were like heavy burdens you had to carry around with you and she was determined to have some good ones to lighten the load. So when was she going to grab the courage to walk away from him, before Renzo did the walking and left her feeling broken and crushed?

'I'm early because I sent your driver away and took the Tube instead,' she explained, brushing excess raindrops from her forest of red curls.

'You sent the driver away?' He frowned as he slid the damp raincoat from her shoulders. 'Why on earth would you do that?'

Darcy sighed, wondering what it must be like to be Renzo Sabatini and live in an enclosed and protected world, where chauffeur-driven cars and private jets shielded you from rain and snow and the worries of most normal folk. Where people did your shopping and picked up your clothes where you'd left them on the bedroom floor the night before. A world where you didn't have to speak to anyone unless you really wanted to, because there was always some minion who would do the speaking for you.

'Because the traffic is a nightmare at this time of day and often we're forced to sit in a queue, moving at a snail's pace.' She took the coat from him and gave it a little shake before hanging it in the cupboard. 'Public transport happens to have a lot going for it during the rush hour. Now, rather than debating my poor timekeeping can I please have a cup of tea? I'm f-f-freezing.'

But he didn't make any move towards the kitchen as most people might have done after such a wobbly request. He took her in his arms and kissed her instead. His lips were hard as they pressed against hers and his fingers caressed her bottom through her uniform dress as he brought her up close to his body. Close enough for her to feel the hardness of his erection and the warmth of his bare chest as he deepened the kiss. Darcy's eyelids fluttered to a close as one hard thigh pushed insistently against hers and she could feel her own parting in automatic response. And suddenly her coldness was forgotten and tea was the last thing on her mind. Her questions and insecurities dissolved as he deepened the kiss and all she was aware of was the building heat as her chilled fingers crept up to splay themselves over his bare and hair-roughened torso.

'Hell, Renzo,' she breathed.

'Is it really hell?' he murmured.

'No, it's…' she brushed her lips over his '…heaven, if you must know.'

'That's what I thought. Are you trying to warm your hands on my chest?'

'Trying. I don't think I'm having very much luck. You do many things very well, but acting as a human hot-water bottle isn't one of them.'

'No. You could be right. My skills definitely lie in other directions. Perhaps I could demonstrate some of them to you right now.' He moved his hand from her bottom and curled his fingers round hers as he guided her hand towards his groin. 'In which case I think you'd better join me in the shower, don't you?'

She couldn't have said no even if she'd wanted to. One touch from Renzo was like lighting the touchpaper. Two seconds in his arms and she went up in flames.

In the bathroom, he unzipped her drab beige uniform, soft words of Italian falling from his lips as her breasts were revealed to him. Disproportionately big breasts which had always been the bane of her life, because she'd spent her life with men's attention being constantly homed in on them. She'd often thought longingly of a breast reduction—except who could afford an operation like that on the money she earned waiting tables? So she'd made do with wearing restrictive bras, until Renzo had taught her to love her body and told her that her breasts were the most magnificent thing he'd ever seen. To enjoy being suckled or having his teeth tease the sensitive flesh until she was crying out with pleasure. He'd started to buy lingerie for her, too—the only thing she'd ever allowed him to buy for her and only because he'd insisted. He couldn't understand why she wouldn't let him spend money on her, but her reasons were raw and painful and she had no intention of letting him in on her secret.

But she let him buy her pretty underclothes, because he insisted that it enhanced their sex play—balcony bras and tiny matching panties, which he said made the most of her curvy hips. And didn't it make her feel rather decadent when she was at work, knowing she was wearing the finest silk and lace beneath the drab check of her waitress uniform? Hadn't he told her that he *wanted* her to think about him when he wasn't there? That when he was far away on business he liked to imagine her touching herself until she was wet between the legs and her body bucking helplessly as she thought about *him*. And although his fantasy about how she lived when he wasn't there was just that—fantasy—she couldn't deny that it also turned her on. But then, everything about Renzo Sabatini turned her on. His tall and powerful frame. His black hair and black eyes and those dark-rimmed spectacles he wore when he was working on one of his detailed plans. That way he had of watching her as she moved around the room. And stroking her until she was trembling with helpless need for him. Like now.

Her dress fell to the floor and the delicate underwear quickly followed. A master in the art of undressing, her Italian lover was soon as naked as she, and Darcy sucked in an instinctive gasp when she saw how aroused he was.

'Daunting, isn't it?' His sensual lips curved into a mocking smile. 'Want to touch me?'

'Not until I've got hot water gushing over me. My hands are so cold you might recoil.'

'I don't think so,' he said softly.

His eyes glittered as he picked her up and carried her into the wet room, where steaming water streamed down from a huge showerhead and the sensory impact of the experience threatened to overwhelm her. Hot water on icy skin and a naked Renzo in her arms. In the steamy environment, which made her think of a tropical forest, his lips were hungry, one hand stroking between her legs while the other played with one aching nipple. The warm water relaxed her, made her aware of the fierce pounding of her heart and the sudden rush of warmth at her groin. She ran her hands over the hard planes of his body, enjoying the sensation of honed muscle beneath his silken olive skin. Boldly she reached down to circle his erection, sliding her thumb and forefinger lightly up and down the rocky shaft the way she knew he liked it. He gave a groan. Hell. *She* liked it, too. She liked everything he did to her...and the longer it went on, the more difficult it was to imagine a life without him.

She closed her eyes as his fingers moved down over her belly until they were tangling in the wet hair at the juncture of her thighs. One finger took a purposeful route farther, until it was deep inside her and she gave a little yelp of pleasure as he strummed the

finger against swollen flesh, the rhythmical movement taking her closer to the edge. And now it was
her turn to writhe her hips against him, wanting release—and wanting oblivion, too.

'Now,' she breathed. 'Make love to me now.'

'You are impatient, little one.'

Of course she was impatient. It had been nearly a
month since she'd seen him. A month when he'd been
hard at work in Japan, before flying to South America
to oversee the enormous new hotel complex he'd designed which was creating a lot of waves in the high-
octane world of architecture. And yes, there had been
the occasional email—an amusing description about
a woman who had propositioned him after a boardroom meeting, which Darcy had managed to laugh
off and act as if it didn't hurt. He'd even phoned her
once, when his plane had been delayed at the airport
in Rio de Janeiro and presumably he must have had
time to kill. And even though she'd been battling
through the wind on her way back from the discount
supermarket at the time, she'd managed to find shelter in a shop doorway and make like it was a normal
conversation. She'd tried to tell herself that she didn't
mind his total lack of commitment. That they didn't
have an ordinary relationship and that was what made
it so interesting.

He'd told her right from the start what she could
expect and what she must not expect, and number
one on his list had been commitment, closely followed by love. She remembered turning round as he'd
spoken, surprising an unexpectedly bleak look in his
gaze—unexpected because those ebony eyes usually
gave nothing away. But she hadn't probed further be-

cause she'd sensed he would clam up. Actually, she never probed—because if you asked someone too many questions about themselves, they might just turn around and ask them back and that was the last thing she wanted.

And she had agreed to his emotionally cold terms, hadn't she? She'd acted as if they were the most reasonable requests in the world. To be honest, she hadn't been able to think beyond the next kiss—and every kiss had the effect of binding her ever tighter to him. But several months had passed since he'd extracted that agreement from her and time changed everything. It always did. Time made your feelings start to deepen and made you prone to foolish daydreams. And what could be more foolish than imagining some kind of future with the billionaire designer with his jet-set lifestyle and homes all around the world? She, without a single qualification to her name, whose only skill was her ability to multitask in a restaurant?

She pressed her lips against his shoulder, thinking how best to respond to his question—to show him she still had some control left, even if it was slipping away by the second. 'Impatient?' she murmured into his wet, bare skin. 'If I'm going too fast for you, we could always put this on hold and do it later. Have that cup of tea after all. Is that what you'd like, Renzo?'

His answer was swift and unequivocal. Imprisoning her hands, he pushed her up against the granite wall of the wet room, parted her legs and thrust into her, as hot and hard as she'd ever felt him. She gasped as he filled her. She cried out as he began to move. From knowing nothing, he'd taught her everything and she had been his willing pupil. In his arms, she came to life.

'Renzo,' she gasped as he rocked against her.

'Did you miss me, *cara*?'

She closed her eyes. 'I missed…this.'

'But nothing else?'

She wanted to say that there *was* nothing else, but why spoil a beautiful moment? No man would want to hear something like that, would they—even if it was true? Especially not a man with an ego the size of Renzo's. 'Of course,' she said as he stilled inside her. 'I missed you.'

Did he sense that her answer was less than the 100 per cent he demanded of everything and everyone? Was that why he slowed the pace down, dragging her back from the brink of her orgasm to tantalise her with nearly there thrusts until she could bear it no more?

'Renzo—'

'What is it?'

How could he sound so calm? So totally in control. But control was what he was good at, wasn't it? He was the master of control. She squirmed. 'Don't play with me.'

'But I thought you liked me playing with you. Perhaps…' he bent his head to whisper in her water-soaked ear '…I shall make you beg.'

'Oh, no, you won't!' Fiercely, she cupped his buttocks and held him against her and he gave an exultant laugh as at last he gave her exactly what she wanted. He worked on her hard and fast, his deep rhythm taking her up and up, until her shuddered cries were blotted out by his kiss and he made that low groaning sound as he came. It was, she thought, about the only time she'd ever heard him sound helpless.

Afterwards he held her until the trembling had subsided and then soaped her body and washed her hair with hands which were almost gentle—as if he was attempting to make up for the almost-brutal way he'd brought her gasping to orgasm. He dried her carefully, then carried her into the bedroom and placed her down on the vast bed which overlooked the whispering treetops of Eaton Square. The crisp, clean linen felt like heaven against her scented skin as he got into bed beside her and slid his arms around her waist. She was sleepy and suspected he was, too, but surely they needed to have some sort of *conversation* instead of just mating like two animals and then tumbling into oblivion.

But wasn't that all they were, when it boiled down to it? This affair was all about sex. Nothing except sex.

'So how was your time away?' she forced herself to ask.

'You don't want to know.'

'Yes, I do.'

'All good.' He yawned. 'The hotel is almost complete and I've been commissioned to design a new art gallery just outside Tokyo.'

'But you're tired?' she observed.

His voice was mocking. '*Sì, cara.* I'm tired.'

She wriggled her back against him. 'Ever thought of easing off for a while? Taking a back seat and just enjoying your success?'

'Not really.' He yawned again.

'Why not?' she said, some rogue inside her making her persist, even though she could sense his growing impatience with her questions.

His voice grew hard. 'Because men in my position don't *ease off.* There are a hundred hot new architects who would love to be where I am. Take your eye off the ball and you're toast.' He stroked her nipple. 'Why don't you tell me about your week instead?'

'Oh, mine was nothing to speak about. I just *serve* the toast,' she said lightly.

She closed her eyes because she thought that they might sleep but she was wrong because Renzo was cupping her breasts, rubbing his growing erection up against her bottom until she gave an urgent sound of assent and he entered her from behind, where she was slick and ready.

His lips were in her hair and his hands were playing with her nipples as he moved inside her again. Her shuddered capitulation was swift and two orgasms in less than an hour meant she could no longer fight off her fatigue. She fell into a deep sleep and sometime later she felt the bed dip as Renzo got up and when she dragged her eyelids open it was to see that the spring evening was still light. The leaves in the treetops outside the window were golden-green in the fading sunlight and she could hear a distant bird singing.

It felt surreal lying here. The prestigious square on which he lived sometimes seemed like a mirage. All the lush greenery gave the impression of being in the middle of the country—something made possible only by the fact that this was the most expensive real estate in London. But beyond the treetops near his exclusive home lay the London which was *her* city. Discount stores and tower blocks and garbage fluttering on the pavements. Snarled roads and angry drivers. And somewhere not a million miles from here, but which felt as if it might as well be in a different universe, was the tiny bedsit she called home. Sometimes it seemed like something out of some corny old novel—the billionaire boss and his waitress lover. Because things like this didn't usually happen to girls like her.

But Renzo hadn't taken advantage of her, had he? He'd never demanded anything she hadn't wanted to give. She'd accepted his ride home—even though some part of her had cried out that it was unwise. Yet for once in her life she'd quashed the voice of common sense which was as much a part of her as her bright red hair. For years she had simply kept her head down and toed the line in order to survive. But not this time. Instead of doing what she knew she *should* do, she'd succumbed to something she'd really wanted and that something was Renzo. Because she'd never wanted anyone the way she'd wanted him.

What she was certain he'd intended to be just one night had become another and then another as their unconventional relationship had developed. It was a relationship which existed only within the walls of his apartment because, as if by some unspoken agreement, they never went out on dates. Renzo's friends were wealthy and well connected, just like him. Fast-living powerbrokers with influential jobs and nothing in common with someone like her. And anyway, it would be bizarre if they started appearing together in public because they weren't really a *couple*, were they?

She knew their relationship could most accurately be described as 'friends with benefits,' though the benefits heavily outweighed the friendship side and the arrogant Italian had once told her that he didn't really have any female *friends*. Women were for the bedroom and kitchen—he'd actually said that, when he'd been feeling especially uninhibited after one of their marathon sex sessions, which had ended up in the bath. He'd claimed afterwards that he'd been joking but Darcy had recognised a grain of truth behind his words. Even worse was the way his masterful arrogance had thrilled her, even though she'd done her best to wear a disapproving expression.

Because when it boiled down to it, Darcy knew the score. She was sensible enough to know that Renzo Sabatini was like an ice cream cone you ate on a sunny day. It tasted amazing—possibly the most amazing thing you'd ever tasted—but you certainly didn't expect it to last.

She glanced up as he walked back into the bedroom carrying a tray, a task she performed many times a day—the only difference being that he was completely naked.

'You're spoiling me,' she said.

'I'm just returning the favour. I'd like to ask where you learned that delicious method of licking your tongue over my thighs but I realise that—'

'I learned it from you?'

'Esattamente.' His eyes glittered. 'Hungry?'

'Thirsty.'

'I expect you are,' he said, bending over to brush his lips over hers.

She took the tea he gave her and watched as he tugged on a pair of jeans and took his glass of red wine over to his desk, sitting down and putting on dark-framed spectacles before waking his computer from sleep mode and beginning to scroll down. After a couple of minutes he was completely engrossed in something on the screen and suddenly Darcy felt completely excluded. With his back on her, she felt like an insignificant cog in the giant wheel which was his life. They'd just had sex—twice—and now he was burying himself in work, presumably until his body had recovered enough to do it to her all over again. And she would just lie back and let him, or climb on top of him if the mood took her—because that was her role. Up until now it had always been enough but suddenly it didn't seem like nearly enough.

Did she signal her irritation? Was that why he rattled out a question spoken like someone who was expecting an apologetic denial as an answer?

'Is something wrong?'

This was her cue to say no, nothing was wrong. To pat the edge of the bed and slant him a compliant smile because that was what she would normally have done. But Darcy wasn't in a compliant mood today. She'd heard a song on the radio just before leaving work. A song which had taken her back to a place she hadn't wanted to go to and the mother she'd spent her life trying to forget.

Yet it was funny how a few random chords could pluck at your heartstrings and make you want to screw up your face and cry. Funny how you could still love someone even though they'd let you down, time after time. That had been the real reason she'd sent Renzo's driver away. She'd wanted to walk to the Tube so that her unexpected tears could mingle with the rain. She'd hoped that by coming here and having her Italian lover take her to bed, it might wipe away her unsettled feelings. But it seemed to have done the opposite. It had awoken a new restlessness in her. It had made her realise that great sex and champagne in the shadows of a powerful man's life weren't the recipe for a happy life—and the longer she allowed it to continue, the harder it would be for her to return to the real world. Her world.

She finished her tea and put the cup down, the subtle taste of peppermint and rose petals still lingering on her lips. It was time for the affair to fade out, like the credits at the end of the film. And even though she was going to miss him like crazy, she was the one who needed to start it rolling.

She made her voice sound cool and non-committal. 'I'm thinking I won't be able to see you for a while.'

That had his attention. He turned away from the screen and, putting his glasses down on the desk, he frowned. 'What are you talking about?'

'I have a week's holiday from work and I'm planning to use it to go to Norfolk.'

She could see he was slightly torn now because he wasn't usually interested in what she did when she wasn't with him, even if he sometimes trotted out a polite question because he obviously felt it was expected of him. But he was interested now.

'What are you doing in Norfolk?'

She shrugged her bare shoulders. 'Looking for a place to rent. I'm thinking of moving there.'

'You mean you're leaving *London*?'

'You sound surprised, Renzo. People leave London all the time.'

'I know. But it's...' He frowned, as if such an option was outside his realm of understanding. 'What's in Norfolk?'

She'd been prepared to let him think that she just wanted a change—which was true—and to leave her real reasons unspoken. But his complete lack of comprehension angered her and when she spoke her voice was low and trembling with an anger which was directed as much at herself as at him.

'Because there I've got the chance of renting somewhere that might have a view of something which isn't a brick wall. As well as a job that doesn't just feature commuters who are so rushed they can barely give me the time of day, let alone a *please* or a thank you. The chance of fresh air and a lower cost of living, plus a pace of life which doesn't wear me out just thinking about it.'

He frowned. 'You mean you don't like where you're living?'

'It's perfectly adequate for my *needs*,' she said carefully. 'Or at least, it has been until now.'

'That's a pretty lukewarm endorsement.' He paused and his frown deepened. 'Is that why you've never invited me round?'

'I guess.' She'd actually done it to save his embarrassment—and possibly hers. She'd tried to imagine him in her humble bedsit eating his dinner off a tray or having to squeeze his towering frame into her tiny bathroom or—even worse—lying on her narrow single bed. It was a laughable concept which would have made them both feel awkward and would have emphasised the vast social gulf between them even more. And that was why she never had. 'Would you really have wanted me to?'

Renzo considered her question. Of course he wouldn't, but he was surprised not to have got an invite. You wouldn't need to be a genius to work out that her life was very different from his and perhaps if he'd been confronted by it then his conscience would have forced him to write a cheque, and this time be more forceful in getting her to accept it. He might have told her to buy some new cushions, or a rug or even a new kitchen, if that was what she wanted. That was how these things usually worked. But Darcy was the proudest woman he'd ever encountered and, apart from the sexy lingerie he'd insisted she wear, had stubbornly refused all his offers of gifts. Why, even his heiress lovers hadn't been averse to accepting diamond necklaces or bracelets or those shoes with the bright red soles. He liked buying women expensive presents—it made him feel he wasn't in any way *beholden* to them. It reduced relationships down to what they really were…transactions. And yet his hard-up little waitress hadn't wanted to know.

'No, I wasn't holding out for an invite,' he said slowly. 'But I thought you might have discussed your holiday plans with me before you went ahead and booked them.'

'But you never discuss your plans with me, Renzo. You just do as you please.'

'You're saying you want me to run my schedule past you first?' he questioned incredulously.

'Of course I don't. You've made it clear that's not the way you operate and I've always accepted that. So you can hardly object if I do the same.'

But she was missing the point and Renzo suspected she knew it. *He* was the one who called the shots because that was also how these things worked. He was the powerbroker in this affair and she was smart enough to realise that. Yet he could see something implacable in her green gaze, some new sense of determination which had settled over her, and something else occurred to him. 'You might stay on in Norfolk,' he said slowly.

'I might.'

'In which case, this could be the last time we see one another.'

She shrugged. 'I guess it could.'

'Just like that?'

'What were you expecting? It had to end sometime.'

Renzo's eyes narrowed thoughtfully. Up until a couple of hours ago it wouldn't *really* have bothered him if he'd been told he would never see her again. Oh, he might have experienced a faint pang of regret and he certainly would have missed her in a physical sense, because he found her enthusiastic lovemaking irresistible. In fact, he would go so far as to say that she was the best lover he'd ever had, probably because he had taught her to be perfectly attuned to the needs of *his* body. But nothing was for ever. He knew that. In a month—maybe less—he would have replaced her with someone else. Someone cool and presentable, who would blend more easily into his life than Darcy Denton had ever done.

But she was the one who was doing the withdrawing and Renzo didn't like that. He was a natural predator—proud and fiercely competitive. Perhaps even prouder than Darcy. Women didn't leave *him*… He was the one who did the walking away—and at a time of *his* choosing. And he still wanted her. He had not yet reached the crucial boredom state which would make him direct her calls straight to voicemail or leave a disproportionately long time before replying to texts. Lazily, he flicked through the options available to him.

'What about if you took a holiday with me, instead of going to Norfolk on your own?'

He could tell from the sudden dilatation of her eyes that the suggestion had surprised her. And the hardening of her nipples above the rumpled bedsheet suggested it had excited her. He felt the sudden beat of blood to his groin and realised it had excited him, too.

Her emerald eyes were wary. 'Are you serious?'

'Why not?'

He got up from the chair, perfectly aware of the powerful effect his proximity would have on her as he sat down on the edge of the bed. 'Is that such an abhorrent suggestion—to take my lover on holiday?'

She shrugged. 'It's not the type of thing we usually do. We usually stay in and don't go out.'

'But life would be very dull if only the expected happened. Are you telling me that the idea of a few days away with me doesn't appeal to you?' He splayed his palm possessively over the warm weight of her breast and watched as her swanlike neck constricted in a swallow.

She chewed on her lip. 'Renzo—'

'Mmm…?'

'It's…it's quite difficult to think straight when you're touching my nipple like that.'

'Thinking in the bedroom can be a very overrated pastime,' he drawled, subtly increasing the pressure of his fingers. 'What's to think about? My proposition is perfectly simple. You could come out to Tuscany with me. I need to make a trip there this weekend. We could spend a few days together and you would still have time to go to Norfolk.'

She leaned back against the pillows and her eyes closed as he continued to massage her breast. 'You have a house there, don't you?' she breathed. 'In Tuscany.'

'Not for much longer. That's why I'm going. I'm selling it.' The pressure on her breast increased as his voice hardened. 'And you can keep me company. I have to take an earlier flight via Paris to do some business but you could always fly out separately.' He paused. 'Doesn't the idea tempt you, Darcy?'

His words filtered into her distracted mind as he continued to tease her exquisitely aroused nipple and her lashes fluttered open. His black eyes were as hard as shards of jet but that didn't affect the magic he was creating with the slow movement of his fingers as she tried to concentrate on his question.

Her tongue flicked out to moisten her lips. Of course a few days away with him tempted her—but it wasn't the thought of flying to Tuscany which was making her heart race like a champion stallion.

He tempted her. Would it be so wrong to grab a last session of loving with him—but in a very different environment? Because although his apartment was unimaginably big, it had its limitations. Despite the pool in the basement, the heated roof terrace and huge screening room, she was starting to feel like part of the fixtures and fittings. Couldn't she go out to Italy and, in the anonymous setting of a foreign country, pretend to be his *real* girlfriend for a change? Someone he really cared about—rather than just someone whose panties he wanted to rip off every time he saw her.

'I guess it does tempt me,' she said. 'A little.'

'Not the most enthusiastic response I've ever had,' he commented. 'But I take it that's a yes?'

'It's a yes,' she agreed, relaxing back into the feathery bank of pillows as he turned his attention to her other aching breast.

'Good.' There was a pause and the circular movement of his fingers halted. 'But first you're going to have to let me buy you some new clothes.'

Her eyes snapped open and she froze—automatically pushing his hand away. 'When will you get it into your thick skull that I'm not interested in your money, Renzo?'

'I think I'm getting the general idea,' he said drily. 'And although your independence is admirable, I find it a little misguided. Why not just accept gracefully? I like giving presents and most women like receiving them.'

'It's a very kind thought and thank you all the same,' she said stiffly, 'but I don't want them.'

'This isn't a question of *want*, more a case of *need*

and I'm afraid that this time I'm going to have to in-sist,' he said smoothly. 'I have a certain…*position* to maintain in Italy and, as the woman accompanying me, you'll naturally be the focus of attention. I'd hate you to feel you were being judged negatively because you don't have the right clothes.'

'Just as you're judging me right now, you mean?' she snapped.

He shook his head, his lips curving into a slow smile and his deep voice dipping. 'You must have realised by now that I prefer you wearing nothing at all, since nothing looks better than your pale and perfect skin. But although it's one of my biggest fan-tasies, I really don't think we can have you walking around the Tuscan hills stark naked, do you? I'm just looking out for you, Darcy. Buy yourself a few pretty things. Some dresses you can wear in the evenings. It isn't a big deal.'

She opened her mouth to say that it *was* a big deal to her but he had risen to his feet and his shadow was falling over her so that she was bathed in darkness as she lay there. She looked up into lash-shuttered eyes which gleamed like ebony and her heart gave a funny twist as she thought about how much she was going to miss him. How was she going to return to a life which was empty of her powerful Italian lover? 'What are you doing?' she croaked as he began to unzip his jeans.

'Oh, come on. Use your imagination,' he said softly. 'I'm going to persuade you to take my money.'

CHAPTER TWO

RENZO LOOKED AT his watch and gave a click of impatience. Where the hell *was* she? She *knew* he detested lateness, just as she knew he ran his diary like clockwork. In the exclusive lounge at Florence airport he crossed one long leg over the other, aware that the movement had caused the heads of several women instinctively to turn, but he paid them no attention for there was only one woman currently on his mind—and not in a good way.

The flight he had instructed Darcy to catch—in fact, to purchase a first-class ticket for—had discharged its passengers twenty minutes earlier and she had not been among their number. His eyes had narrowed as he'd stared at the hordes of people streaming through the arrivals section, fully expecting to see her eagerly pushing her way through to see him, her pale face alight with excitement and her curvy body resplendent in fine new clothes—but there had been no sight of her. A member of staff had dealt with his irritation and was currently checking the flight list while he was forced to consider the unbelievable... *that she might have changed her mind about joining him in Italy.*

He frowned. Had her reluctance to take the cash he had insisted she accept gone deeper than he'd imagined? He'd thought she was simply making a gesture—hiding the natural greed which ran through the veins of pretty much every woman—but perhaps he had misjudged her. Perhaps she really *was* deeply offended by his suggestion that she buy herself some decent clothes.

Or maybe she'd just taken the money and done a runner, not intending to come here and meet him at all.

Renzo's mouth hardened, because wasn't there a rogue thought flickering inside his head which almost wished that to be the case? Wouldn't he have welcomed a sound reason to despise her, instead of this simmering resentment that she was preparing to take her leave of him? That she had been the one to make a decision which was usually *his* province. He glanced again at his wristwatch. And how ironic that the woman to call time on a relationship should be a busty little red-headed waitress he'd picked up in a cocktail bar rather than one of the many more eligible women he'd dated.

He hadn't even been intending to go out the night he'd met her. He'd just planned to have a quick drink with a group of bankers he'd known from way back who had been visiting from Argentina and wanted to see some London nightlife. Renzo didn't particularly like nightclubs and remembered the stir the six men had made as they'd walked into the crowded Starlight Room at the Granchester Hotel, where they'd ordered champagne and decided which of the women sipping cocktails they should ask to dance. But Renzo hadn't been interested in the svelte women who had been smiling invitingly in his direction. His attention had been caught by the curviest little firecracker he'd ever seen. She'd looked as if she had been poured into the black satin dress which had skimmed her rounded hips, but it had been her breasts which had caused the breath to dry in his throat. *Madonna, che bella!* What breasts! Luscious and quivering, they had a deep cleavage he wanted to run his tongue over and that first sight of them was something he would remember for as long as he lived.

He had ended up dancing with no one, mainly because he'd been too busy watching her and his erection had been too painful for him to move without embarrassment. He'd ordered drinks only from her, and wondered afterwards if she noticed he left them all. Each time he'd summoned her over to his table he could sense the almost palpable electricity which sizzled in the air—he'd certainly never felt such a powerful attraction towards a total stranger before. He'd expected her to make some acknowledgement of the silent chemistry which pulsed between them, but she hadn't. In fact the way her eyelids had half shielded her huge green eyes and the cautious looks she'd been directing at him had made him think she must either be the world's greatest innocent, or its most consummate actress. If he had known it was the former, would he still have pursued her?

Of course he would. Deep down he recognised he wouldn't have been able to stop himself because hadn't he been gripped by a powerful hunger which insisted he would never know peace until he had possessed her?

He'd been waiting outside when eventually she had emerged from the club and had thanked the heavens for the heavy downpour of rain which had been showering down on her. She hadn't looked a bit surprised to see him as she'd opened up her umbrella and for a moment it had crossed his mind that she might take a different man home with her every night, though even that had not been enough to make him order his driver to move on. But when he'd offered her a lift she'd refused, in an emphatic manner which had startled him.

'No, thanks.'

'No?'

'I know what you want,' she'd said, in a low voice. 'And you won't get it from me.'

And with that she'd disappeared into the rain-wet night and Renzo had sat in the back seat of the limousine, watching her retreating form beneath her little black umbrella, his mouth open and his body aching with frustration and unwilling admiration.

He'd gone to the club the next night and the weekend when he'd returned from a work trip to New York. Some nights she'd been there and some she hadn't. He'd discovered she only worked there at weekends and it had only been later he'd found out she had a daytime job as a waitress somewhere else. Extracting information from her had been like trying to get blood from a stone. She was the most private woman he'd ever met as well as the most resistant and perhaps it was those things which made Renzo persist in a way he'd never had to persist before. And just when he'd been wondering if he was wasting his time, she had agreed to let him drive her home.

His voice had been wry as he'd looked at her. '*Madonna mia!* You mean you've decided you trust me enough to accept the lift?'

Her narrow shoulders had shrugged, causing her large breasts to jiggle beneath the shiny black satin of her dress and sending a shaft of lust arrowing straight to his groin. 'I guess so. All the other staff have seen you by now and you've been captured on CCTV for all eternity, so if you're a murderer then you'll be apprehended soon enough.'

'Do I look like a murderer?'

She had smiled then, and it had been like the sun coming out from behind a cloud.

'No. Although you look just a little bit dangerous.'

'Women always tell me that's a plus.'

'I'm sure they do, though I'm not sure I agree. Anyway, it's a filthy night, so I might as well get a lift with you. But I haven't changed my mind,' she'd added fiercely. 'And if you think I'm going to sleep with you, then you're wrong.'

As it happened, she was the one who'd been wrong. They'd driven through the dark wet streets of London and he'd asked her to come in for coffee, not thinking for a moment she'd accept. But maybe the chemistry had been just as powerful for her. Maybe her throat had also been tight with tension and longing and she'd been finding it as difficult to speak as he had, as she'd sat beside him in the leather-scented car. He'd driven her to his apartment and she'd told him primly that she didn't really like coffee. So he'd made her tea flavoured with peppermint and rose petals, and for the first time in his life he'd realised he might lose her if he rushed it. He'd wondered afterwards if it was his unfamiliar restraint which had made her relax and sink into one of his huge sofas—so that when at last he'd leaned over to kiss her she'd been all quivering acquiescence. He'd done it to her right there—pulling her panties down and plunging right into her—terrified she might change her mind during the long walk from the sitting room to the bedroom.

And that had been when he'd discovered she was a virgin—and in that moment something had changed. The world had tipped on its axis because he'd never had sex with a virgin before and had been unprepared for the rush of primitive satisfaction which had flooded through him. As they'd lain there afterwards, gasping for breath among all the cushions, he'd pushed a damp curl away from her dewy cheek, demanding to know why she hadn't told him.

'Why would I? Would you have stopped?'

'No, but I could have laid you at the centre of my big bed instead of the sofa if I'd known this was your first sexual adventure.'

'What, you mean like some sort of medieval sacrifice?' she'd murmured and that had confused him, too, because he would have expected high emotion at such a moment, not such a cool response.

Had it been her coolness which had made him desire her even more? Possibly. He'd thought it would be one night, but he'd been mistaken. He'd never dated a waitress before and he acknowledged the cold streak of snobbery in his nature which told him it would be unwise to buck that trend. But Darcy had confounded him. She read just as many books as an academic he'd once dated—although admittedly, she preferred novels to molecular biology. And she didn't follow the predictable path of most women in a sexual relationship. She didn't bore him with stories of her past, nor weigh him down with questions about his own. Their infrequent yet highly satisfying meetings, which involved a series of mind-blowing orgasms, seemed to meet both their needs. She seemed instinctively to understand that he wasn't seeking a close or lasting connection with a woman. Not now and not ever.

But sometimes an uncomfortable question strayed into his mind to ask why such a beauty would have so willingly submitted her virginity to a total stranger. And didn't he keep coming up with the troublesome answer that maybe she had been holding out for the highest bidder—in this case, an Italian billionaire...?

'Renzo?'

The sound of her voice dragged him away back into the present and Renzo looked up to see a woman walking through the airport lounge towards him, pulling behind her a battered suitcase on wheels. His eyes narrowed. It was Darcy, yes—but not Darcy as he knew her, in her drab waitress uniform or pale and naked against his pristine white sheets. Renzo blinked. This was Darcy in a dress the colour of sunshine, dotted with tiny blue flowers. It was a simple cotton dress but the way she wore it was remarkable. It wasn't the cut or the label which was making every man in the place stare at her—it was her youthful body and natural beauty. Fresh and glowing, her bare arms and legs were honed by honest hard work rather than mindless sessions in the gym. She looked *radiant* and the natural bounce of her breasts meant that no man could look at her without thinking about procreation. Renzo's mouth dried. Procreation had never been on *his* agenda, but sex most definitely was. He wanted to pull her hungrily into his arms and to kiss her hard on the mouth and feel those soft breasts crushing against him. But Renzo Sabatini would never be seen in any airport—let alone one in his homeland—making such a public demonstration of affection.

And wasn't it time he reinforced the fact that no-body—nobody—ever kept him waiting?

'You're late,' he said repressively, throwing aside his newspaper and rising to his feet.

Darcy nodded. She could sense his irritation but that didn't affect her enjoyment of the way he was looking at her—if only to reassure her she hadn't made a terrible mistake in choosing a cheap cotton dress instead of the clothes he must have been expecting her to wear. Still, since this was going to be the holiday of a lifetime it was important she got it off to a good start and the truth of it was that she *was* late. In fact, she'd started to worry if she would get here at all because that horrible vomiting bug she'd had at the beginning of the week had really laid her low.

'Yes, I know. I'm sorry about that.'

He commandeered her wheeled case and winced slightly as he took her hand luggage. 'What have you got in here? Bricks?'

'I put in a few books,' she said as they set off towards the exit. 'Though I wasn't sure how much time I'd have for reading.'

Usually he would have made a provocative comment in response to such a remark but he didn't and the unyielding expression on his face told her he wasn't ready to forgive her for making him wait. But he didn't say anything as they emerged into the bright sunshine and Darcy was too overcome by the bluest sky she'd ever seen to care.

'Oh, Renzo—I can't believe I'm in Italy. It's so beautiful,' she enthused as she looked around, but still he didn't answer. In fact, he didn't speak until his shiny black car had pulled out of the airport and was heading towards a signpost marked Chiusi.

'I've been waiting at the damned airport for over an hour,' he snapped. 'Why weren't you on the flight I told you to get?'

Darcy hesitated. She supposed she could come up with some vague story to placate him but hadn't she already shrouded so much of her life with evasion and secrets, terrified that someone would examine it in the harsh light of day and judge her? Why add yet another to the long list of things she needed to conceal? And this was different. This wasn't something she was ashamed of—so why not be upfront about the decision she'd made when he had stuffed that enormous wad of cash into her hand and made her feel deeply uncomfortable?

'Because it was too expensive.'

'Darcy, I *gave* you the money to get that flight.'

'I know you did and it was very generous of you.' She drew in a deep breath. 'But when I saw how much it cost to fly to Florence first class, I just couldn't do it.'

'What do you mean, you couldn't do it?'

'It seemed a ludicrous amount of money to spend on a two-hour flight so I bought a seat on a budget airline instead.'

'You did *what*?'

'You should try it sometime. It's true they ran out of sandwiches and the tea was stone-cold, but I saved absolutely loads of money because the price difference was massive. Just like I did with the clothes.'

'The clothes,' he repeated uncomprehendingly.

'Yes. I went to that department store you recommended on Bond Street but the clothes were stupidly overpriced. I couldn't believe how much they were asking for a simple T-shirt so I went to the high street and found some cheaper versions, like this dress.' She smoothed the crisp yellow cotton down over her thighs and her voice wavered a little uncertainly. 'Which I think looks okay, doesn't it?'

He flashed a glance to where her hand was resting. 'Sure,' he said, his voice sounding thick. 'It looks okay.'

'So what's the problem?'

He slammed the palm of his hand against the steering wheel. 'The problem is that I don't like being disobeyed.'

She laughed. 'Oh, Renzo. You sound like a headmaster. You're not my teacher, you know—and I'm not your pupil.'

'Oh, really?' He raised his eyebrows. 'I thought I'd been responsible for teaching you rather a lot.'

His words made her face grow hot as they zoomed past blue-green mountains, but suddenly Darcy was finding the sight of Renzo's profile far more appealing than the Tuscan countryside. He was so unbelievably gorgeous. Just the most gorgeous man she'd ever seen. Would she ever feel this way about anyone again, she wondered—with a chest which became so tight when she looked at him that sometimes it felt

as if she could hardly *breathe*? Probably not. It had
never happened before, so what were the chances of it
happening again? How had Renzo himself described
what had happened when they first met? *Colpo di
fulmine*—that was it. A lightning strike—which everyone knew was extremely rare. It was about the
only bit of Italian she knew.

She sneaked another glance at him. His black hair
was ruffled and his shirt was open at the neck—olive
skin glowing gold and stunningly illuminated by the
rich Tuscan light. His thighs looked taut beneath his
charcoal trousers and Darcy could feel the sudden in-
crease of her pulse as her gaze travelled along their
muscular length. She'd rarely been in a car with him
since the night he had seduced her—or rather, when
she had fallen greedily into his arms. She'd hardly
been *anywhere* with him other than the bedroom and
suddenly she was glad about something which might
have bothered other women.

Because with the amazing landscape sliding past
like a TV commercial, she thought how easy it would
be to get used to this kind of treatment. Not just the
obvious luxury of being driven through such beautiful countryside, but the chance to be a bona fide
couple like this. And she mustn't get used to it, because it was a one-off. One last sweet taste of Renzo
Sabatini before she began her new life in Norfolk
and started to forget him—the man with the cold
heart who had taught her the definition of pleasure.
The precise and brilliant architect who turned into a
tiger in the bedroom.

'So what exactly are we going to be doing when
we get to this place of yours?' she said.

'You mean apart from making love?'

'Apart from that,' she agreed, almost wishing he hadn't said it despite the instant spring of her breasts in response. Did he need to keep drumming in her sole purpose in his life? She remembered the hiking shoes she'd packed and wondered if she'd completely misjudged the situation. Was he planning to show her anything of Tuscany, or would they simply be doing the bed thing, only in a more glamorous location? She wondered if he had sensed her sudden discomfiture and if that was the reason for his swift glance as they left the motorway for a quieter road.

'The man who is buying the estate is coming for dinner,' he said, by way of explanation.

'Oh? Is that usual?'

'Not really, but he's actually my lawyer and I want to persuade him to keep on the staff who have worked at Vallombrosa for so long. He's bringing his girlfriend with him, so it'll be good to have you there to balance the numbers.'

Darcy nodded. To balance the numbers. Of course. She was there to fill an empty chair and warm the tycoon's bed—there was nothing more to it than that. Stupidly, his remark hurt but she didn't show it—something in which she'd learned to excel. A childhood of deprivation and fear had taught her to hide her feelings behind a mask and present the best version of herself to the world. The version that prospective foster parents might like if they were looking for a child to fit into their lovely home. And if sometimes she wondered what she might reveal if that mask ever slipped, she didn't worry about it for too long because she was never going to let that happen.

'So when were you last abroad?' he questioned, as they passed a pretty little hilltop village.

'Oh, not for ages,' she answered vaguely.

'How come?'

It was a long time since she'd thought about it and Darcy stared straight ahead as she remembered the charity coach trip to Spain when she'd been fifteen. When the blazing summer sun had burned her fair skin and the mobile home on the campsite had felt like sleeping in a hot tin can. They were supposed to be grateful that the church near the children's home had raised enough money to send them on the supposed trip of a lifetime and she had really tried to be grateful. Until somebody had drilled a peephole into the wall of the female showers and there had been a huge fuss about it. And someone had definitely stolen two pairs of her knickers when she'd been out swimming in the overcrowded pool. Somehow she didn't think Renzo Sabatini's Tuscan villa was going to be anything like that. 'I went on a school trip when I was a teenager,' she said. 'That was the only time I've been abroad.'

He frowned. 'You're not much of a traveller, then?'

'You could say that.'

And suddenly Darcy scented danger. On the journey over she'd been worried she might do something stupid. Not something obvious, like using the wrong knife and fork at a fancy dinner, because her waitressing career had taught her everything there was to know about cutlery.

But she realised she'd completely overlooked the fact that proximity might make her careless. Might make her tongue slip and give something away—

something which would naturally repulse him. Renzo had told her that one of the things he liked about her was that she didn't besiege him with questions, or try to *dig deep* to try to understand him better. But that had been a two-way street and the fact he didn't ask about *her* past had suited her just fine. More than fine. She didn't want to tell any lies but she knew she could never tell him the truth. Because there was no point. There was no future in this liaison of theirs, so why tell him about the junkie mother who had given birth to her? Why endure the pain of seeing his lips curve with shock and contempt as had happened so often in the past? In a world where everyone was striving for perfection and judging you, it hadn't taken her long to realise that the best way to get on in life was to bury all the darkness just as deep as she could.

But thoughts of her mother stabbed at her conscience, prompting her to address something which had been bothering her on the flight over.

'You know the money I saved on my airfare and clothes?' she began.

'Yes, Darcy. I know. You were making a point.' He shot her a glance, his lips curving into a sardonic smile. 'Rich man with too much money shown by poor girl just how much he could save if he bothered to shop around. I get the picture.'

'There's no need to be sarcastic, Renzo,' she said stiffly. 'I want you to have it back. I've put most of it in an envelope in my handbag.'

'But I don't want it back. When are you going to get the message? I have more than enough money. And if it makes you feel better, I admire your resourcefulness and refusal to be seduced by my wealth. It's rare.'

For a moment there was silence. 'I think we both know it wasn't your wealth which seduced me, Renzo.'

She hadn't meant to say it but her quiet words reverberated around the car in an honest explanation of what had first drawn her to him. Not his money, nor his power—but him. The most charismatic and compelling man she'd ever met. She heard him suck in an unsteady breath.

'Madonna mia,' he said softly. 'Are you trying to tempt me into taking the next turning and finding the nearest layby so that I can do what I have been longing to do to you since last I saw you?'

'Renzo—'

'I don't want the damned money you saved! I want you to put your hand in my lap and feel how hard I am for you.'

'Not while you're driving,' said Darcy and although she was disappointed he had turned the emotional into the sexual, she didn't show it. Because that was the kind of man he was, she reminded herself. He was never emotional and always sexual. She didn't need to touch him to know he was aroused—a quick glance and she could see for herself the hard ridge outlined beneath the dark trousers. Suddenly her lips grew dry in response and she licked them, wishing they *could* have sex right then. Because sex stopped you longing for things you were never going to have. Things other women took for granted—like a man promising to love and protect you. Things which seemed as distant as those faraway mountains. With an effort she dragged her attention back to the present. 'Tell me about this place we're going to instead.'

'You think talking about property is a suitable substitute for discovering what you're wearing underneath that pretty little dress?'

'I think it's absolutely vital if you intend keeping your mind on the road, which is probably the most sensible option if you happen to be driving a car.'

'Oh, Darcy.' He gave a soft laugh. 'Did I ever tell you that one of the things I admire about you is your ability to always come up with a smart answer?'

'The *house*, Renzo. I want to talk about the house.'

'Okay. The house. It's old,' he said as he overtook a lorry laden with a towering pile of watermelons. 'And it stands against a backdrop that Leonardo should have painted, instead of that village south of Piacenza which is not nearly as beautiful. It has orchards and vineyards and olive groves—in fact, we produce superb wines from the Sangiovese grape and enough olive oil to sell to some of the more upmarket stores in London and Paris.'

The few facts he'd recited could have been lifted straight from the pages of an estate agent's website and Darcy felt oddly disappointed. 'It sounds gorgeous,' she said dutifully.

'It is.'

'So…why are you selling it?'

He shrugged. 'It's time.'

'Because?'

Too late, she realised she had asked one question too many. His face grew dark, as if the sun had just dipped behind a cloud and his shadowed jaw set itself into a hard and obdurate line.

'Isn't one of the reasons for our unique chemistry that you don't plague me with questions?'

She heard the sudden darkness underpinning his question. 'I was only—'

'Well, don't. Don't pry. Why change what up until now has been a winning formula?' His voice had harshened as he cut through her words, his hands tensing as a discreet sign appeared among the tangle of greenery which feathered the roadside. 'And anyway. We're here. This is Vallombrosa.'

But his face was still dark as the car began to ascend a tree-lined track towards an imposing pair of dark wrought-iron gates which looked like the gates of heaven.

Or the gates of hell, Darcy thought with a sudden flash of foreboding.

CHAPTER THREE

'HOW ON EARTH am I going to converse with every-one?' questioned Darcy as she stepped out onto the sunny courtyard. 'Since my Italian is limited to the few words I learnt from the phrasebook on the plane and that phrase about the lightning strike?'

'All my staff are bilingual,' Renzo said, his show of bad temper in the car now seemingly forgotten. 'And perfectly comfortable with speaking your mother tongue.'

The words mocked her and Darcy chewed on her lip as she looked away. Mother tongue? Her own mother had taught her to say very little—other than things which could probably have had her prosecuted if she'd repeated them to the authorities.

'Pass Mummy that needle, darling.'

'Pass Mummy those matches.'

'If the policewoman asks if you've met that man before, tell her no.'

But she smiled brightly as she entered the shaded villa and shook hands with Gisella, the elderly house-keeper, and her weather-beaten husband, Pasquale, who was one of the estate's gardeners. A lovely young woman with dark hair helped Gisella around the house and Darcy saw her blush when Renzo introduced her as Stefania. There was also a chef called Donato, who apparently flew in from Rome whenever Renzo was in residence. Donato was tanned, athletic, amazingly good-looking and almost certainly gay.

'Lunch will be in an hour,' he told them. 'But sooner if you're hungry?'

'Oh, I think we can wait,' said Renzo. He turned to Darcy. 'Why don't we take a quick look around while our bags are taken to our room?'

Darcy nodded, thinking how *weird* it felt to be deferred to like that—and to be introduced to his staff just like a real girlfriend. But then she reminded herself that this was only going to work if she didn't allow herself to get carried away. She followed him outside, blinking a little as she took in the vastness of his estate and, although she was seeing only a fraction of it, her senses were instantly overloaded by the beauty of Vallombrosa. Honeybees flitted over purple spears of lavender, vying for space with brightly coloured butterflies. Little lizards basked on baked grey stone. The high walls surrounding the ancient house were covered with scrambling pink roses and stone arches framed the blue-green layers of the distant mountains beyond. Darcy wondered what it must be like growing up somewhere like here, instead of the greyness of the institution in the north of England, which had been the only place she'd ever really called home.

'Like it?' he questioned.

'How could I not? It's beautiful.'

'You know, you're pretty beautiful yourself,' he said softly as he turned his head to look at her.

Remembering the way he'd snapped at her in the car, she wanted to resist him, but the light touch of his hand on her hip and brush of his fingers against her thighs made resistance impossible and Darcy was shaking with longing by the time they reached the shuttered dimness of his bedroom. It was a vast wood-beamed room but there was no time to take in her surroundings because he was pulling her into his arms, his lips brushing hungrily over hers and his fingers tangling themselves in her curls.

'Renzo,' she said unsteadily.

'What?'

She licked her lips. 'You know what.'

'I think I do.' His lips curved into a hard smile. 'You want this?'

Sliding down the zip of her cotton dress, he peeled it away from her and she felt the rush of air against her skin as it pooled to the ground around her ankles. 'Yes,' she breathed. 'That's what I want.'

'Do you know,' he questioned as he unclipped her lacy bra and it joined the discarded dress, 'how much I have been fantasising about you? About this?'

She nodded. 'Me, too,' she said softly, because the newness of the environment and the situation in which she found herself was making her feel almost *shy* in his presence.

But not for long. The beat of her heart and the heat of her blood soon overwhelmed her and had her fumbling for his belt, her fingers trembling with need. Very quickly she was naked and so was he—soft, shuttered light shading their bodies as he pushed her down onto the bed and levered his powerful form over hers. She gripped at the silken musculature of his broad shoulders as he slowly stroked his thumb over her clitoris. And she came right then—so quickly it was almost embarrassing. He laughed softly and eased himself into her wet heat and for a moment he was perfectly still.

'Do you know how good that feels?' he said as he began to move inside her.

She swallowed. 'I've… I've got a pretty good idea.'

'Oh, Darcy. It's you,' he groaned, his eyes closing. 'Only you.'

He said the words like a ragged prayer or maybe a curse—but Darcy didn't read anything into them because she knew exactly what he meant. She was the first and only woman with whom he hadn't needed to wear a condom, because her virginity had elevated her to a different status from his other lovers—he'd told her that himself. He told her she was truly pure. He'd been fascinated to find a woman of twenty-four who'd never had a lover before and by her fervent reply when he'd asked if she ever wanted children.

'Never!'

Her response must have been heartfelt enough to convince him because in a rare moment of confidence he told her he felt exactly the same. Soon afterwards he had casually suggested she might want to go on the pill and Darcy had eagerly agreed. She remembered the first time they'd left the condom off and how it had felt to have his naked skin against hers instead of *'that damned rubber'*—again, his words—between them. It had been…*delicious*. She had felt dangerously close to him and had needed to give herself a stern talking-to afterwards. She'd told herself that the powerful feelings she was experiencing were purely physical. Of course sex felt better without a condom—but it didn't *mean* anything.

But now, in the dimness of his Tuscan bedroom, he was deep inside her. He was filling her and thrusting into her body and kissing her mouth until it throbbed and it felt so amazing that she could have cried. Did her low, moaning sigh break his rhythm? Was that why, with a deft movement, he turned her over so that she was on top of him, his black eyes capturing hers?

'Ride me, *cara*,' he murmured. 'Ride me until you come again.'

She nodded as she tensed her thighs against his narrow hips because she liked this position. It gave her a rare feeling of power, to see Renzo lying underneath her—his eyes half-closed and his lips parted as she rocked back and forth.

She heard his groan and bent her head to kiss it quiet, though she was fairly sure that the walls of this ancient house were deep enough to absorb the age-old sounds of sex. He tangled his hands in her hair, digging his fingers into the wayward curls until pleasure—intense and unalterable—started spiralling up inside her. She came just before he did, gasping as he clasped her hips tightly and hearing him utter something urgent in Italian as his body bucked beneath her. She bent her head to his neck, hot breath panting against his skin until she'd recovered enough to peel herself away from him, before falling back against the mattress.

She looked at the dark beams above her head and the engraved glass lampshade, which looked as if it was as old as the house itself. Someone had put a small vase of scented roses by the window—the same roses

which had been scrambling over the walls outside—
and all the light in that shadowy room seemed to be
centred on those pale pink petals.

'Well,' she said eventually. 'That was some welcome.'

Deliberately, Renzo kept his eyes closed and his
breathing steady because he didn't want to talk.
Not right now. He didn't need to be told how good
it was—that was a given—not when his mind was
busy with the inevitable clamour of his thoughts.

He'd felt a complex mixture of stuff as he'd driven
towards the house, knowing soon it would be under
different ownership. A house which had been in his
mother's family for generations and which had had
more than its fair share of heartbreak. Other people
might have offloaded it years ago but pride had made
him hold on to it, determined to replace bad memories with good ones, and to a large extent he'd succeeded. But you couldn't live in the past. It was time
to let the place go—to say goodbye to the last clinging fragments of yesterday.

He looked across the bed, where Darcy was lying
with her eyes closed, her bright red hair spread all
over the white pillow. He thought about her going to
Norfolk when they got back to London and tried to
imagine what it might be like sleeping with someone
else when she was no longer around, but the idea of
some slender-hipped brunette lying amid his tumbled
sheets was failing to excite him. Instinctively he flattened his palm over her bare thigh.

'And was it the perfect welcome?' he questioned
at last.

'You know it was.' Her voice was sleepy. 'Though

I should go and pick my dress up. It's the first time I've worn it.'

'Don't worry about it.' He smiled. 'I'll have Gisella launder it for you.'

'There's no need for that.' Her voice was suddenly sharp as her eyes snapped open. 'I can do my own washing. I can easily rinse it out in the sink and hang it out to dry in that glorious sunshine.'

'And if I told you I'd rather you didn't?'

'Too bad.'

'Why are you so damned stubborn, Darcy?'

'I thought you *liked* my stubbornness.'

'When appropriate, I do.'

'You mean, when it suits *you*?'

'*Esattamente.*'

She lay back and looked up at the ceiling. How could she explain that she'd felt his housekeeper looking at her and seeing exactly who she was—a servant, just as Gisella was. Like Gisella, she waited tables and cleared up around people who had far more money than she had. That was who she was. She didn't want to look as if she'd suddenly acquired airs and graces by asking to have her clothes laundered. She wasn't going to try to be someone she wasn't—someone who would find it impossible to settle back into her humble world when she got back to England and her billionaire lover was nothing but a distant memory.

But she shouldn't take it out on Renzo, because he was just being Renzo. She'd never objected to his high-handedness before. If the truth were known, she'd always found it a turn-on—and in a way, his arrogance had provided a natural barrier. It had stopped her falling completely under his spell, forcing her to be realistic rather than dreamy. She leaned over and brushed her mouth against his. 'So tell me what you've got planned for us.'

His fingers slid between the tops of her thighs. 'Plans? What plans? The sight of your body seems to have completely short-circuited my brain.'

Halting his hand before it got any further, Darcy enjoyed her brief feeling of power. 'Tell me something about Vallombrosa—and I'm not talking olive or wine production this time. Did you live here when you were a little boy?'

His shuttered features grew wary. 'Why the sudden interest?'

'Because you told me we'd be having dinner with the man who's buying the place. It's going to look a bit odd if I don't know anything about your connection with it. Did you grow up here?'

'No, I grew up in Rome. Vallombrosa was our holiday home.'

'And?' she prompted.

'And it had been in my mother's family for generations. We used it to escape the summer heat of the city. She and I used to come here for the entire vacation and my father would travel down at weekends.'

Darcy nodded because she knew that, like her, he was an only child and that both his parents were dead. And that was pretty much all she knew.

She circled a finger over the hardness of his flat belly. 'So what did you do when you were here?'

He pushed her hand in the direction of his groin. 'My father taught me to hunt and to fish, while my mother socialised and entertained. Sometimes friends came to visit and my mother's school friend Mariella always seemed to be a constant fixture. We were happy, or so I thought.'

Darcy held her breath as something dark and steely entered his voice. 'But you weren't?'

'No. We weren't.' He turned his head to look at her, a hard expression suddenly distorting his features. 'Haven't you realised by now that so few people are?'

'I guess,' she said stiffly. But she'd thought...

What? That other people were strangers to the pain she'd suffered? That someone as successful and as powerful as Renzo had never known emotional deprivation? Was that why he was so distant sometimes—so shuttered and cold? 'Did something happen?'

'You could say that. They got divorced when I was seven.'

'And was it...acrimonious?'

He shot her an unfathomable look. 'Aren't all divorces acrimonious?'

She shrugged. 'I guess.'

'Especially when you discover that your mother's best "friend" has been having an affair with your father for years,' he added, his voice bitter. 'It makes you realise that when the chips are down, women can never be trusted.'

Darcy chewed on her lip. 'So what happened?'

'After the divorce, my father married his mistress but my mother never really recovered. It was a double betrayal and her only weapon was me.'

'Weapon?' she echoed.

He nodded. 'She did everything in her power to keep my father out of my life. She was depressed.' His jaw tightened. 'And believe me, there isn't much a child can do if his mother is depressed. He is—

quite literally—helpless. I used to sit in the corner of the room, quietly making houses out of little plastic bricks while she sobbed her heart out and raged against the world. By the end of that first summer, I'd constructed an entire city.'

She nodded in sudden understanding. Had his need to control been born out of that helplessness? Had the tiny plastic city he'd made been the beginnings of his brilliant architectural career? 'Oh, Renzo—that's... *terrible*,' she said.

He curled his fingers over one breast. 'What an innocent you are, Darcy,' he observed softly.

Darcy felt guilt wash over her. He thought she was a goody-goody because she suspected he was one of those men who divided women into two types— Madonna or whore. Her virginity had guaranteed her Madonna status but it wasn't that simple and if he knew why she had kept herself pure he would be shocked. Married men having affairs was hardly ground-breaking stuff, even if they chose to do it with their wife's best friend—but she could tell him things about *her* life which would make his own story sound like something you could read to a child at bedtime.

And he wasn't asking about *her* past, was he? He wasn't interested—and maybe she ought to be grateful for that. There was no point in dragging out her dark secrets at this late stage in their relationship and ruining their last few days together. 'So what made you decide to sell the estate?'

There was a pause. 'My stepmother died last year,' he said flatly. 'She'd always wanted this house and I suppose I was making sure she never got her hands on it. But now she's gone—they've all gone—and somehow my desire to hang on to it died with her. The estate is too big for a single man to maintain. It needs a family.'

'And you don't want one?'

'I thought we'd already established that,' he said and now his voice had grown cool. 'I saw enough lying and deceit to put me off marriage for a lifetime. Surely you can understand that?'

Darcy nodded. Oh, yes, she understood all right. Just as she recognised that his words were a warning. A warning not to get too close. That just because she was here with him in the unfamiliar role of girlfriend, nothing had really changed. The smile she produced wasn't as bright as usual, but it was good enough to convince him she didn't care. 'Shouldn't we think about getting ready for lunch?' she questioned, her voice growing a little unsteady as his hand moved from her breast to the dip of her belly. 'Didn't…didn't Donato say it would be ready in an hour?'

The touch of her bare skin drove all thoughts from Renzo's mind until he was left with only one kind of hunger. The best kind. The kind which obliterated everything except pleasure. He'd told her more than he usually told anyone and he put that down to the fact that usually she didn't ask. But she needed to know that there would be no more confidences from now on. She needed to know that there was only one reason she was here—and the glint of expectation in her eyes told him that she was getting the message loud and clear. He felt his erection grow exquisitely hard as he looked at the little waitress who somehow knew how to handle him better than any other woman.

'I employ Donato to work to my time frame, not

his,' he said arrogantly, bending his head and sucking at her nipple.

'Oh, Renzo.' Her eyes closed as she fell back against the pillow.

'Renzo, what?' he taunted.

'Don't make me beg.'

He slid his finger over her knee. 'But I like it when you beg.'

'I know you do.'

'So?'

She groaned as her hips lifted hungrily towards his straying finger. 'Please…'

'That's better.' He gave a low and triumphant laugh as he pulled her towards him. 'Lunch can wait,' he added roughly, parting her thighs and positioning himself between them once more. 'I'm afraid this can't.'

CHAPTER FOUR

'This?' Darcy held up a glimmering black sheath, then immediately waved a flouncy turquoise dress in front of it. 'Or this?'

'The black,' Renzo said, flicking her a swift glance before continuing to button up his shirt.

Her skin now tanned a delicate shade of gold, Darcy slithered into the black dress, aware that Renzo was watching her reflection in the glass in the way a hungry dog might look at a butcher, but she didn't care. She found herself wishing she had the ability to freeze time and that the weekend wasn't drawing to a close because it had been the best few days of her life.

They'd explored his vast estate, scrambling up hilly roads to be rewarded with spectacular views of blue-green mountains and the terracotta smudge of tiny villages. Her hiking boots had come in useful after all! He'd taken her to a beautiful village called Panicale, where they'd drunk coffee in the cobbled square with church bells chiming in stereophonic all around them. And even though Renzo had assured her that May temperatures were too cold for swimming, Darcy wasn't having any of it. She'd never been anywhere with a private pool before—let alone a pool as vast and inviting as the one at Vallombrosa.

Initially a little shy about appearing in her tiny bikini, she'd been quickly reassured by the darkening response in his eyes—though she'd been surprised when he'd changed his mind and decided to join her in the pool after all. And Renzo in sleek black swim shorts, olive skin gleaming as he shook water from his hair, was a vision which made her heart race. She could have spent all afternoon watching his powerful body ploughing through the silky water. But he'd brought her lazy swim to a swift conclusion with some explicit suggestions whispered in her ear and they had returned to his bedroom for sex which had felt even more incredible than usual.

Was it because her senses had been heightened by fresh air and sunshine that everything felt so amazing? Or because Renzo had seemed unusually accessible in this peaceful place which seemed a world away from the hustle and bustle of her normal life? Darcy kept reminding herself that the reasons why were irrelevant. Because this was only temporary. A last trip before she moved to Norfolk—which was probably the only reason he had invited her to join him. And tonight was their final dinner, when they were being joined by Renzo's lawyer, who was buying the Sabatini estate.

Their eyes met in the mirror.

'Will you zip me up?'

'Certo.'

'So tell me again,' she said, feeling his fingers brushing against her bare skin as he slid the zip of the close-fitting dress all the way up. 'The lawyer's name is Cristiano Branzi and his girlfriend is Nicoletta—'

'Ramelli.' There was a moment of hesitation and his eyes narrowed fractionally. 'And—just so you know—she and I used to have a thing a few years back.'

In the process of hooking in a dangly earring, Darcy's fingers stilled. 'A *thing*?'

'You really are going to have to stop looking so shocked, *cara*. I'm thirty-five years old and in Rome, as in all cities, social circles are smaller than you might imagine. She and I were lovers for a few months, that's all.'

That's all. Darcy's practised smile didn't waver. Just like her. Great sex for a few months and then goodbye—was that his usual pattern? Had Nicoletta been rewarded with a trip abroad just before the affair ended? But as she followed Renzo downstairs she was determined not to spoil their last evening and took the champagne Stefania offered, hoping she displayed more confidence than she felt as she rose to greet their guests.

Cristiano was a powerfully built man with piercing blue eyes and Darcy thought Nicoletta the most beautiful woman she'd ever seen. The Italian woman's sleek dark hair was swept up into a sophisticated chignon and she wore a dress which was obviously designer made. Real diamond studs glittered at her ears, echoing the smaller diamonds which sparkled in a watch which was slightly too loose for her narrow wrist. Darcy watched as she presented each smooth cheek in turn to be kissed by Renzo, wondering why she hadn't worn the turquoise dress after all. Why hadn't she realised that of *course* the Italian woman would also wear black, leaving the two of them wide open for comparison? How cheap her own glimmering gown must seem in comparison—and how wild her untameable red curls as they spilled down over her shoulders towards breasts which were much too large by fashionable standards.

'So…' Nicoletta smiled as they sat down to prosciutto and slivers of iced melon at a candlelit table decorated with roses. 'This is your first time in Italy, Darcy?'

'It is,' answered Darcy, with a smile.

'But not your last, I hope?'

Darcy looked across the table at Renzo, thinking it might bring the mood down if she suddenly announced that they were in the process of splitting up.

'Darcy isn't much of a traveller,' he said smoothly.

'Oh?'

Something made her say it. Was it bravado or stupidity? Yet surely she wasn't *ashamed* of the person she really was. Not unless she honestly thought she could compete with these glossy people, with their Tuscan estates and diamond wristwatches which probably cost as much as a small car.

'To be honest, I don't really have a lot of money to go travelling.' She slanted Nicoletta a rueful smile. 'I'm a waitress.'

'A *waitress*?' Nicoletta's silver fork was returned to her plate with a clatter, the dainty morsel she'd speared remaining untouched. 'That is a very unusual job.' There was a slightly perplexed pause. 'So how did you and Renzo actually meet?'

Darcy registered the faint astonishment on Nicoletta's face, but what had she expected? And now she had dropped Renzo in it. He was probably going to bluster out some story about how he'd bumped into her in a bookshop or been introduced at a party by a friend of a friend. Except he'd told her very specifically that he didn't like lies, hadn't he?

'I met Darcy when she was working in a nightclub in London,' Renzo said. 'I walked in with some visiting colleagues and saw her serving cocktails to the people on the next table. She turned round and looked at me and that was it. I was completely blown away.'

'I'm not surprised,' murmured Cristiano. 'I have never seen hair as bright as yours before, Darcy. I believe this is what they call the show-stopping look?'

The compliment was unexpected and Darcy met Renzo's eyes, expecting to find mockery or anger in them but there was none. On the contrary, he looked as if he was *enjoying* the praise being directed at her and suddenly she wanted to turn and run from the room. Or tell him not to look at her that way because it was making her fantasise about a life which could never be hers.

She cleared her throat, trying to remember back to when she'd worked in that very hip restaurant which had been frequented by the media crowd. To remember how those high-profile people used to talk to each other when she arrived to offer them a bread roll, which they inevitably refused. They used to play everything down, didn't they? To act as if nothing really mattered.

'Oh, that's quite enough about me,' she said lightly. 'I'd much rather talk about Tuscany.'

'You like it here?' questioned Nicoletta. 'At Vallombrosa?'

'Who could fail to like it?' questioned Darcy simply. 'There can't be anywhere in the world as beautiful as this. The gardens are so lovely and the view is to die for.' She smiled as she reached for a piece of bread. 'If I had the money I'd snap it up in a shot. You're a very lucky man, Cristiano.'

'I'm very aware of that.' Cristiano's blue eyes crinkled. 'Nobody can quite believe that Renzo has put it on the market at last, after years of everyone offering him vast amounts of money to sell it. And he won't say what has suddenly changed his mind.'

But Darcy knew why. She'd seen the pain in his eyes when he'd talked about his parents' divorce and suspected his stepmother's death had made him want to let all that painful past go. He hadn't said that much but it surprised her that he'd confided in her at all. For a little while it had made her feel special—more than just his 'friend with benefits.' But that was fantasy, too. It was easy to share your secrets with someone you knew was planning to leave you.

Except for her, of course. She was one of those people whose secrets were just too dark to tell.

Course after course of delicious food was served—stuffed courgette flowers, ultra-fine pasta with softshell crab and a rich dessert of cherries and cream—all accompanied by fine wines from Renzo's cellar. Nicoletta skilfully fired a series of questions at her, some of which Darcy carefully avoided answering but fortunately Nicoletta enjoyed talking about herself much more. She waxed lyrical about her privileged upbringing in Parioli in Rome, her school in Switzerland and her fluency in four languages. It transpired that she had several dress shops in Rome, none of which she worked in herself.

'You should come visit, Darcy. Get Renzo to buy you something pretty.'

Darcy wondered if that was Nicoletta's way of subtly pointing out that the cheapness of her clothes hadn't gone unnoticed, but if it was, she didn't care. All she could think about right then was being alone with Renzo again as she tried not to focus on time slipping away from them. She returned to their room while he waved their guests goodbye and was naked in bed waiting for him when at last he came in and shut the door behind him.

'You were very good during dinner,' he said, unbuckling the belt of his trousers.

'Good? In what way?'

'A bewitching combination. A little defiant about your lowly job,' he observed as he stepped out of his boxer shorts. 'And there's no need to look at me that way, Darcy, because it's true. But your heartfelt praise about the property pleased Cristiano very much, though he's always been a sucker for a pretty girl. He's going to keep Gisella, Pasquale and Stefania on, by the way. He told me just before they left for Rome.'

'So all's well that ends well?' she questioned brightly.

'Who said anything about it ending?' he murmured, climbing into bed and pulling her into his arms so that she could feel the hard rod of his arousal pushing against her. 'I thought the night was only just beginning.'

They barely slept a wink. It was as if Renzo was determined to leave her with lasting memories of just what an amazing lover he was as he brought her to climax over and over again. As dawn coated the dark room with a pale daffodil light, Darcy found herself enjoying the erotic spectacle of Renzo's dark head between her thighs, gasping as his tongue cleaved over her exquisitely aroused flesh, until she quivered helplessly around him.

She was slow getting ready the next morning and when she walked into the dining room, Renzo glanced up from his newspaper.

'I need to leave for the airport soon,' she said.

'No, you don't. We'll fly back together on my jet,' he said, pouring her a cup of coffee.

Darcy sat down and reached for a sugar cube. *Start as you mean to go on. And remember that your future does not contain billionaire property tycoons with an endless supply of private transport.*

'Honestly, there's no need,' she said. 'I have a return ticket and I'm perfectly happy to go back on FlyCheap.'

The look he gave her was a mixture of wry, indulgent—but ultimately uncompromising. 'I'm not sending you back on a budget airline, Darcy. You're coming on my jet, with me.'

And if Darcy had thought that travelling in a chauffeur-driven car was the height of luxury, then flying in Renzo's private plane took luxury onto a whole new level. She saw the unmistakable looks of surprise being directed at her by two stewardesses as they were whisked through passport control at Florence airport. Were they thinking she didn't look like Renzo's usual *type*, with her cheap jewellery, her bouncing bosom and the fact that she was clearly out of her comfort zone?

But Darcy didn't care about that either. She was just going to revel in her last few hours with her lover and as soon as he'd dismissed the flight crew she unzipped his jeans. As she pulled down his silk boxers she realised this was the last time she would ever slide her lips over his rocky length and hear his helpless groan as he jerked inside her mouth. The last time he would ever give that low, growling moan as he clamped his hands possessively around her head to anchor her lips to the most sensitive part of his anatomy. Afterwards, he made love to her so slowly that she felt as if she would never come down to earth properly.

But all too soon the flight was over and they touched down in England where his car was waiting. Darcy hesitated as the driver held open the door for her.

'Could you drop me off at the Tube on the way?'

Renzo frowned, exasperation flattening his lips. 'Darcy, what is this? I'm not dropping you anywhere except home.'

'No. You don't have to do that.'

'I know I don't.' He paused before giving a flicker of a smile. 'You can even invite me in for coffee if you like.'

'Coffee?'

'There you go. You're sounding shocked again.' He shook his head. 'Isn't that what normally happens when a man takes a woman home after the kind of weekend we've just had? I've never even seen where you live.'

'I know you haven't. But you're not interested in my life. You've always made that perfectly clear.'

'Maybe I'm interested now,' he said stubbornly.

And now was too late, she thought. Why hadn't he done this at the beginning, when it might have meant something? He was behaving with all the predictability of a powerful man who had everything he wanted—his curiosity suddenly aroused by the one thing which was being denied him.

'It's small and cramped and all I can afford, which is why I'm moving to Norfolk,' she said defensively. 'It's about as far removed from where you live as it's possible to be and you'll hate it.'

'Why don't you let me be the judge of that? Unless you're ashamed of it, of course.'

Furiously, she glared at him. 'I'm not *ashamed* of it.'

'Well, then.' He shrugged. 'What's the problem?'

But Darcy's fingers were trembling as she unlocked her front door because she'd never invited *anyone* into this little sanctuary of hers. When you'd shared rooms and space for all of your life—when you'd struggled hard to find some privacy—then something which was completely your own became especially precious. 'Come in, then,' she said ungraciously.

Renzo stepped into the room and the first thing he noticed was that the living, dining and kitchen area were all crammed into the same space. And…his eyes narrowed…was that a narrow *bed* in the corner?

The second thing he noticed was how clean and unbelievably tidy it was—and the minimalist architect in him applauded her total lack of clutter. There were no family photos or knick-knacks. The only embellishment he could see was a cactus in a chrome pot on the window sill and an art deco mirror, which reflected some much-needed extra light into the room. And books. Lots of books. Whole lines of them, neatly arranged in alphabetical order.

He turned to look at her. She had been careful about sitting in the Tuscan sun but, even so, her fair skin had acquired a faint glow. She looked much healthier than she'd done when she'd arrived at Vallombrosa, that was for sure. In fact, she looked so pretty in the yellow dress with blue flowers which she had stubbornly insisted on laundering herself, that he felt his heart miss a beat. And suddenly Renzo knew he wasn't ready to let her go. Not yet. He thought about the way she'd been in his arms last night. The way they'd taken their coffee out onto the terrace at Vallombrosa to stare at the moon, and he'd known a moment of unexpected peace. Why end something before it fizzled out all of its own accord, especially when it still had the potential to give him so much pleasure?

He glanced over towards her neat little kitchenette. 'So... Aren't you going to offer me coffee?'

'I've only got instant, I'm afraid.'

He did his best to repress a shudder. 'Just some water, then.'

He watched as she poured him a glass of tap water—he couldn't remember the last time he'd drunk *that*—and added an ice cube. But when she put the drink down on the table, he didn't touch it. Instead, he fixed her with a steady gaze.

'I've had a good weekend,' he said slowly.

'Me, too. Actually, it was more than good.' She gave him a quick smile. 'Thank you.'

There was a pause. 'Look, this move to Norfolk seems a little…hasty. Why don't you stay in London a bit longer?'

'I told you why—and now you've seen for yourself my reasons. I want to start living differently.'

'I can understand that. But what if I told you I had an apartment you could use—somewhere much bigger and more comfortable than this? What then?'

'What, just like that? Let me guess.' Her emerald gaze bored into him. 'Even if you don't have one available, you'll magically "find" an apartment for me? Browse through your extensive property portfolio or have one of your staff discreetly rent somewhere? Thanks, but no, thanks. I'm not interested, Renzo. I have no desire to be a "kept woman" and fulfilling the stereotype of being a rich man's mistress, even if that's the way I'm currently heading.'

Her stubbornness infuriated him but it also produced another spark of admiration. How could a woman with so little be so proud and spirited and turn down an offer anyone else in her position would have leapt at? Renzo picked up the iced water and sipped it before walking over to the window and looking out at a red-brick wall. He wondered what it must be like to wake up to this view every morning, before putting on some drab uniform to spend the rest of the day carrying trays of food and drink.

He turned round. 'What if I asked you to delay going to Norfolk?'

She raised her eyebrows. 'And why would you do that?'

'Oh, come on, Darcy,' he said softly. 'You may have been an innocent when I bedded you, but you're not so innocent now. I have taught you a great deal—'

'Perhaps there's some kind of certificate I could nominate you for, if it's praise you're after?'

He gave a low laugh, turned on by an insolence he encountered from nobody else. He could see the wariness on her face as he took a step towards her, but he could also see the darkening of her eyes and the sudden stiffness of her body, as if she was using every bit of willpower not to give into what she really wanted. And Renzo knew enough about women to realise that this wasn't over. Not yet.

'It's not praise I want,' he said softly. 'It's you. I'm not ready to let you go.' He reached out to smooth down her riotous curls and felt the kick of lust as he pulled her into his arms. 'What if I told you that I liked the way you were with Cristiano and Nicoletta? That I find you charming in company as well as exquisite in bed and that maybe I'd like to take you out a little more. Why shouldn't we go to the theatre, or a party or two? Perhaps I've been a little selfish keeping you locked away and now I want to show you off to the world.'

'You make it sound as if I've passed some sort of hidden test!' she said indignantly.

'Maybe you have,' came his simple reply.

Darcy was torn, because his words were dangerous. She didn't want him *showing her off to the world*. What if someone remembered her? Someone who knew who she really was? And yet Renzo was only echoing the things she'd been thinking. Things she'd been trying and failing to deny—that she wasn't yet ready to walk away either.

'What if I gave you a key to my apartment?' His voice broke into her thoughts.

'A key?' she echoed.

'Why not? And—just so you know—I don't hand out keys every day of the week. Very few people are given access to my home because I value my privacy very highly.'

'So why me? To what do I owe this huge honour?'

'Because you've never asked me for anything,' he said quietly. 'And nobody's ever done that before.'

Darcy tried telling herself it was just another example of a powerful man being intrigued by the unfamiliar. But surely it was more than that. Wasn't the giving of a key—no matter how temporary—a sign that he *trusted* her? And wasn't trust the most precarious yet most precious thing in the world, especially considering Renzo's lack of it where women were concerned?

She licked her lips, tempted beyond reason, but really—when she stopped to think about it—what was holding her back? She'd escaped her northern life and left that dark world behind as she'd carved out a new identity for herself. She'd been completely underqualified and badly educated but night classes had helped make up for her patchy schooling—and her sunny disposition meant she'd been able to find waitressing work whenever she had put her mind to it. She wasn't quite sure where she wanted to be but she knew she was on her way. And who would possibly remember her after all this time? She'd left Manchester for London when she was sixteen and that was a long time ago. Didn't she deserve a little fun while she had the chance?

He was watching her closely and Darcy was savvy enough to realise her hesitation was turning him on. Yet she wasn't playing games with him. Her indecision was genuine. She really *was* trying to give him up, only it wasn't as easy as she'd imagined. She was beginning to suspect that Renzo Sabatini was becoming an addiction and that should have set off every alarm bell in her body because it didn't matter if it was drink or drugs or food—or in this case a man— addictions were dangerous. She knew that. Her personal history had taught her that in the bleakest way possible.

But now he was pulling her against him and she could feel all that hard promise shimmering beneath the surface of his muscular body. Enveloped by his arms, she found herself wanting to sink further into his powerful embrace, wanting to hold on to this brief sense of comfort and safety.

'Say yes, Darcy,' he urged softly, his breath warm against her lips. 'Take my key and be my lover for a little while longer.'

His hand was on her breast and her knees were starting to buckle and Darcy knew then that she wasn't going to resist him anytime soon.

'Okay,' she said, closing her eyes as he began to ruck up her dress. 'I'll stay for a bit longer.'

CHAPTER FIVE

THE LIMOUSINE SLID to a halt outside the Granchester
Hotel as Renzo was caressing Darcy's thigh and he
found himself thinking that she'd never looked more
beautiful than she did tonight. Hungrily, he ran his
gaze over the emerald shimmer of her gown, thinking
that for once she looked like a billionaire's mistress.

He gave an almost imperceptive shake of his head.
Didn't she realise that, despite her initial reluctance,
she was entitled to a mistress's perks? He'd tried to
persuade her that it would be easier all round if she
enjoyed *all* the benefits of his wealth and made herself more available to him by giving up her lowly job,
but she had stubbornly refused to comply. She'd told
him he should be grateful she was no longer working
in the nightclub and he had growled at the thought
of her curvy body poured into that tight black satin
while men drooled over her.

But tonight, a small victory had been won. For
once she'd accepted his offer of a custom-made gown
to wear to the prestigious ball he was holding in aid
of his charity foundation, though it had taken some
persuasion. His mouth flattened because where once
her stubborn independence had always excited him,

her independence was starting to rankle, as was her determination to carry on waiting tables even though it took up so much of her time.

'The princess is supposed to be smiling when she goes to the ball,' he observed wryly, feeling her sequin-covered thigh tense beneath his fingers. 'Not looking as if she's walking towards her own execution.'

'But I'm not a princess, Renzo. I'm a waitress who happens to be wearing a gown which cost as much as I earn in three months.' She touched her fingertips to one of the mother-of-pearl clips which gleamed like milky rainbows against the abundant red curls. 'If you must know, I feel like Cinderella.'

'Ah, but the difference is that your clothes will not turn into rags at midnight, *cara*. When the witching hour comes you will be doing something far more pleasurable than travelling home in a pumpkin. So wipe that concerned look from your face and give me that beautiful smile instead.'

Feeling like a puppet, Darcy did as he asked, flashing a bright grin as someone rushed forward to open the car door for her. Carefully, she picked up the fishtail skirt of her emerald gown and stepped onto the pavement in her terrifyingly high shoes, thinking how quickly you could get used to being driven around like this and having people leap to attention simply because you were in the company of one of the world's most powerful men. What was not so easy was getting rid of the growing feeling of anxiety which had been gnawing away inside her for weeks now—a sick, queasy feeling which just wouldn't shift.

Because she was starting to realise that she was

stuck. Stuck in some awful limbo. Living in a strange, parallel world which wasn't real and locked into it by her inability to walk away from the only man who had ever been able to make her feel like a real woman.

The trouble was that things had changed and they were changing all the time. Why hadn't she realised that agreeing to accept the key to his apartment would strengthen the connection between them and make it even harder for her to sever her ties with him? It had made things…*complicated*. She didn't want her heart to thunder every time she looked at him or her body to melt with instant desire. Her worst fears had been realised and Renzo Sabatini had become her addiction. She ran her tongue over her lips. She knew he was bad for her yet she couldn't seem to give him up.

Sometimes she found herself longing for him to tire of her and kick *her* out since she didn't have the strength to end it herself. Wouldn't such a move force her to embrace the new life in Norfolk which she'd done absolutely nothing about—not since the day he'd given her his key and then made her come on the narrow bed in her humble bedsit, which these days she only ever visited when Renzo was away on business?

She could hear him telling his driver to take the rest of the night off and that they'd get a taxi home when the ball was over and she wished he wouldn't be so thoughtful with his staff. No wonder they all thought the world of him. But Darcy didn't need any more reasons to like him. Hadn't it been easier not to let her heart become involved when their affair had been more low-key, rather than this new-found openness with trips to the opera and theatre and VIP balls?

And now he was taking her arm and leading her towards the red-carpeted marble staircase where the paparazzi were clustered. She'd known they were going to be there, but had also known she couldn't possibly avoid them. And anyway, they weren't going to be looking at *her*. They would be far too busy focussing on the Hollywood actress who was wearing the most revealing dress Darcy had ever seen, or the married co-star she was rumoured to be having an affair with.

Flashbulbs exploded to light up the warm night and although Darcy quickly tried to turn her head away, the press weren't having any of it. And wasn't that a TV camera zooming in on her? She wondered why she had let the dress designer put these stupid clips in her hair which meant she couldn't hide behind the usual comforting curtain of her curls. This was the most high-profile event they'd attended as a couple but there had been no way of getting out of it—not when it was Renzo's foundation and he was the man who'd organised it.

She felt like a fox on the run as they entered the ballroom but the moment she was swallowed up by all that glittering splendour, she calmed down. The gilded room had been decked out with giant sprays of pink-and-white cherry blossoms, symbolising the hope which Renzo's foundation brought to suffering children in war-torn areas of the world. Tall, guttering candles gave the place a fairy-tale feel. On a raised dais, a string quartet was playing and the exquisitely dressed guests were mingling in small chattering groups. It was the fanciest event she'd ever attended and dinner had been prepared by a clutch of award-winning chefs. But the moment the first rich course was placed in front of her, Darcy's stomach did an intricate kind of twist, which meant she merely pushed the food around her plate and tried not to look at it. At least Renzo didn't notice or chide her for her lack of appetite as he might normally have done—he was too busy talking to fundraisers and donors and being photographed next to the diamond necklace which was the star lot for the night's auction.

But after disappearing into one of the restrooms, where a splash of her face with cold water made her queasiness shift, Darcy became determined to enjoy herself. *Stop living so fearfully*, she chided herself as she chatted attentively whenever she was introduced to someone new and rose eagerly to her feet when Renzo asked her to dance. And that bit felt like heaven. His cheek was warm against hers and her body fitted so snugly into his that she felt like one of those salt and pepper shakers you sometimes found in old-fashioned tea rooms—as if they were made to be together. But they weren't. Of course they weren't.

She knew this couldn't continue. She'd been seduced into staying but if she stayed much longer she was going to have to tell him the truth. Open up about her past. Confess to being the daughter of a junkie and all the other stuff which went with it. He would probably end their affair immediately and a swift, clean cut might just be the best thing. She would be heartbroken for a while of course, but she would get over it because you could get over just about anything if you worked at it. It would be better than forcing herself to walk away and having to live with the stupid spark of hope that maybe it *could* have worked.

'So… How is the most beautiful woman in the

room?' He bent his head to her ear. 'You seem to be enjoying yourself.'

She closed her eyes and inhaled his sultry masculine scent. 'I am.'

'Not as bad as you thought it was going to be?'

'Not nearly so bad.'

'Think you might like to come to something like this again in the future?'

'I *could* be persuaded.'

He smiled. 'Then let's go and sit down. The auction is about to begin.'

The auctioneer stepped onto the stage and began to auction off the different lots which had been donated as prizes. A holiday in Mauritius, a box at the opera and a tour of Manchester United football ground all went under the hammer for eye-watering amounts, and then the diamond necklace was brought out to appreciative murmurs.

Darcy listened as the bidding escalated, only vaguely aware of Renzo lifting a careless finger from time to time. But suddenly everyone was clapping and looking at *them* and she realised that Renzo had successfully bid for the necklace and the auctioneer's assistant had handed it to him and he was putting it on *her* neck. She was aware of every eye in the room on them as he fixed the heavy clasp in place and she was aware of the dazzle of the costly gems.

'In truth you should wear emeralds to match your eyes,' he murmured. 'But since diamonds were the only thing on offer they will have to do. What do you think, *cara*?'

Darcy couldn't get rid of the sudden lump in her throat. It felt like a noose. The stones were heavy and the metal was cold. But there was no time to protest because cameras were flashing again and this time they were all directed at her. Sweat beaded her forehead and she felt dizzy, only able to breathe normally when the rumour went round that the Hollywood star was exiting through the kitchens and the press pack left the ballroom to follow her.

Darcy turned to Renzo, her fingertips touching the unfamiliar stones. 'You do realise I can't possibly accept this?' she questioned hoarsely.

'And you do realise that I am not going to let you give it back? Your tastes are far too modest for a woman in your position. You are the lover of a very wealthy man, Darcy, and I want you to wear it. I want you to have some pretty jewels for all the pleasure you've given me.'

His voice had dipped into a silken caress, which usually would have made her want to melt, but he made it sound like payment for services rendered. Was that how he saw it? Darcy's smile felt as if someone had stitched it onto her face with a rusty needle. Shouldn't she at least try to look as a woman *should* look when a man had just bought something this valuable? And wasn't she in danger of being a hypocrite? After all, she had a key to his Belgravia home—wasn't that just a short step to accepting his jewels? What about the designer dress she was wearing tonight, and the expensive shoes? He'd bought those for her, hadn't he?

Something like fear clutched at her heart and she knew she couldn't put it off any longer. She was going to have to come clean about her mum and the children's home and all the other sordid stuff.

So tell him. Explain your aversion to accepting gifts and bring this whole crazy relationship to a head, because at least that will end the uncertainty and you'll know where you stand.

But in the car he kissed her and when they reached the apartment he kissed her some more, unclipping the diamond choker and dropping it onto a table in the sitting room as casually as if it had been made of paste. His hands were trembling as he undressed her and so were hers. He made love to her on one of the sofas and then he carried her into the bedroom and did it all over again—and who would want to talk about the past at a moment like that?

They made love most of the night and because she'd asked for a day off after the ball, Darcy slept late next morning. When she eventually woke, it was getting on for noon and Renzo had left for the office long ago. *And still she hadn't told him.* She showered and dressed but her queasiness had returned and she could only manage some mint tea for breakfast. The morning papers had been delivered and, with a growing sense of nervousness, she flicked through the pages until she found the column which listed society events. And there she was in all her glory—in her mermaid dress of green sequins, the row of fiery white diamonds glittering at her throat, with Renzo standing just behind her, a hint of possessiveness in the sexy smile curving his lips.

She stood up abruptly, telling herself she was being paranoid. Who was going to see, or, more important, to *care* that she was in the wretched paper?

The morning slipped away. She went for a walk, bought a bag of oranges to put through the squeezer and was just nibbling on a piece of dry toast when the doorbell rang and Darcy frowned. It never rang when Renzo wasn't here—and not just because his wasn't a lifestyle where people made spontaneous visits. He'd meant what he said about guarding his privacy; his home really was his fortress. People just didn't come round.

She pressed the button on the intercom.

'Yes?'

'Is that Darcy Denton?' It was a male voice with a broad Manchester accent.

'Who is this?' she questioned sharply.

'An old friend of yours.' There was a pause. 'Drake Bradley.'

For a minute Darcy thought she might pass out. She thought about pretending to be someone else—the housekeeper perhaps. Or just cutting the connection while convincing herself that she didn't have to speak to anyone—let alone Drake Bradley. But the bully who had ruled the roost in the children's home had never been the kind of person to take no for an answer. If she refused to speak to him she could imagine him settling down to wait until Renzo got home and she just imagined what he might have to say to him. Shivering, she stared at her pale reflection in the hall mirror. What was it they said? Keep your friends close but your enemies closer.

'What do you want?'

'Just a few minutes of your time. Surely you can spare that, Darcy.'

Telling herself it was better to brazen it out, Darcy pressed the buzzer, her heart beating out a primitive tattoo as she opened the door to find Drake standing there—a sly expression on his pockmarked face. A decade had made his hair recede, but she would have recognised him immediately and her blood ran cold as the sight of him took her back to a life she'd thought she'd left for ever.

'What do you want?' she asked again.

'That's not much of a welcome, is it? What's the matter, Darcy? Aren't you going to invite me in? Surely you're not ashamed of me?'

But the awful thing was that she *was*. She'd moved on a lot since that turbulent period when their lives had merged and clashed, yet Drake looked as if he'd been frozen in time. Wearing clothes which swamped his puny frame, he had oil beneath his fingernails and on the fingers of his left hand were the letters *H, A, T, E. You have no right to judge him*, she told herself. He was simply another survivor from the shipwreck of their youth. Surely she owed him a little hospitality when she'd done so well for herself.

She could smell stale tobacco and the faint underlying odour of sweat as she opened the door wider and he brushed past her. He followed her into the enormous sitting room and she wondered if he was seeing the place as she had seen it the first time she'd been here, when she'd marvelled at the space and light and cleanliness. And, of course, the view.

'Wow.' He pursed his lips together and whistled as he stared out at the whispering treetops of Eaton Square. 'You've certainly landed on your feet, Darcy.'

'Are you going to tell me why you're here?'

His weasel eyes narrowed. 'Not even going to offer me a drink? It's a hot day outside. I could murder a drink.'

Darcy licked her lips. *Don't aggravate him. Tolerate him for a few minutes and then he'll go.* 'What would you like?'

'Got a beer?'

'Sure.'

Her underlying nausea seemed to intensify as Darcy went to the kitchen to fetch him a beer. When she returned he refused her offer of a glass and began to glug greedily from the bottle.

'How did you find me?' she asked, once he had paused long enough to take a breath.

He put the bottle down on a table. 'Saw you on the news last night, walking into that big hotel. Yeah. On TV. Couldn't believe my eyes at first. I thought to myself, that can't be Darcy Denton—daughter of one of Manchester's best known hookers. Not on the arm of some rich dude like Sabatini. So I headed along to the hotel to see for myself and hung around until your car arrived. I'm good at hanging around in the shadows, I am.' He smiled slyly. 'I overheard your man giving the address to the taxi driver so I thought I'd come and pay you a visit to catch up on old times. See for myself how you've come up in the world.'

Darcy tried to keep her voice light. To act as if her heart weren't pounding so hard it felt as if it might burst right out of her chest. 'You still haven't told me what you want.'

His smile grew calculating. 'You've landed on your feet, Darcy. Surely it's no big deal to help out an old friend?'

'Are you asking for money?' she said.

He sneered. 'What do you think?'

She thought plenty but nothing she'd want *him* to

hear. She thought about how much cash she had squir-relled away in her bank account. She'd amassed funds since she'd been with Renzo because he wouldn't let her pay for anything. *But it was still a pitiful amount by most people's standards, and besides…if you gave in to blackmail once then you opened up the flood-gates.*

And she didn't need to give into blackmail be-cause hadn't she already decided to tell Renzo about her past? This might be the push she needed to see if he still wanted her when he discovered who she re-ally was. Her mouth dried. Dared she take that risk?

She had no choice.

Drawing her shoulders back, she looked straight into Drake's shifty eyes. 'You're not getting any money from me,' she said quietly. 'I'd like you to leave and not bother coming back.'

His lip curled and then he shrugged. 'Have it your own way, Darcy.'

Of course, if she'd thought it through properly, she might have wondered why he obeyed her quite so eagerly…

Renzo's eyes narrowed as the man with the pock-marked face shoved his way past, coming out of *his* private elevator as if he had every right to do so. His frown deepened. Had he been making some kind of delivery? Surely not, dressed like *that*? He stood for a moment watching his retreating back, instinct alert-ing him to a danger he didn't quite understand. But it was enough to cast a shadow over a deliciously high mood which had led to him leaving work early—

something which had caused his secretary to blink at him in astonishment.

In truth, Renzo had been pretty astonished himself. Taking a half-day off wasn't the way he usually operated, but he had wanted to spend the rest of the afternoon with Darcy. Getting into bed with her. Running his fingers through her silky riot of curls. Losing himself deep in her tight, tight body with his mouth on her breast. Maybe even telling her how good she made him feel. Plus he'd received an urgent message reminding him that he needed to insure the necklace he'd spent a fortune on last night.

After watching the man leave the building, Renzo took the penthouse elevator where the faint smell of tobacco and beer still tainted the air. He unlocked the door to his apartment just as Darcy tore out of the sitting room. But the trouble was she didn't look like the Darcy of this morning's smouldering fantasies, when somehow he'd imagined arriving home to see her clad in that black satin basque and matching silk stockings he'd recently bought. Not only was she wearing jeans and a baggy shirt—her face was paler than usual and her eyes looked huge and haunted with something which looked like guilt. Now, why was that? he wondered.

'Renzo!' she exclaimed, raking a handful of bouncing red curls away from her forehead and giving him an uncertain smile. 'I wasn't expecting you.'

'So I see.' He put his briefcase on the hall table. 'Who was the man I saw leaving?'

'The man?' she questioned, but he could hear the sudden quaver in her voice.

Definitely guilt, he thought grimly.

'The man I met coming down in the elevator. Bad skin. Bad smell. Who was he, Darcy?'

Darcy met the cool accusation in Renzo's eyes and knew she had run out of reasons not to tell him.

'I need to talk to you,' she said.

He didn't respond straight away, just walked into the sitting room leaving her to follow him, her senses alerted to the sudden tension in his body and the forbidding set of his shoulders. Usually, he pulled her into his arms and kissed all the breath out of her when he arrived home but today he hadn't even touched her. And when he turned around, Darcy was shocked by the cold expression on his face.

'So talk,' he said.

She felt like someone who'd been put on stage in front of a vast audience and told to play a part she hadn't learnt. Because she'd never spoken about this before, not to anyone. She'd buried it so deep it was almost inaccessible. But she needed to access it now, before his irritation grew any deeper.

'He's someone I was in care with.'

'In care?'

She nodded. 'That's what they call it in England, although it's a bit of a misnomer because you don't actually get much in the way of care. I lived in a children's home in the north for most of my childhood.'

His black eyes narrowed. 'What happened to your parents?'

Darcy could feel a bead of sweat trickling its way down her back. Here it was. The question which separated most normal people from the unlucky few. The question which made you feel a freak no matter which way you answered it. Was it any wonder she'd spent her life trying to avoid having to do so?

And yet didn't it demonstrate the shallowness of her relationship with Renzo that in all the time she'd known him—this was the first time he'd actually asked? Dead parents had been more than enough information for him. He hadn't been the type of person to quiz her about her favourite memory or how she'd spent her long-ago Christmases.

'I'm illegitimate,' she said baldly. 'I don't know who my father was and neither did my mother. And she... Well, for a lot of my childhood, she wasn't considered fit to be able to take care of me.'

'Why not?'

'She had...' She hesitated. 'She had a drug problem. She was a junkie.'

He let out a long breath and Darcy found herself searching his face for some kind of understanding, some shred of compassion for a situation which had been out of her control. But his expression remained like ice. His black eyes were stony as they skimmed over her, looking at her as if it was the first time he'd seen her and not liking what they saw.

'Why didn't you tell me any of this before?'

'Because you didn't ask. And you didn't ask because you didn't want to know!' she exclaimed. 'You made that very clear. We haven't had the kind of relationship where we talked about stuff like this. You just wanted...sex.'

She waited for him to deny it. To tell her that there had been more to it than that—and Darcy realised she was already thinking of their relationship in the past tense. But he didn't deny it. His sudden closed look made his features appear shuttered as he walked over to the table near where he'd undressed her last night and her heart missed a beat as she saw him looking down at the polished surface, on which stood a lamp and nothing else.

Nothing else.

It took a moment for her to register the significance of this and that moment came when he lifted his black gaze to hers and slanted her an unfathomable look. 'Where's the necklace?' he questioned softly.

Darcy's mind raced. In the heat of everything that had happened, she'd forgotten about the diamond necklace he'd bought last night for her at the auction. She vaguely remembered the dazzle of the costly gems as he'd dropped them onto the table, but his hands had been all over her at the time and it had blotted out everything except the magic of his touch. Had she absent-mindedly tidied it away when she was picking up her clothes this morning? No. It had definitely been there when...

Fear and horror clamped themselves around her suddenly racing heart.

When...

Drake! Her throat dried as she remembered leaving him alone in the room while she went to fetch him a beer. Remembered the way he'd hurriedly left after his half-hearted attempt at blackmail. Had Drake stolen the necklace?

Of course he had.

'I don't—'

His voice was like steel. 'Did your friend take it?'

'He's not—'

'What's the matter, Darcy?' Contemptuously, he

cut through her protest. 'Did I arrive home unexpectedly and spoil your little plan?'

'What *plan*?'

'Oh, come on. Isn't this what's known in the trade
as a scam? To rob me. To cheat on me.'

Darcy stared at him in disbelief. 'You can't honestly believe that?'

'Can't I? Perhaps it's the first clear-headed thought
I've had in a long time, now that I'm no longer completely mesmerised by your pale skin and witchy
eyes.' He shook his head like a man who was emerging from a deep coma. 'Now I'm beginning to wonder whether something like this was in your sights
all along.'

Darcy felt foreboding icing her skin. 'What are
you talking about?' she whispered.

'I've often wondered,' he said harshly, 'what you
might give a man who has everything. Another house,
or a faster car?' He shook his head. 'No. Material
wealth means nothing when you have plenty. But innocence—ah! Now that is a very different thing.'

'You're not making sense.'

'Think about it. What is a woman's most prized
possession, *cara mia*?' The Italian words of endear-
ment dripped like venom from his lips. '*Sì*. I can see
from your growing look of comprehension that you
are beginning to understand. Her virginity. Precious
and priceless and the biggest bartering tool in the
market. And hasn't it always been that way?'

'Renzo.' She could hear the desperation in her
voice now but she couldn't seem to keep it at bay.
'You don't mean that.'

'Sometimes I would ask myself,' he continued,

still in that same flat tone, 'why someone as beautiful and sensual as you—someone hard-up and working in a dead-end job—hadn't taken a rich lover to catapult herself out of her poverty before I came along.'

Desperation morphed into indignation. 'You mean…use a man as a meal ticket?'

'Why are you looking so shocked—or is that simply an expression you've managed to perfect over the years? Isn't that what every woman does ultimately—feed like a leech off a man?' His black gaze roved over her. 'But not you. At least, not initially. Did you decide to deny yourself pleasure—to look at the long game rather than the lure of instant gratification? To hold out for the richest man available, who just happened to be me—someone who was blown away by your extraordinary beauty coupled with an innocence I'd never experienced before?' He gave a cynical smile. 'But you were cunning, too. I see that now. For a cynic like me, a spirited show of independence was pretty much guaranteed to wear me down. So you refused my gifts. You bought cheap clothes and budget airline tickets while valiantly offering me the money you'd saved. What a touching gesture—the hard-up waitress offering the jaded architect a handful of cash. And I fell for it—hook, line and sinker! I was sucked in by your stubbornness and your pride.'

'It wasn't like that!' she defended fiercely.

'You must have thought you'd hit the jackpot when I gave you the key to my flat and bought you a diamond necklace,' he bit out. 'Just as I did when you gave yourself so willingly to me and I discovered you were a virgin. I allowed my ego to be flattered and to blind myself to the truth. How could I have *been* so blind?'

Darcy felt her head spin and that horrible queasy feeling came washing over her again, in giant waves. This couldn't be happening. In a minute she would wake up and the nightmare would be over. But it wouldn't, would it? She was living her nightmare and the proof was right in front of her eyes. In the midst of her confusion and hurt she saw the look of something like satisfaction on Renzo's face. She remembered him mentioning his parents' divorce and how bitterly he'd said that women could never be trusted. Was he somehow pleased that his prejudices had been reinforced and he could continue thinking that way? Yes, he was, she realised. He *wanted* to believe badly of her.

She made one last attempt because wasn't there still some tiny spark of hope which existed—a part which didn't want to let him go? 'None of that—'

'Save your lying words because I don't want to hear them. You're only upset because I came home early and found you out. How were you going to explain the absence of the necklace, Darcy?' he bit out. 'A "burglary" while you were out shopping? Shifting the blame onto one of the people who service these apartments?'

'You think I'd be capable of that?'

'I don't know what you're capable of, do I?' he said coldly. 'I just want you to listen to what I'm going to say. I'm going out and by the time I get back I want you out of here. Every last trace of you. I don't ever want to see your face again. Understand? And for what it's worth—and I'm sure you realise it's a lot— you can keep the damned necklace.'

'You're not going to go to the police?'

'And advertise exactly what kind of woman my girlfriend really is and the kind of low-life company she keeps? That wouldn't exactly do wonders for my reputation, would it? Do whatever you'd planned to do with it all along.' He paused and his mouth tightened as his black gaze swept down over her body. 'Think of it as payment for services rendered. A clean-break pay-off, if you like.'

It was the final straw. Nausea engulfed her. She could feel her knees buckling and a strange roaring in her head. Her hand reached out to grab at the nearest chair but she missed and Darcy felt herself sliding helplessly to the ground, until her cheek was resting on the smooth silk of the Persian rug and her eyes were level with his ankles and the handmade Italian shoes which swum in and out of focus.

His voice seemed to come from a long way off. 'And you can spare me the histrionics, Darcy. They won't make me change my mind.'

'Who's asking you to change your mind?' she managed, from beneath gritted teeth.

She saw his shadow move as he stepped over her and a minute later she heard the sound of the front door slamming shut.

And after that, thankfully, she passed out.

CHAPTER SIX

'YOU CAN'T GO ON like this, Darcy, you really can't.'

The midwife sounded both kind and stern and Darcy was finding it difficult keeping her lips from wobbling. Because stern she could handle. Stern was something she was used to. It was the kindness which got to her every time, which made her want to cover her face with her hands and howl like a wounded animal. And she couldn't afford to break down, because if she did—she might never put herself back together again.

Her hand slipped down to her belly. 'You're sure my baby's okay?' she questioned for the fourth time.

'Your baby's fine. Take a look at the scan and see. A little bit on the small side perhaps, but thriving. Unlike you. You're wearing yourself out,' continued the midwife, a frown creasing her plump face. 'You're working too hard and not eating properly, by the look of you.'

'Honestly, I'll try harder. I'll…I'll cut down on my hours at work and start eating more vegetables,' said Darcy as she rolled up her sleeve. And she would. She would do whatever it took because all she could think about was that her baby was safe. *Safe.* Relief washed over her in almost tangible waves as the terror she'd experienced during that noisy ambulance ride began to recede. 'Does that mean I can go home?'

'I wanted to talk to you about that. I'm not very happy about letting you go anywhere,' said the midwife. 'Unless you've got somebody who can be there for you.'

Darcy tried not to flinch. She supposed she could pretend she had a caring mother or protective sister or even—ha, ha, ha—a loving husband. But that would be irresponsible. Because it wasn't just her she was looking out for any more. There was a baby growing inside her. Her throat constricted. Renzo's baby.

She tried not to tense up as the midwife began to measure her blood pressure. Things hadn't been easy since Renzo had left her lying on the floor of his Belgravia apartment, accusing her of histrionics before slamming the door behind him. But Darcy's unexpected faint hadn't been caused by grief or anger, though it had taken a couple of weeks more to realise why a normally healthy young woman should have passed out for no apparent reason. It was when she'd found herself retching in the bathroom that she'd worked it out for herself. And then, of course, she wondered how she could have been so stupid to have not seen it before. It all added up. But her general queasiness and lack of appetite—even the lateness of her period—had been easy to overlook after Renzo had dumped her.

Of course she'd hoped. Hoped like mad she'd somehow got her dates muddled, but deep down she'd known she hadn't because the brand-new aching in her breasts had told her so. She'd gone out to buy a pregnancy kit and the result had come as a shock but no great surprise. Heart racing, she'd sat on the floor of her bathroom in Norfolk staring at the blue line, wondering who to tell. But even if she *had* made some friends in her new home town, she knew there was only one person she *could* tell. Tears of injustice had stung her eyes. The man who thought she was a thief and a con woman. Who had looked at her with utter contempt in his eyes. But that was irrelevant. Renzo's opinion of her didn't really matter—all that mattered was that she let him know he was going to be a father.

If only it had been that easy. Every call she'd made had gone straight through to voicemail and she'd been reluctant to leave him her news in a message. So she'd telephoned his office and been put through to one of his secretaries for another humiliating experience. She'd felt as if the woman was reading from a script as she'd politely told her that Signor Sabatini was un- available for the foreseeable future. She remembered the beads of sweat which had broken out on her fore- head as she'd asked his secretary to have him ring her back. And her lack of surprise when he hadn't.

'Why...?' Her voice faltered as she looked up into the midwife's lined face. 'Why do I have to have someone at home with me?'

'Because twenty-eight weeks is a critical time in a woman's pregnancy and you need to take extra care. Surely there must be someone you could ask. Who's the baby's father, Darcy?'

Briefly, Darcy closed her eyes. So this was it. The point where she really needed to be self-sacrificing and ignore pride and ego and instinct. For the first time in a long time images of Renzo's darkly rugged face swam into her mind, because she'd been trying her best not to think about him. To forget that chiselled jaw and lean body and the way he used to put on those sexy, dark-rimmed glasses while he was working on plans for one of his buildings. To a large extent she had succeeded in forgetting him, banishing memories of how it used to feel to wake up in his arms, as she concentrated on her new job at the local café.

But now she must appeal for help from the man who had made her feel so worthless—whose final gesture had taken her back to those days when people used to look down their noses at her and not believe a word she said. She told herself it didn't matter what Renzo thought when the hospital phoned him. That she didn't care if he considered her a no-good thief because she knew the truth and that was all that mattered. Her hand reached down to lie protectively over her belly, her fingers curving over its hard swell. She would do anything to protect the life of this unborn child.

Anything.

And right at the top of that list was the need to be strong. She'd been strong at the beginning of the affair and it had protected her against pain. She'd done her usual thing of keeping her emotions on ice and had felt good about herself. Even during that weekend when he'd taken her to Tuscany and hinted at his trust issues and the fickleness of women, she had still kept her feelings buried deep. She hadn't expected anything—which was why it had come as such a surprise to her when they'd got back to England and he'd offered her the key to his apartment.

Had that been when she'd first let her guard down

and her feelings had started to change? Or had she just got carried away with her new position in life? Her plans to move to Norfolk had been quietly shelved because she'd enjoyed being his mistress, hadn't she? She'd enjoyed going to that fancy ball with him, when—after her initial flurry of nerves—she'd waltzed in that cherry blossom–filled ballroom in his arms. And if things hadn't gone so badly wrong and Drake hadn't turned up, it probably wouldn't have taken long for her to get used to wearing Renzo's jewels either.

She'd been a fool and it was time to stop acting like a fool.

Never again would she be whimpering Darcy Denton, pleading with her cruel Italian lover to believe her. He could think what the hell he liked as long as he helped take care of her baby.

She opened her eyes and met the questioning look in the midwife's eyes.

'His name is Renzo Sabatini,' she said.

Feeling more impotent than he'd felt in years, Renzo paced up and down the sterile hospital corridor, oblivious to the surreptitious looks from the passing nurses. For a man unused to waiting, he couldn't believe he was being forced to bide his time until the ward's official visiting hours and he got the distinct impression that any further pleas to be admitted early would by vetoed by the dragon-like midwife he'd spoken to earlier, who had made no secret of her disapproval. With a frown on her face she'd told him that his girlfriend was overworked and underfed and clearly on the breadline. Her gaze had swept over him, taking in his dark suit, silk tie and handmade Italian shoes and he could see from her eyes that she was sizing up his worth. He was being judged, he realised—and he didn't like to be judged. Nor put in the role of an absentee father-to-be who refused to accept his responsibilities.

But amid all this confusion was a shimmering of something he couldn't understand, an emotion which licked like fire over his cold heart and was confusing the life out of him. Furiously, he forced himself to concentrate on facts. To get his head around the reason he was here—why he'd been driven to some remote area of Norfolk on what had felt like the longest journey of his life. And then he needed to decide what he was going to do about it. His head spun as his mind went over and over the unbelievable fact.

Darcy was going to have a baby.

His baby.

His mouth thinned.

Or so she said.

Eventually he was shown into the side room of a ward where she lay on a narrow hospital bed—her bright hair the only thing of colour in an all-white environment. Her face was as bleached as the bed sheets and her eyes were both wary and hostile as she looked at him. He remembered the last time he'd seen her. When she'd slid to the floor and he had just let her lie there and now his heart clenched with guilt because she looked so damned fragile lying propped up against that great bank of pillows.

'Darcy,' he said carefully.

She looked as if she had been sucking on a lemon as she spoke. 'You came.'

'I had no choice.'

'Don't lie,' she snapped. 'Of course you did! You could have just ignored the call from the hospital, just like you've ignored all my other calls up until now.'

He wanted to deny it but how could he when it was true? 'Yes,' he said flatly. 'I could.'

'You let my calls go through to voicemail,' she accused.

Letting out a breath, Renzo slowly nodded. At the time it had seemed the only sane solution. He hadn't wanted to risk speaking to her, because hadn't he worried he would cave in and take her back, even if it was for only one night? Because after she'd gone he hadn't been able to forget her as easily as he'd imagined, even though she had betrayed his trust in her. Even when he thought about the missing diamonds and the way she'd allowed that creep to enter his home—that still didn't erase her from his mind. He'd started to wonder whether he'd made a big mistake and whether he should give her another chance, but pride and a tendency to think the worst about women had stopped him acting on it. He'd known that 50 per cent of relationships didn't survive—so why go for one which had the odds stacked against it from the start? Yet she'd flitted in and out of his mind in a way which no amount of hard work or travelling had been able to fix.

'Guilty as charged,' he said evenly.

'And you told your secretary not to put me through to you.'

'She certainly would have put you through if she'd known the reason you were ringing. Why the hell didn't you tell her?'

'Are you out of your mind? Is that how you like to see your women, Renzo?' she demanded. 'To have them plead and beg and humiliate themselves? *Yes, I know he doesn't want to speak to me, but could you please tell him I'm expecting his baby?* Or would you rather I had hung around outside the Sabatini building, waiting for the big boss to leave work so I could grab your elbow and break my news to you on a busy London street? Maybe I should have gone to the papers and sold them a story saying that my billionaire boyfriend was denying paternity!'

'Darcy,' he said, and now his voice had gentled. 'I'm sorry I accused you of stealing the necklace.'

Belligerently, she raised her chin. 'Just not sorry enough to seek me out to tell me that before?'

He thought how tough she was—with a sudden inner steeliness which seemed so at odds with her fragile exterior. 'I jumped to the wrong conclusions,' he said slowly, 'because I'm very territorial about my space.' But he had been territorial about her, too, hadn't he? And old-fashioned enough to want to haul that complete stranger up against the wall and demand to know what he'd been doing alone with her. 'Look, this isn't getting us anywhere. You shouldn't be getting distressed.'

'What, in my *condition*?'

'Yes. Exactly that. In your condition. You're pregnant.' The unfamiliar word sounded foreign on his lips and once again he felt the lick of something painful in his heart. She looked so damned vulnerable lying there that his instinct was to take her in his arms and cradle her—if the emerald blaze in her eyes weren't defying him to dare try. 'The midwife says you need somebody to take care of you.'

Darcy started biting her lip, terrified that the stupid tears pricking at the backs of her eyes would start pouring down her cheeks. She hated the way this new-found state of hers was making her emotions zigzag all over the place, so she hardly recognised herself any more. She was supposed to be staying strong only it wasn't easy when Renzo was sounding so...*protective*. His words were making her yearn for something she'd never had, nor expected to have. She found herself looking up into his darkly handsome face and a wave of longing swept over her. She wanted to reach out her arms and ask him to hold her. She wanted him to keep her safe.

And she had to stop thinking that way. It wasn't a big deal that he'd apologised for something he needed to apologise for. She needed to remind herself that Renzo Sabatini wouldn't even *be* here if it weren't for the baby.

'It's the unborn child which needs taking care of,' she said coldly. 'Not me.'

His gaze drifted down to the black-and-white image which was lying on top of the locker. 'May I?'

She shrugged, trying to ignore the tug at her heart as he picked it up to study it, as engrossed as she had ever seen him. 'Suit yourself.'

And when at last he raised his head and looked at her, there was a look on his face she'd never seen before. Was that wonder or joy which had transformed his dark and shuttered features?

'It's a boy,' he said slowly.

She'd forgotten about his precise eye and attention

to detail, instantly able to determine the sex of the baby where most men might have seen nothing but a confusing composition of black and white.

'It is,' she agreed.

'A son,' he said, looking down at it again.

The possessive way his voice curled round the word scared her. It took her back to the days when she'd been hauled in front of social services who'd been trying to place her in a stable home. Futile attempts which had lasted only as long as it took her mother to discover her new address and turn up on the doorstep at midnight, high on drugs and demanding money in 'payment' for her daughter. What had those interviews taught her? That you should confront the great big elephant in the room, instead of letting it trample over you when you weren't looking.

'Aren't you going to ask whether it's yours?' she said. 'Isn't that what usually happens in this situation?'

He lifted his gaze and now his eyes were flinty. 'Is it?'

Angered by the fact he'd actually *asked* despite her having pushed him into it, Darcy hesitated—tempted by a possibility which lay before her. If she told him he wasn't the father would he disappear and let her get on with the rest of her life? No, of course not. Renzo might suffer from arrogance and an innate sense of entitlement but he wasn't stupid. She'd been a virgin when she met him and the most enthusiastic of lovers during their time together. He must realise he was the father.

'Of course it's yours,' she snapped. 'And this baby will be growing up with me as its mother, no matter how hard you try to take him away!'

As he put the photo back down with a shaking hand she saw a flash of anger in his eyes. 'Do you really think I would try to take a child away from its mother?'

'How should I know what you would or wouldn't do?' Her voice was really shaking now. 'You're a stranger to me now, Renzo—or maybe you always were. So eager to think badly of someone. So quick to apportion blame.'

'And what conclusion would you have come to,' he demanded, 'if you'd arrived home to find a seedy stranger leaving and a costly piece of jewellery missing?'

'I might have stopped to ask questions before I started accusing.'

'Okay. I'll ask them now. What was he doing there?'

'He turned up out of the blue.' She pushed away a sweat-damp curl which was sticking to her clammy cheek. 'He'd seen a photo of me at the ball. He was the last person I expected or wanted to see.'

'Yet you offered him a beer.'

Because she'd been afraid. Afraid of the damage Drake could inflict if he got to Renzo before she did because she hadn't wanted her golden present to come tumbling down around her ears. But it had come tumbling down anyway, hadn't it?

'I thought he would blackmail me by telling you about my mother,' she said at last, in a low voice. 'Only now you know all my secrets.'

'Do I?' he questioned coolly.

She didn't flinch beneath that quizzical black gaze. She kept her face bland as her old habit for self-preservation kept her lips tightly sealed. He knew her mother had been a drug addict and that was bad enough, but what if she explained how she had funded her habit? Darcy could imagine only too well how that contemptuous look would deepen. Something told her there were things this proud man would find intolerable and her mother's profession was one of them. Who knew how he might try to use it against her?

Suddenly, she realised she would put nothing past him. He had accused her of all kinds of things—including using her virginity as some kind of bartering tool. Why shouldn't she keep secrets from him when he had such a brutal opinion of her?

'Of course you do. I'm the illegitimate daughter of a junkie—how much worse could it be?' She sucked in a deep breath and willed herself to keep her nerve. 'Look, Renzo, I know I'm expecting your baby and it must be the last thing you want but maybe we can work something out to our mutual satisfaction. I don't imagine you'll want anything more to do with me but I shan't make any attempt to stop you from having regular contact with your son. In fact, I'll do everything in my power to accommodate access to him.' She forced a smile. 'Every child should have a father.'

'That's good of you,' he said softly before elevating his dark eyebrows enquiringly. 'So what do you propose we do, Darcy? Perhaps you'd like me to start making regular payments until the baby is born? That way you could give up work and not have to worry.'

Hardly able to believe he was being so acquiescent, Darcy sat up in bed a little, nervously smoothing the thin sheet with her hand. 'That's a very generous offer,' she said cautiously.

'And in the meantime you could look for a nice house to live in for when our son arrives—budget no obstacle, obviously. In the country of your choice—that, too, goes without saying.'

She flashed him an uncertain smile. 'That's… that's unbelievably kind of you, Renzo.'

'And perhaps we could find you a street paved with gold while we're at it? That way you could bypass me completely and simply help yourself to whatever it was you wanted?'

It took a moment or two for her to realise he was being sarcastic but the darkly sardonic look on his face left her in no doubt. 'You were joking,' she said woodenly.

'Yes, I was *joking*,' he bit back. 'Unless you think I'm gullible enough to write you an open cheque so you can go away and bring up my son in whatever chaotic state you choose? Is that your dream scenario? Setting yourself up for life with a rich but absent babyfather?'

'As if,' she returned, her fingers digging into the thin hospital sheet. 'If I had gone looking for a wealthy sperm donor, I'd have chosen someone with a little more heart than you!'

Her words were forceful but as Renzo absorbed her defiant response he noticed that her face had gone as white as the sheet she was clutching. 'I don't want to hurt you, Darcy,' he said, self-reproach suddenly rippling through him.

'Being able to hurt me would imply I cared.' Her mouth barely moved as she spoke. 'And I don't. At least, not about you—only about our baby.'

Her fingers fluttered over the swell of her belly

and Renzo's heart gave a sudden leap as he allowed his gaze to rest on it. 'I am prepared to support you both.' His voice thickened and deepened. 'But on one condition.'

'Let me guess. Sole custody for you, I suppose? With the occasional access visit for me, probably accompanied by some ghastly nanny of your choice?'

'I'm hoping it won't come to that,' he said evenly. 'But I will not have a Sabatini heir growing up illegitimately.' He walked over to the window and stared out at the heavy winter clouds before turning back again. 'This child stands to inherit my empire, but only if he or she bears my name. So yes, I will support you, Darcy—but it will be on my terms. And the first, non-negotiable one is that you marry me.'

She stared at him. 'You have to be out of your mind,' she whispered.

'I was about to say that you have no choice but it seems to me you do. But be warned that if you refuse me and continue to live like this—patently unable to cope and putting our child at risk—I will be on my lawyers so fast you won't believe it. And I will instruct them to do everything in their power to prove you are an unfit mother.'

Darcy shivered as she heard the dark determination in his voice. Because wouldn't that bit be easy? If that situation arose he would start digging around in her past—and what a bonanza of further unsavoury facts he would discover. The drug addict bit was bad enough, but would the courts look favourably on the child of a prostitute without a single qualification to her name, one who was struggling to make ends meet and who had been admitted to hospital with severe exhaustion? Of course they wouldn't. Not when she was up against a world-famous architect with more money than he knew what to do with.

She licked her lips, naked appeal in her eyes. 'And if the marriage is unbearable, what then? If I *do* want a divorce sometime in the future, does that mean you won't give me one?'

He shook his head. 'I'm not going to keep you a prisoner, Darcy—you have my word on that. Perhaps we could surprise ourselves by negotiating a relationship that works. But that isn't something we need to think about today. My priority is to get you out of here and into a more favourable environment, if you agree to my terms.' His gaze swept over her, settling at last on her face so that she was captured by the dark intensity of that look. 'So...do I have your consent? Will you be my wife?'

A hundred reasons to refuse flooded into her mind but at that precise moment Darcy felt her son kicking. The unmistakable shape of a tiny heel skimmed beneath the surface of her belly and a powerful wave of emotion flooded over her. All she wanted was the best for her child, so how could she possibly subject him to a life like the one she had known? A life of uncertainty, with the gnawing sense of hunger. A life spent living on the margins of society with all the dangers that entailed. Secondhand clothes and having to make do. Free meals at school and charity trips to the seaside. Did she want all that for her little boy?

Of course she didn't.

She stared into Renzo's face—at all the unshakable confidence she saw written on his shuttered features. It would be easier if she felt nothing for him but she wasn't self-deluding enough to believe that. She thought how infuriating it was that, despite his arrogance and determination to get his own way, she should still want him. But she did. Her mind might not be willing but her flesh was very weak. Even though he'd wounded her with his words and was blackmailing her into marriage—she couldn't deny the quiver of heat low in her belly whenever he looked at her.

But sex was dangerous. Already she was vulnerable and if she fell into Renzo's arms and let him seduce her, wouldn't that make her weaker still? Once their relationship had been about passion but now it was all about possession and ownership. And power, of course—cold, economic power.

But a heady resolve flooded through her as she reminded herself that she'd coped with situations far worse than this. She'd cowered in cupboards and listened to sounds no child should ever have had to hear. She'd stood in courtrooms where people had talked about her future as if she weren't there, and she'd come through the other side. What was so different this time?

She nodded. 'Yes, Renzo,' she said, with a bland and meaningless smile. 'I will marry you.'

CHAPTER SEVEN

DARCY ALMOST LAUGHED at the pale-faced stranger in the mirror. What would the child she'd once been have thought about the woman whose reflection stared back at her? A woman dressed in clothes which still made her shudder when she thought about the price tag.

Her floaty, cream wedding gown had been purchased from one of Nicoletta's boutiques in Rome and the dress cleverly modified to conceal her baby bump but nonetheless, Darcy still felt like a ship in full sail. Her curls had been tied and tamed by the hairdresser who'd arrived at the Tuscan villa they were renting now that Vallombrosa had been sold, and from which they had been married that very morning. Darcy had wanted to wear normal clothes for her marriage to Renzo, as if to reinforce that it was merely a formality she was being forced to endure, but her prospective husband had put his foot down and insisted that she at least *looked* like a real bride...

'What difference does it make whether I wear a white dress or not?' she'd questioned sulkily.

'The difference is that it will feel more real if you wear white and carry flowers. You are a very beautiful woman, *cara*—and you will make a very beautiful bride.'

But Darcy had not felt at all real as she'd walked downstairs—though she couldn't deny that the dark blaze in Renzo's eyes *had* made her feel briefly beautiful. He had insisted they marry in Italy, presumably on the advice of his lawyers, who seemed to be running the whole show. But that part Darcy didn't mind. A wedding in Italy was bound to be more low-key than a wedding in England, where the press were much more curious and there was the possibility of someone from her past getting wind of it. With all the necessary paperwork in place, they had appeared before the civil registrar in the beautiful medieval town of Barga, with just Gisella and Pasquale as their witnesses. And just four days later they had been legally allowed to wed.

It had been the smallest and most formal of ceremonies in an ancient room with a high, beamed ceiling and although Gisella had voiced a slight wistfulness that they weren't having a religious service, Darcy, for one, was glad. It was bad enough having to go through something you knew was doomed, without having to do so before the eyes of the church.

But there had been a point when her heart had turned over and she'd started wishing it *were* real and that had been when Renzo had smiled at her once they'd been legally declared man and wife— his black eyes crinkling with a smile which had reminded her of the first time she'd met him. With his dark suit echoing the raven hue of his hair he'd made a sensational groom. And when he'd looked at her that way, he'd looked as if he actually *cared*—and she'd had to keep reminding herself that he didn't. It had all been an act for the benefit of those around them. She was here because she carried his child and for no other reason. But it had been difficult to remember that when he'd pulled her into his arms in full view of everyone.

She'd felt so torn right then. Her instinctive response had been to hug him back because that was how she always responded and they hadn't touched one another in any way since he'd turned up at the hospital with his ultimatum of a marriage proposal. But too much had happened for her to ever go back to that easy intimacy. How could she possibly lie in his arms and let him kiss her after all the cruel and bitter things which had been done and said? How could she bear to feel him deep inside her body when he'd been so eager to think badly of her?

She remembered freezing as his hands went to her expanded waist, feeling as if her body had suddenly turned to marble. 'Please, Renzo,' she'd whispered, her words a soft protest, not a plea.

But he hadn't let her go or changed his position. He'd dipped his head and spoke to her in low and rapid English, his fingers spanning the delicate fabric of the dress and increasing the points at which he'd been in contact with her.

'You are dressed to play the part of my bride and therefore you will act the part of my bride,' he'd said softly. 'Let's show the world that I have married a flesh-and-blood woman and not some pale-faced doll.'

It was then that he'd bent his head to claim her lips and it had been the weirdest kiss of her life. At

first her determination had made it easy not to respond, but the sensation of his lips on hers had soon
melted away her reservations and she'd sunk into
that kiss with an eagerness she hadn't been able to
disguise. She'd felt powerless beneath that brief but
thorough exploration. She hadn't been able to hold
back her gasp as she'd felt that first sweet invasion
of his tongue. Heat had flooded over her. Her hands
had reached up to hold on to him as the beat of her
heart had become erratic but suddenly the movement
had become about so much more than support. Suddenly she'd been clinging to him and revelling in the
feel of all that rock-hard flesh beneath her fingertips. She'd wanted him so much that she hadn't even
cared about his triumphant laugh of pleasure as he'd
drawn his lips away because it had felt like for ever
since he'd kissed her and it had tasted as delicious as
having a drink after a dusty walk. Like the first hint
of sweetness on your tongue when you badly needed
the boost of sugar.

A kiss like that was the inevitable forerunner of
intimacy and she must not let it happen again. She
dared not…

'You look miles away.' Renzo's low drawl broke
into Darcy's reverie and she watched his reflected
body as he strolled in from the en-suite bathroom of
their honeymoon suite, wearing nothing but a too-
small white towel slung low over his hips. Crystalline
droplets of water glittered like diamonds in his ebony
hair and, despite knowing she shouldn't be affected
by his near-nakedness, Darcy's brain was refusing to
listen to reason and instead was sending out frantic
messages to her pulse points.

It was the first time she'd seen him in a state of undress since the night of the ball, when they'd come home and he'd made rapturous love to her. The night before Drake had visited and the necklace had disappeared and her whole world had come crashing down around her. A necklace Renzo had been prepared to write off in his eagerness to be rid of her. It all seemed like a dream now and yet suddenly all that honed silken flesh was haunting her with everything she'd been missing.

'So why,' he questioned, his voice growing sultry as he walked over and stood behind her and wound one long finger around an errant curl, 'did you let them put your hair up like that?'

Darcy swallowed because, from this position, far too much of his flesh was on show and his skin was still damp and soap-scented from the shower. 'The hairdresser said loose hair would look untidy.'

'But perhaps your husband doesn't like it to look *tidy*,' he mocked, pulling out one pearl-topped pin quickly followed by another. 'He likes it to look wild and free.'

'Which is slightly ironic given that you're the most precise and ordered man on the planet. And I don't remember giving you permission to do that,' she protested as he continued to remove them.

'I'm your husband now, Darcy. Surely I don't have to ask permission to take your hair down?'

Glad for the tumble of curls concealing the reluctant lust which was making her cheeks grow so pink, Darcy stared down at her lap. 'You're my husband in name only,' she said quietly.

'So you keep saying. But since we're sharing a room and a bed—'

'Yes, I wanted to talk to you about that. Tell me again *why* we're sharing a bed.'

'Because I need to keep an eye on you. I promised the midwife and the doctor.' His black eyes glittered. 'And that being the case—just how long do you think you can hold off from letting me make love to you when you're as jumpy as a scalded cat whenever I come near?'

'I think *making love* a rather inaccurate way to describe what we do,' she said, sighing as the last curl tumbled free and he added the final pearl pin to the neat little line he'd assembled on the dressing table. 'I wish we didn't have this wedding party tonight.'

'I know. You'd much rather be alone with me.'

'I didn't say that.'

'I know you didn't.' His dark gaze was full of mockery. 'But a wedding is a wedding and it is fitting to celebrate such a momentous occasion with friends. We don't want them thinking our union is in name only, do we?'

'Even if it is?'

'Even if it is. So why not try playing your part with enthusiasm? Who knows? Sooner or later you might find the feelings have rubbed off.' He stroked her hair. 'You won't have anything to do, if that's what's worrying you. The food, the wine and the guests have all been taken care of.'

'And in the meantime I'm to be brought down and paraded around in my white dress like a cow in the marketplace?'

He gave a soft laugh. 'Looking at you now, that's

the very last image which springs to mind.' He leaned forward, his hands on her shoulders, his mouth so close that she could feel his warm breath fanning the curls at the back of her neck. And suddenly his voice was urgent. 'Listen to me, Darcy. Neither of us wanted this to happen but it's what we've ended up with. I didn't want to get married and I certainly didn't plan to be a parent and neither, presumably, did you.'

Her lips folded in on themselves. 'No.'

In the reflection of the glass their eyes met and Renzo wondered why, even in the midst of all this unwanted emotional drama, their chemistry should be as powerful as ever. Did she feel it too? She must.

He could see her nipples pushing against the silk of her wedding gown and the darkening of her emerald eyes, but the tight set of her shoulders and her unsmiling lips were telling him quite clearly to stay away. Once he had known her body completely, but not any more. Her bulky shape was unfamiliar now, just as she was. She was spiky, different, wary. It was difficult being around her without being able to touch her and, oh, how he wanted to touch her. That had not changed, despite everything which had happened. Her skin was luminous, her eyes bright, and the rampant red curls even more lustrous than before. Didn't people say that a woman with child developed a glowing beauty all of her own? He'd never really thought about it before now—why would he?—but suddenly he knew exactly what they meant. He noticed the way she kept moving her hand to her growing bump, as if she were in possession of the world's greatest secret.

Pregnant.

His mouth dried. It was still hard for him to get his head around that. To believe that a whole new life was about to begin and he must be responsible for it. He'd meant it when he told her he never wanted a family and not just because he recognised all the potential for pain which a family could bring. He had liked his life the way it was. He liked having to answer to no one except himself. And if every female who'd fallen into his arms had thought they'd be the one to change his mind, they had been wrong. He'd managed to get to the age of thirty-five without having to make any kind of commitment.

Had Darcy done what nobody else had been able to do—and deliberately got herself pregnant? But if that had been the case then he must take his share of the blame. He'd been so blown away by discovering she was a virgin that he couldn't wait for her to go on the pill. He remembered the first time he'd entered her without wearing a condom and the indescribable pleasure he'd felt. It had been primitive, powerful and overwhelming but it hadn't been wise. He had allowed sexual hunger to blind him to reason. He'd allowed her to take sole responsibility for birth control and look what had happened. His heart clenched tightly with an emotion he didn't recognise as he stared into her green eyes.

'Did you mean to get pregnant?' he demanded.

He saw her flinch and compose herself before answering.

'No,' she answered quietly. 'I had some sort of bug just before we went to Tuscany and I didn't realise…'

'That sickness would stop the pill from working?'

'Apparently.'

He raised his eyebrows. 'You weren't warned that could happen?'

'Probably—but with all the excitement about the holiday, I forgot all about it. It wasn't deliberate, Renzo—if that's what you're thinking.' She gave a wry smile. 'No woman in her right mind would want to tie herself to a man with ice for a heart, no matter how rich or well-connected he might be.'

And he believed her. He might wish he didn't but he did. His pale-faced bride in the floaty dress was telling the truth. 'So it seems we have a choice,' he said. 'We can go downstairs to our guests with good grace or I can take you kicking and screaming every inch of the way.'

'I won't embarrass you, if that's what you're worried about. I have no desire to make this any more difficult than it already is.'

'Good.'

Turning away, he dropped the towel and Darcy was treated to the distracting sight of his bare buttocks— each hard globe a paler colour than the dark olive of his back. She could see the hair-roughened power of those thighs and hated the way her stomach automatically turned over when she was doing everything in her power to fight her attraction.

'Tempted?' His voice was full of sensual mockery—as if he had the ability to read her expression even with his back turned. And she mustn't let him realise the accuracy of his taunt. If she wanted to protect herself, she mustn't let him get close to her—not in any way.

'Tempted by what—our wedding feast?' she questioned, sniffing at the air as if trying to detect the rich scents of cooking which had been drifting through the downstairs of the house all morning. 'Absolutely! To be honest, I do have a little of my appetite back. I could eat a horse.'

He gave a low laugh as Darcy scuttled into the bathroom where she spent a long time fiddling with her hair, and when she returned to the bedroom it was to find him dressed in that head-turning way which only Italian men seemed able to pull off. His dark suit emphasised his broad shoulders and powerful physique and he'd left his silk shirt open at the neck to reveal a sexy smattering of dark hair.

Uncertainly, she skimmed her hand down over her dress. 'Won't I look a little overdressed?'

'Undoubtedly,' he said drily. 'But probably not in the way you imagine.'

Her cheeks were still pink by the time they walked into the formal salon, which had been transformed with bridal finery by Gisella and a team of helpers from the nearby village. The cold winter weather meant they couldn't venture out into the huge grounds, but instead enormous fires were blazing and dark greenery festooned the staircases and fireplace. There were white flowers, white ribbons and sugar-dusted bonbons heaped on little glass dishes. A towering *croquembouche* wedding cake took pride of place in the dining room and on a table at the far end of the room—a pile of beautifully wrapped presents which they'd expressly stated they didn't want!

A loud burst of applause reached them as they walked in, along with cries of *'Congratulazioni!'* and *'Ben fatto, Renzo!'* The guests were all Renzo's friends, and although he'd told her he would pay for anyone she wanted to fly out to Tuscany for the celebration, Darcy hadn't taken him up on his offer. Because who could she invite when she'd lived her life a loner—terrified of forming any lasting commitments because of her past and the very real fear of rejection?

But she was pleased to see Nicoletta and not just because the glamourous Italian had helped with her trousseau. She'd realised that Renzo no longer had any lingering feelings about the woman he'd once had a 'thing' with. Darcy might have had an innate lack of self-confidence brought about by years of neglect, but even she couldn't fail to see the way her husband was looking at her tonight—a sentiment echoed by Nicoletta.

'I have never seen Renzo this way before,' she confided as Darcy sucked *limonata* through a straw. 'He can barely tear his eyes away from you.'

Darcy put her glass down. Because he was one of life's winners, that was why. He would want his marriage to succeed in the way that his business had succeeded and because his own parents' marriage had failed. That was why he was suddenly being so nice to her. And that scared her. It made her want to fight her instinctive attraction and to pull away from him. She didn't dare sink into a false state of security which would leave her raw and hurting when their marriage hit the skids. Because it would. Of course it would. How long would it take before her brilliant husband tired of her once reality kicked in? Had he even stopped to consider how a wife at the mercy of fluctuating hormones might fit into his calm and ordered life, let alone all the change which a new baby would bring?

But the evening fared better than she would have imagined. Renzo's obvious appreciation—whether faked or not—seemed to make everyone eager to welcome her into their midst. His friends were daunting, but essentially kind. She met lawyers, bankers and an eminent heart surgeon and although each and every one of them spoke to her in perfect English, she vowed to learn Renzo's native tongue. Because suddenly, she caught a glimpse of what the future could be like if she wasn't careful. Of Renzo and their son speaking a language which the new *mamma* couldn't understand, with her inevitably being cast into the role of outsider.

And that could also be dangerous. Renzo had been reasonable before the marriage, but now she had his ring on her finger there was no longer any need for him to be. If she didn't watch her back she would become irrelevant. She looked around at the elegant room her new husband was renting for what she considered an extortionate amount of money. Could she really envisage their son willingly accompanying her back to an unknown England and an uncertain future if the marriage became unbearable, and leaving all this privilege and beauty behind?

But she ate, chatted and drank her *limonata*, waiting until the last of their guests had gone before following Renzo up to their suite, her heart rattling loudly beneath her ribcage. She undressed in the bathroom, emerging wearing a nightgown Nicoletta had insisted on gifting her. It was an exquisite piece for a new bride to wear and one designed to be removed almost as soon as it had been put on. Despite the hard curve of her baby bump, the ivory silk-satin coated her body as flatteringly as a second skin. Edged with ivory lace, the delicate fabric framed the skin above her engorged breasts and the moment she walked into the bedroom Darcy saw Renzo's eyes darken.

Her own answering tug of lust made her reconsider her decision to distance herself from him, because surely physical intimacy would provide some kind of release and lessen the unmistakable tension which had sprung up between them. But sexual intimacy could also be dangerous, especially in their situation. Something was growing inside her which was part of him and how could she bear to cheapen that by having sex which was nothing but a physical *release*?

She sat down heavily on the side of the bed, not realising that she'd given a little groan until he glanced across at her.

'You must be tired.'

She nodded, suddenly feeling as if all the stuffing had been knocked out of her. 'I am. But I need to talk to you.'

'About…?'

'Stuff.'

His smile was slow, almost wolfish. 'Be a little bit more explicit, Darcy. What kind of stuff?'

She shrugged. 'Where we're going to live. Practicalities. That kind of thing. And we need to decide soon because I won't be allowed to fly once I'm past thirty-six weeks.'

His self-assured shake of his head was tinged with the arrogant sense of certainty which was so much a part of him. 'I have my own jet, Darcy. We can fly when the hell we like, provided we take medical support with us.'

She nodded as she pulled back the covers and got into the king-size bed, rolling over as far as possible until she had commandeered one side of it. 'Whatever,' she said. 'But we still need to discuss it.'

'Just not tonight,' he said, the bed dipping beneath his weight as he joined her. 'You're much too tired. We'll talk in the morning. And—just for the record— if you lie much closer to the edge, you're going to fall off it in the middle of the night and, apart from the obvious danger to yourself, you might just wake me up.' She heard the clatter as he removed his wristwatch and put it on the bedside table. 'Don't worry, Darcy, I'm reading your body language loud and clear and I have no intention of trying to persuade a woman to make love if she has set her mind against it.'

'Something which has never happened to you before, I suppose?' she questioned waspishly.

'As it happens, no,' he drawled. He snapped off the light. 'Usually I have to fight them off.'

Darcy's skin stung with furious heat. It was a lesson to never ask questions unless you were prepared to be stupidly hurt by the answer you might receive. Lying open-eyed in the darkness, almost immediately she heard the sounds of Renzo's deep and steady breathing and fearfully she foresaw a restless night ahead, plagued by troubled thoughts about the future. But to her surprise she felt warm and cosseted in that big bed with a brand-new wedding ring on her finger. And, yes, even a little bit *safe*.

As the keen Tuscan wind howled outside the ancient house Darcy snuggled down into her pillow and, for the first time in a long time, slept soundly.

CHAPTER EIGHT

RENZO INSISTED ON a honeymoon—cutting through Darcy's automatic protests when she went down-stairs the following morning to find him in the throes of planning it. As she glanced at the road map he'd spread out on the dining-room table, she told him it would be hypocritical; he said he didn't care.

'Maybe you're just doing it to make the marriage look more authentic than it really is,' she observed, once she had selected a slice of warm bread from the basket. 'Since we haven't actually consummated it.'

'Maybe I am,' he agreed evenly. 'Or maybe it's because I want to show you a little of my country and to see you relax some more. You slept well last night, Darcy.' His black eyes gleamed but that was the only reference he made to their chaste wedding night, though she felt a little flustered as his gaze lingered on the swell of her breasts for slightly longer than was necessary. 'And we can consummate it anytime you like,' he said softly. 'You do realise that, don't you?'

She didn't trust herself to answer, though her burn-ing cheeks must have given away the fact that the sub-ject was very much on her mind. Sharing a bed so he could keep an eye on her was more straightforward in theory than in practice. Because a bed was a bed, no matter how big it was. And wasn't it true that at one point during the night her foot had encountered one of her new husband's shins and she'd instinctively wanted to rub her toes up and down his leg, before hastily rolling away as if her skin had been scorched?

She told herself their situation was crazy enough but at least she was in full control of her senses—and if she had sex with him, she wouldn't be. And she was afraid. Afraid that the pregnancy was making her prone to waves of vulnerability she was supposed to have left behind. Afraid he would hurt her if he saw through to the darkness at the very core of her. Because something had changed, she recognised that. He was being *gentle* with her in a way he'd never been before. She knew it was because she was carrying his baby but even so… It was intoxicating behaviour coming from such an intrinsically cold man and Darcy might have been bewitched by such a transformation, had she not instinctively mistrusted any type of kindness.

But she couldn't get out of the 'honeymoon' he was planning and perhaps that was a good thing. It would be distracting. There would be things to occupy them other than prowling around their beautiful rented villa like two wary, circling tigers, with her terrified to even meet those brilliantine black eyes for fear he would read the lust in hers and act on it…

So she packed her suitcase with the warm clothes which had also been purchased from Nicoletta's boutique and Renzo loaded it into the back of his sports car. The air was crisp as they drove through the mountains towards Italy's capital, the hills softly green against the ice-blue sky as the powerful car swallowed up the miles. They stopped in a small, hilltop town for an early lunch of truffled pasta followed by *torta della nonna* and afterwards walked through narrow cobbled streets to the viewpoint at the very top, looking down on the landscape below, which was spread out like a chequered tablecloth of green and gold.

Darcy gave a long sigh as her elbows rested on the balustrade and Renzo turned to look at her.

'Like it?' he questioned.

'It's beautiful. So beautiful it seems almost unreal.'

'But there are many beautiful parts of England.'

She shrugged, her eyes fixed on some unseen spot in the distance. 'Not where I grew up. Oh, there were lots of lovely spaces in the surrounding countryside, but unless they're on your doorstep you need funds to access them.'

'Was it awful?' he questioned suddenly.

She didn't answer immediately. 'Yes,' she said, at last.

He heard the sadness in that single word and saw the way her teeth chewed on her bottom lip and he broke the silence which followed with a light touch to her arm. 'Come on. Let's try and get there before it gets dark.'

She fell asleep almost as soon as she got in the car and as Renzo waited in line at a toll gate, he found himself studying that pale face with its upturned freckled nose. Her red curls hung over one shoulder in the loose plait she sometimes wore and he thought that today she looked almost like a teenager, in jeans and a soft grey sweater. Only the bump reminded him that she was nearly twenty-five and soon going to have his baby.

Could they make it work? His leather-gloved fingers gripped the steering wheel as they moved forward. They *had* to make it work. There was no other choice, for he would not replicate his own bleak and fatherless childhood. He realised how little she'd actually told him about her own upbringing, yet, uncharacteristically, she had mentioned it today. And even though that haunted look had come over her face, he had found himself wanting to know more.

Wasn't that his role now, as husband and prospective father—to break the ingrained rules of a lifetime and find out as much about Darcy as possible? And wasn't the best way to do that to tell her something about *him*—the kind of stuff women had quizzed him about over years, to no effect. Because communication was a two-way street, wasn't it? At least, that was what that therapist had told him once. Not that he'd been seeing her professionally. To him she was just a gorgeous brunette he'd been enjoying a very physical relationship with when she'd freaked him out by telling him that she specialised in 'family therapy' and he could confide in her anytime she liked. His mouth thinned. Maybe he should have taken her up on her offer and gathered tips about how to deal with his current situation.

Darcy woke as they drove into the darkening city whose ancient streets were deeply familiar to him from his own childhood. Taking a circuitous route, Renzo found himself enjoying her murmured appreciation of the Campidoglio, the Coliseum and other famous monuments, but he saw her jaw drop in amazement when he stopped outside the sixteenth-century *palazzo* on the Via Condotti, just five minutes from the Spanish Steps.

'This isn't yours?' she questioned faintly, after he'd parked the car and they'd travelled up to the third floor.

'It is now. I bought it a couple of years ago,' he replied, throwing open the double doors into the main salon, with its high ceilings, gilded furniture and matchless views over the ancient city. 'Although the Emperor Napoleon III happened to live here in 1830.'

'Here? Good grief, Renzo.' She stood in the centre of the room, looking around. 'It's gorgeous. Like… well, like something you might see in a book. Why don't you live here? I mean, why London?'

'Because my work is international and I wanted to establish a base in London and the only way to do that properly is to be permanently on-site. I don't come back here as often as I should, but maybe some day.'

'Renzo—'

But he cut her off with a shake of his head. 'I know. You want to talk—but first you should unpack. Get comfortable. We need to think about dinner but first I need to do a little work.'

'Of course,' she said stiffly.

'Come with me and I'll show you where the main bedroom is.'

Down a high-ceilinged corridor she followed him to yet another room which defied expectation. The enormous wooden bed had a huge oil painting on the wall behind it, with elaborate silk drapes on either side, which made it seem as if you were looking out of a window onto mountains and trees. Darcy blinked as she stared at it. *How am I even* here? she wondered as she unwound the soft blue scarf which was knotted around her neck. She looked around the room, taking in the antique furniture, the silken rugs and the priceless artwork. Yet this staggering display of a wealth which many people would covet had little meaning for her. She didn't want *things*—no matter how exquisite they were. She wanted something which was much harder to pin down and which she suspected would always elude her.

She showered and changed into a cashmere tunic with leggings, padding barefoot into the salon to see her new husband at his computer, the familiar sight of one of his spectacular designs dominating the screen. But despite her noiseless entrance he must have heard her because he turned round, those dark-rimmed spectacles on his nose giving him that sexy, geeky look which used to make her heart turn over.

Still did, if she was being honest.

'Room to your satisfaction?' he questioned.

'Bit cramped, actually.'

He gave the glimmer of a smile. 'I know. Makes you claustrophobic. Hungry?'

'After that enormous lunch?' She wrinkled her nose. 'Funnily enough, I am.'

'Good.' His gaze roved over her, black eyes gleaming as they lingered a little too long. 'Looks like you have some catching up to do. You need to put some meat on those bones.'

She didn't reply to that. She wasn't going to tell him that she felt all breasts and bump. She wanted to tell him not to look at her body any more than was absolutely necessary.

And yet she wanted him to feast his eyes on it all day and make her glow inside.

'We could eat out,' he continued. 'I could take you to Trastevere, where you can eat some real Italian food and not something designed to try to appeal to an international palate. Or...'

She raised her eyebrows questioningly. 'Or?'

'We could order in pizza.'

'Here?'

'Why not?'

She shrugged as she stared through an arch to see a long, softly polished dining table set with tall silver candelabra. 'It seems way too grand.'

'A table is there to be used, Darcy, no matter what you're eating.'

It seemed decadent to find themselves there an hour later sitting on ormolu chairs, eating pizza with their fingers. As if they had broken into a museum and had temporarily set up home for the night.

'Good?' questioned Renzo as she popped the last piece of anchovy in her mouth and licked bright orange oil from her fingers.

'Heaven,' she sighed.

But it still seemed like a dream—as if it were happening to someone else—until they returned to the main salon and he asked her if she wanted mint tea. She didn't know what made her ask if he had hot chocolate and was surprised when he said he'd find out—and even more surprised when he returned a few minutes later with a creamy concoction in a tall mug. A potent memory squeezed at her heart as she took the drink from him—perhaps it was the sweet smell of the chocolate which made the words slip out before she could stop them.

'Wow! I haven't had this since…'

She caught herself on but it was too late.

'Since when?'

She kept her voice airy. 'Oh, nothing to interest you.'

'I'm interested,' he persisted.

She wondered if the shaky way she put the mug down gave away her sudden nerves. 'You've never been interested before.'

'True,' he agreed drily. 'But you're carrying my baby now and maybe I need to understand the mother of my child.'

And Darcy knew she couldn't keep avoiding the issue—just as she knew that to do so would probably intrigue him. Even worse—it might make him start to do his own investigative work and *then* what might he discover? Her heart sank. She knew exactly what he would discover. He would discover the reason for the deep dark shame which still festered inside her. She stared at the cooling chocolate, wishing she could turn back time and that this time he wouldn't ask. But you couldn't turn back time. Just as you couldn't hide everything from a man who was determined to find out.

'It sounds so stupid—'

'Darcy,' he said, and his voice sounded almost *gentle*.

She shrugged. 'The chocolate reminded me of going out to a café when I was a little girl. Going to meet some prospective new foster parents.'

The image came back to her, unbearably sharp and

achingly clear. She remembered strawberry-covered cakes gleaming behind glass frontage and the waitresses with their starched aprons. It had been one of those awkward but hopeful meetings, with Darcy's social worker the referee—observing the interaction between a little girl who badly needed a home and two adults who wanted to give her one. They'd bought her hot chocolate in a glass mug, topped with a hillock of whipped cream and a shiny cherry on top. She'd stared at it for a long time before she could bear to disturb its perfection and when she'd drunk from it at last, the cream had coated her upper lip with a white moustache and made everyone laugh. The laughter was what she remembered most.

'Foster parents?' prompted Renzo, his deep voice dissolving the image.

'I didn't have the most…stable of childhoods. My mother was seventeen when she was orphaned. The roads were icy and her father took the bend too fast. They said he'd been…drinking. The police knocked at her door on Christmas Eve and said she'd better sit down. She once told me that after they'd gone she looked at the Christmas tree and all the presents underneath it. Presents which would never be opened…' Her voice trailed off. It had been a rare moment of insight and clarity from a woman whose life had been lived in pursuit of a constant chemical high. 'And it… Well, it freaked her out.'

'I'm not surprised. Did she have any relatives?'

Darcy shook her head. 'No. Well, there were some on the west coast of Ireland but it was too late for her to get there in time for the holiday. And she couldn't face intruding on someone else's Christmas. Being the spectre at the feast. Being pitied. So she spent the holiday on her own and soon after she went to Manchester with the money she'd inherited from her parents but no real idea about a career. In fact, she had nothing to commend her but her looks and her new-found ability to party.'

'Did she look like you?' he questioned suddenly.

'Yes. At least, at the beginning she did.' Darcy closed her eyes. She'd seen pictures of a feisty-looking redhead with green eyes so like her own. Seen her tentative smile as that young woman cradled the infant Darcy in her arms. She didn't want to tell Renzo what had happened to those looks—not when she couldn't bear to think about it herself. 'Before the drugs took hold. I was first taken into care at the age of two and I stayed there until I was eight, when my mother went to the courts to try to "win" me back, as she put it.'

'And did she succeed?'

'She did. She could put on a good performance when the need arose.'

'And what was that like—being back with her?'

Darcy swallowed. How much could she tell him? How much before a look of disgust crossed his face and he started to worry whether she might have inherited some of her poor mother's addictive traits— or the other, even more unpalatable ones? 'I'll leave that to your imagination,' she said, her voice faltering a little. 'She used me to interact with her dealer, or to answer the door when people she owed money to came knocking. There's nothing quite like a child in an adult's world for throwing things off balance.'

'And were you *safe*?' he demanded.

'I was lucky,' she said simply. 'Lucky that some kind social worker went over and above the call of duty and got me out of there. After that I went to the children's home—and, to be honest, I felt glad to be there.'

Not safe. Never really safe. But *safer*.

'And what did you do when you left there?'

'I came to London. Went to night school and caught up with some of the education I'd missed. It's why I ended up waitressing—nobody really cares if you've got a GCSE in Maths if you can carry a tray of drinks without spilling any.'

There was no sound in the room, other than the ticking of some beautiful freestanding clock which Darcy suspected might have been in place when Napoleon himself was living there.

'So…' His voice was thoughtful now; his black eyes hooded. 'Seeing as so much of your childhood was spent with people making decisions for you, where would *you* like to live when our baby is born, Darcy?'

Not only was it not the reaction she'd been expecting, it was also the most considerate question anyone had ever asked her and Darcy was terrified she was going to start blubbing—an over-the-top response from someone who'd experienced little real kindness in her life. But she needed to keep it together. She'd been given enough false hope in life to build Renzo's offer up into something it wasn't.

'I would prefer to be in England,' she said slowly. 'Italy is very beautiful and I love it here but I feel like a foreigner.' She forced a laugh. 'Probably because I am.'

'My apartment in Belgravia, then?'

She shook her head. 'No. That won't do. I don't really want to go back there.'

He looked faintly surprised, as she supposed anyone might be if their new wife had just rejected a luxury apartment worth millions of pounds. 'Because?'

Should she tell him that she felt as if she'd lived another life there? She'd behaved like someone she no longer recognised—with her balcony bras and her tiny panties. She'd been nothing but his plaything, his always-up-for-it lover who was supposed to have been expendable before all this happened. How could she possibly reconcile that Darcy with the woman she was now and the mother she was preparing to be? How could she bear to keep reminding herself that he'd never planned for her to become a permanent fixture in his life? 'It's not a place for a baby.'

He raised his dark eyebrows. 'You're not suggesting we decamp to that tiny cottage you were renting in Norfolk?'

'Of course not,' she said stiffly. 'I think we both know that wouldn't work. But I would like to bring up the baby away from the city.' She licked her lips and her tongue came away with the salty flavour of capers. 'Somewhere with grass and flowers and a park nearby. Somewhere you can work from, so it doesn't necessarily have to be a long way out of London, just so long as it's *green*.'

He nodded and gave a small smile. 'I think we can manage that.'

'Thank you.'

Hearing her voice tremble, Renzo frowned. 'And you need to get to bed. Now. You look washed out.'

'Yes.' Awkwardly, she rose to her feet and walked across the room, feeling the soft silk of a Persian rug beneath her bare feet. But despite her initial reservations at having told him more than she'd ever told anyone, Darcy was amazed by how much *lighter* she felt. And she was grateful to him, too—stupidly relieved he'd managed to keep his shock and disgust to himself because most people weren't that diplomatic. All she wanted now was to climb into bed and have him put his arms round her and hold her very tight and tell her it was going to be all right. She closed her eyes. Actually, she wanted more than that. Could they be intimate again? Could they? Hadn't that book on pregnancy explained that sex in the latter stages was perfectly acceptable, just as long as you didn't try anything too adventurous?

For the first time in a long time, she felt the faint whisper of hope as she brushed her teeth, her hands wavering as she picked up the exquisite silk nightgown she'd worn on her wedding night, feeling the slippery fabric sliding between her fingers. It was beautiful but it made her feel like someone she wasn't. Or rather, somebody she no longer was. Wouldn't it be better to be less *obvious* if she wanted them relaxed enough to get to know one another again? Shouldn't it be a slow rediscovery rather than a sudden wham-bam, especially given the circumstances in which they found themselves?

Pulling on one of Renzo's T-shirts, which came to halfway down her thighs, she crept beneath the duvet and waited for him to come to bed.

But he didn't.

She tried to block the thoughts which were buzzing in her mind like a mosquito in a darkened room, but some thoughts just wouldn't go away. Because apart from that very public kiss when he'd claimed her as his bride, he hadn't come near her, had he? And something else occurred to her, something which perhaps *she* had been too arrogant to take into account. What if he no longer wanted her? If he no longer desired her as a man was supposed to desire a woman.

Tossing and turning in those fine cotton sheets, she watched the hand of the clock slowly moving. Soon her heart rate overtook the rhythmical ticking. Eleven o'clock. Then twelve. Shortly before one she gave in to the exhaustion which was threatening to crush her and Darcy never knew what time Renzo came to bed that night, because she didn't hear him.

CHAPTER NINE

'So... What do you think? Does it meet with your approval?' Renzo's eyes didn't leave Darcy's profile as they stood in the grounds of the imposing manor house. A seagull heading for the nearby coast gave a squawk as it flew overhead and he could definitely detect the faint tang of salt in the air. A light breeze was ruffling his wife's red curls, making them gleam brightly in the sunshine. How beautiful she looked, he thought—and how utterly unapproachable. And how ironic that the woman he'd spent more time with than anyone else should remain the most enigmatic woman of them all. 'You haven't changed your mind about living here now that it's actually yours?'

Slowly she turned her head and returned his gaze, those glittering emerald eyes filled with emotions he couldn't begin to understand.

'Ours, you mean?' she said. 'Our first marital home.'

He shook his head. 'No. Not mine. I've spoken with my lawyers and the deeds have been made over to you. This is yours, Darcy. Completely yours.'

There was a moment of silence before she frowned and blinked at him. 'But I don't understand. We talked about it in Rome and I thought we'd agreed that a house in England was going to be the best thing for us.' She touched the ever-increasing girth of her belly. 'All of us.'

Was she being deliberately naïve, he wondered—or just exceptionally clever? Did she know she had him twisted up in knots and he didn't have a damned clue how to handle her? Because he was starting to realise that, despite his experience with women, he had no idea how to sustain a long-term relationship. He'd never had to try before. In the past he had always just walked away—usually because boredom had set in and he'd found the increasing demands tedious. But with Darcy he couldn't do that. Furthermore, he didn't want to. He wanted this baby so badly. It scared him just how badly. For a man who'd spent his life building things for other people—someone who considered himself urbane, sophisticated and cool—he hadn't reckoned on the fierce and primitive pride he felt at having created the most precious thing of all.

Life.

But Darcy remained a mystery he couldn't solve. She'd closed herself off to him since that night in Rome. She'd told him more about what he'd already known and the brutal facts had horrified him when he'd thought how tough her childhood must have been. He'd sat up for a long time that night after she'd rushed off to bed, drinking whisky until it had tasted stale in his mouth and gazing into space as he'd wondered how best to deal with the information. But he had dealt with it in the same way he dealt with anything emotional. He'd compartmentalised it. Filed it away, meaning to do something about it sometime but never getting round to it. She'd been asleep by the time he'd slid into bed beside her, her fecund body covered in one of his oversized T-shirts, sending out a silent signal to stay the hell away from her. He remembered waking up to a beautiful Roman morning with the air all clear and blue. They'd gone out for coffee and *cornetti* and he hadn't said a word about her revelations and neither had she. She'd closed herself off from him again and he sensed that he could frighten her away if he didn't let her take this thing at her own pace.

But it hadn't worked.

Because now she looked at him so warily by day, while at night she still wore those infernal all-enveloping T-shirts and lay there quietly, holding her breath—as if daring him to come near. Had he handled it badly? If it had been any other woman he would have pulled her into his arms and kissed her until she was wet and horny—reaching for him eagerly, the way she used to.

But she was not *any other woman*. She was his wife. His pregnant wife. How could he possibly ravish her when she was both bulky and yet impossibly fragile? Her skin looked so delicate—the blue tracery of her veins visible beneath its porcelain fragility—as if to even breathe on her might leave some kind of mark. And against her tiny frame, the baby looked huge—as if what her body had achieved was defying both gravity and logic, something which continued to amaze him. He'd even taken to working solely from home these past weeks, cancelling a trip to New York and another to Paris, terrified she was

going to go into labour early even though there were
still three weeks to go.

'Let's get inside,' he said abruptly. He unlocked
their new front door and stood back to let her pass
and their footsteps sounded loud in a house which was
still largely empty, save for the few pieces of furniture which had already been delivered. But at least it
wasn't cold. Despite the bite of early spring, the estate
agent must have put on the heating—knowing that
today was their first visit as official owners. The door
swung closed behind them and he realised that she
was still looking at him with confusion in her eyes.

'Why have you put the house in my name, Renzo?
I don't understand.'

'Because you need to have some kind of insurance
policy. Somewhere to call home if—'

'If the marriage doesn't work out?'

'That's right.'

She nodded as if she understood at last for her
face had whitened, her eyes appearing darkly emerald against her pale skin.

'But you said—'

'I know what I said,' he interrupted. 'But I didn't
factor in that the situation might prove more difficult
than I'd anticipated.'

'You mean, my company?'

'No, not your *company*,' he negated impatiently,
and then suddenly the words came bubbling out of
nowhere, even though he hadn't intended to say them.
'I mean the fact that I want you so damned much and
you don't seem to want me any more. The fact that
you're always just out of reach.'

Shocked, Darcy stared at him. So she *hadn't* been

imagining it. It *had* been lust she'd seen in his eyes
and sexual hunger which made his body grow tense
whenever she walked in the room. So why hadn't he
touched her? Why did he keep coming to bed later
and later while keeping their days ultrabusy by whisking her from property to property until at last she'd
fallen in love with this East Sussex house which was
only eight miles from the sea?

The truth was that he hadn't come near her since
that night in Rome, when she'd told him everything
about her mother. She felt her stomach clench. Actually, not quite everything—and hadn't she been
thankful afterwards that she hadn't blurted out the
whole truth? Imagine his reaction if she'd told him
that, when he was already repulsed by what he knew,
even though he'd done his best to hide it. And it was
funny how the distance between a couple could grow
almost without you realising. They'd been wary in
each other's company. As the space between them
had increased, she'd found the presence of her Italian husband almost…*forbidding.*

But if she had read it all wrong, then where did that
leave her? If he hadn't been making value judgments
about her, then why was she being so passive—always waiting for Renzo to make the first move? Yes,
he was an alpha man with an instinctive need to dominate but it wasn't beyond the realms of possibility
that he was simply being cautious around the baby
she carried in her belly. He'd never had a pregnant
lover before. He had taught her so much—wasn't this
her chance to teach *him* something?

She walked over to him and, without warning,
raised herself up on tiptoe to press her lips against

his—feeling him jerk with surprise before sliding his arms around her waist to support her. Their tongues met as he instantly deepened the kiss but although Darcy could feel herself begin to melt, she forced herself to pull away.

'No,' she whispered. 'Not here. Not like this. Let's go upstairs. I need to lie down.'

'To bed?'

She took his hand and began to walk towards the stairs. 'Why not? It just happens to be about the only piece of furniture we have.'

An old-fashioned boat bed had been delivered to the master bedroom, her only instruction to the removal men being that the thick plastic covering the mattress should be taken away and disposed of. The wooden-framed structure dominated an otherwise empty room and on its king-size surface lay the embroidered coverlet she'd found when she and Renzo had been rooting around in one of Rome's antiques markets. She hadn't asked for it to be placed there but now it seemed like a sign that this had been meant to happen.

'Get undressed,' she whispered as she pulled off her overcoat and dropped it to the ground.

His eyes were fixed on hers as he removed his jacket, his sweater and trousers. Soon their discarded clothes were mingled in a heap beside the bed and at last Darcy stood in front of him. She was naked and heavily pregnant and feeling more than a little awkward, yet the look of desire in his eyes was melting away any last trace of shyness.

'I feel…bulky,' she said.

'Not bulky,' he corrected, his voice husky. 'Beautiful. Luscious and rounded—like the ripest of fruits about to fall from the tree.'

She shivered as he spoke and he took her into his arms.

'You're cold,' he observed.

She shook her head, still reeling from his words and the way he'd looked at her as he said them. 'No, not cold. Excited.'

'Me, too.' He gave a low laugh as he unfolded the coverlet and shook it out over the mattress.

'It almost looks as if we're planning on a picnic,' she said, her voice suddenly betraying a hint of uncertainty.

'That's exactly what I'm planning. I'm going to feast on you, *mia bella*.' But his face suddenly darkened as he pulled her into his arms and their bare flesh met for the first time in so long. 'I'm out of my depth here, Darcy,' he groaned. 'I've never made love to a pregnant woman before and I'm scared I'm going to hurt you. Tell me what you want me to do.'

'Just kiss me,' she whispered as they sank down onto the mattress. 'And we'll make it up as we go along.'

He kissed her for a long time. Tiny, brushing kisses at first and then deeper ones. And for a while, there were hard kisses which felt almost angry—as if he was punishing her for having kept him away for so long. But his anger soon passed and the kisses became exploratory as he licked his way inside her mouth and they began to play a silent and erotic game of tongues.

And then he started to touch her as Darcy had ached for him to touch her night after lonely night, waiting in vain for him to come to bed. At first he simply skated the palms of his hands down over her, as if discovering all the different contours and curves which had grown since last time they'd been intimate. No area of skin escaped the light whisper of his fingertips and she could feel every nerve ending growing acutely sensitised. Slowly, he circled each breast with his thumb, focussing his attention on each peaking nipple and putting his mouth there to lick luxuriously until she was squirming with frustrated longing. She wanted him to hurry yet she wanted him to take all day. But the rhythmical movements of his hand relaxed her completely, so that she was more than ready for his leisurely exploration of her belly when it came.

Their gazes met as his fingers splayed over the tight drum, his black eyes filled with question. 'This is okay?' he breathed.

'This is more than okay,' she managed, her voice growing unsteady as he slipped his hand down beyond to the silky triangle of hair, fingering her honey-eyed flesh so that she gasped with pleasure and the scent of her sex filled the air.

She reached for him, her pleasure already so intense that she could barely think straight as she tangled her fingers through his thick black hair, before hungrily reacquainting herself with the hard planes of his body. His shoulders were so broad and powerful; his pecs iron-hard. She loved the smattering of hair which roughened the rocky torso. Her fingertips skated lightly over his chest, feeling the rock-like definition of his abs. She thought his skin felt like oiled silk and she traced a lingering path over the dip of his belly before her fingers curled around the hardness of his erection, but he shook a cautionary head and pulled her hand away.

'It's been too long,' he said unevenly.

'You're telling me!'

'And I need to do it to you right now before I go out of my mind—the only question is, how?'

In answer, Darcy turned onto her side, wiggling her bottom against his groin in blatant invitation. 'Like this, I think.'

'But I can't see you.'

'Doesn't matter. And it never used to bother you. Go on.' She wiggled again and he groaned and she could feel how big he was as his moist tip positioned enticingly against her wet heat. 'You can feel me now and look at me later.'

He gave a low laugh and said something softly profound in Italian as he eased inside her. But the moan he gave was long and Darcy thought she'd never heard such an exultant sound before.

'Okay?' he bit out, holding himself perfectly still.

'More than okay,' she gasped.

'I'm not hurting you?'

'No, Renzo, but you're frustrating the hell out of me.'

His laugh sounded edgy but he began to move. In slow motion, he stroked himself in and out of her, his palms cupping her heavy breasts, his lips on her neck—kissing her through the thick curtain of curls. Darcy closed her eyes as she gave into sensation, forgetting that this was the only time they ever seemed truly equal. Forgetting everything except for the pulse points of pleasure throbbing throughout her body and the inexorable building of her orgasm as Renzo made love to her. Insistent heat pushed towards her. She could feel it coming—as inevitable as a train hurtling along the track—and part of her wanted to keep it at bay, to revel in that sweet expectation for as long as possible. But Renzo was close, as well—she could sense that, too. She'd had him come inside her too many times not to realise when he was near the edge. So she let go. Let pleasure wash over her—wave after sweet wave of it—until his movements suddenly quickened. He thrust into her with a deeper sense of urgency until at last he quivered and jerked and she felt the burst of his seed flooding into her.

Afterwards he lay exactly where he was and so did she. His skin was joined to hers, his body, too. It felt warm and sticky and intimate. Darcy just wanted to savour the moment and her deep sense of contentment as she waited for his verdict on that deeply satisfying interlude. Still remembering the dreamy things he'd murmured when they'd started to make love, part of her anticipating just what his next words might be. But when they came, it felt as if someone had ripped through that lazy contentment like a knife ripping through delicate silk.

'So… Was that my reward, I wonder, *cara mia*?' he questioned softly.

She pulled away from him, aware of the sudden pounding of her heart and the general indignity of turning to face a man when any kind of action was proving laborious. Especially when you were completely naked beneath the gaze of a pair of eyes which looked suddenly distant. She told herself not to read unnecessary stuff into his words—not to always imagine the worst. *He told you he wanted you and that he's been lusting after you...so go with that.*

'I'm afraid I'm not with you,' she said lightly.

'No?' He turned onto his back and yawned. 'You mean that wasn't your way of thanking me for buying you a home of your own? For finally getting the independence you must have craved for all these years?'

Darcy froze as the meaning of his words sank in and suddenly all that vulnerability which was never far from the surface began to rise in a dark unwanted tide. Groping down over the side of the bed, she managed to retrieve her overcoat and slung it over herself to cover her nakedness.

'Let's just get this straight.' Her voice was trembling. 'You think I had sex with you because you made me an overgenerous offer I hadn't actually asked for?'

'I don't know, Darcy.' His tone had changed. It rang out, iron-hard—like the sound of a hammer hitting against a nail. And when he turned his head to look at her, his eyes were icy. Like the black ice you sometimes saw when you were out on the roads in winter. Or didn't see until it was too late. 'I just don't get it with you. Sometimes I think I know you and other times I think I don't know you at all.'

'But aren't all relationships like that?' she questioned, swallowing down her fear. 'Didn't some songwriter say that if our thoughts could be seen, they'd probably put our heads in a guillotine?'

His eyes were narrowed as they studied her. 'And if I promised to grant you leniency, would you give me access to your thoughts right now?'

Darcy didn't react. She could tell him the rest of

her story—and maybe if it had been any other man than Renzo she would have done so. But he had already insulted her by thinking she'd had sex with him just because he'd bought her this house. To him, it all boiled down to a transaction and he didn't really trust himself to believe anything different. He thought of everything in terms of barter between the sexes because he didn't really *like* women, did he? He'd told her that a long time ago. He might want her but he didn't trust her and even though she could try to gain that trust by confessing her biggest secret, surely it was too big a gamble?

'I'm just wondering why you seem determined to wreck what chance we have of happiness,' she said, in a low voice. 'We have a lovely new home and a baby on the way. We're both healthy and we fancy each other like crazy. We've just had amazing sex—can't we just enjoy that?'

Black eyes seared into her for a long moment until eventually he nodded, his hand snaking around her waist and pulling her closer so that she could feel the powerful beat of his heart.

'Okay,' he said as he stroked her hair. 'Let's do that. I'm sorry. I shouldn't have said that. It's just all very new to me and I don't do trust very easily.'

Silently, she nodded, willing the guilt and the tears to go away. All she wanted was to live a decent life with her husband and child. She wanted what she'd never had—was that really too much to ask? She relaxed a little as his hand moved from her hair to her back, his fingertips skating a light path down her spine. Couldn't she be the best kind of wife to him, to demonstrate her commitment through her actions rather than her words?

He leaned over her, black fire blazing as he bent his face close. 'Are you tired?'

She shook her head. 'Not a bit. Why?'

His thumb grazed the surface of her bottom lip and she could feel his body hardening against her as he gave a rueful smile. 'Because I want you again,' he said.

CHAPTER TEN

DARCY'S FIRST INKLING that something was wrong
came on a Monday morning. At first she thought it
was nothing—like looking up at the sky and thinking
you'd imagined that first heavy drop of rain which
heralded the storm.

Renzo was in London unveiling his design for the
Tokyo art gallery at a press conference—having left
the house at the crack of dawn. He'd asked if she'd
wanted to accompany him but she'd opted to stay, and
was in the garden pegging out washing when the call
came from one of his assistants, asking if she was
planning to be at home at lunchtime.

Darcy frowned. It struck her as a rather strange
question. Even if she wasn't home, Renzo knew she
wouldn't have strayed much further than the local
village—or, at a pinch, the nearby seaside town of
Brighton. All that stuff they said about pregnant
women wanting to nest was completely true and she'd
built a domestic idyll here while awaiting the birth
of their baby. And hadn't that nesting instinct made
her feel as though life was good—or as good as it
could be? Even if sometimes she felt guilt clench at
her heart unexpectedly, knowing that her husband

remained ignorant of her biggest, darkest secret. But why rock the boat by telling him? Why spoil something which was good by making him pity her and perhaps despise her?

Placing the palm of her hand over the tight drum of her belly, she considered his assistant's question. 'Yes, I'm going to be here at lunchtime. Why?'

'Signor Sabatini just asked me to make sure.'

Darcy frowned. 'Is something wrong? Is Renzo around—can I speak to him, please?'

The assistant's voice was smooth but firm. 'I'm afraid that won't be possible. He's in a meeting. He said to tell you he'll be with you soon after noon.'

Darcy replaced the receiver, trying to lose the sudden feeling of apprehension which had crept over her, telling herself it was only because that fractured phone call felt a little like history repeating itself which had made her nervous. At least it hadn't been the same assistant who had stonewalled her attempts to get through to Renzo to tell him she was pregnant. That assistant had suddenly been offered a higher position in a rival company, something which Darcy suspected Renzo had masterminded himself. He'd seemed to want to put the past behind them as much as she did. *So stop imagining trouble where there isn't any.*

But it didn't matter how much she tried to stay positive, she couldn't seem to shake off the growing sense of dread which had taken root inside her. She went inside and put away the remaining clothes pegs—something her billionaire husband often teased her about. He told her that hanging out washing was suburban; she told him she didn't care. She knew he wanted to employ a cleaner and a housekeeper, and to keep a driver on tap instead of driving herself— in the fairly ordinary family car she'd chosen, which wasn't Renzo's usual style at all. The private mid-wife who lived locally and could be called upon at any time had been her only concession to being married to a billionaire.

But she wanted to keep it real, because reality was her only anchor. Despite Renzo's enormous power and wealth, she wanted theirs to be as normal a family as it was possible to be. And despite what she'd said when he'd railroaded her into the marriage, she badly wanted it to work. Not just because of their baby or because of their unhappy childhoods. She looked out the window, where her silk shirt was blowing wildly in the breeze. She wanted it to work because she had realised she loved him.

She swallowed.

She loved him.

It had dawned on her one morning when she'd woken to find him still sleeping beside her. In sleep he looked far less forbidding but no less beautiful. His shadowed features were softened; the sensual lips relaxed. Two dark arcs of eyelashes feathered onto his olive skin and his hair was ruffled from where she'd run her hungry fingers through it sometime during the night. She remembered the powerful feeling which had welled up inside her as the full force of her feelings had hit her and she wondered how she could have failed to recognise it before.

Of course she loved him. She'd been swept away by him from the moment she'd looked across a crowded nightclub and seen a man who had only had eyes for her. A once-in-a-lifetime man who'd made her feel a once-in-a-lifetime passion, despite the fact that he could be arrogant, tricky and, at times, downright difficult. And if fate—or rather pregnancy—had given her the opportunity to capitalise on those feelings and for passion to evolve into love, then she had to make the most of it. He might not feel the same way about her but she told herself that didn't matter because she had more than enough love to go round. She planned to make herself indispensable—not just as the mother of his child, but as his partner. To concentrate on friendship, respect and passion and reassure herself that maybe it could be enough. And if sometimes she found herself yearning for something more—well, maybe she needed to learn to appreciate what she had and stop chasing fantasy.

She spent the next hour crushing basil leaves and mashing garlic, trying to perfect a pesto sauce as good as the one they'd eaten in Rome on the last evening of their honeymoon. Then she picked a handful of daffodils and put them in a vase and had just sat down with a cup of tea to admire their yellow frilliness, when she heard the front door slam.

'I'm in here!' she called. She looked up to see Renzo framed in the doorway, her smile and words of welcome dying on her lips when she saw the darkness on his face. She put the cup down with a suddenly shaking hand. 'Is something wrong?'

He didn't answer and that only increased her fear. His hands were white-knuckled and a pulse was beating fast at his temple, just below a wayward strand of jet-black hair. She could sense an almost palpable tension about him—as if he was only just clinging on to his temper by a shred.

'Renzo! What's wrong?'

He fixed her with a gaze which was cold and hard. 'You tell me,' he said.

'Renzo, you're scaring me now. What is it? I don't understand.'

'Neither did I.' He gave a harsh and bitter laugh. 'But suddenly I do.'

From his pocket he took out an envelope and slapped it onto the table. It was creased—as if somebody had crushed it in the palm of their hand and then changed their mind and flattened it out again. On the cheap paper Renzo's name had been printed—and whoever had written it had spelt his surname wrong, she noted automatically.

His lip curved. 'It's a letter from your friend.'

'Which *friend*?'

'Shouldn't take you long to work that one out, Darcy. I mean, it isn't like you have a lot of friends, is it?' His mouth twisted. 'I never really understood why before. But suddenly I do.'

She knew then. She'd seen the look often enough in the past not to be able to recognise it. She could feel the stab of pain to her heart and the sickening certainty that her flirtation with a normal life was over.

'What does it say?'

'What do you think it says?'

'I'd like to hear it.' Was she hoping for some sort of reprieve? For someone to be writing to tell him that she'd once told a policewoman a lie—or that she'd missed school for a whole three months while her mother kept her at home? She licked her lips and looked at him. 'Please.'

With another contemptuous twist of his lips he pulled out the lined paper and began to read from it, though something told her he already knew the words by heart.

> '"Did you know that Pammie Denton was a whore? Biggest hooker in all of Manchester. Ask your wife about her mam."'

He put the note down. 'It's pointless asking if you recognise the writing, since it's printed in crude capitals, but I imagine Drake Bradley must be the perpetrator and that this is the beginning of some clumsy attempt at blackmail. Don't you agree?' he added coolly.

Her normal reaction would have been to shut right down and say she didn't want to talk about it because that had been the only way she'd been able to cope with the shame in the past, but this was different. Renzo was her husband. He was the father of her unborn baby. She couldn't just brush all the dirty facts under the carpet and hope they would go away.

And maybe it was time to stop running from the truth. To have the courage to be the person she was today, rather than the person forged from the sins of yesterday. Her heart pounded and her mouth grew suddenly dry. To have the courage to tell him what maybe she should have told him a long time ago.

'I'd like to explain,' she said, drawing in a deep breath.

He gave her another unfathomable look as he

opened up the refrigerator and took out a beer and Darcy blinked at him in consternation because cool and controlled Renzo Sabatini never drank during the day.

'Feel free,' he said, flipping the lid and pouring it into a glass. But he left the drink untouched, putting it down on the table and leaning against the window sill as he fixed her with that same cold and flinty stare. 'Explain away.'

In a way it would have been easier if he'd been angry. If he'd been hurling accusations at her she could have met those accusations head-on. She could have countered his rage with, not exactly *reason*— but surely some kind of heartfelt appeal, asking him to put himself in her situation. But this wasn't easy. Not when he was looking at her like that. It was like trying to hold a conversation with a piece of stone.

'My mother was a prostitute.'

'I think we've already established that fact and I think I know how prostitution works,' he said. 'So what exactly was it you wanted to *explain*, Darcy?'

It was worse than she'd thought because there *was* anger, only it was quiet and it was brooding and it was somehow terrifying. Because this was a man she scarcely recognised. It was as if his body had become encased in a thick layer of frost. As if liquid ice were running through his veins instead of blood.

She looked at him, wanting to convey a sense of what it had been like, trying to cling on to the certainty that there *was* something between her and Renzo—something which was worth fighting for. There had to be. He might take his parental responsibilities very seriously but deep down she knew he wouldn't have married her or contemplated staying with her unless they had *something* in common. 'She was an addict. Well, you know that bit. Only… Well, drugs are expensive—'

'And a woman can always sell her body?' he interposed acidly.

She nodded, knowing this time there was no going back. That she needed to tell him the truth. The cruel, unedited version she'd never even been able to admit to herself before, let alone somebody else.

'She can,' she said. 'Until her looks start to go— and that tends to happen sooner rather than later where addicts are concerned. My mother had once been beautiful but her looks deserted her pretty quickly. Her…her hair fell out and then…'

She flushed with shame as she remembered the kids at school taunting her and she remembered that she'd once thought she would never tell him this bit, but she knew she had to. Because why was she trying to protect her mother's memory, when she had uncaringly gone out and wrecked as many lives as it took to get that hypodermic syringe plunging into her arm?

'Then her teeth,' she whispered, staring down at the fingers which were knotted together in her lap. 'And that was the beginning of the end, because she kept losing her dentures whenever she got stoned. She was still able to get clients—only the standard of client went rapidly downhill, as I'm sure you can imagine, and so did the amount of money she was able to charge.'

And that had been when it had got really scary. When she hadn't wanted to go home from school at night—even though she was so stressed that learning had become impossible. She'd never know what she'd find when she got there—what kind of lowlife would be leering at her mother, but, worse, leering at *her*. That had been where her mistrust of men had started and if that kindly social worker hadn't stepped in, she didn't know what would have happened. To most people, going back to the children's home would have seemed like the end of the road—but to her it had felt like salvation.

'It sounds a nightmare,' he said flatly.

Sensing a sea change in his mood, Darcy looked up but the hope in her heart withered immediately when she saw that his stony expression was unchanged. 'It was. I just want you to understand—'

'No,' he said suddenly, cutting across her words. 'I'm not interested in understanding, Darcy. Not any more. I want you to know that something was destroyed when I received this letter.'

'I realise it was shocking—'

He shook his head. 'No. You're missing the point. I'm not talking about *shocking*. Human behaviour has always been shocking. I'm talking about trust.'

'T-trust?'

'Yes. I can see the bewilderment on your face. Is that word such an alien concept to you?' His mouth twisted. 'I guess it must be. Because I asked you, didn't I, Darcy? I asked you not once, but twice, whether you were keeping anything else from me. I thought we were supposed to be embracing a new openness—an honest environment in which to bring up our child, not one which was tainted by lies.'

She licked her lips. 'But surely you can understand why I didn't tell you?'

'No,' he snapped. 'I can't. I knew about your mother's addiction. Did you expect me to judge you when I found out how she paid for that addiction?'

'Yes,' she said helplessly. 'Of course I did. Because I've been judged by every person who ever knew about it. Being the daughter of Manchester's biggest hooker tends to saddle you with a certain reputation. People used to sneer at me. I could hear them laughing behind my back. And even though my social worker said it was because I was attractive and people would try to bring me down by exploiting my vulnerability, that didn't stop the hurt. It's why I left and came to London. It's why I never was intimate with a man before I met you.'

'Why you never accepted the gifts I tried to give you,' he said slowly.

'Yes!' she answered, desperately searching for a chink in the dark armour which made him look so impenetrable. Searching for the light of understanding in his eyes which might give her hope.

But there was none.

'You do realise, Darcy,' he questioned, 'that I can't live with secrets?'

'But there aren't any—not any more. Now you know everything about me.' Her heart was crashing wildly against her ribcage as she pleaded her case like a prisoner in the dock. 'And I need never lie to you again.'

He shook his head. 'You just don't get it, do you?' he said and his voice sounded tired. 'You knew that my childhood was tainted with secrets and lies. I told you a long time ago that I had trust issues and I meant it. How the hell can I ever trust you again? The truth is that I can't.' He gave a bitter laugh. 'And the even bigger truth is that I don't even want to.'

She was about to accuse him back. To tell him that he'd never trusted her in the first place. Look how he'd reacted when he'd discovered she was pregnant—showering her with suspicious questions when she'd lain in her hospital bed. He'd even thought she'd had wild sex with him just because he'd bought her a house. But her accusations remained unspoken because what was the point? No matter what she did or said, something in him had died—she could tell that from the emptiness in his eyes when he looked at her.

She nodded. 'So what do you want to do?'

He lifted the glass of beer now and drank it down in a draught, before slowly putting the empty glass back down on the table. 'I'm going back to London,' he said and Darcy could hear the bitterness in his tone. 'Because I can't bear to be around you right now.'

'Renzo—'

'No, please. Let's keep this dignified, shall we? Don't let's either of us say anything we might later regret, because we're still going to have to co-parent. We'll obviously need to come to some sort of formal agreement about that but it isn't something we need to discuss right now. I think you know me well enough to know that I won't be unreasonable.'

She nearly broke then—and what made it worse was the sudden crack in his voice as he said those words. As if he was hurting as much as she was. But he wasn't, was he? He couldn't be. Because nobody could possibly share this terrible pain which was searing through her heart and making it feel as if it had exploded into a million little pieces.

'You have the services of the midwife I've employed,' he continued. 'I spoke to her from the car on the way here and explained the circumstances and she has offered to move into the annex if that would make you feel more secure.'

'No, it would not make me feel more secure!' Darcy burst out. 'I don't want a total stranger living here with me.'

He gave a short, sarcastic laugh. 'No. I can't imagine you do. Living with a stranger isn't something I'd particularly recommend.'

And then he turned his back on her and walked out, closing the door with a click behind him. Darcy struggled to her feet to watch him walking down the garden path, past the washing line. The wind was blowing the sleeves of her shirt so that they flapped towards him, as if they were trying to pull him back, and how she wished they could. She considered rushing down the path after him, cumbersome in her late pregnancy, grabbing the sleeve of his handmade Italian suit and begging him to give her another chance. To stay.

But dignity was the one thing she had—maybe the only thing she had left.

So she watched him go. Watched him get into the back of the luxury car with the sunlight glinting off dark hair as blue-black as a raven's wing. His jaw set, he kept his gaze fixed straight ahead, not turning round as the powerful vehicle pulled away. There was no last, lingering look. No opportunity for her eyes to silently beseech him to stay.

The only thing she saw was his forbidding profile as Renzo Sabatini drove out of her life.

CHAPTER ELEVEN

AFTER HE'D GONE, a wave of desolation swept over Darcy—a desolation so bleak that it felt as if she were standing on the seashore in the depths of winter, being buffeted by the lashing sea. As his car disappeared from view she stumbled away from the window, trying to keep her wits about her, telling herself that her baby was her primary focus—her *only* focus—and she needed to protect the innocent life inside her. Briefly she closed her eyes as she thought about what Renzo had just found out—the shameful truth about her mother being a common prostitute. Would she be forced to tell her son about the kind of woman his grandmother had been? Yet surely if there was enough love and trust between her and her little boy, then anything was possible.

She swallowed because nothing seemed certain—not any more. She could understand her husband's anger but it had been impossible to penetrate. It had been a controlled reaction which shouldn't have surprised her—but another aspect of it had and that was what was confusing her. Because he hadn't threatened her with the full force of his wealth and power after making his sordid discovery, had he? Wouldn't another man—a more ruthless man—have pressured her with exposure if she didn't relinquish her role as primary carer to their baby?

Brushing away the sweat which was beading her brow, she knew she ought to sit down but she couldn't stop pacing the room as her jumbled thoughts tried to assemble themselves into something approaching clarity. His voice had been bitter when he'd spoken to her—almost as if he'd been hurt. But Renzo didn't *do* hurt, did he? Just as he didn't do emotion.

Surely he must recognise why she'd kept her terrible secret to herself—why the shame of the past had left her unable to trust anyone, just as *he* had been unable to trust anyone.

But Renzo had trusted *her*, hadn't he?

The thought hit her hard.

How many times had he trusted her?

He'd trusted her to take the pill and, even though that method of birth control had failed, he'd trusted her enough to believe her explanation.

He'd trusted her enough to confide in her when he first took her out to Tuscany and told her things he need never have said. And then, when they'd got back to England, he'd trusted her enough to give her the key to his apartment. He might not have wooed her with words but words were cheap, weren't they? Anyone could say stuff to please a woman and not mean it. But Renzo's actions had demonstrated trust and regard and that was pretty amazing. It might not have been love but it came a pretty close second. And she had blown it.

Tears welled up in her eyes as she stared at the yellow blur of daffodils in the vase. She had blown it by refusing to trust *him*—by not lowering the defences she'd erected all those years ago, when the police had asked her questions and she'd been too frightened to tell the truth, for fear her mother would go to jail. Renzo hadn't judged her because her mother had been an addict and he wouldn't have judged her because she'd been a prostitute—what had made him turn away with that tight-lipped face was the fact that she'd lied to him. Again and again, she'd kept her secrets to herself.

So what was she going to do about it? She looked at the bright blue sky outside, which seemed to mock her. Stay here with the midwife on standby, while she waited for the baby to arrive? Day following day with remorse and regret and the feeling that she'd just thrown away the best thing which had ever happened to her? Or have the courage to go to Renzo. Not to plead or beg but to put her feelings on the line and tell him what she should have told him a long time ago. It might be too late for him to take her back, but surely he could find it in his heart to forgive her?

Picking up the car keys, she went to the garage and manoeuvred the car out on the lane, sucking in lots of deep and calming breaths just as they'd taught her in the prenatal relaxation classes. Because she had a very precious passenger on board and there was no way she should attempt to drive to London if she was going to drive badly.

She let out the clutch and pulled away, thinking that she should have been scared but she'd never felt so strong or so focussed. She kept her mind fixed firmly on the traffic as the country roads gave way to the city and she entered the busy streets of London,

glad she was able to follow the robotic instructions
of the satnav. But her hands were shaking as eventually she drew up outside the towering skyscraper
headquarters of Sabatini International. She left the
car by the kerb and walked into the foyer, where a security guard bustled up importantly, barring her way.

'I'm afraid you can't park there, miss.'

'Oh, yes, I can. And it's Mrs, actually—or Signora,
if you prefer. My husband owns this building. So
if you wouldn't mind?' Giving a tight smile at his
goggle-eyed expression, she handed him her car keys.
'Doing something with my car? I'd hate Renzo to
get a ticket.'

She was aware of people staring at her as she
headed for the penthouse lift but maybe that wasn't
surprising. Among the cool and geeky workers mill-
ing around, she guessed a heavily pregnant woman
with untidy hair would be a bit of a talking point.
The elevator zoomed her straight up to the thirty-second floor, where one of Renzo's assistants must have
been forewarned because she stood directly in Darcy's path, her fixed smile not quite meeting her eyes.

'Mrs Sabatini.' She inclined her head. 'I can't let
you disturb him. I'm afraid your husband is tied up
right now.'

Suddenly tempted by a wild impulse to ask
whether Renzo had suddenly been converted to the
pleasures of bondage, Darcy looked at her and nodded, but she didn't feel anger or irritation. The woman
was only doing her job, after all. In the past she might
have crumbled—gone scuttling back downstairs with
a request that Renzo contact her when he had a free
moment. But that was then and this was now. She'd

overcome so much in her life. Seen stuff no child should ever see. She'd come through the other side of all that and yet…

Yet she had still let it define her, hadn't she? Instead of shutting the door on the past and walking away from it, she had let it influence her life.

Well, not any more.

'Watch me,' Darcy said as she walked across the carpeted office towards Renzo's office, ignoring the woman's raised voice of protest.

She pushed open the door to see Renzo seated at the top of a long boardroom table with six other people listening to what he was saying, but his words died away the moment he glanced up and saw her. Comically, every head swivelled in her direction but Darcy didn't pay them any attention; she was too busy gazing into the eyes of her husband and finding nothing in their ebony depths but ice. But she was going to be strong. As strong as she knew she could be.

'Darcy,' he said, his eyes narrowing.

'I know this isn't a convenient time,' she said, preempting his dismissal and drawing herself up as tall as she could. 'But I really do need to speak to you, Renzo. So if you people wouldn't mind giving us five, we'll make sure this meeting is rescheduled.'

Almost as if they were being controlled by some unseen puppet master, six heads turned to Renzo for affirmation.

He shrugged. 'You heard what the lady said.'

Darcy's heart was pounding as they all trooped out, shooting her curious looks on their way, but Renzo still hadn't moved. His expression remained completely impassive and only the sudden movement of his fingers as he slammed his pen onto the table gave any indication that he might be angry at her interruption.

'So what are you doing here?' he questioned coolly. 'I thought we'd said everything there is to say.'

She shook her head. 'But we haven't. Or rather, I haven't. You did a lot of talking earlier only I was too shocked and upset to answer.'

'Don't bother,' he said, sounding almost...*bored*. 'I don't want to hear any more of your lies. You want to hold on to your precious secrets, Darcy? Then go right ahead! Or maybe find a man you trust enough to tell the truth.'

She let out a shuddered breath, struggling to get out the words she knew she needed to say. 'I trust you, Renzo. It's taken me this long to dare admit it, but I do. I trust you enough to tell you that I've been scared...and I've been stupid. You see, I couldn't believe someone as good as you could ever be part of my life and I thought...' Her voice stumbled but somehow she kept the tears at bay. 'I thought the only way I could hold on to it was to be the person I thought you'd want me to be. I was terrified that if you knew who I really was, that you would send me away— baby or no baby—'

'You can't—'

'No,' she said fiercely, and now the tears *had* started and she scrubbed them away furiously with the back of her fist. 'Let me finish. I should have celebrated my freedom from the kind of life I'd grown up in. I should have rejoiced that I had found a man who was prepared to care for me, and to care for our baby. I should have realised that it was a pretty big deal for you to tell me stuff about your past and give me a key to your apartment. I should have looked for the meaning behind those gestures instead of being too blind and too scared to dare. And rather than keeping my feelings locked away, I should have told you the biggest secret of all.'

He froze. 'Not another one?'

'Yes,' she whispered. 'The final one—and I'm about to let you in on it. Not because I want something in return or because I'm expecting something back, but because you need to know.' Her voice trembled but she didn't care. This was her chance to put something right but it was also the truth—shining, bold and very certain, no matter the consequences. 'I love you, Renzo. I've loved you from the first moment I saw you, when the thunderbolt hit me, too. Because that feeling never went away. It just grew and grew. When we made love that first time, it was so powerful—it blew me away. I've never wanted to be intimate with a man before you and I know that, if you don't want me, I won't ever find somebody who makes me feel the way you do.'

There was a silence when all Darcy could hear was the fierce pounding of her heart and she could hardly bear to look at him for fear that she might read rejection in his face. But she had to look at him. If she had learned anything it was that she had to face up to the truth, no matter how painful that might be.

'How did you get here?' he demanded.

She blinked at him in confusion. 'I...drove.'

He nodded. 'You parked your car in the middle of the city when you've only recently passed your test?'

'I gave the keys to the security guard.' She licked her lips. 'I told him I was your wife.'

'So you thought you'd just drive up here and burst into my building and disrupt my meeting with a few pretty words and make it all better?'

'I did…' She drew in a deep breath. 'I did what I thought was best.'

'Best for you, you mean?'

'Renzo—'

'No!' he interrupted savagely and now all the cold-ness had gone—to be replaced with a flickering fire and fury which burned in the depths of his black eyes. 'I don't want this. *Capisci?* I meant what I said, Darcy. I don't want to live this way, wondering what the hell I'm going to find out about you next. Never knowing what you're hiding from me, what secrets you're concealing behind those witchy green eyes.'

She searched his face for some kind of softening but there was none. And who could blame him? She'd known about his trust issues and she'd tested those issues to the limit. Broken them beyond repair so that they lay in shattered ruins between them. The hope which had been building inside her withered and died. Her lips pressed in on themselves but she would not cry. *She would not cry.*

She nodded. 'Then there's nothing more to be said, is there? I'll leave you so that you can get on with your meeting. You're right. I should have rung ahead beforehand, but I was afraid you wouldn't see me. I guess I would have been right.' She swallowed. 'Still, I'm sure we can work something out. The best and most amicable deal for our baby. I'm sure we both want that.' There was a pause as she took one long last look at him, drinking in the carved olive features, the sensual lips and the gleam of his black eyes. 'Goodbye, Renzo. Take…take good care of yourself.'

And then, with her head held very high, she walked out of his office.

Renzo stared at her retreating form, his mind spinning, aware of the door closing before opening again and his assistant rushing in.

'I'm sorry about that, Renzo—'

But he waved an impatient hand of dismissal until the woman left him alone again. He paced the floor space of his vast office, trying to concentrate on his latest project, but all he could think about was the luminous light of Darcy's green eyes and the brimming suggestion of unshed tears. And suddenly he found himself imagining what her life must have been like. How unbearable it must have been. All the sordid things she must have witnessed—and yet she had come through it all, hadn't she? He thought how she'd overcome her humble circumstances and what she had achieved. Not in some majorly highpowered capacity—she'd ended up waitressing rather than sitting on the board of some big company. But she'd done it with integrity. She'd financed her studies and read lots of novels while working two jobs—yet even when she'd been poured into that tight satin cocktail dress she had demonstrated a fierce kind of pride and independence. She'd never wanted to take a single thing from him, had she? She'd refused much more than she'd accepted and it hadn't been an act, had it? It had been genuine. From the heart. A big heart, which she'd been scared to expose for fear that she'd be knocked back, just as she must have been knocked back so many times before.

And he had done that to her. Knocked her back and let her go, right after she'd fiercely declared her love for him.

Her *love* for him.

He was prepared to give up that, along with her beauty and her energy, and for what?

For *what*?

A cold dread iced his skin as swiftly he left his office, passing his assistant's desk without saying a word as he urgently punched the button of the elevator. But the journey down to the basement seemed to take for ever, and Renzo's fist clenched as he glanced at his watch, because surely she would have left by now.

It took a moment for his eyes to focus in the gloomy light of the subterranean car park but he couldn't see her. Only now it wasn't his fist which clenched but his heart—a tight spear of pain which made him feel momentarily winded. What if she'd driven off after his callous rejection and was negotiating the busy roads to Brighton as she made her way back towards an empty house?

Pain and guilt washed over him as his eyes continued to scan the rows of cars and hope withered away inside him. And then he saw her on the other side of the car park in the ridiculously modest vehicle she'd insisted she wanted, in that stubborn way which often infuriated him but more often made his blood sing. He weaved his way through the cars, seeing her white face looking up at him as he placed the palm of his hand against the glass of the windscreen.

'I'm sorry,' he mouthed, but she shook her head.

'Let me in,' he said, but she shook her head again and began putting the key in the ignition with shaking fingers.

He didn't move, but placed his face closer to the window, barely noticing that someone from the IT department had just got out of the lift and was staring at him in open-mouthed disbelief. 'Open the door,' he said loudly. 'Or I'll rip the damned thing off its hinges.'

She must have believed him because the lock clicked and he opened the door and sat in the passenger seat before she could change her mind. 'Darcy,' he said.

'Whatever it is you want to say,' she declared fiercely, 'I don't want to hear it. Not right now.'

She'd been crying. Her face was blotchy and her eyes red-rimmed and he realised that he'd never seen her cry—not once—she, who probably had more reason to cry than any other woman he'd known.

He wanted to take her in his arms. To feel her warmth and her connection. To kiss away those drying tears as their flesh melted against each other as it had done so many times in the past. But touching was cheating—it was avoiding the main issue and he needed to address that. To face up to what else was wrong. Not in her, but in him. Because how could she have ever trusted him completely when he kept so much of himself locked away?

'Just hear me out,' he said, in a low voice. 'And let me tell you what I should have told you a long time ago. Which is that you've transformed my life in every which way. You've made me feel stuff I never thought I'd feel. Stuff I didn't want to feel, because I was scared of what it might do to me, because I'd seen hurt and I'd seen pain in relationships and I didn't want any part of that. Only I've just realised…' He drew in a deep breath and maybe she thought he wasn't going to continue, because her eyes had narrowed.

'Realised what?' she questioned cautiously.

'That the worst pain of all is the pain of not having you in my life. When you walked out of my office just now I got a glimpse of just what that could be like—and it felt like the sun had been blotted from the sky.'

'Very poetic,' she said sarcastically. 'Maybe your next girlfriend will hear it before it's too late.'

She wasn't budging an inch but he respected her for that, too. If it had been anyone else he wouldn't have stayed or persisted or cared. But he was fighting for something here. Something he'd never really thought about in concrete terms before.

His future.

'And there's something else you need to know,' he said softly. 'And before you look at me in that stubborn way, just listen. All those things I did for you, things I've never done for anyone else—why do you think they happened? Because those thunderbolt feelings never left me either, no matter how much I sometimes wished they would. Because I wanted our baby and I wanted you. I like being with you. Being married to you. Waking up to you each morning and kissing you to sleep every night. And I love you,' he finished simply. 'I love you so much, Darcy. Choose what you do or don't believe, but please believe that.'

As she listened to his low declaration of love,

Darcy started to cry. At first it was the trickle of a solitary tear which streaked down her cheek and ended up in a salty drip at the corner of her mouth. She licked it away but then more came, until suddenly they were streaming her face but the crazy thing was that she didn't care.

In the close confines of the car she stared at him through blurry vision and as that vision cleared the dark beauty of his face no longer seemed shuttered. It seemed open and alight with a look she'd always longed to see there, but never thought she would. It was shining from his eyes as a lighthouse shone out to all the nearby ships on the darkest of nights. 'Yes, I believe you,' she whispered. 'And now you need to hold me very tightly—just to convince me I'm not dreaming.'

With a soft and exultant laugh Renzo pulled her into his arms, smoothing away the tangle of curls before bending his head to kiss away the tears which had made her cheeks so wet. She clung to him as their mouths groped blindly together and kissed as they'd never really kissed before. It was passionate and it was emotional—but it was superseded by a feeling so powerful that Darcy's heart felt as if it were going to spill over with joy, until she suddenly jerked away—tossing her head back like a startled horse.

'Oh, I love you, my beautiful little firecracker,' he murmured as she dug her fingers into his arms.

'The feeling is mutual,' she said urgently. 'Only we have to get out of here.'

He frowned. 'You want to go back to Sussex?'

She flinched and closed her eyes as another fierce contraction gripped her and she shook her head. 'I don't think we're going to make it as far as Sussex. I know it's another two weeks away, but I think I'm going into labour.'

It was a quick and easy birth—well, that was what the cooing midwives told her, though Darcy would never have described such a seismic experience as *easy*. But she had Renzo beside her every step along the way. Renzo holding her hand and mopping her brow and whispering things to her in Italian which—in her more lucid moments—she knew she shouldn't understand, but somehow she did. Because the words of love were universal. People could say them and not mean them. But they could also say them in a foreign language and you knew—you just *knew*—what they meant and that they were true.

It was an emotional moment when they put Luca Lorenzo Sabatini to her breast and he began to suckle eagerly, gazing up at her with black eyes so like his daddy's. And when the midwives and the doctor had all left them, she glanced up into Renzo's face and saw that his own eyes were unusually bright. She lifted her hand to the dark shadow of growth at his unshaven jaw and he met her wondering gaze with a shrug of his powerful shoulders. Was he *crying*?

'*Scusi,*' he murmured, bending down to drop a kiss on his son's downy black head before briefly brushing his lips over Darcy's. 'I'm not going to be a lot of use to you, am I—if I start letting emotion get the better of me?'

And Darcy smiled as she shook her head. 'Bring it on,' she said softly. 'I like seeing my strong and powerful man reduced to putty by the sight of his newborn baby.'

'It seems as if my son has the same power over me as his mother,' Renzo responded drily. He smoothed back her wild red curls. 'Now. Do you want me to leave and let you get some rest?'

'No way,' she said firmly, shifting across to make space for him, her heart thudding as he manoeuvred his powerful frame onto the narrow hospital bed. And Darcy felt as if she'd never known such joy as when Renzo put his arm around her and hugged her and Luca close. As if she'd spent her life walking along a path—much of the time in darkness—only to emerge into a place full of beautiful light.

'It's not the most comfortable bed in the world, but there's room on it for the three of us. And I want you beside me, Renzo. Here with me and here with Luca.' And that was when her voice cracked with the emotion which had been building up inside her since he'd told her he loved her. 'In fact, we're never going to let you go.'

EPILOGUE

KICKING OFF HER shoes and flopping onto the sofa with a grateful sigh, Darcy frowned as Renzo handed her a slim leather box. 'What's this?' she questioned.

He raised his brows. 'Isn't the whole point of presents that they're supposed to be a surprise?'

'But it isn't my birthday.'

'No,' he said steadily. 'But it's Luca's.'

'Yes.' The box momentarily forgotten, Darcy looked into her husband's ebony eyes and beamed. Hard to believe that their beautiful son had just celebrated his first birthday. A year during which he'd captivated everyone around him with his bright and inquisitive nature, which at times showed more than a glimpse of his mother's natural stubbornness.

Today, with streamers and balloons and a bit too much cake, they'd held a party for all his little friends in Sussex—while the mothers had each sipped a glass of pink champagne. Confident in her husband's love, and freed from the shame of the past, Darcy had started to get to know people—both here in Sussex and in their London house, as well as the beautiful Tuscan villa where they spent as many holidays as they could. Invitations had started to arrive as, for the first time in her life, she'd begun to make friends. Real friends—though her best friend was and always would be her husband. She looked at him now with bemusement.

'Open it,' he said softly.

She unclipped the clasp and stared down at the necklace. A triple row of square-cut emeralds gleamed greenly against the dark velvet and there was a moment of confusion before she lifted her eyes to his. She remembered how, just after Luca's birth, he'd gone to see Drake Bradley and persuaded the blackmailer to tell him where he'd pawned the diamond necklace. He'd got Drake's confession on tape of course and, with the threat of prosecution and prison very real, Renzo had surprised everyone by refusing to turn him in to the police. Instead, he'd given Drake a chance—offering him a job working on the site clearance of one of his new projects in England. Employment Drake had eagerly accepted—possibly his first ever legitimate job and one which, against all the odds, he excelled at. For ever after, he treated Renzo with the dedication and loyalty a badly beaten dog might display towards the man who had rescued him.

Keep your friends close... Renzo had whispered to her on the night when the diamond necklace was back in his possession, after she'd finished remonstrating with him for putting himself in possible danger. But his expression had been rueful as she had held the dazzling diamond neckpiece as if it were an unexploded bomb.

'I guess you wouldn't get a lot of pleasure out of wearing this now?'

Darcy had shaken her head. 'Nope. Too much bad history. And I'm no big fan of diamonds, you know that.'

The next day Renzo had returned the piece to the charity, telling them to auction it again. And he hadn't mentioned jewellery since.

Until now.

'Renzo,' Darcy whispered, her gaze dazzled by the vivid green fire of the emeralds. 'This is too much.'

'No,' he said fiercely. 'It isn't. Not nearly enough. If I bought up the contents of every jewellery shop in the world, it still wouldn't be enough. Because I love you, Darcy. I love what you've given and shown me. How you've made me the man I am today, and I like that man much better than the one I was before.' His voice dipped, his gaze dark as the night as it blazed over her. 'And didn't I always say you should have emeralds to match your eyes?'

Very wet eyes now, she thought, but she nodded as he kissed away her tears. And the jewels were suddenly forgotten because, when it boiled down to it, they were just pretty pieces of stone. The most precious thing Darcy had was her love—for her son and for her husband. And the chance to live her life without shame and without secrets.

'Come here, *mia caro*,' she whispered, practising her ever-increasing Italian vocabulary as she pulled him down onto the sofa next to her.

'What did you have in mind?'

'I just want to show you…' she smiled as her fingertip stroked his cheek until she reached the outline of his sensual mouth, which softened as she edged her own lips towards it '…how very much I love you.'

* * * * *

A PAWN IN THE
PLAYBOY'S GAME

CATHY WILLIAMS

To my three wonderful and inspiring daughters

CHAPTER ONE

'DON'T KNOW WHAT you're doing here.' Roberto Falcone glared at his son. He had shuffled to the front door and now he remained standing in front of it like a bouncer blocking entry to a club. 'Told you not to bother coming and meant it.'

Alessandro felt that familiar tension invade his body, the way it always did on those occasions when he was in his father's company. Usually, though, they at least managed pleasantries before he felt like spinning on his heel and walking as fast as he could in the opposite direction. This time, there was no polite surface small talk and Alessandro braced himself for an impossibly difficult weekend.

Which they would both have to endure because there was no choice.

'Are you going to let me in or are we going to have this conversation on the doorstep? Because if we are, I'll get my coat from the car. I'd rather not die from frostbite just yet.'

'You won't die from frostbite,' Roberto Falcone scoffed. 'It's practically tropical here.'

Alessandro didn't bother to argue. He'd had a lot of experience when it came to disagreeing with his father. Roberto Falcone might be eighty years old but there was nothing he gave up without a fight, and arguing about whether eight degrees Celsius counted as cold or not was just one of those things. He was a hardy soul who lived in Scotland and thought that blizzard conditions were a bracing challenge. Real men cleared snowdrifts half-naked and barefoot! His son was a softie who lived in London and switched on the central heating the second the sun went behind a cloud.

And never the twain would meet.

Which was why duty visits were limited to three times a year and lasted as long as it took for the limited well of polite conversation to run dry.

Except this was more than a duty visit and he had known that his father wasn't going to make things easy.

'I'll get my coat.'

'Don't bother. Now that you've landed here, I suppose I don't have much choice but to let you in, but if you think that I'm going to be heading down to London with you, then you've got another think coming. I'm not budging.'

In the cold, gathering gloom, they stared at one another, Alessandro's expression veiled, his father's fiercely determined.

'We'll discuss this when I'm inside,' Alessandro said. 'Why have you answered the door? Where's Fergus?'

'It's the weekend. Man deserves a break.'

'You had a stroke six months ago and you're still recovering from a fractured pelvis. The man's paid enough to give up his breaks.'

Roberto scowled but Alessandro didn't back down. Frankly, this wasn't the time for pussyfooting round the issue. Like it or not, his father was going to return to London with him in three days' time. The contents of the house could be packed up and shipped south once the place had been vacated.

His mind was made up and once Alessandro had made his mind up on anything, he was not open to discussion, far less persuasion. His father could no longer cope with the rolling Victorian mansion, even if he could afford an army of hired help if he chose. Neither could he cope with the acres of lawns and garden. He liked plants. Alessandro would introduce him to the marvels of Kew Gardens.

The brutal truth was that Roberto Falcone was now frail, whether he wanted to admit it or not, and he needed somewhere small, somewhere closer to Alessandro, somewhere in London.

'I'll get my bag,' Alessandro said abruptly. 'You go in and I'll join you in the sitting room. I take it you haven't dispatched *all* the help...because you felt they needed some time out from doing what they're so handsomely paid to do?'

'You might be lord of that manor of yours in London,' Roberto retorted, 'and I wouldn't think of questioning you if you chose to give whoever works for you a weekend off, but this is *my* manor and I can do whatever I want.'

'Let's not kick off this weekend on an argument,' Alessandro said heavily. He looked at the elderly man in front of him, still leonine in appearance with his thick head of steel-grey hair, his piercing dark eyes and his impressive height, at six foot one only a couple of inches shorter than him. The only hint of his frailty was the walking stick and, of course, a thick wad of medical notes residing in the hospital ten miles due west.

'Freya is here. There's food in the kitchen, which is where you will find me. Had I known you were going to descend on me, I might have asked her to prepare something a little less simple, but you're here now and salmon and potatoes is going to have to do.'

'You knew I was coming,' Alessandro pointed out patiently. A sharp gust of wind, carrying the sort of bitter cold rarely experienced in London, blew his dark hair away from his face. 'I emailed you.'

'Must have slipped my mind.'

Clenching his jaw in pure frustration, Alessandro watched as his father shuffled away, leaving the front door wide open.

The move to London was going to be a big step, for both of them. They barely had anything to say to one another. Lord only knew how more frequent meetings were going to play out, but there was no way he could continue making laborious trips to the depths of Scotland every time his father had a mishap, and there were no siblings with whom he could share the burden.

Just him. An only child shunted off to boarding school at the age of seven, returning back to their vast, cold mansion every holiday, where nannies and cooks and cleaners had picked up the role of parent because his father had rarely been in evidence, appearing only at the end of the day when they had dined at opposite ends of the formal dining table, waited on by the very people with whom Alessandro had spent his day.

Until, of course, he had become old enough to begin spending the occasional holidays with friends. His father had not once objected. Alessandro suspected that he had probably been quietly relieved. There was only so much polite conversation to be made across the length of a twenty-seat table.

The polite conversation was still made but at least now Alessandro could take it in his stride, at least he had stopped trying to find reasons behind his father's coldness, stopped wondering whether things might have been different had he remarried after the death of Muriel Falcone, stopped trying not to be a disappointment. That particular youthful sentiment had long disappeared.

Hitching his overnight bag over his shoulder and remotely locking his glossy black SUV, Alessandro decided that he would have to find some hobbies for his father the second he arrived in London.

Hobbies that would take him out of the luxurious three-bedroom ground-floor apartment in a small, portered Georgian block, which had been bought for him. A man with hobbies would be a happy man. Or at least a relatively invisible one. Too much visibility was not going to work for either of them.

Returning to Standeth House, for Alessandro, was like returning to a mausoleum. Same cold feel, although now that it would shortly be put on the market he found that he could better appreciate the impressive flagstoned hallway and all the period features that he would never have dreamed of having in anywhere he personally owned but which, he conceded, had a certain something.

And, with as much money as you could fling a stick at, it had been well maintained. His father had been born into wealth, had maintained and increased it in his lifetime and had not stinted when it came to spending it on his surroundings. He had always been generous financially if parsimonious when it came to everything else.

He found his father in the kitchen, where, despite what he had said, there was no housekeeper.

Alessandro frowned. 'You said Freya would be here to take care of the food.'

Roberto looked at his son from under grey, bushy brows. 'Left at four. Note on the cooker jogged my memory. Forgot to mention it.' He ladled a generous portion of food onto his plate and went to the kitchen table, leaving Alessandro to help himself. 'Sick dog. Had to take it to the vet. It happens. And before you launch into a conversation about how you've come here to tear me away from my house and my land, eat some food and talk about something else. Been months since you ventured up here.

You must have something to talk about aside from rescuing me from my old age.'

'Work's fine.' Alessandro looked at the slab of salmon on his plate with distaste. Freya was in her mid-sixties and had been his father's cook for the past fifteen years. She was as thin as a rake, only smiled on high days and bank holidays and would never be asked to cook for the queen. Or anyone with halfway decent tastebuds. Her productions were as spartan as she was. Potatoes, some vegetables and fish, which were unadorned with anything that could fall under the heading of tasty.

'I've added a niche publishing house to my portfolio, along with three small hotels on the other side of the Atlantic. It's a little comic relief from my IT companies and telecommunications.' He might have benefited from being the son of a wealthy man, might have been to the finest schools, been given the most pocket money, treated to the fastest car at an age when fast cars and young boys should never have had even a nodding acquaintance, but he had refused point-blank to show the slightest interest in his father's empire. When it came to earning a living, Alessandro had always known that he would go it without any help from his austere and distant parent.

Not that Roberto had asked. Until a decade ago he had still been running his empire himself.

Neither had Alessandro accepted any start-up money. He had used his brains to super-achieve at university and he had continued using his brains to super-achieve at everything that had followed. As far as he was concerned, the less he had to do with Roberto Falcone, the better. They maintained contact, paid lip service to their relationship, and that was that. It worked.

'And still chasing the same idiots you were chasing when I last saw you? What was the name of that one you dragged up here? Acted as though she didn't recognise what mud was and refused to go near the garden because it had rained and her high heels couldn't take the strain.' Roberto guffawed.

'Sophia,' Alessandro said through gritted teeth. This was the first time his father had come right out and voiced his scathing disapproval of the women he had met in the past, girlfriends Alessandro had taken with him because a third party, even an intellectually challenged third party, was worth her weight in gold when it came to smoothing over pregnant pauses.

And it had to be said that the women he dated more than made up for their sometimes limited conversation with their looks. He liked them leggy, long-haired, slender and outrageously good-looking. The size of their IQs didn't really come into it. Just as long as they pleased him, looked good, said yes when he wanted them to say yes and didn't get attached.

'Sophia...that's the one. Nice-looking girl with all that bouncy hair but difficult to have a conversation with. I'm guessing that doesn't bother you, though. Where is she now?' He looked around him as though suddenly alert to the possibility that the six-foot-tall brunette might be hiding behind the kitchen door or underneath the counter.

'It didn't work out.' The gloves were certainly off if his father was diving into his personal life. Polite was beginning to look like a cosy walk in the park in comparison. Was this how Roberto intended to retaliate to the winds of change? By getting too close to the bone for comfort?

'Reason I brought that up...' Roberto finished his salmon and shoved the plate to one side '...is if that's the kind of people who hang around the rich in that city of yours, then it's just another reason why I won't be joining you. So you can start looking for tenants for that apartment you bought.'

'There are lots of different kinds of people in London.' And who, exactly, were his father's friends here anyway? He'd met one or two couples, bumped into them while out to dinner locally with his father over the years, but how often did he mix with them?

Like vast swathes of his father's life, that was just another mystery. For all Alessandro knew, his father could be cooped up in his country estate from dawn till dusk with nothing but the hired help and his plants for company.

He had long trained himself to feel no curiosity. The door had been shut on him a long time ago and it wasn't going to reopen.

'And some of them might have more to talk about than the weather, the tidal changes and salmon fishing. On another note, I see Freya is continuing to shine as a cordon bleu chef...'

'Simple food for a simple man,' Roberto returned coldly. 'If I wanted anything fancier, I would have employed one of those TV chef types who have fish restaurants in Devon and use ingredients nobody's ever heard of.'

For the first time in living memory, Alessandro felt his lips twitch with amusement at his father's asperity.

But then he reminded himself that humour wasn't behind this conversation. These were all little warning jabs before the real battle began in the morning.

He stood up, irritated that on a Friday evening there was no one around to at least clear the table. Alessandro didn't have anyone working for him, aside from a cleaner three times a week and his driver, but if he had he would have damned well made sure that they were available to work when he needed them, instead of skipping off to give their dog cuddles and cough syrup.

'I have some work to get through by ten tonight.' He

looked at his watch and then at his father, who had not moved a muscle to stand up.

'No one's keeping you.' Roberto fluttered his hand in the general direction of the kitchen door.

'Heading up to bed now?'

'Maybe not. Maybe I should have a late-night walk through the grounds so that I can appreciate the open space before you start manhandling me into a flat in that city of yours.'

'Freya in tomorrow? Or will her dog still require her urgent attention?' Alessandro wasn't going to be provoked into a simmering argument that he would take to bed with him. 'Because if she plans on spending the weekend with her sick dog, I'll head into town first thing in the morning and stockpile some food that's easy to cook.' He stood up and began clearing the table. 'Just enough to last the weekend,' he threw over his shoulder.

'Don't need you cooking for me. Perfectly capable of throwing something in a pan.'

'It's not a problem.'

'If she doesn't come, she might send someone in her place. Sometimes does that.'

'How reliable *is* this bloody woman?' Alessandro turned to his father's face and scowled. 'I had a look at the accounts the last time I was here, and she's paid a fortune! Are you telling me that she skives off when she feels like it?'

'I'm telling you that it's *my* money and I'll spend it any damn way I want to! If I want to pay the woman to show up every other weekend and dance on the table, that's *my* shout!'

Alessandro looked at his father narrowly and eventually shrugged.

'If she doesn't show up,' Roberto inserted grudgingly, 'she'll send someone in her place.'

'Fine. In that case, I'll leave all the dirty dishes so that she or her replacement has something to do when they get here. And now I'm heading off to do some work. I take it you won't be needing your study?'

'What would an old, feeble man with an old, feeble brain need a study for?' He waved his hand, dismissing Alessandro without sparing him a glance. 'It's all yours.'

Laura Reid finally hopped on her bike and headed out of the terraced house she shared with her grandmother forty-five minutes later than planned.

Things moved at a different speed here. She had now lived here for nearly a year and a half and she was still getting used to the change of pace. She wasn't sure whether she would ever completely get used to it.

On a bright, cold Saturday morning, her intentions might have been to start the day at the crack of dawn, get all the little chores done and dusted by nine and then cycle up to the big house, but intentions counted for nothing here.

People had dropped by. Her grandmother had taken herself off to Glasgow to visit her sister for two weeks and every well-wishing friend had popped around to make sure she was all right, as if her grandmother's absence might herald all sorts of untold disasters. Was she making sure to eat properly? Curious, concerned eyes peered into the kitchen in the hope of spotting a pie or two. Had she remembered that the garbage people had changed their collection day because old Euan's son had gone to hospital and his brother was covering?

Was she remembering to make sure the logs were kept dry? Edith would have a fit if she returned to find them soaked through and who knew what the weather would bring in the next ten days. And make sure to lock all the doors! Mildred had told Shona who had told Brian who had told his daughter Leigh that there had been a spate of petty thefts in the neighbouring village and you couldn't be too careful.

The wind on her face felt great as she began cycling away from the town.

It meant freedom and peace and was always a time when she replayed her life in slow motion in her head, the way it had turned full circle so that she was right back where she had started.

The young girl who had gaily gone to London to take up a position as PA to a CEO in an upwardly mobile, just-gone-public company was no more. At least now, when she thought of that time in her life, her mouth no longer filled with bitterness and despair. Instead, she could put it all in perspective and see her experiences as a valuable learning curve.

She had worked for a busy, aggressive company, which, coming from this small town, had been a first. She had seen the bright lights and felt the buzz of big-city excitement. She had hopped on the Underground and jostled with the crowds at rush hour. She had eaten on the run and gone to wine bars with new friends.

And two years into her bright, shiny life she had met a guy, someone so wildly different from every guy she had ever met that was it any wonder she had fallen hopelessly in love with him?

The only downside was that he had been her boss. Not *directly* her boss, but far, far higher than her in the company food chain, recently transferred back to London from New York.

And naive as she had been, all the warning signs that

would have been flagged up to any woman with just a bit more experience had passed her by.

Rich guy...top job...cute, with little dimples and floppy blond hair...thirty-four and single...

Laura had been over the moon. She hadn't minded the weekends he'd been unable to spend with her because he'd visited his ailing father in the New Forest area...hadn't cared that meals out had always been in small, dark places miles away from the city centre...hadn't really twigged when he'd told her that once an arrangement was made, it was set in cement...no need for her to call him and, besides, he was just one of those guys who hated long, rambling telephone conversations on mobiles.

'There's never a time when it's convenient!' he had joked teasingly. 'You're either in the supermarket, about to hand over your credit card...or on the Underground, hanging on to a strap for dear life...or about to step into the shower... Leave the calling to me!'

She had for nearly a year until she had seen him out, quite by chance, with a sandy-haired woman hanging on to his arm and a little toddler sucking a lollipop, twisting round from her pushchair to look at him.

So much for love. She'd fallen for a married guy, had fallen for surface charm and a clever way with words.

She had worked out her notice and left and now she was ninety-nine per cent convinced that it had all been for the best. Secretarial work hadn't been for her. The job had been buzzy and well paid but the teaching job she did now was much more emotionally rewarding.

Plus everyone had to have a learning curve. She would never make the mistake of even *looking twice* at any man who was out of her league. If it looked too good to be true, it probably was.

It was a dull, cloudy morning and she could feel icy fin-

gers trying to wriggle through the layers of her clothes…
the vest, jumper, padded sleeveless waterproof that bulked
her up so that she looked like a beach ball in search of a
stretch of sand.

When she glanced over her shoulder, the little town had
been left behind and there was roaming, rambling countryside all around her, stretching as far as the eye could see.

She slowed down. There was no place on earth as beautiful as Scotland. No place where you could practically
hear the silence and the small sounds of nature, living,
breathing nature. This was where she had grown up. Not
this precise spot in this exact town, but in a very similar
small town not a million miles away. She had moved to live
with her grandmother when her parents had died. She had
been just seven at the time. She had adjusted over time to
the loss of her parents and it had taken her a lot less time
to adjust to life in this part of Scotland because the scenery was so familiar to her.

She crested a hill, on either side of which russets,
browns and stark, naked fields, stripped bare of colour,
filled her with a sense of freedom, and there, just ahead
of her, she could see the entrance to the long drive that led
up to Roberto's house.

She slowed down, took her time pedalling her way up
the drive. She never tired of this familiar route. In summer it was stunning, vibrant with green, the trees bending
over the drive. In winter the bare trees were equally impressive, stretching up like talons reaching for the clouds.

The unexpected sight of a black SUV brought her to a
halt and she slowly began walking the bike towards the
front door.

Surprises were rarely of the good kind and this was a
surprise because Roberto seldom had visitors. At least,
not ones that weren't of the local variety. He had friends

in the village…her grandmother was very pally with him, somewhat more than pally, she suspected, and of course he went to the usual things arranged for older people because there was quite a thriving community in the village for the over-sixties, but strangers appearing out of nowhere…?

Which only left one possibility and that made her heart sink. She'd never met the son and, in fairness, Roberto didn't dwell on him very much but the little he had said had not left a good impression either with her or with her grandmother.

She rang the doorbell and waited, heart beating fast.

Inside the house, specifically inside the office to which he had retreated after a tense breakfast with his father that had achieved less than zero, if that was possible, Alessandro heard the sharp ring of the doorbell and cursed fluently under his breath.

The vanishing hired help had remained vanished. His father, who was hell-bent on not listening to common sense, had taken himself off to his massive greenhouse, where, he said, he could have more fruitful conversation with his plants. Alessandro's plan to buy some food and do something with it had changed. He had decided to take his father out for dinner in the town because if his father was in a restaurant, there was just so far he could go when it came to dodging the inevitable conversation.

He reached the front door and pulled it open, his mood already foul because he could see the word *wasted* stamped all over his weekend.

The girl standing in front of him, gripping the handlebars of a bike that looked like a relic from a different era, took him momentarily by surprise.

She was a short, round little thing with copper-coloured hair that had been dragged back into a ponytail and eyes…

The purest, greenest eyes he had ever seen.

'About time.'

'I beg your pardon?' Laura had been expecting Roberto to answer the door. Instead, finding herself staring up at the most beautiful man she had ever seen in her life, her breathing had become jerky and her pulse was all over the place.

This would be the son and he was nothing like the mental picture she'd had in her head.

Her mental picture had been of a pompous, puffed-up, frankly ugly little guy who had his nose stuck in the air and never ventured out of London if he could help it. He hardly showed his face in Scotland and when he did, Roberto was always subdued afterwards, as if recovering from a virus.

Unfortunately, the man staring down at her with a glacial expression was too disturbingly good-looking for anybody's good. He positively towered over her and every inch of his body was hard-packed muscle. The black, long-sleeved T-shirt lovingly advertised that, as did the faded, low-slung black jeans.

'Finished staring?' he asked coolly, and Laura went bright red. 'Because if you are, you can come in, head directly to the kitchen and begin doing what you're paid to do.'

'Sorry?' Laura blinked and stared at him in bewilderment before remembering the way he had sneered at her for staring, which made her immediately shift her gaze to the ivy clambering up the wall behind him.

Alessandro didn't bother answering. Instead, he stepped to one side and headed to the kitchen, expecting her to follow him.

Laura stared at his departing back with mounting anger.

'I'd like to know what's going on,' she demanded, having flung her bike to the ground and sprinted in his wake.

'What's going on…' Alessandro turned to face her and spread his arms wide '…is a kitchen that needs tidying. Which is what you're paid to do. Correct me if I'm wrong.' He leaned against the granite counter and looked at the round little bundle poised resentfully by the door. No one liked being reprimanded, but needs must, he thought. 'I understand that Freya couldn't make it to work yesterday because her dog was feeling under the weather, but it beggars belief that she couldn't be bothered to send her replacement until today and it's even more astonishing that her replacement can't be bothered to turn up until after ten in the morning!'

Placid by nature, Laura was discovering that it was remarkably easy to go from cool to boiling in seconds. She folded her arms and glared at him. 'If the kitchen needed tidying, why didn't you tidy it yourself?'

'I'll pretend I just didn't hear that!'

'I'd like to see Roberto…'

'And why would that be?' Alessandro drawled silkily. He folded his arms and stared at her. 'You might be able to get past him with some fairy-tale sob story about not being able to do the job you're paid to do because the dog's cousin got a cold or the rain was falling in the wrong direction so you just couldn't make it on time, but I'm made of tougher stuff. You should have been here at eight, as far as I'm concerned, and your pay will be docked accordingly!' Not, in all events, that that was going to be much of a concern considering his father would be out of the house, if not this weekend, then certainly by the end of the month.

'Are you *threatening* me?'

'It's not a threat. It's a statement of fact and frankly you should consider yourself lucky that I don't sack you on the spot.'

'This is too much! Where is Roberto?'

'*Roberto?*' He couldn't remember Freya addressing his father by his first name. Eyes narrowed now on her flushed face, Alessandro slowly pushed himself away from the counter and strolled towards her.

Like a predator with prey in its sight, he circled her before coming to a stop right in front of her, arms still folded, and this time his expression was thoughtful.

'Interesting,' he mused softly.

'What? What's interesting?' Laura inched back a little because his presence was so suffocating. She worked out that it wasn't just to do with the fact that the man was sinfully, unfairly sexy. There was also something about him, something intangible that sent shivers racing up and down her spine.

'Interesting that the hired help is now on a first-name basis with my father, who is a very rich man indeed.'

'I'm not following you.'

'Young girl…reasonably attractive…elderly man… loaded… I'm doing the maths and not liking the solution to the conundrum.'

Blood leached out of her face and there was a roaring in her ears. 'Are you accusing me of…of…of…?'

'I know. Incomprehensible, isn't it? My father is pushing eighty, has more money than he knows what to do with, and a whippersnapper who couldn't be more than… what?…twenty-two addresses him by his first name and seems pretty desperate to see him because, presumably, you know he'll rescue you from an uncomfortable situation. Smacks of unhealthy cosiness but, then, maybe I'm just being unfairly cynical.'

'Twenty-six, actually. I'm twenty-six.' A gold-digger? Was that what she was being accused of? A *reasonably attractive* gold-digger? Could there be any more insults stashed up his sleeve?

'Twenty-two…twenty-six. Doesn't really make much of a difference. You're still young enough to be his granddaughter. Thank God I've come along and seen for myself what goes on here.'

'And I'm not the hired help.'

'No?' Alessandro's eyebrows shot up. Hired help or no hired help, the woman was still an opportunist, although he had to admit that the old man had reasonably good taste. Up close, her eyes were even more amazing, her skin satiny smooth with a sprinkling of freckles across the bridge of her nose, and her mouth…

His eyes dipped lazily to her mouth, which was full and perfectly shaped.

She might not be a model but she certainly wasn't a woman you would throw out of your bed on a rainy night.

She was fresh-faced and that in itself was oddly appealing. No wonder she had managed to inveigle herself into his father's good graces. God knew how much she had managed to con out of him thus far.

'No!' Her skin burned under his scrutiny but she maintained eye contact, even though every nerve in her body was reacting with tight hostility to his accusations.

'So who are you?'

'I'm Laura. I'm a friend. As you would discover if you went and got him!'

'Oh, I'll get him,' Alessandro said in a voice that made her teeth snap together in impotent fury. 'Just as soon as you and I have had a nice little chat. So why don't you have a seat at the table, *Laura*, and we'll…how do I put this?… get to know one another… No, wrong choice of words. *I'll* get to know *you* and *you'll* get to understand where *I'm* coming from.'

He smiled and she stared back angrily at him because

chilling though the smile was it was still horribly, horribly sexy.

'Fine,' she snapped, because if *he* wanted to have a word with her, he'd find that she had a few words of her own to share. She stalked off towards the kitchen table and in one easy movement yanked off the annoying waterproof and turned to face him with a toss of her head. 'And then I want to see your father.'

CHAPTER TWO

'YOU KNOW WHO I AM.' This was getting better and better. He had no idea who she was and yet she knew who he was. If she was a *friend*, then she was a *special* one, because he knew his father and one thing was for sure—Roberto Falcone was tight-lipped when it came to conversation. He was a man, and had always been a man, who spoke only when the situation demanded speech.

Alessandro could remember many a meal consumed in silence once the formalities of polite conversation had been exhausted.

'Of course I know who you are. Why wouldn't I? You're Alessandro, the son who never comes up to Scotland if he can help it.'

Alessandro flushed darkly. 'My father said that?'

'He didn't have to. You import your father down to London when you want to see him because it's easier. When was the last time you were here anyway?'

'How do you know my father?' Alessandro asked abruptly, cutting short any attempts to try to derail the conversation. So she wasn't the hired help and he should have recognised that from the get-go. Hired help didn't look like her and they certainly didn't have that stubborn tilt to their heads. His eyes roved over a body that, now that it was divested of the bulky parka, was rounded in all the right places. Small, voluptuous and...especially when

you combined it with her fresh-faced, make-up-free look...
downright sexy.

He sat down at the opposite end of the table. The
kitchen was one of the few really informal places in the
splendid mansion and Alessandro had never ceased to be
amazed that his father had given the go-ahead for it to be
furnished with weathered pine, a softly upholstered sofa
to the side, an oven that was well-worn and distressed
cupboards. Not at all a reflection of the stern, tight-lipped
man he was.

'I'm not here for an inquisition. I don't have to answer
your questions. Where is he? I came to ask whether there
was anything he needed from the shops. I didn't expect
to find you here.'

Alessandro found pretty much everything she said
highly offensive, from the tone of her voice to her refusal to
answer his questions to the implication that he was somehow vaguely responsible for his father's non-appearance.
Did she think that he had stashed Roberto away in a cupboard somewhere? To be retrieved a little later when it
suited him?

'And furthermore,' Laura added for good measure, 'I
resent your insinuation that because I'm young I'm only
friends with your father because he's rich. You have no
right to accuse me of something like that. You don't even
know who I am!' She leaned forward, her cheeks flushed,
more angry than she had ever been in her life. Angrier, it
felt, than when she had discovered that the so-called love
of her life was a married man with a toddler. Every single
thing about the arrogant man staring at her with forbidding
iciness got under her skin and made her see red.

'Frankly, I don't really care whether you resent my in-
sinuations or not,' Alessandro said coolly. 'I intend to protect my father's interests and if that means seeing off *a*

friend, then so be it. Answer my questions and we can move forward. Sit there foaming at the mouth…and back on your bike you go.'

'I am *not* foaming at the mouth!'

'How long have you known my father?'

Frustrated, Laura yanked her hair out of its constricting ponytail and ran her fingers through its thick length, and for a few seconds the air was sucked out of his lungs. It was a rich mane of colour and very long, longer than fashionably chic, cascading over her shoulders. He tore his eyes away and frowned, unsettled.

'Off and on for years.' Laura reluctantly gave him the information he wanted because she had a feeling that he wouldn't stop until she had told him what he wanted to know. Frankly, he probably wouldn't let her out of the kitchen until she told him what he wanted to know. He would probably strap her to the chair, shine a torch on her face and keep asking his wretched questions until she answered him.

And maybe he had a point. Roberto *was* very, very wealthy and could potentially be a target for gold-diggers. And she *was*, after all, seriously young to be his friend, even if she was only *passably attractive*. It was one thing to have no illusions about the way you looked. It was another thing to have someone point out your physical shortcomings without even bothering to be nice about it.

She *knew* that she wasn't blessed with knock-'em-dead looks. She had lived in London long enough to realise that the tall and skinny ruled the roost when it came to what was deemed sexy and attractive.

But had there been any need for him to point it out? The throwaway insult hovered at the back of her mind like a thorn. Odious man.

'Years…' Alessandro said, frowning. She wasn't lying.

Her face couldn't have been more transparent, and yet how was it that he hadn't even known of her existence?

'Before I went to London,' Laura confirmed. 'He belonged to the same gardening group as me and…as me. He loves horticulture, you know. And playing chess. Ever since I returned from London I've been playing chess with him once a week. He's a brilliant chess player.'

'You're telling me that the only interest you have in my father is as fellow chess player and gardener.'

'It's not solely about the gardening.' Laura bristled. 'It's the thrill of spotting rare plants, trying to produce interesting hybrids…' She noted the blank expression on his face. 'I don't suppose you have any plants where you live,' she tacked on. 'Roberto says that you live in a flat.'

'Penthouse apartment, and, no, no plants that I can think of offhand,' Alessandro responded automatically. 'So you play chess and talk about plants.'

'Pretty much.' The silence stretched between them until she began to fidget uncomfortably. 'It's called having hobbies. You must have some of those…'

'I work,' Alessandro replied shortly. 'And…' he suddenly smiled and just like that his face was transformed, the harsh, unyielding lines smoothed out to give a picture of mind-blowing sexiness '…I play. I consider both to be my hobbies…'

Colour had invaded her cheeks. Her green eyes were locked to his face. When she nervously licked her lips, she saw the way his eyes absently followed the movement and that made her go even redder. 'Play?' she asked feebly. Her brain seemed to have gone AWOL. He was still half smiling, his head inclined slightly to one side, and she was still beetroot red, uncomfortable in her own skin and not liking the sensation.

'Oh, yes,' he said smoothly. 'I'm very good at playing.'

Laura blinked and came back down to earth. 'Well, your father enjoys his chess and his plants and...'

'And?'

'This and that. He's had to take it easy after the stroke and, of course, he's only really now back on his feet properly after the fall, but he'll be back in the swing of things in no time at all.'

'What's *this and that*?' Trampolining? Abseiling? White-water rafting? He'd had no idea that his father was an active member of the local horticultural society so the *this and that* could literally, in his books, have applied to anything at all.

Laura shrugged evasively. 'Usual. The point is that he can start back doing all the stuff he enjoys now. So you can go back down to London, safe in the knowledge that he's well looked after. No need to feel duty bound to rush up here and check him over. Not to mention check over his friends and the people who work for him. No need for you to think that you have to keep an eye and give people the sack or dock their pay or whatever else you think might be necessary...'

Alessandro looked in wonderment at the pink-faced woman glaring defiantly at him. When was the last time he had encountered someone with such barefaced cheek? Actually, had he *ever*? Whatever angle women took with him, it never included being lippy.

'Before we get on to the juicy bit of what I have to say...' Alessandro relaxed back and crossed his legs, ankle resting lightly on his knee, hands linked on his lap. 'I'm curious.'

'What about?' Laura didn't care for his loose-limbed, relaxed pose because it resembled the looseness of a predator just before it homed in for a kill.

'About what brought you back from London to this...'

he looked around him, as though in search of an inspiring adjective '...backwater.'

Laura bristled. He was doing it again. Turning her into a self-defensive, shrieking harridan, which was not her at all.

She breathed in deeply and tried to think Zen thoughts. 'This isn't a *backwater*.' Her voice was quiet and even, even if her blood was boiling. 'If you took the time to really look around you, you'd see that it's one of the most beautiful places in the world. There's everything you could possibly hope to want in Scotland. There are castles, lochs, rivers and lakes, mountains... It's a wonderfully peaceful place...'

'Interesting travelogue. I'm more of an urban guy myself but is that an invitation to show me the sights and win me over?'

'It most certainly is not!'

Alessandro laughed, really laughed, with humour, his dark eyes lazy and amused as they rested on her flushed face.

'Shame,' he mused pensively. 'A personal tour might really go the distance in winning me over to its charms. So you moved here because there are castles and lakes and it's peaceful.'

Laura didn't actually think that her reasons for moving back to Scotland were any of the man's business but would he keep pressing? Secrets always engendered curiosity in other people and naturally she didn't care one way or another whether he was curious or not but still...why make things harder for herself?

'Partly, and also because my grandmother had a turn...' Which was somewhat true and left out the bigger part of her reason, namely her ill-advised, foolish love affair.

'Had a turn?'

'Was getting dizzy spells, suffering with her balance.
She lives on her own and I wanted to be here for her.' She
looked wistfully off into the distance. 'She was there for
me when my parents died. I didn't begrudge returning to
be here for her.'

Alessandro swiftly dispelled the glaring contradictions
between them. He was here on behalf of his father, to take
him down to London even though he might protest the
move. It was for his own good! For a start, there was just so
much choice when it came to various medical treatments,
and having had both a stroke and a fall, who knew what
medical treatment the future held for him? In London, he
would receive the best!

'Big of you,' Alessandro murmured. 'I can only think
that it must have been a wrench leaving the bright city
lights and returning to all this peace and tranquillity. What
was your job in London?'

He wasn't interested. Not really. He was simply estab-
lishing her credentials, working out whether she was a
threat to his father's fortune or not. She knew that.

She wondered what had possessed her to come cycling here today and, having seen that SUV skewed in
the courtyard, what had further possessed her to ring
the doorbell, knowing that Roberto's son would be on
the premises.

Fate had really decided to have a laugh at her expense.

'I worked as a PA.' She lowered her eyes, a little flicker
of movement that Alessandro's keen antennae picked up.

'What company?'

'I don't know what that has to do with anything!' she
snapped, bright spots of colour on her cheeks.

'You're right. It hasn't. And I wouldn't have asked if I'd
known that I was getting too close to state secrets.'

'It's no big deal.' And yet, for some reason, she was reluctant to say the name of the firm out loud. Was it because she would be reminded of Colin? And the mortification of finding out that he had been lying to her? The horror of realising just how naive she had been to have handed over her trust to a smooth-talker? The shame when she thought that he had seen how green round the gills she'd been and had known that she would have lacked the experience to figure out what a bastard he really was?

She surfaced to find Alessandro's dark eyes pinned thoughtfully to her face and she tilted her chin stubbornly and told him the name of the company.

'Not,' she repeated, 'that it's any of your business.'

'I know the company,' he murmured, still looking at her in a way that made her feel as though he could see right down deep into the very core of her. 'And naturally I'm interested in finding out about one of my father's friends… Why wouldn't I be?'

'I didn't think you were ever interested before,' Laura pointed out. 'I mean, you could have come to visit when there have been things going on…joined in…'

'Things? What sort of things?'

'Oh, you know…we yokels try to have a barn dance at least once a month and let's not forget the annual hog roast while we all stand outside and admire the peaceful countryside…'

He burst out laughing. Suddenly those thoughtful eyes were dark with lazy appreciation.

Sexy, sharp-tongued, lippy…funny.

'I prefer the barn dances in London,' he told her with mock seriousness. 'And the hog roasts are good, too, although, of course, we all tend to stand outside and admire the pollution. Happy times…'

Laura didn't want to laugh but she had to fight the urge. 'It's good of you to visit him,' she admitted grudgingly.

'I suppose you've been worried but, like I said, there's no need. I try to check on him every day after work.'

'Oh? You managed to find yourself another PA job here?' He wasn't even sure what companies existed in the small town. He definitely wouldn't have put it down as somewhere with a flourishing employment sector.

'I realised that working as someone's personal assistant wasn't what I wanted to do.'

'No?'

'When I came back here, I landed a teaching job and it's very fulfilling. I teach at the local primary school. It's small and there are only a handful of kids in each class, but it's extremely rewarding.'

'Teacher.'

'The hours are convenient and, of course, there are the holidays and half-terms, and because it's a small village school I know all the mums on a one-to-one basis.' It was a terrific job, nothing to be ashamed of, and yet Laura couldn't stop the feeling of being just a little drab, just a tiny bit of a country bumpkin.

'Cosy.'

'I expect you must find it all very boring, but not everyone is consumed with wanting to live in a city and make pots of money.'

'I can't recall saying anything about finding what you do boring, although I question how much personal satisfaction you must get in a place as small as this, especially after living in London.'

'I got sick of the rat race,' she told him shortly, and his eyebrows shot up.

'Bit young to be jaded about that, wouldn't you say? Normally that's something that tends to afflict the over-forties. What about all the excitement?'

'I'd had it with excitement.'

'Ah,' Alessandro murmured, and she shot him a sharp, narrowed look, which he returned with bland innocence.

'Is that all? Have you finished questioning me? Maybe you could point me in the direction of your father, if, of course, I've passed the test.'

'He's in his greenhouse.' Alessandro jerked his head in the general direction of the back gardens but his eyes remained pinned to her face.

So she'd returned to her grandmother to lick her wounds. Maybe her grandmother really had had some kind of turn but he was sharp enough to get the lie of the land…she'd had some sort of unpleasant experience in London involving a guy, probably someone she worked with, judging from the shifty way she had talked about her place of work. She might wax lyrical about the peace and tranquillity and lakes and rivers, but the truth was that she'd had her heart broken and had returned to her comfort zone to patch herself up.

He found himself wondering what sort of guy she had got involved with and promptly nipped his curiosity in the bud because after this weekend he doubted he would ever lay eyes on the woman again.

Which was something of a shame. In fact, something of a shame he hadn't laid eyes on her before, on one of his rare forays into the Scottish wilds. She would certainly have made his duty visits a lot more alluring. Biting winds, depressingly bleak and empty countryside and his father's challenged conversational skills would definitely have been easier to endure…

'Right.' Laura stood up and thought that she should be feeling more relieved to be out of the presence of this odious man than she actually was.

'I wouldn't bother having the food conversation, though.'

'What are you talking about?'

'You mentioned that you had cycled over to do your Good Samaritan duty…an offer to go food shopping for him, as if my father doesn't have the wherewithal to pay someone to do that on his behalf. Actually—and I'm sure you know this—he could pay a chef to buy the food and cook it if he wanted. It would certainly spare him the stuff Freya churns out…'

Laura did her best not to agree with him. She had a good enough relationship with Freya, who occasionally cracked a half-smile in her presence, but no one could say that the woman produced haute cuisine.

'Your father likes plain, simple food.'

'Just as well. With sour-faced Freya at the helm, it's all he's ever likely to get.'

'Why shouldn't I ask him if he needs anything?'

'Because there's no point filling the cupboards only to empty them again in the space of a few days. Waste of time.'

'What? What are you talking about?' Laura stared at that drop-dead-gorgeous, arrogant face and subsided back into her chair like a puppet whose strings had suddenly been cut.

'There's a reason I've come up here,' Alessandro explained calmly. 'I've spoken to my father about this on a number of occasions, and I've emailed him…' He sighed heavily and flung his head back, half closing his eyes as he thought about the frustration of dealing with someone who didn't want to face the inevitable. It shouldn't be like this. He knew that. Of course, history couldn't be altered any more than the present could be changed…but it shouldn't be like this, a constant uphill struggle.

'I'm confused,' Laura said urgently. 'Spoken to him about what? Emailed him about what?'

Alessandro opened his eyes and looked at her in silence

for a few seconds. 'He hasn't confided in you, then. Odd, considering you're supposed to be best buddies.'

'Please stop being sarcastic and tell me what's going on.'

'I've come up here to take my father back down to London with me.'

'Take him?' Laura looked at him in complete bewilderment. 'Take him down for a few days?'

'Not quite,' he said gently. 'Brace yourself. Roberto's stint here in Scotland is at an end. I'm taking him down to London with me and he won't be returning. The house will be packed up, necessities shipped down to London, the rest removed for auction. I've bought him an apartment in Chelsea. It's the right size and if he's in London I can keep an eye on him.'

Laura was finding it hard to keep track of what he was saying because none of it made any sense.

'You're kidding. Aren't you?'

'I never kid about things like that. Hasn't he mentioned any of this to you? On any of your Little Red Riding Hood visits?'

For a second, Laura wanted to throw something at him. How could he just sit here, discussing the future of an old man, talking about it in a voice that was dry and cool and caustic?

'You,' she hissed in a driven undertone, 'are the most… the most…'

'Spit it out. I assure you I won't take it personally.'

'The most *obnoxious* person I have *ever* met in my entire life! It's no wonder that…'

'That *what*?'

They stared at each other in silence. Laura could hear the pounding of her heart, could feel the blood rushing hotly through her veins. 'That nothing…' she muttered, casting her eyes downwards. She had raced towards a cliff and almost flung herself over the side. What did she know of the relationship between father and son? She surmised. Roberto had never come out and said anything derogatory about Alessandro, but the cold distance between them was as obvious as a neon sign in a dark street.

The truth was that it was not really her business. And because the man sitting opposite her rattled her, it did not give her the excuse to say things that shouldn't be said or to voice thoughts that should remain in her head.

Alessandro chose to let that go.

Did he really want to find out what might have been said about him behind his back? No! This was how it was between his father and himself but he wasn't going to put himself through unnecessary irritation by having an out-side party share their opinion on the situation. No way.

He looked at her coldly, noting her discomfort and choosing not to relieve her of it.

'He hasn't breathed a word of this to me or to... Well, I'm shocked. Beyond shocked. I can't believe you're going to try to wrench poor Roberto away from everything he... he holds dear and fling him into the mad chaos of London life. You can't. You just can't!'

'No need to panic,' Alessandro murmured in a soft voice that sent chills racing through her. 'It's a spacious three-bedroom apartment. All mod cons, including en suite bathrooms. I'm sure he'll keep a bedroom free for his spe-cial friends.' He was repulsed by the thought of her having anything to do with his father beyond the purely platonic. Yes, she had denied that connection, but if that were the case, why the horror and dismay?

Why the extreme reaction? She looked as distraught as Chicken Little when the sky was falling down.

His lips thinned and she knew exactly what he was

getting at. Where was a heavy object when you needed one? she fumed.

'And if he hasn't mentioned anything to you,' Alessandro inserted smoothly, 'I put that down to denial. Because I've been having this conversation with my father for the past six months.'

Laura looked at him in stunned silence.

'He's old…'

'My point exactly! The stroke…the fractured pelvis… He can't deal with this bloody great big mansion. He needs somewhere more compact. He needs to be able to make it to his bedroom from the kitchen in under three hours.'

'Please don't exaggerate. Like you said, Roberto could afford as much help as he wants to. At the moment he just has Freya and Fergus, but I'm sure he would employ someone else to help him if he thought he needed it.'

'This isn't a subject that's open to debate. I'm not thrusting him into a rabbit hutch in the centre of the city. He'll adjust. London is full of exciting things.'

'Old people don't want excitement,' Laura said flatly. 'They want routine. They want stability. They want to be surrounded by the people and faces they're familiar with.'

Alessandro stared at her with incredulity. Were they talking about the same man?

'And how often are you going to visit him?' she pursued, ignoring his closed expression. 'Are you going to make sure he settles in? Will you be taking him under your wing? Or will you be visiting him four times a year but happily with a much shorter journey?'

Alessandro scowled. 'Your concern is touching but I assure you…he'll be just fine. And, incidentally, who are these familiar faces he needs to surround himself with?'

'He has lots of friends in the village.'

'Aside from you?'

'Yes, aside from me! What do you think he does during the days? I mean, I know his health hasn't been great recently, but before that? And now that he's on the mend?'

Alessandro looked at her blankly.

'You don't know, do you? You haven't got a clue. You want to drag him away from his home and you can't even be bothered to find out what he'll be missing! What his life here is all about!'

'You're shouting.'

'I *never* shout!' Her voice reverberated in the silence and she glared at him. 'I *usually* never shout,' she amended, 'but I'm just so…angry. And stop staring at me. I suppose you've never been shouted at by anyone in your life before?'

'Correct.'

Drawn out of her state of shock, Laura peered suspiciously at him. 'No one ever gets mad at you?' she asked incredulously. 'Ever?'

'You're looking at me as though you find that hard to believe,' Alessandro returned coolly. Taking away the physical side of things, on every level this woman offended him on all fronts. He had no thoughts one way or another on other people and the choices they made in terms of relationships. As far as he was concerned, the rest of humanity could hurl themselves into pointless marriages like lemmings jumping off a cliff, only to find themselves picking up the pieces and counting the pennies when those marriages crashed and burned. Which most of them did.

As for himself, he had no intention, and never had, of getting wrapped up with any woman. He had led a life that was ruled by his head and he liked that. Maybe the cold withdrawal of his only parent had pointed him down that path. It wasn't something he had wasted his time analysing. He just knew that, for him, women were there to be savoured and enjoyed until the time came for him to push on. They were his stress-free zone, a welcome break from the enjoyable frenzy of being at the top of the game in the world of business.

A woman who shouted did not constitute a stress-free zone.

'I do,' Laura said truthfully.

'Women, especially, fall into that category.'

'I find that even harder to believe.'

'I don't encourage temper tantrums,' he said smoothly. 'There's something about a screaming woman I don't find a turn-on.'

Just as well my aim isn't to turn you on, Laura thought. The pulse in her throat kicked up a steady beat. She took in his lazy sprawl, the brooding night-dark gaze of his eyes, the harsh, perfect contours of his face, and something inside her flared into unwelcome, unexpected life.

Suddenly confused, she banked it down.

'I just think that before you start trying to pull the rug from underneath someone's feet, you should make an effort to understand where they're coming from and what they would lose. Doesn't your father have any say in this? Or are you going to stampede through his objections and do what *you* think is best?'

'This conversation is going round in circles.' Alessandro raked his fingers impatiently through his hair, spared her a searing glance and then stood up to help himself to a bottle of water from the fridge, which he drank in one long swallow. Then he leaned against the kitchen counter and looked at her. 'I'll do what I consider best for my father and you can pull all the hysterical, emotive language out of the bag, but nothing is going to change that. Like I told you, I've talked to my father about this. If he chose not to keep you in the loop, then what can I say?' He shrugged and stared at her flushed face.

'There's something you should know,' Laura said grudgingly, and Alessandro stilled.

'I'm all ears.'

'It's not just that your father has a social life in the village, and if...' she looked at him with a flare of uncharacteristic rebellion in her wide, green eyes '...he chose to keep you out of the loop, then what can I say? He's also... well...you probably have cut-and-dried opinions on love, but he's involved with someone locally...'

For a few seconds, and for maybe the first time in his life, Alessandro was rendered speechless. Her words filtered into his consciousness, tried to take shape but then dissolved before they could link up and make any sense.

'Did you just hear what I said?'

'I heard you. I'm just not following... You're telling me that my father *has a girlfriend*?'

'My gran.'

Perplexed, Alessandro shook his head in an attempt to get the connections in his brain to start working.

Laura saw his bewilderment and suddenly, out of nowhere, she felt a sharp pang of sympathy and compassion for him. Didn't this say everything there was to say about the kind of relationship he had with Roberto? One in which nothing personal was ever discussed? In which no emotion was ever allowed to surface? How on earth had that happened?

'My father is going out with your...your grandmother? How does that even make sense?'

'It's easy,' Laura said drily. 'They met ages ago and have been friends for a long time, but in the past few months, a bit longer, actually, they've begun seeing one another. Going on dates, that kind of thing…'

'My father *goes on dates*?'

'It happens. Two people have a solid friendship…one thing leads to another… He's still an attractive guy. I'd bet there are a few ladies in the gardening club who have had their eye on him.'

Alessandro walked back to the table, sat down, stared off for a few frowning moments into space, then focused on the woman looking at him, head inclined, her soft lips parted.

'Details.'

'I beg your pardon?'

'How long exactly has this dating game been going on? And your grandmother…where does she live? Widowed? Divorced? How old is she?'

Laura tensed, predicting the direction of his assumptions. 'You've accused me of being a gold-digger,' she said coldly. 'You couldn't have been further from the truth. And don't you even dare think of implying that my grandmother is after your dad's money, either! They're just two people who get along and enjoy one another's company. If you want the bare details, here they are.

'My grandmother lives in a little house on the outskirts of the village about twenty minutes away. She's lived here all her life and, yes, she's widowed. My grandfather passed on more years ago than I care to think. She never really thought about ever finding anyone else, least of all someone she's known since for ever, but, then, it's really only in the past ten years or so that your father has really begun integrating himself into the community. He was quite reclusive before that. I guess work kept him away a lot…and of course my gran would have been busy working in the neighbouring town. She ran the garden centre there. Only gave up five years ago because the travel was getting a bit of a nuisance, especially in the winter. 'Course, she drove there, but you have no idea how freez—'

'I'm getting the picture. Age?'

'Huh? Oh. Right. Seventy-six. So that's just one of the reasons why it would be heartbreaking for you to charge up here and try to force him to leave.'

'Charge? Force? Heartbreaking?'

But this put a new spin on things. Maybe he should personally check out the situation. His father was dating someone whose granddaughter was his best buddy. Cynicism was ingrained in Alessandro, as much a vital part of him as drawing breath. Could this pair be working in tandem? It was far-fetched but sometimes far-fetched turned out to be reality and it always paid to be on the safe side, especially when tens of millions of pounds were at stake.

'You're right.'

'I am?' Laura looked at him warily, trying to see behind that thoughtful, speculative expression.

'If my father is to leave this place, then it's not up to me to be heavy-handed. I need to persuade him that there's life beyond the Scottish boundaries...'

'He won't be persuaded, I'm sure of that.'

Alessandro dealt her a slashing smile. So this weekend might not happen, but that was fine. He was the kind of guy who could think outside the box when it came to dealing with unexpected situations. Like this. And, being perfectly honest, the lush appeal of the woman currently looking at him as though she expected him to produce a bomb from up his sleeve would certainly introduce a bit of entertainment to the menu.

'But worth a try, wouldn't you agree? I mean, you've spent the past hour wringing your hands and wailing that

I'm being unfair. So I'm sure you'd have no objections to…
showing me first-hand this fuzzy, warm social life my father would be so loath to leave behind…'

CHAPTER THREE

'BOY'S LATE. PROBABLY changed his mind. Probably decided that it'd be better to airlift me out of my own damned house than go through this charade of pretending he's interested in anything I do!'

Laura looked at Roberto anxiously. Alessandro was half an hour late and who better than she to know the vagaries of transport? Trains that laughed in the face of timetables. Cabs that got stuck in traffic and crawled along as though they were submerged in treacle. Planes that hovered and circled and hovered and circled because they were at the back of a queue.

'He said he'd come,' she told him firmly while sneaking a glance at her watch. It was nearly six and the two of them were hovering like maiden aunts waiting for their wayward charge to return home.

It was ridiculous.

'My son has his own damned personal schedule! Lives for his work!' He repositioned his tie and banged his walking stick on the wooden floor. 'Probably got a call and, of course, any call would take precedence over coming to Scotland! Never *could* stand the place! Always preferred that namby-pamby London life!' He threw her a sly look. ''Course, something else could have held him up!'

'Yes?' She looked at Roberto affectionately. He still belonged to an era when ties were de rigueur, whatever the occasion, and trousers were always belted firmly at the waist. He was dressed in a jumper with the crisp white shirt underneath neatly buttoned to the neck, the knot of his dark, striped tie crisply in place and a pair of his most casual slacks, which were still pressed into submission with no-nonsense creases down the middle of the legs. His shoes gleamed. He looked such a vision that she had taken a picture of him on her phone so that she could send it to her grandmother. He had, naturally, grumbled, although she'd noticed that he had surreptitiously neatened his thick silver hair with his hand before the shot.

'Floozy.'

'Sorry?'

'Floozy. Has enough of them chasing behind him! Met one or two myself. Silly little airheads but sometimes even the smartest of men can't resist a—'

'I get the picture, Roberto!' She led him away from that subject back to plants and gardens and the cookery club her grandmother wanted him to join.

The last thing she needed was to hear about Alessandro and his so-called floozies.

In fact, the last thing she wanted was to be here, on a Friday evening, wearing a long-sleeved, knee-length dress and boots and waiting for a guy who had managed to get under her skin in a very, very irritating way. She had spent the past week thinking about him, hadn't been able to shake him out of her head, and having to face him again was not what she wanted.

But here she was because Roberto had told her that the three of them would be going out.

'Got it into his head that the old man's life's suddenly interesting!' Roberto had announced. 'Told him it was a damned sight more interesting than one that was just work, work, work and some floozies in between!' After that he had sat her down and explained the whole business of the move he didn't want and wasn't going to be forced into. He hadn't been able to bring himself to discuss it with her grandmother and she wasn't to say a word. He would talk to Edith himself when she returned, not, he insisted, that he was going anywhere.

'But if the boy wants to try to move me, then he can try all he wants! He'll soon find out that this old bugger won't be going anywhere!'

Laura had picked up the thread of trepidation running through his bravado and had instantly agreed to be by his side when Alessandro arrived. She would not, emphatically *would not*, be sticking around for the entire weekend but, yes, she would accompany them to dinner at the newly opened fish restaurant in the neighbouring town.

Now Roberto was fretting but before she could start soothing him all over again they heard an overhead roar and they both hurried over to the big bay window, peered out and registered the presence of a helicopter, which was circling, finding the right spot in the immense garden outside, before landing. The blindingly bright beam cutting through the darkness was an impressive sight. Laura would put money on every single person in the town craning their necks out of their windows and wondering what the heck was going on.

'Might have guessed he wouldn't have come like any other person!' He was already hobbling out of the sitting room, where they had been chatting in front of a pot of tea, and Laura sprinted after him, reaching the front door just as it was opened and there he was, as tall, as sinfully good-looking, as aristocratically arrogant as she remembered.

'Hope you haven't set that thing down on any of my plants!' Roberto bellowed as the rotors wound down to a noisy din.

Alessandro glanced wryly past him to catch Laura's eye and her skin was suddenly on fire.

'And thank you for that warm welcome.' Alessandro turned back to signal something to his pilot, then stepped into the hall, shutting the door behind him. His sharp eyes didn't miss a thing. His father still had the same mutinous expression on his face as he had had the weekend before, when Alessandro had tried to get him to talk about moving, and Laura...

She'd been on his mind. He hadn't been able to work that one out. Was it because, in a sea of predictable women, she had been the only one to have ever contradicted him? Had the novelty of being criticised got under his skin and provoked a reaction? Like nettle rash? Something annoying you couldn't ignore? Or had the lack of a female presence in his life had something to do with it? It had been a couple of months since he had seen off his last girlfriend.

He didn't analyse the reaction. He just knew that the weekend planned had lain in front of him, glittering like a gem on the horizon. And that, in itself, was spectacular, considering how reluctant his visits had been in the past, obligatory visits to be endured before returning to the sanity of city life.

'You're late. Was about to head to the kitchen and take something out of the fridge!'

He glanced at Laura to see whether she, like him, was irritated with his father's impatience, but when he looked at her it was to see that she was smiling indulgently at Roberto, her hand resting lightly on his forearm, a gesture of affection that his father appeared to take for granted.

'If Freya stocks the fridge,' Alessandro said evenly, 'then I wouldn't count on the contents to be inspiring. I'll be ten minutes at the most. I need to send a quick email.'

Laura frowned. She knew that Roberto had been

dressed and waiting for the past hour and a half. She'd helped him with his tie and she'd seen, from the other three ties draped over the back of the chair, that he'd had a task choosing the one he wanted to wear.

'I think we should head off sooner rather than later,' she murmured, catching Alessandro's eye and holding it. 'Roberto always has an early night.'

'Roberto can go to bed whenever he damned well wants to!' Roberto announced, but she felt him relax a little when Alessandro immediately nodded and dumped his case on the floor.

'I'm having a car delivered to me in the morning.' Alessandro fished his mobile out of his pocket. 'What's the number for the local taxi company?'

'No need,' Laura said briskly. She hooked her arm through Roberto's and then turned to him and tucked his scarf neatly into his overcoat.

'You're always faffing and fussing, girl!'

But again Alessandro was made aware of a relationship he had never even known existed, a relationship from which he was made to feel like an outsider. His father, grumbling and chiding, was clearly pleased to have her fuss over him.

'Someone has to when my grandmother isn't around,' she murmured, and Roberto shot his son a sidelong look before shooing her away. 'There's no need to call a taxi.' She stood back, head cocked, making sure everything was up to her inspection with Roberto's outfit. 'I've brought my car.'

'You're going to drive us?' Alessandro let them pass and slammed the door behind them.

'Don't tell me you don't feel comfortable with a woman behind the wheel,' she said with saccharine sweetness. 'Because if that's the case, then you're a dinosaur.'

'Girl speaks her mind!' Roberto chortled smugly. 'Something you'll have to get used to, my boy!' He absently patted her hand as they trundled towards the side of the house.

'You intend to take us out in *that*?' Squatting directly under one of the security lights that surrounded the house was an ageing Morris Minor. 'I thought those cars were extinct,' he murmured. 'Along with the dinosaurs you mentioned.'

'It's very reliable,' Laura told him tartly.

'Except for last winter,' Roberto pointed out, and for the duration of the drive they launched into an extended anecdote about the unpredictability of her car, which, Alessandro assumed, he was supposed to find uproariously hilarious. He wondered why his father didn't just buy her something more reliable and then grimaced because had he done that, Alessandro knew that *he* would have been the first to point out that his father was being ripped off.

He had intended to bring up the matter of the move but, over a surprisingly good meal, he found every effort thwarted.

They had in-jokes. They talked about people in the village. They spent way too long discussing some orchids someone or other had done something or other with, only desisting when Alessandro was forced to butt in and shut down that particular topic or risk falling asleep. He heard his father laugh. Twice. The sound was so unusual that he wondered whether his ears had been playing up but, no, at the end of an hour and a half he could see for himself that the life he had envisioned his father having might have been slightly off target.

And he had known nothing about it.

'So how long will you be staying?' Laura asked politely,

when, engine still running, they were back at the manor house.

'This has been the most uncomfortable journey of my life,' Alessandro informed her as he levered his big body out of the back seat. 'Why is your engine still running? I take it you're coming in.'

'I hadn't intended to.'

'Girl's got to be on her way!' Roberto announced.

'In that case,' Alessandro countered, 'we can have some time to discuss your move.'

'Not tonight, my boy. This old man needs his beauty sleep!'

'I'll come in for a couple of minutes.'

Roberto, on his way to the front door, paused to look at the two of them, eyes narrowed. 'Can't think Edith will want you gallivanting all over the country at this time of the night!'

Laura laughed as she joined them to walk to the front door. Roberto's bushy brows were drawn together in a frown. 'Hardly *gallivanting* all over the country,' she soothed. 'My grandmother worries too much.'

'With good cause,' Roberto muttered, rapping his walking stick on the front door impatiently as Alessandro jangled a bunch of keys, hunting out the right one. 'After all those shenanigans in London!'

'Here we go!' Laura trilled, hoping to drown out that utterly, utterly inappropriate remark and mentally vowing to warn her grandmother about any more confidences while Alessandro was on the scene, earwigging. 'Back home and I must say the meal was delicious!'

Much as she didn't want to spend time in Alessandro's company, she knew that she would have to, at least for half an hour or so. First, she wanted to find out how long he intended staying in Scotland, because having a car delivered was not a good sign. Second, she was desperate to know whether he was rethinking his silly decision to try to browbeat Roberto into moving down to London.

She had seen the way Roberto had deflected all attempts to manoeuvre the conversation to the move and she knew that whatever relationship the two had, it would crash and burn completely if Alessandro kept hammering away at his father, trying to force a move that wasn't wanted.

Couldn't he see that?

Did he care?

And how on earth had these two ended up at such loggerheads...?

She was curious. She shouldn't be but she was. She was waved aside when she offered to walk Roberto up the stairs and it was only when he had disappeared from sight that she felt the power of Alessandro's presence wrap around her like a stranglehold.

In the busyness of leaving the house and driving to the restaurant and then doing her utmost to carry the conversation to any topic that would demonstrate Roberto's ties to the community, she had forgotten how uncomfortable she felt in the dress.

Now, as those dark eyes settled on her, she had to stop herself from tugging it down.

'Drink?' He looked at her for a few seconds. She was wearing a dress that was never going to win prizes at a fashion show. It was an awkward length and, twinned with serviceable boots, gave the impression of someone who wasn't into clothes. His was a rich diet of catwalk models but he had still found his eyes straying time and time again over dinner to the way the fabric stretched over her full breasts, the way the neckline offered just a glimpse of cleavage, enough for his imagination to take flight. 'Because I'm guessing that the only reason you volunteered to come in was because there's something you want to say to me. A stiff gin and tonic might move things along.'

Laura scowled. With no Roberto around, he was back to being the arrogant, obnoxious guy who thought it was amusing to needle her. She could also tell from the way his eyes had skimmed over her that he found her get-up funny—the dress, which hadn't seen the light of day since London, and even then had only been worn once, the boots, which were sturdy, useful and most of all warm, but hardly the height of fashion.

He headed towards the kitchen and she traipsed along behind him. In a dark jumper and dark trousers, he was just impossibly sexy and she really resented the way she even *noticed* that when she didn't want to. She halted at the door and watched as he sauntered towards a cupboard, fetched two squat glasses and poured them both a drink.

'So,' he drawled, handing her a glass, 'are you going to remain standing by the door like a sentry or are you going to sit down and say what you have to say?'

His fingers had brushed against hers and every muscle and nerve in her body had reacted.

'You never mentioned how long you intended staying here…' She inched her way towards the table and sat down. The first sip of the gin and tonic was pretty frightful but the second sip was much better and helped her relax.

'Undecided. Why? Do I make you feel uncomfortable? I wouldn't want to put a spoke in the wheel, but…' he shrugged, sipped his drink and looked at her over the rim of his glass '…needs must.'

'What needs?'

'That's a somewhat leading question, wouldn't you say?' If they were referring to *his* needs, then he might very well meet them by staying.

He had a vivid image of her in his bed, sprawled in all

her glorious, lush beauty, her delicate, heart-shaped face heated with desire, her body his for the taking. He imagined her huge, green eyes riveted to his nakedness, her arms spread wide, her legs likewise...

Blood surged through him and he felt a fast, hard, painful erection.

'You were desperate for me to discover the ins and outs of my father's busy life here and if I'm to do that I'm going to have to rely on more than a question-and-answer session.' His voice was terse as he dispelled the sudden eroticism of his thoughts. 'For starters, answering questions has never been my father's speciality. When it comes to answering *personal* questions...well, put it this way, I don't foresee him putting out the welcome mat. Father-and-son chats have just never gone down that road.'

'Why?'

'Come again?'

'You should be able to have an honest, heart-to-heart conversation with Roberto when it comes to something as important as this. He should tell you why he doesn't want to move to London.'

'And yet, as you've seen for yourself, that sort of explanation hasn't been forthcoming, which is why I've gone ahead and done what I've considered best all round.'

'So why are you bothering to stay here if you've already made your mind up?'

'Because I want to see first-hand what the situation is with my father and your grandmother,' he said bluntly.

'Meaning?'

'I want to make sure that it's all above board.'

'I can't believe you just said that!'

'Why?' He shrugged. 'We've been through this before. You might as well accept that I'm not one of these idealistic, trusting types who takes whatever's told to him as the whole truth and nothing but the truth.'

'You are just *so cynical*. Isn't it enough that your father has found someone at his age? Someone who makes his life a better place?'

'Beautiful. And even more beautiful if that someone has his physical well-being at heart and frankly couldn't care less about the well-being of his bank account.'

Laura ground her teeth and glared at him. How was it that someone so good-looking could be so...cold?

But, then, Colin had been good-looking as well, hadn't he? And he'd turned out to be as genuine as a three-pound note. She obviously had a problem when it came to her judgement. She obviously was one of those people who could be swayed by good looks. Well, it had happened once before and it wasn't going to happen again.

And there was a big difference between Colin and Alessandro. Colin had been suave and charming. Alessandro was just...outspoken, arrogant and downright *charmless*.

If he had any reserves of charm, he wasn't going to use up any of his supply on *her*, at any rate.

And when it came to attractiveness...the differences were extreme as well, once you started looking a little more closely. Colin had been attractive in a *sanitised* way. His blond hair had always looked ever so slightly *helped along with products*, his smile had dazzled, his body had been slim and trim but not overtly muscular.

Alessandro, on the other hand, was good-looking in a more raw, untamed way. Underneath the sophistication you could half sense something more elemental, something powerful that was barely leashed.

And thank the Lord for that, she thought. Because that made her far safer from his brand of good looks!

'Gran is away until next week.' She reined in the desire to get into a shouting fit with him.

'And I can't wait to meet her.'

'And once you've sized her up, what do you intend to do?'

'I enjoy crossing bridges when I get to them.' Not strictly speaking true. He was a guy who had always preferred to plan in advance. However, in this instance he would have to think out of the box and react accordingly. The disturbing truth was that he had planned on a more clear-cut situation and was realising that that was not the case. He had counted on his father's stubbornness. What he hadn't counted on was the fact that that stubbornness was not misplaced if he saw himself as being dragged away from connections he would find difficult to replace in London.

But the thorny issue of trekking back and forth remained. Maybe if he and his father had had anything remotely resembling a functioning relationship, that situation might have been different. Maybe then those journeys wouldn't have been seen as a nuisance. But why beat around the bush? They didn't and Alessandro wasn't thrilled at the thought of having to make more and more inconvenient trips, staying for longer and longer periods of time, should his father's health nosedive.

He might not be lining up to receive the son of the year award, but neither was he so lacking in a sense of filial duty that he would be able to switch off completely.

'Don't you have to be…er…back in London? Running your company?'

'Companies. Plural. I have more than one and, no, I can take some time out to assess this situation.' He sighed suddenly and raked his fingers through his hair. 'It's not ideal,' he admitted. 'I didn't think I'd end up having to spend time here, checking up on a life I had no idea my father had. It makes things…slightly more problematic.'

Laura swallowed the last of her drink. She'd had nothing to drink over dinner as she had been driving and now the gin and tonic rushed pleasantly to her head, warming her and making her feel relaxed, not as defensive. He looked weary. Still sexy as hell, but weary.

'I don't know why you have the relationship you have with Roberto,' she was startled to hear herself say, 'but if you try to force his hand, it'll backfire. You might end up dragging him down to London but it would be against his will and he'll resent you for it for the rest of his life.'

'I don't recall asking for your opinion.'

'Do you *ever* ask for anyone's opinion?'

'No.'

'Sometimes it pays to hear what other people have to say.' She felt some of her Dutch courage ooze away in the face of his icy stare. 'You can't be a rock all of the time…'

Except he was and always had been. He'd grown up knowing that he was on his own and he had acquired the necessary independence from an early age. She, it would appear, had not. Even though…

'How old were you when you lost your parents?' He gave in to the curiosity that had been nibbling at the edges of his consciousness. He didn't encourage deep and meaningful conversations with women because deep and meaningful unfailingly gave rise to awkward forward thinking on their part. There was nothing he disliked more than a woman with plans and too much interest from him engendered plans. But…this was different. Exceptional circumstances. Curiosity was permitted.

'Seven.' She was startled at his digression.

'And then you moved in with your grandmother.'

'She was my closest living relative and we'd always been close.'

'And despite the loss of your parents, you remain an optimistic, upbeat person. That…' he sat forward, scarcely believing that he was having this conversation '…is because your grandmother was a constant. I think you're viewing the relationship I have with my father through rose-tinted spectacles.

'He paid the exorbitant school fees for my boarding school, lavished as much pocket money on me as any boy could possibly want or need, paid for ridiculously expensive holidays, which I took with various trusted members of staff, and those were the constant. His presence wasn't because I seldom laid eyes on him and when I did, we were forced into agonisingly polite conversation that we were both very happy to bring to an end as soon as we could.' He couldn't believe he had said as much as he had. It was so unlike him to confide in anyone. It made him feel annoyed and uncomfortable at the same time but he told himself that it had been necessary, if only to combat her perky optimism. She was a one-woman cheerleading team.

'What about your mother?' Laura's heart went out to him. In fact, she wanted to close the distance between them and place her hand over his.

'What about her?' This was a subject that was closed to all. It was something he rarely thought about. He had put to bed all questions about his mother a long time ago. His mother had died when he had been young enough not to have remembered her…an unexpected heart complication that had sprung from nowhere. That was the sum total of what he knew.

'Your father has never mentioned her,' Laura said wistfully. 'I know he came here without a wife all those years ago. No one saw much of him at all. He was never around.

He lived in the big house and half the time no one knew whether he was in the house or not.'

'And no doubt everyone had a theory.'

'I don't know. I was busy at school, then I went away to university and then down to London. By then he had stopped working, I guess, and had begun to appear in the town with a little more regularity.'

'I'm struggling to picture my father strolling into the village on a Sunday morning for a cup of tea and chit-chat with the locals.'

'That might be because you don't really know him.'

Alessandro's lips thinned. 'And it's so important to really get to know people, isn't it?' he remarked with smooth assurance. He strolled to pour them both another drink and she half-heartedly swatted the offer away.

'I have to drive back.'

Alessandro didn't answer that. He perched on the table, which meant that she had to look up at him, and their eyes met. The slow flush that crawled into her cheeks was telling him something and he never, ever, got it wrong when it came to those little signals women emanated.

His dark eyes dropped to her mouth and he deliberately let them linger there, and the way she nervously licked her lips was also telling him something.

The fire that had been running through his veins like a deep, underground, fast-flowing river began surfacing.

He wasn't into self-denial when it came to sex. What was the point? If it was there, he took it. It was there now. Did she even know that? Was she even aware of the attraction she felt towards him or was she too busy trying to analyse him and probe beneath the surface?

'And, yes, it's important you really get to…er…you know, find out about Roberto before you do anything that could…um…really throw him into turmoil…' Laura's eyes skittered away from his, although her skin felt as hot as fire. She could still feel those deep, dark eyes of his locked onto her and it was rousing stuff in her that she didn't want.

Alessandro Falcone was off limits and it had a lot more to do with the complicated situation between them.

He was off limits because he was just plain wrong on every single level.

He was everything she didn't want in her life. When she'd walked away from London, from her job and from a guy who had strung her along with his charm and his dashing good looks, she had made a quiet resolution to herself that she would not get involved with anyone who wasn't open, sincere and basically just like her. Normality was what she wanted in a guy. Even if she were to have a fling, it would be with someone whose values she shared and who wasn't out to get what he could. It wouldn't be with one of life's takers.

So why was it that she felt naked and exposed when he looked at her like that?

'We could spend the rest of the night discussing my father,' Alessandro murmured. He moved, strolled to the window, which offered the view of a pitch-dark night outside, strolled back to the table and resumed his position, perching on it but this time closer to her. Close enough for her breathing to feel a little restricted.

'But let's talk about you instead. You've done a lot of low-level, amateur psychoanalysis on me... Fair's fair. What was my father referring to when he mentioned your shenanigans in London?'

'I don't know what you're talking about.'

'Please tell me that you're not one of those hypocrites who are forthright and direct when it comes to mouthing off their opinions on other people's lives but clam up the second someone tries to get a straight answer out of them about their own lives. That would be disappointing…'

Laura glared at him angrily. Hypocrite? That was one accusation that had never been levelled against her! Too outspoken, yes. Naive, yes. Too honest for her own good, definitely! But hypocritical? No.

'Lost for words?' Alessandro asked silkily. 'And yet you've been so vocal up until now…'

'You know what the older generation is like,' she hedged through gritted teeth. 'They gossip.'

'I never took my father for a gossiper,' Alessandro commented truthfully.

'Well, he is when he's with my grandmother. And you know…people of that generation think that walking in a park holding hands with someone if you're not engaged to be married comes under the heading of *shenanigans*!'

'Have you buried yourself here to escape a broken relationship?'

The mildness of his voice was disconcerting because his eyes were shrewd and perceptive.

'I don't consider this a graveyard.'

'So you had an ill-advised fling with someone you worked with. It fell apart at the seams. It happens.'

'Who told you that?' She looked at him narrowly. 'I suppose Roberto let slip.'

'Like I told you, my father and I are not on such familiar terms. I guessed and it seems that I was right.'

She looked away. Her hands were trembling and she linked her fingers together, stilling them. She didn't want to talk about this, wasn't going to talk about it, and yet wasn't he right when he'd said that she had felt free to probe but when the shoe was on the other foot, she wasn't quite so ready to confide?

Was this her Achilles' heel? The place where her insecurities lay? Being brought up by her grandmother had been good, better than good, but she had never really caught on to make-up and feminine wiles—not in the way her other classmates had. Her grandmother had simply been beyond all that by the time Laura had hit her teens. When it came to the art of flirting, she was at a loss and so Colin and the way he had used her inexperience had hit her hard, had reinforced all those insecurities.

She couldn't shake it off because she didn't know how. She wasn't casual enough when it came to men. Would she *ever* be able to shake it off? Alessandro was right, wasn't he? She'd buried herself here and she wondered, in a sudden surge of panic, whether she would remain buried. Would she ever venture out into the big, bad world again? Dip her feet back into the water?

Or would that prospect seem scarier and scarier the more time passed by? The only interaction with guys she had here was with the partners of the friends she had grown up with, who had left and returned or else had never left. She would end up batty and alone and talking to herself at inappropriate times in public places.

'You're not going to cry on me, are you?'

'No, I'm not!' Laura snapped fiercely. 'And, *yes*, I did have a situation with someone I worked with. Satisfied? He strung me along and then I found out that he was married!'

'He was just another bastard.'

'You don't understand! I really trusted Colin Scott. I thought he was a decent kind of guy but it turned out that he was a liar without any morals. So, yes, I came back here. Go on, say it… I'm a loser and an idiot.'

'Is that what you think?'

'What else?' she asked bitterly.

'You were blindsided by a creep but you don't have to bury yourself and lick your wounds.'

'No? What would you suggest?' she muttered. 'I'm not licking my wounds. I'm just…taking time out…'

'Well, there *is* one thing I would suggest.'

'What's that? I'm all ears, as you would say.'

'Step back into those muddy waters.' He stood up and flexed his muscles. It had been a while since he had done any chasing. He wondered whether he was rusty but, no, she was looking up at him with dawning comprehension. He wondered whether it was a good idea to go there but, then, they were both adults, weren't they? And once the ground rules were laid…

'Only next time round,' he said softly, 'make sure you know exactly what you're dealing with. I find that works for me. I'm honest upfront. Sex with no strings attached. No future plans made. No promises to be broken.' He smiled crookedly and stroked a stray tendril of hair away from her face, felt her breathing quicken, saw the way her pupils dilated.

'From where I'm standing, that's the way forward. The waters might still be a little muddy but they'd be a hell of a lot safer than quicksand…'

CHAPTER FOUR

HEART BEATING SO hard she felt as though she might pass out, Laura inched back in the chair but she couldn't peel her eyes away from his face.

'I should be leaving,' she managed to croak. 'I don't... don't want to be driving late at night.'

'Why? The only thing you're likely to pass are a couple of stray sheep. If you like, I can drive back to your house with you, make sure you get home safe and sound.'

Laura wildly thought that *safe and sound* were not words that she would naturally associate with being in his presence. *Unsafe* and *at risk* would have been nearer the mark, as far as her pulse rate and blood pressure were concerned, at any rate.

'And how would you get back here?' She did her best to get her breathing under control, knowing that he was picking up on her flustered behaviour and drawing his own conclusions.

'Walk.' Alessandro shrugged.

'Hand-made Italian leather shoes aren't made for walking miles on country lanes.' She stood up, legs feeling like jelly, and with some alarm she watched as he followed suit, standing up as well and crowding her with his towering presence.

'These shoes would do what I tell them to,' Alessandro murmured.

Laura gripped the back of the chair and drew in a deep, steadying breath. 'Is that how it works for you?'

'What are you talking about?' He frowned, perched once more on the table so that they were now eyeball to eyeball. She had the most expressive face of any woman he had ever seen. Her eyes were wide and clear and her freckles were standing out against the waxy pallor of her skin. She was hot and bothered and there was no way she could hide it. He liked that. It made all those cool, ultra-beautiful models he had dated in the past seem like plastic dolls in comparison.

This was a living, breathing, one hundred per cent sexy woman.

'You always get your own way?'

'Would it be a bad thing if I told you that I did? Ninety-nine per cent of the time?'

'No wonder you're so…so…*arrogant*!' She could barely think straight and yet there he was, as cool as a cucumber, making her feel as though *she* was the one making a mountain out of a molehill! Her fingers itched to smack that self-assured gleam right off his face and her anger felt a lot safer than that disturbing pull towards him.

'What's arrogant about telling it like it is?' he asked softly, unruffled. 'And, by the way, you're extremely cute when you're angry. I have a feeling you don't get angry very often.'

Laura gritted her teeth together, not wanting to stay where she was but somehow unable to unglue her feet from the floor and walk away.

'I don't fancy you,' she said in a strangled voice, 'and I'm certainly not interested in having a fling!'

'You do fancy me, you know.'

'You're the most egotistic man I have ever met!'

'If you didn't,' he pointed out in an ultra-reasonable

voice, 'you wouldn't be glaring at me and spitting fire. If you didn't fancy me, what I just said to you wouldn't have got under your skin the way it has. You would have been mildly amused, mildly insulted, largely indifferent. You might even have accepted my company back to your house because you wouldn't have felt threatened.' He grinned, eyebrows raised. 'We could always solve this vexing situation by putting it to the test...' he murmured, as though suddenly hitting upon the perfect solution.

He didn't give her time to think. He couldn't. He was so close to her that he could smell the clean, flowery smell of whatever scent she was wearing, and that fragrant scent matched the scent of her hair. With just the slightest hint of provocation, he thought that he might take her right here, in the kitchen, on the kitchen table. His erection was bulging, painful, and it was even more painful when he imagined her cool hands on it, followed by her cool, cool mouth. Since when had he ever had such an X-rated imagination?

He had to kiss her.

Laura sensed his intent before his mouth descended. She raised her hands to ward him off, mentally prepared to shove him firmly away, but...

Something happened. He kissed her gently. When his tongue flicked to probe the moistness of her mouth, she stifled a whimper. Her whole body trembled against him. Somehow, she had closed the gap between them and she could feel his hardness throbbing against her, a flagrant indication of how turned on he was.

She curled her fingers into his shirt and tugged him towards her. Every nerve in her shameless body was shrieking in hot response. Her breasts felt heavy, her nipples tingled, wanting more than just this kiss.

'So...' Alessandro reluctantly set her back gently. For a few seconds she could barely focus through the daze but when she did, mortification washed over her in a tidal wave of pure, undiluted horror.

'I don't know what just happened there,' she whispered.

'Lust.'

'I…I want to go now…' She looked away but was still hyper-aware of him standing close to her, his warmth mingling with hers in an agonising reminder of the kiss they had just shared. She was mortally horrified to admit to herself that she wanted to be back in his arms, kissing him and being kissed by him.

'Why?'

'What does that *mean*?' Her eyes flashed as they tangled with his and the breath caught in her throat.

Lust.

Hadn't she learned her lesson? She'd fallen victim to lust before and look at where it had got her! Except when she thought about Colin she couldn't remember feeling anything like what she had felt just then. That kiss, which had been meant to *prove* something, to *prove* that she was attracted to him, had sent her soaring into some crazy place where she hadn't even been able to *think*!

Colin's approach had been stealthy, like a serpent in the grass. He had charmed her, dismantled her doubts and inhibitions. Alessandro had just…swept in like a conquering marauder, intent on plunder.

She didn't even approve of him! She didn't even like him. So how on earth had he managed to…steamroller through all the defences she had so carefully put in place after her catastrophe with Colin?

'You don't want to go. You want to run away. We both know that we could easily have ended up—'

'I don't want to talk about this,' she said tightly. 'It shouldn't have happened. In fact, it probably only did because I had that drink. I'm not accustomed to drinking shorts. I wasn't thinking straight!'

'Tut-tut. You don't really believe that, do you?'

'You can't just come here and take what you want because you're bored,' she said, drawing in a deep breath and finally meeting his gaze and holding it.

'Whoever said anything about being bored?' He still wanted to touch her, wanted to feel the softness of her body without the barrier of clothes. The dress might not have been an overcoat but it might as well have been.

Laura squeezed her arms tightly around her body. 'I'm not looking for a guy like you.'

'A guy like me?' was the first response that came to hand, even though, more appropriately, he could have told her that if she wasn't looking for a guy like him, then he, likewise, wasn't interested in her or anyone else finding him and thinking they'd hooked him.

He wasn't into the business of encouraging false hope. He shoved away the uneasy thought that he had already managed to tell her a hell of a lot more than he had ever dreamed of telling any other woman in his life before.

Circumstances.

'You're everything I disapprove of. I don't know what the problem is with your father but you don't even make an effort! In all these years you've never shown any interest in trying to get to know him! In finding out what his life here is like... Do you know that he was actually *excited* at the thought of you coming up here twice? Taking us out for dinner? He had a problem choosing the right tie!'

For a few seconds Alessandro was lost for words. He stood up and prowled through the kitchen before leaning against the kitchen counter.

She couldn't read his expression. Was there *uncertainty*

behind that glower? Surely not. Surely he wasn't someone who was *ever* uncertain.

'Don't be ridiculous,' he muttered, standing directly in front of her, legs spread squarely apart, fingers hooked into the waistband of his trousers.

'Don't tell me I'm being ridiculous!'

'I don't think it's possible for my father to get excited over my appearance here, especially given the circumstances surrounding it. Actually, I doubt it's possible for my father to get excited over anything to do with me.' His mouth twisted into a wry smile before he abruptly turned away, to say over his shoulder, 'It's an understanding we share. As few displays of emotion as possible. It works.'

'He was excited because you were showing some interest in his life here. You should be so grateful you have him,' she said quietly, to his averted back.

That had him turning round to look at her. 'I count my blessings every night before I go to sleep.'

Are you always sarcastic? Laura wanted to ask him. And then it struck her that everyone had their defence mechanisms. That was his. He wasn't just an arrogant bastard who was here to complete a mission that would make his life easier, even if it meant railroading Roberto into doing something he didn't want to do.

He was far more complex than that.

'I would give anything to have a parent,' she said wistfully, 'even one I didn't get along with.'

'That's because you're sentimental,' Alessandro responded deflatingly. 'I'm betting there are damp tissues all round whenever you watch a tearjerker at the movies.'

'Would anything change your mind as far as removing your father is concerned? Are you just sticking around so that you can size my grandmother up and make sure she's not going to nick the silver the minute your back's turned?'

Alessandro shrugged. 'I'm taking it as it comes.'

'But it's a good thing,' Laura mused thoughtfully, 'because you've had to actually put yourself out to integrate into your father's life.'

'Let's not dress this up, Laura. It's a two-way street.' He had no idea what was propelling him to unpick scabs that had hardened over the years. Neither could he work out how they had managed to digress from the topic of when and where they were going to do something about the chemistry burning between them. Which was a far more interesting topic for discussion.

She lowered her eyes and didn't say anything. Frustrating woman, Alessandro thought. Any other woman would have been pressing to continue the conversation. The slightest shred of confidential information being shared would have opened the door to all sorts of thoughts of *really getting to know him*...the *real* him...

But, then, this woman was different, wasn't she? She might be hellishly attracted to him, but that still didn't make him *her type*. And since he wasn't *her type*, she wasn't looking for a way in to him via trying to lead him down the path of touchy-feely conversation. She was probably away with the fairies right now, thinking sentimental thoughts about her past.

'I don't know my father,' Alessandro heard himself say through gritted teeth, 'because he's always made sure to be unavailable.'

'Unavailable?'

'I was brought up by a selection of hired help,' he pointed out neutrally. 'Some excellent nannies, it has to be said. I barely remember my father being around when I was a kid. He spent most of his time abroad. He even...' Alessandro laughed mirthlessly '...went on holidays without me. Not that I didn't enjoy everything that vast sums of money could buy. I did. I had holidays few could dream of…in the company of the reliable hired help. At seven I was shipped off to the finest boarding school in the country and so the tale of our serviceable but distant relationship goes on…'

'I'm sorry.' Laura took a few steps towards him and Alessandro, cursing himself for the ease with which the natural fortress he had built around himself had been invaded, shot her a wolfish half-smile.

'Sorry enough to come to bed with me?' he murmured. 'Trust me when I tell you that I'm not at all against a sympa—'

'Stop it!' White-faced, Laura looked at him with blazing eyes. Was that what it had all been about? Had that unexpected crack in his self-assured, forbidding exterior been a deliberate ploy to try to get her to sleep with him?

She remembered the way Colin had infiltrated himself into her life, playing on her emotions and saying whatever he thought she might want to hear. In retrospect, it had been so obvious.

Was she so transparent that Alessandro Falcone was ready to pull the same stunt?

She placed her hands firmly on her hips and glared at him, seething. 'That was crude!'

Alessandro had the grace to flush. Yes, it had been, and crude was something he had never resorted to in his life before.

'My apologies.' He raked his fingers through his hair and stared at her, and for a few seconds she was so taken aback by the apology that she couldn't find anything to say. 'You're right. It's getting late. You should go. What was it my father said about your grandmother not wanting you to be gallivanting all over the country?'

Released from the awkward situation, Laura hovered

for a few seconds. She licked her lips and noticed the way he absently followed that little gesture with his eyes.

He wasn't coming closer to her, not by an inch. In fact, she could almost feel him pulling away, distancing himself, but the *heat* was still there. She could feel it like something tangible and alive between them.

Of course it would be madness to even think about going there, but it still gave her a heady kick to know that he found her attractive and she didn't honestly think it was because he happened to be here, in the middle of nowhere, bored and restless.

She wanted to shove him in the same bracket as Colin because it somehow felt safer, but he wasn't Colin.

'So…' She unconsciously stepped a tiny bit towards him. She wasn't even aware that she was doing it.

'So? So what?'

She shrugged, mesmerised by the smouldering darkness of his eyes.

'You really shouldn't, you know…'

'Shouldn't what?'

'Kiss me the way you kissed me…hot and hard and urgent…and then pull away and wipe your lips and somehow try to make-believe that it didn't happen and if it did, it wasn't your fault…'

'I never—'

He overrode her feeble interruption in the same dangerously soft voice. 'And then, when I take a step back, look at me as though you'd love nothing more than for me to kiss you all over again. Is that what you want? For me to kiss you all over again? Would you like me to lock the kitchen door, sweep the glasses off the table and make love to you right there? With the lights on so neither of us misses a thing?'

A thousand erotic images flashed through Laura's head.

Her mouth went dry and she knew that her whole body was aroused beyond belief. Moisture was dampening her underwear, pooling between her legs. It was somehow all the more of a turn-on because he was still keeping his distance. She felt giddy.

'No…' she managed, in a voice she didn't recognise.

'Sure? Because if you do…just say the word…'

'I've had one narrow escape when it comes to flinging myself into something…something…wrong…'

Alessandro shrugged. 'Like I said, there would be no wrongs or rights, because I'm not in it for the long haul.' Her body was so exquisitely provocative, especially as she seemed oblivious to that. He was holding himself back by sheer willpower but he had to. There was no way he intended to coerce anyone into bed with him, even if he knew that she wanted him.

She either came to him or she didn't.

His eyes darkened when he contemplated the possibility of her walking away. If he ended up being denied the promise of touching and making love to that glorious body, which he couldn't seem to get out of his head, he would have to instil a rigid regime of cold showers.

Never had the outcome of any encounter with any woman been so precariously balanced and he wondered whether that was why he could scarcely contemplate the thought of her turning her back on him for airy-fairy, woolly reasons that made no sense, because they were both adults and they both fancied each other. End of story.

'And I won't be using persuasive arguments to try to convince you that what we have needs to be…sated…'

'This is crazy!'

'When does your grandmother return from her holiday?'

'Huh?'

'We've covered the subject of sex,' he imparted with a

wave of his hand, 'so, before you go, I want to arrange a time and a place for me to meet her.'

Laura's brain seemed to be lagging behind. It seemed to have snagged somewhere between him asking her whether she wanted him to kiss her all over again and telling her that she just had to say the word.

Now he was moving on and that in itself said it all about the way he could compartmentalise sex, put it into a box that was quite separate from emotions or feelings or thoughts of the long-term.

She landed back down on earth and focused on him. 'Right. Yes. My grandmother.' Deep breath in, deep breath out. 'She's back on Friday. I'm going to pick her up from the airport. She could get a taxi back but, you know, she always thinks that taxi drivers are hell-bent on ripping her off by taking long, unnecessary detours...' She knew that she was babbling but she couldn't help it. And she wished he would stop looking at her like that, with his head ever so slightly inclined to one side, as though he was think-ing all sorts of stuff that had nothing to with what she was talking about.

'In that case, Saturday. You and your grandmother can come here.'

'For tea? A drink?'

'Dinner. Maybe I'll do our digestive systems a favour and give Freya the evening off...fly my guy in. He could stay for the weekend.'

'Fly your guy in?'

'I have someone I can call on who cooks for me if I happen to eat at home.'

'Your father may have lots of money,' Laura said, 'but I don't think he would be happy with that situation.'

'No.' Alessandro gave her one of those slow, amused smiles that could knock her for six. 'I think he's so accustomed to Freya's challenged cooking that he might be confused if anything too edible came his way.'

'That's unkind.' She didn't want to, but he could bring a smile to her face without trying.

'Seven?' Alessandro asked, and she nodded.

Meeting her grandmother would be the last thing he would want to do when it came to finding out about the life his father would be leaving behind, the final piece of the jigsaw puzzle.

Laura couldn't imagine him kicking his heels in Scotland for much beyond that, even though he had sorted out an office for himself and appeared to be working quite efficiently.

'We'll be there.'

'No need for you to have arranged all this nonsense!' Roberto glared at his son from the stiff-backed chair where he sat, unhelpfully critical of the evening's arrangements.

'Don't you want me to meet the…ah…woman in your life?' Alessandro looked at his father and marvelled, yet again, at how simple conversation could end up feeling so tortured.

Not that strides forward hadn't been made. Ever since Laura had confided, a few days ago, about the dilemma with the tie, Alessandro had loosened up a little, had found it easier not to let his hackles rise after three seconds.

He had been invited to go over his father's company accounts and over dinner, the night before, they had actually managed a halfway decent conversation about the gradual sale of some of his father's interests now that he was fully retired.

Business was a safe topic of conversation and it was a damn sight more stimulating than the leaden silence that usually settled between them and to which they had become accustomed over the years.

'Old men don't have *women*.' Roberto adjusted his navy tie and eyed his gleaming shoes with a jaundiced eye. 'They have *companions*, my boy! Don't see why the sudden interest in meeting Edith anyway! Never had much time for what was going on in my life in the past!'

'But I wasn't trying to convince you to leave these goings-on before, was I?' Alessandro pointed out, because his father had developed an annoying and efficient habit of sweeping all talk of his move to London under the carpet.

'Must be missing your *women* in London...' Roberto said slyly. 'Must be hordes of 'em walking up and down outside your house, waiting for you to return... Nothing better to do with themselves, judging from the couple I met! Certainly couldn't get a job anywhere! Not with sawdust for brains!'

Alessandro, standing by the imposing Victorian fireplace, half smiled to himself because right now the last thing he was missing were women in London. Right now, this felt like a game and it was an exciting one. All he needed was the one woman right here on his doorstep, thank you very much.

'I'm doing just fine,' he murmured and missed the sharp look his father threw at him.

'Ever think of settling down?'

Alessandro looked at his father, shocked at this unexpected departure from their normal regime of polite conversation.

'Not if I can help it,' he said smoothly.

'You should,' Roberto grizzled. 'Marriage makes a man.'

Saved by the doorbell, Alessandro didn't get a chance to

quiz him on that because he had no idea what the quality of his father's marriage had been, but he could only assume that it had been a dictatorship in which his long-suffering mother had had to put up with the same sort of silent treatment from a man who had only spoken when absolutely necessary. He had a mental picture of two people moving around one another in silence.

Except…how much did he actually know for sure? He was about to answer the door to a friend in her twenties he had never known existed and a woman who was his father's girlfriend, someone else whose existence he had known nothing about.

Opening the front door, Alessandro dispelled the unsettling feeling of the floor shifting under his feet.

Laura had prepared her grandmother by telling her that Roberto's son wanted to meet her.

'I wondered when I'd get to meet him,' Edith had replied crisply. 'About time Roberto and his son sorted themselves out! Communication! That's all it takes!'

Laura had been too busy thinking her own thoughts to pay much attention to that remark.

What to wear? What did a girl wear when she was about to see a guy to whom she was stupidly attracted, a guy who had made her insides flip over with one kiss, a guy she most certainly did *not* want to have a fling with…

But was still driven to impress?

It was freezing cold outside but she wore a short-sleeved, deep blue, tight-fitting top with more of a plunging neckline than she would normally feel comfortable wearing and a long, black skirt with ballet pumps. Of course, she had to layer up and she could see her grandmother looking curiously at her dressy get-up, but it was no big deal. When someone invited you to dinner at their house, it was customary to show up in something other than jeans and a shapeless woollen jumper! She left her hair loose and it tumbled down her back, held back from her face with two blue clips on either side.

'Quite a picture,' her grandmother had said approvingly. 'Dress to impress?'

Which had almost made her take the whole lot off and climb back into her usual garb but she didn't and she was glad she hadn't when Alessandro opened the door and…

Black jeans, a faded black polo-neck jumper…he was so drop-dead gorgeous that her mouth went dry. She made sure not to look at him as they were ushered inside but she could feel his eyes on her as coats were removed and in just the tight top and her long skirt she was as conscious of the plunging neckline as she'd feared she might be.

'Fetching outfit,' Alessandro murmured, as Roberto and Edith walked towards the sitting room. 'Did you wear the top because you knew I wouldn't be able to take my eyes off you?'

'This old thing?' Laura said airily. 'I just stuck on the first thing in the wardrobe that came to hand.'

'What else is there in that wardrobe? I'm curious…'

'I told you that I'm not interested in…in anything… so…'

'I know.' He put both hands up in a gesture of mock surrender. 'You only kissed me because you had a couple of sips of gin and tonic and suddenly all your reservations were washed away! But I'm not your type because I'm an arrogant bore.'

'I never said you were boring.'

'So you find me scintillating company and as sexy as hell…it's almost impossible to keep your hands off me… but you're going to do your best to resist because some loser you met in London let you down.'

'This isn't the time or the place to be talking about this!' She looked surreptitiously at Roberto and her grandmother. Edith was doing a lot of talking and Roberto was laughing at something she had said. They were as absorbed in one another as a couple of teenagers on a first date.

'I like it. You can't run away. You never said what he did to you. Promised you the earth and then failed to deliver? Like I said, relationships are so much more straightforward when you lay down the boundary lines from the start.'

Laura stopped and looked up at him. 'He strung me along and I found out that it really wasn't going anywhere because he was married.' Remembered shame washed over her.

'What a class-A bastard,' Alessandro murmured softly. He looked down into those sea-green eyes and wanted to strangle the creep who had let her down. 'But you can't take that with you for ever and let it hang round your neck like an albatross.'

'I can learn from it.'

'Granted you can learn from it and then move on or else you can become so risk-averse that you never take a chance again.'

'I can reduce the odds by not having a stupid fling with someone who's totally unsuitable. I can wait until I meet the right guy for me. I don't think that's being risk-averse. I think that's being *sensible*!'

'Yes, but where's the fun in that?'

'It's not all about fun. When it comes to relationships, it's much more than having fun.'

'I bet your grandmother wouldn't agree. She looks a feisty lady. Should I ask her?'

'Don't you dare!'

She was so wrapped up in their conversation that she only noticed Roberto and her grandmother looking at them out of the corner of her eye, then she smiled a little faintly and cleared her throat.

'What's going on here?' Roberto tapped his way towards them and looked at both of them narrowly.

'Nothing,' Laura said.

'Good! Now, come along. No more of this hush-hush nonsense! Wasn't my idea to have a dinner party but now that it's happening, then into the sitting room you both go! No more standing out here and whispering! Bad damned manners!'

'Don't blame me!' Laura laughed and linked her arm through his. 'Blame your son!'

'Hope…' Roberto turned to look at Alessandro through narrowed eyes '…I won't have to.'

CHAPTER FIVE

HE WOULD LEAVE for the week and return on the weekend. It made sense.

'Bloody waste of your time,' Roberto grumbled. 'Don't see the point of it myself.'

'What's my choice?' Alessandro shrugged nonchalantly. 'Edith has returned the dinner invitation for next Saturday. What's a polite guy like me supposed to do? She looks like she might attack me with a rolling pin if I bail.'

'She's spirited, that one,' Roberto agreed.

'And we're getting nowhere with the decision about London.' He had now spent more time solidly in the company of his father than he ever had in his life before, and counting. At the rate he was going, he may as well import his PA and set up camp for the long haul.

Time and big business waited for no man.

Strangely, though, he was missing the cut and thrust of city life less than he had anticipated. Despite living in the middle of nowhere, the broadband connection was fast and for the past week he had established a routine that worked.

'London Schmondon,' his father contributed unhelpfully. 'More to life than pollution and smog.'

Stalemate.

But Alessandro was happy to take time out with this particular stalemate situation.

Indeed, as he returned to Scotland the following Thursday, a couple of days earlier than anticipated, he was in high spirits. He could have travelled by helicopter but had instead chosen a first-class compartment on the train and had managed to get a considerable amount of work done. Few people kicked off before eight-thirty in the morning, by which time he was on his way, and by ten, when his phone began buzzing, he had already signed off two deals and had had his conference call to his people on the other side of the world.

By mid-afternoon he was at the closest station to the town and on the spur of the moment he set the satnav in the SUV he had conveniently left in the station car park to direct him to the school where Laura worked.

She would be finishing around now. She always stayed after close of day to mark books and get the classroom ready for the following morning.

Over dinner with her grandmother and his father he had told her that it sounded like a terminally tedious routine and then had enjoyed the way her cheeks had gone pink and her eyes had flashed. Even her *hair* had looked annoyed. She spent a lot of her time being annoyed with him, but underneath the annoyance ran a river of desire as strong as an ocean undercurrent. He'd never spent so much time dwelling on one woman, never mind a woman he hadn't taken to his bed. She was becoming a delicious obsession and he couldn't wait for the day when she came to him, when her defences had finally been broken down.

The school was perched at the edge of the village. Stepping out of the taxi, he spotted her car neatly parked in one of the spots for staff. It was just mid-afternoon, but the light was already fading fast and the playground, which was in front of the brick building, was empty of children.

This was the smallest school he had ever seen in his life and there was no way in unless you buzzed and announced yourself. So he buzzed and was let in by a middle-aged woman with rimless specs and a tightly pursed mouth after he explained that he was there to see Laura Reid.

'We all know who you are.' The woman's expression fell into a smile. Her pursed lips were obviously there to tackle any unwanted visitors to the school. 'Roberto's son. Maud at the post office bumped into the lady who does for Edith and she told us that you were here. You must be worried sick over the little turn your father had but he'll be right as rain in no time at all! Similar thing happened to my sister, bless her soul. Had a little stroke and then fell and broke her leg. She was off work for six months! And she bounced right back after that, so don't you go worrying unduly over your father. He's a robust one!'

All the time they were walking through a maze of corridors with classrooms on either side. It was bigger inside than it appeared from the outside. The walls were decorated with bright paintings and there was a low bookcase that ran the length of the corridor, stuffed with books.

He saw her before she noticed he was there. Straight from London and the wine bar, city crowds, he was knocked back at just how artless she was, sitting at her desk with a pile of exercise books on one side, frowning as she leaned over, marking. Her hair was escaping its ponytail, tendrils curling along her cheek, and she was absently chewing the top of her pencil.

'Thanks, I'll take it from here.' He smiled politely at the older woman who had shown him to the classroom and extracted his mobile from his pocket.

He stood to one side, slanting a glance through the small rectangular glass pane on the door so that he could just about see her, see her as she fumbled in her bag for her phone and then picked it up on the fourth ring.

'Just want to say,' he drawled, 'that chewing pencils

can be dangerous for your health…' He saw the way her face lit up, just for that split second when she recognised who was on the other end of the line, and he knew… She could push him away with one hand but she was beckoning him to come closer with the other. He felt the powerful kick of victory and it was an intensely satisfying sensation.

He pushed open the classroom door and she half stood, mobile phone still in her hand as she pressed the disconnect button. 'What are you doing here?'

That little frisson she had felt when she had heard his voice was gone. He could see from the tight expression on her face that she was going to do her best to just block him out because as long as she blocked him out she wouldn't have to deal with the sizzling chemistry between them.

And the harder she tried to block him out, the more he wanted to have her.

His eyes travelled the length of her, from tousled hair to fur-booted feet and then back up, noting the faded jeans and the bright red jumper.

'Thought I'd come a little earlier. So…this is where you work?' He looked around him and then strolled towards the pictures and essays that were tacked to the walls.

'Yes, it is,' Laura said tersely. She wanted to fling herself in front of the drawings he was inspecting with overdone interest because having him here, in the classroom, felt way too intimate. Or maybe it felt intimate because she'd been thinking about him. Correcting an essay while her mind had played and replayed that kiss. Even when he wasn't physically present, he could still manage to get under her skin and rattle her and she didn't like it.

'Nice. Homely.' He swung round to look at her. She was so determined to resist him. He felt that she would run for the hills if she only knew how much he relished the prospect of proving her wrong. As if either of them could resist what was between them.

'Why did you decide to come up here early?'

'A few things I wanted to run past you so I thought I'd see if you were still here. And you are. Why don't you stop…marking those books and have a coffee with me? There must be somewhere here we can go…is there?'

'I still have work to do.'

'Bring it with you. I can help you mark and then when we've finished we can have something to eat and I can talk to you about one or two things that have been on my mind.'

'Don't be silly,' she said, flustered. She smiled weakly past him at Evelyn, the deputy head, who was peering through the open doorway with lively curiosity. 'Just… er…'

'Yes, we met! Showed him in!'

Alessandro smiled at the woman who had ushered him to Laura's classroom and Evelyn blushed like a teenager.

'Perhaps,' he drawled, 'you could convince this stubborn little minx that she can leave with me so that I can take her out for a coffee…or something stronger…'

Laura didn't pay any attention to their bantering conversation but as soon as she and Alessandro were on their own, heading out to his car, she turned on him furiously.

'Thanks very much, Alessandro!'

'You're welcome. Next time you need rescuing from the monotony of marking books, feel free to call on me.'

'That's not what I was talking about!'

'No? Then you need to be a little clearer. I can't really follow you just going from your heated expression. Where's the quaint coffee shop? Or pub? I seem to remember that the town down the road is a little more vibrant when it comes to places to sit and pass the time of day.' He started the engine and began pulling out of the car park.

Was it his imagination or was the formidable middle-aged woman who had shown him in hovering by one of the windows?

'You don't come up here often,' Laura hissed, 'so you probably don't know just how fast the grapevine works!'

'Don't you get a little bored?'

'What are you talking about?'

'Sitting in a classroom, marking exercise books in a village that has twenty residents.'

'Are we back to your comments about it being a back-water? Because we just have to agree to disagree on that one.'

'Do you find it constricting, living with your grand-mother?'

'Why would I?'

'Because you've lived on your own in London, had all the freedom you wanted. It might have suited you while you felt that Edith needed your presence, but she seems in full working order now, from what I've seen.'

'You didn't barge into my classroom so that we can discuss whether I enjoy living here with my grandmother or not.'

'So that's a no...you don't really enjoy it... What's that pub like? Any good?'

Laura glared at him. He was just so damned sure of himself! When she and her grandmother had joined him and Roberto for dinner, she had felt his dark, lazy eyes on her, as tangible as a caress, making her want to squirm, forcing her into awkward speech so that she stumbled over her words, blushing like a gawky teenager.

Had either her grandmother or Roberto noticed? She didn't know, and she had made sure to talk about him as little as she possibly could afterwards, even though her grandmother had asked leading, nosy questions.

'It's fine. Getting back to Evelyn—'

'Evelyn? Who's Evelyn?'

'The deputy head.'

'Never met the woman in my life before but, by all means, let's get back to her.' He pulled into a space, killed the engine and then relaxed back in the seat to look at her.

'She showed you to my classroom.'

'Ah. *That* lady... It took a while for her to crack a smile, but I sense an empathetic person. Remind me why we're talking about her?' The lights in the car park of the pub glinted off her vibrant hair, which was still in a ponytail. The expression on her heart-shaped face was cross and earnest. She had dragged a shapeless black coat over the red jumper outfit. It drowned her but that made no difference to her sex appeal. She still oozed it by the bucketload.

'She's going to wonder who you are.'

'She knew who I was. Someone had told someone who had told someone else who worked for your grandmother. It seems that I'm a talking point without even knowing it!'

Laura groaned. 'Lord knows what she's thinking.'

'Who knows what anyone's thinking?' Alessandro mused softly. He abhorred gossip but he had to admit that he was getting a certain buzz from this situation. 'Sometimes, though, it's easier. For instance, you must know what I'm thinking and here's what I think you're thinking...'

'I don't want to hear.' She looked at him and discovered that she couldn't look away. As fast as his image had crept into her head, she had done her best to dispel it by thinking about Colin and reminding herself that there was no point to learning curves if you just went ahead and ignored them the second they got a little inconvenient.

Colin had worked his charm on her, had used her own trusting nature against her, had played the part of the perfect boyfriend, and she had fallen for all of it, hook, line and sinker.

There was no way that she was going to jump headlong into a similar situation! Alessandro might be more upfront and more straightforward…he might call it *more honest*, but they were essentially made of the same stuff.

She had made a mental promise to herself that the next guy she got involved with would be a normal, considerate, one hundred per cent sincere and honest gentleman. The sort who didn't have a wife and a couple of kids stashed away in a house somewhere. Like Colin.

The sort who didn't change catwalk models as often as he changed his suits. Like Alessandro.

In fact, Alessandro posed a far more dangerous option. Which, frustratingly, was probably why she couldn't get him out of her head.

In fact, and this thought only now occurred to her, she had managed to clear her head of Colin with a lot more success than she was having trying to clear it of Alessandro.

Probably because she had been able to dump her job, dump London and disappear.

While with Alessandro…having made it his duty to avoid Scotland as much as possible, he now seemed to be on the scene all the time…like a guilty conscience.

'Would you like to hear what *I'm* thinking?'

'No!'

'Didn't think so. You'd much rather try to run away from what's between us.'

'There's *nothing* between us!' She was appalled at the edge of hysteria that had crept into her voice and she knew that he had heard it as well, if the knowing, speculative glint in his eyes was anything to go by.

No one could force her to do anything. She knew that. She wasn't going to let emotions or her body guide her actions. She had grown up since her unfortunate experience with Colin. She would use her head to make her choices! So why did she feel so hot and bothered as he continued to look at her with just the sort of pensive, amused speculation that she wished she could wipe off his face?

Why was it so terrifying to think of the way she was attracted to him? When, theoretically, she could control that attraction by boxing it up and ignoring its existence?

'Nothing except raw sexual attraction. You're cropping up in my head when I try to focus on work. It's very bad.'

'That's not my fault,' Laura said faintly, pushing down the little thrill she got from hearing him say that.

'Well, it's not *mine.*'

'There's *nothing* between us,' she repeated, just a little desperately, 'and I don't need the whole village gossiping about something that doesn't exist!'

'Ah, I get it. You think Evelyn the deputy head is going to start spreading unfounded rumours...'

'Yes!'

Personally, Alessandro could think of nothing worse than unfounded rumours. He'd had a couple of unfortunate experiences in that particular field...women who had stupidly spoken to a couple of reporters who had had nothing better to do than run an article or two on the private life of whatever billionaire they could find. They had intimated there had been more to their relationship than had actually been the case and had found to their cost that he could be ruthless when it came to eliminating complications. Women who expected more from him than he was willing to give became complications and women who thought that talking to reporters might somehow pin him down to something he didn't want invariably found themselves dispatched without delay.

Alessandro had never really thought about that side of

his life, the side that refused to become emotionally involved, but on the few occasions when it *had* crossed his mind he had concluded that it had to do with his background.

Love had not been readily shown. He assumed his father cared about him but with reserve and distance, and that reserve and distance had created in him an emotional vacuum that he had never chosen to explore or overcome.

He just wasn't one of those types in search of happy-ever-afters. He relied on what he knew and what he knew was the world of power and big money, the concrete world of business, of deals and machinations and running an empire.

Women were stress-busters. He was upfront with them and if some of them got the wrong idea or started imagining a future that wasn't on the cards, then whose fault was that? Not his. He was nothing if not scrupulously honest when it came to that sort of thing.

So unfounded rumours in a small village...?

He decided that this would be his exception to the rule. What she did to certain parts of his body was worth the inconvenience.

'Doesn't matter, though, does it? Considering they're unfounded?'

'That's not the point.'

'You don't care what people think to the extent that you'd actually pay attention to what they say about something that doesn't even exist, do you?'

Laura met those dark, cynical eyes evenly. 'Yes, I would, because I actually care what people think of me.'

'Why?' Alessandro was genuinely mystified.

'Why don't *you*?'

'Come again?'

'It's not natural to not care *at all* what anyone thinks

of you. Okay, I get it that you don't care what a perfect stranger thinks of you or what you choose to do. I mean, if the milkman peers past you into your hallway and doesn't like your choice of wallpaper, it's no big deal. But don't you care what *anyone* thinks of you or what you do? Isn't there *anyone* whose opinion matters to you?'

'Shall we continue this fascinating conversation over a very early glass of wine?' He reached across to open the car door on her side and his forearm brushed against her breast. He felt her flinch back and half smiled, even though he was still playing around with the annoying question she had posed.

Aside from the gruelling demands of his job, what did he care about? And was not caring a strength or a weakness? Irritated by this sudden bout of introspection, he swept it aside and levered his big body out of the car.

Enthusiastic to be in his company she most certainly was not. Tales of big, bad wolves sprang to mind, with him in the starring role of the big, bad wolf.

Suddenly, it didn't seem as amusing to tease her as it had done minutes before.

Hell, she really cared about what sort of reputation she would get from just being seen with him! They'd done nothing and it was still bugging her.

He toyed idly with the idea of telling her that it was better to be hung for a sheep than a lamb. If the entire village had nothing better to do than twitch their net curtains and speculate, then why not give them something to speculate about?

'You're not trying to run away from an awkward conversation, are you, Alessandro?' She fell into a brisk walk to keep pace with his longer strides.

Wherever he had come from, it hadn't been from sitting behind a desk. He must have changed in his luxurious penthouse apartment before heading up. He oozed casual sex appeal in jeans and a jumper over which he was wearing a mega-expensive trench coat. When it came to practicality in cold Scottish weather, it scored a zero, but in terms of looking indecently good, it was a ten with room to spare.

'I've never run away from anything in my life.' He held the door open and she ducked under his arm. 'And definitely not from idle, wagging tongues, but if you prefer, I'll make sure I keep a healthy distance. What would you like to drink?'

Laura breathed a sigh of relief that the pub was relatively empty and as it wasn't in the village there was less chance of her being recognised, although wasn't Alessandro right? Why should she care? She had cared so much about what had happened with Colin that she had packed her job in without thinking of the repercussions. She could have taken some time off, genuinely because her grandmother had needed her, and then returned to her job, not caring that she might bump into Colin, because he was a bastard so why should she? Not caring if some of her colleagues might have suspected what had been going on, because they hadn't been her close friends so their opinion mattered but within reason.

She could have remained in London because... Living here was fine but there were times when she did feel as though time had been frozen and she wasn't moving forward. She could have quit her job and gone into teaching, but in London...

No. She did *not* want to start thinking of what-ifs and if-onlys!

'A cup of tea would be nice.'

'Tea? It's almost five-fifteen. We can have a glass of wine. I won't tell if you don't...'

She smiled nervously at him but before she could work

out a suitable negative response he was heading towards the bar, where the young girl serving behind the counter dropped what she'd been doing and flew over to take his order.

However cool and detached he was with his father, and however forbidding he could be when he chose to, he could certainly pull the charm out when it suited him, Laura thought wryly. The poor girl could hardly pour the wine into the glasses and she was beetroot red.

'So there's a reason I decided to come up here early and pay you an unexpected visit.' He angled his chair away from her so that he could stretch out his long legs.

His voice was brisk and businesslike. He was keeping a healthy distance between them. She could have been at an informal job interview! Perfect, she thought with a twinge of treacherous disappointment, because his flirting was stupidly addictive.

'Aside, that is, from wanting to see where you work…' He grinned and then steepled his fingers to his lips. 'But starting with Edith…'

'Are you going to tell me that you think she's after your father for his pot of gold?' Laura bristled. She wondered whether she would stop being so attracted to him if she could somehow maintain a state of permanent low-level anger. If she was *angry* with him, then she couldn't be *attracted* to him, could she?

Sometimes, though, it was impossible to respond to him the way her head told her to. Sometimes he just got under her skin and no amount of rubbing could get rid of him.

'Actually, I happen to like your grandmother very much,' Alessandro admitted seriously. 'I don't know what I expected but she…she seems good for my father…'

'And what did you expect?'

'Someone a little more subservient. I'll be honest, my father isn't the easiest of men. I didn't envisage that he would be…attracted…God, have I really said that?…attracted to someone as outspoken.'

'What was your mother like?'

'That remains one of life's mysteries. It's not a subject I have ever discussed with my father and it isn't a subject I intend discussing with you.' He'd tried with his father and had come up against a brick wall of uncooperative evasiveness. He'd stopped trying a long, long time ago.

Laura blushed. His voice had cooled. Sexual innuendo and flirting was fine. A serious conversation apparently wasn't. Whatever he did, he did on his terms and that included how much he wanted to share of himself.

Not that it mattered. This wasn't a show-and-tell, getting-to-know-you session.

'She keeps him in line.' Laura smiled. 'They suit one another. She likes fussing over someone and he enjoys being fussed over. She tells him what he should and shouldn't do and he's like a little lamb when he's with her.'

'I can't believe we're talking about the same person. No matter, the point is…I may possibly have got it wrong when I decided that the only option was to move my father to London.' He sipped some wine and looked at her over the rim of his glass. He really enjoyed the way she was so transparent, so lacking in artifice. 'I hadn't thought that the life he had built here for himself was so… Well, put it this way, I hadn't thought that he'd built *any* life for himself here. It seems that I was wrong and I'm big enough to admit it.'

Laura couldn't help it. She rolled her eyes heavenwards and Alessandro frowned.

'Oh, honestly!' She sighed and laughed lightly, taking in his bemused expression. 'Hasn't anyone *ever* rolled their eyes or clicked their tongue at something you've said?'

'I've just admitted that I may have been wrong. What's the rolling of the eyes all about?'

'You're *big* enough to admit it? What was the other option? That you carry on pretending that he's a lonely old man and drag him down to London rather than admit you'd got it wrong? We *all* misjudge situations once in a while.' He was staring at her with a blank expression and she realised that didn't apply to him. That just wasn't how his world worked. In Alessandro's world misjudging of situations didn't happen but, then, his world was all about stuff that could be measured. Deals, money, business…things that were a million miles away from emotions, feelings and lives, things where misjudgement happened all the time. 'Okay,' she said slowly, 'so now you've recognised that, what happens next?'

'He still needs to move out of that oversized mansion. I always wondered why he bought it in the first place. I am prepared to admit that remaining here might be for the best. The hunt will have to begin to find him somewhere a little more compact, a little more manageable…'

'Aren't you going to discuss this with your father?'

'I'll broach the topic. So…now that's out of the way, let's talk about the weekend.'

'I'm not going anywhere with you.' She couldn't give in to his flirting. She couldn't let herself be overtaken by something as stupid and transitory as physical chemistry. She bristled at the thought that he felt he could just try to dictate how she should spend the little amount of time he designated to spending in a backwater he normally wouldn't be caught dead in. She tried to rustle up Colin's image in her head but all she could see were Alessandro's far too knowing dark eyes focused on her with the sort of lazy intent that sent her nervous system into frantic overdrive.

'I realise that there's some sort of physical attraction between us. I'm not going to deny that, but that doesn't mean that either of us has to succumb to it and, furthermore, it's insulting to think that you just come here and then feel that you can take what you want, never mind the consequences!' She lowered her voice to a meaningful hiss. 'You can't!'

Alessandro inclined his head to one side and the infuriating man didn't say anything.

She looked at her wine glass and realised that it was empty. How had that happened? She rarely drank unless she was out and certainly never at this crazy hour of the evening!

'So you may think you're some kind of saint who can wash his hands of relationships just because you've been kind enough to warn those poor women you date that you're not in it for longer than a couple of days...'

'Hmm... Days... Even for me that would be a rapid turnover.'

Laura ignored him. 'But I'm not one of those women!'

'I never thought that you were.'

'Because I don't happen to be a six-foot-three catwalk model?' she asked bitterly. She had felt so desirable when he had kissed her...nothing had prepared her for the onslaught of lust that would wipe out all her inhibitions as though they had never existed.

But, then, the guy was a force to be reckoned with when it came to the art of seduction. One look at him would tell you that.

'Because I've never had to employ such restraint with any woman in my life before.'

'Well, that may be but it certainly doesn't mean that I'm going to spend the weekend accommodating you!' She tilted her chin at a stubborn angle and glared at him.

'I think you're getting all hot under the collar for no reason,' Alessandro said mildly.

'And I disagree!'

'I wasn't trying to arrange a convenient time to wage an assault on your maidenly virtue, tempting though that option is…' He stared off into the distance, as though wrapped up in all sorts of pleasant thoughts, and then shook his head ruefully. 'I was actually about to say that the weekend might be a good time to start trying to consolidate some of my father's possessions in preparation for a move, should he agree, of course.'

'Oh.'

'Disappointed?'

Laura wanted the ground to open up and swallow her whole. No wonder he was sitting there grinning at her! 'Relieved,' she snapped.

'Good! I will talk to my father this evening and who knows…something might well be sorted out before I leave.'

And once sorted, his life would, of course, return to its normal hectic pace within the confines of his own comfort zone in London.

Or…

He gazed at her flushed face thoughtfully.

Maybe not. The last thing he needed was to leave behind unfinished business…

CHAPTER SIX

'DOWNSIZE? WHAT'S THE point of *that*? Not one for living in a rabbit hutch!'

Alessandro remained silent. His loose-limbed posture in the chair facing Roberto smacked of utter relaxation. Only the stillness of his body betrayed his awareness of the fact that, as always, nothing was going to be easy when it came to his father.

But, for once, he had converts to his cause. Laura and her grandmother had insisted on sitting in on the meeting with his father in a show of moral support, even though Alessandro had told them that it wouldn't be necessary.

'He can be a stubborn old fool,' Edith had announced, as soon as she had been told of Alessandro's decision and given it the green light. Not, Alessandro thought, that a green light from anyone was required, but Edith was not a woman any sane person would pick a fight with. 'Digs his heels in and refuses to budge. Won't be able to pull that one on me, though! I can be a stubborn old fool as well!'

Alessandro had shrugged and so, later that evening, they had all headed up to the manor house, like gunslingers galloping into town to confront the local bad boy.

'And don't…' Roberto wagged his finger at Edith a little later '…you start telling me that you agree with that son of mine!'

'You put that finger away,' Edith said in a clipped voice.

'That son of yours is right and you know it! Who was it who told me not four months ago that he found walking from the kitchen to the bedroom "*a bloody chore*"? And I'm quoting a certain person here. He's sitting not a million miles away, being a stubborn old fool, as I knew he would be!'

Alessandro shot Laura a sideways glance, caught her eye, kept looking until she looked away and then settled down for the count.

It was nearly six-thirty. Yet another unappetising dish prepared by Freya was bubbling away merrily in the oven and in a few minutes he would fetch a chilled bottle of wine, which he decided would be an excellent accompaniment to the thrilling battle of wills unfolding in front of him.

He already knew what the outcome would be. His father might be able to argue for England but he would never be able to hold out against a determined Edith. The woman had missed her calling as a riot-control specialist in a prison block.

At the moment she was reminding Roberto of every conversation they had ever had in which he had complained about the size of the house. There had been a lot, especially in recent months, and she had a very good memory.

'And don't you even bother telling me that you can always live in one wing of the house! Stuff and nonsense!'

'You're a harridan, woman! A harridan!'

'And then there's that garden so-called of yours! How big is it, exactly? Ten acres? What's a man of your age doing with ten acres of garden? You'd need a car to get round the lot! I'll wager you haven't been to the lavender field since last year! And who told me that the greenhouse was getting a little out of control? You won't let any of the gardeners in to tend the plants but you can't tend them all on your own, admit it!'

Alessandro looked at his father's scowling face with amusement. He wore the harried look of someone who'd just found a hole in his defences and simultaneously discovered that he lacked the time and the necessary tools to do a patch-up job.

He had never seen Roberto on the back foot. His father had always made a show of being in command. He had been a towering, forbidding and silent figure in Alessandro's childhood, a largely absent one during his teenage years and a broodingly taciturn and borderline belligerent one as Alessandro had reached adulthood.

That was not the same man sitting in the burgundy covered chair now, glowering at Edith before huffing into silence.

'You're a damned witch, woman!' He looked at her and then said slyly, 'Could you have an ulterior motive for trying to get me out of this house? I hear that house down the road from you is coming up for sale in the next month or so… You know the one I mean…those layabout softies from Edinburgh inherited it when old man Saunders died. Wouldn't fancy getting your hands on me, would you?'

'You should be so lucky!'

'If you'll excuse me…' Alessandro stood up, flexed his muscles '…I'm going to get some wine and, Laura…' he shot a glance at her, eyebrows raised '…why don't you accompany me? You can check on whatever delight Freya's shoved in the oven for us to eat. It's been in there for the past four hours so whatever it's meant to be it'll probably emerge as baby food.'

'Don't you go thinking you've won this round, young man!' Roberto banged his walking stick on the parquet flooring and glared at his son. 'Won't be browbeaten into doing what I don't want to do and...' he transferred his beady eyes to Edith, who wore the smug expression of the victor '...won't be nagged into it, either!'

Alessandro shrugged and left the room with the vague promise that the matter could be revisited over dinner. Behind him, Laura followed. She hadn't said a word, leaving her grandmother to argue with Roberto. She had sat in her chair, her body rigid with tension, her focus exclusively on Roberto, but she had been aware of his son with every pore in her body. Alessandro had relaxed back in the chair, his fingers lightly entwined on his stomach, his legs outstretched and loosely crossed at the ankles. She had sensed his alertness, his watchfulness... Her antennae had picked it up like a gazelle picking up the scent of a jungle cat.

'I think,' he drawled the minute they were in the kitchen, 'that what we have in there is called a foregone conclusion. Maybe we should leave your grandmother to seal the deal and mop up the blood before we take the wine in. I can't believe she got the better of my father! Memorable.' He poured them both a glass of Chablis and watched as she went straight to the oven, removed whatever was being cremated in a cast-iron casserole pot, winced and then rested the pot on the hotplate.

She was doing her best to avoid eye contact. Even when she took the glass of wine from him, those apple-green eyes skittered away hurriedly.

For a few seconds she remained hovering before subsiding into one of the kitchen chairs and taking a long gulp from the long-stemmed glass.

'It would have broken my grandmother's heart if your dad left to live in London. I mean, I know Roberto is probably fond of this place, I know he's lived in it for...well, for as long as any of us can remember, but I think he knows deep down that it's far too big for him. Would you like me to find out whether the cottage at the end of the village will be coming up for sale?' She risked a nervous glance at Alessandro, who was perched against the kitchen counter, staring at her with just the sort of *concentration* that could send her pulse flying to the four winds.

'No need.'

'What do you mean?'

'If you give me the names of whoever owns the place, I'll take it from there.'

'But you won't know who they are and they don't actually live in the cottage. I believe it's a brother and sister. I remember chatting to them when they came to Jim's funeral.' She grimaced. 'They couldn't wait to leave. Since then they've been down a couple of times to make sure the cottage is still standing but they haven't done anything with it and I'm sure they won't be interested in moving in.'

'I just need the names. What's the boy called?' He reached for his mobile and tapped in the name given to him.

'What good is that going to do?'

'I'll get in touch with him.'

'But what if he doesn't want to sell? I know you think that this is just a backwater, but it's possible that they might want it as a holiday home. It's absolutely stunning in the summer months and the salmon fishing is very good...'

'He'll sell because I'll make him an offer he can't refuse. If he wants a holiday home in this part of the world, he can buy one somewhere else. I intend striking while the iron's hot. Give my father a little time to start working on another argument for staying put and I could find myself in the same position as I'm in now this time next year.'

'And that would never do, would it?' Laura said tartly.

'Having to drag yourself away from hectic city life to go through the horror of repeat trips to the backwater?'

Alessandro smiled slowly at her. He sipped some of the wine and carried on looking over the rim of the glass, liking what he saw. Jeans, a checked shirt peeping out from behind a dull red jumper. The same fur-lined boots she had been wearing in the classroom. High fashion wasn't going to be staging a takeover any time soon with her and he really liked that. He also liked the way her skin was tinged pink, the way she was mutinously doing her best to meet his eyes and hold them, the way she didn't wear any make-up so that the sprinkling of freckles across the bridge of her nose stood out against her pale, smooth skin. Her hair wasn't in a ponytail but she had still pulled it back into a single long braid, which she had pulled over her shoulder, and it was tied at the end with a red piece of stretchy elastic.

What was a man to do? he wondered.

She wasn't one of his catwalk models, who were as hard as nails and knew the score before they jumped into bed with him.

She was also nursing a broken heart, although, as far as he was concerned, after a year and a half the heart should not only be mended but would benefit from some energetic exercise. The sort of exercise he was an expert at providing.

And how complicated could it get? They lived in opposite ends of the country and he knew, unerringly, that although she fancied him, she would never look for anything lasting with someone of whom she fundamentally disapproved.

And vice versa. She might make a great change from his predictable diet, but she was as poles apart from him as he was from her. They could have come from different planets and he couldn't wait to explore their differences.

A big plus was that it would make visiting his father a thing of anticipation, at least for a while. Of course, denial would be a safer option because she didn't obey the rules of the game he played when it came to women, but denial was something with which he had little experience. What was the point? When it came to sex, all was fair in love and war between consenting adults. And her consent was simmering just below the surface. He could sense it.

'City life *can* be hectic,' Alessandro agreed. 'Maybe I've been viewing these trips to Scotland in entirely the wrong light.' He glanced around at the kitchen as though pondering whether there was more to it than met the eye, maybe a magic wardrobe concealing a lion and a witch, and then he gazed at her with his head tilted to one side. 'For *backwater*, one can always read *peaceful*. Maybe I haven't thoroughly explored the potential for kicking back here.' He shrugged, still giving the matter some thought. ''Course, my father's endearing ways might have detracted from the temptation to spend longer than a few minutes in the place but I sense we might be getting onto a different footing...'

'You do?' Laura subdued a brief flare of thrilling anticipation at the prospect of him being around, which she immediately squashed, choosing to interpret the way her heart skipped a beat as nothing more than perfectly understandable satisfaction that father and son might manage to work their way to a better relationship.

'He has friends and a social life here,' Alessandro mused, 'so I'm thinking that there might be more to him than has always met the eye. Once or twice I've even caught a flash of humour in something he's said and I've always thought that humour was something he disapproved of on principle. And, of course, I've seen first-hand that he's not as intransigent with the entire human race as I've always been led to believe. Your grandmother knows how to wield a big stick and he obeys. Doesn't take a genius to work out who wears the trousers in that relationship.'

'Roberto is all bark and no bite.'

'I wouldn't go so far as to say that…'

Laura looked at him curiously and he returned her gaze with raised eyebrows. 'I've discovered he has a healthy set of teeth. Trust me. But…' he shrugged and slanted her a crooked smile '…I don't get away much. Might do me good to discover what this part of Scotland has to offer.'

'Why don't you get away much? Don't you enjoy going on holiday?' Laura couldn't fathom why anyone who was as rich as Alessandro didn't feel the urge to take time out. He could afford to go anywhere on the planet.

'Come again?'

'You said you don't get away much. Why not? Surely you must get tired of working all day, every day, without let-up? Your father says you never stop. He tells me that you're always in the newspapers about closing some big, important deal or other. Doesn't it all get a little too much?'

'How would my father know about deals I've closed?' Alessandro queried silkily.

'Because he has a scrapbook of newspaper cuttings.'

Sudden silence filled the room, then Alessandro swirled his glass and finished the remainder of the wine. Scrapbook? What scrapbook? Since when?

'I don't take holidays because I don't have time,' he told her bluntly. He thought of the houses he owned, one in the Caribbean, another in Paris, a third in Tuscany. Aside from the occasional business trip to Paris, when he occasionally might stay in his apartment there, they remained vacant, tended by paid help, waiting in readiness for the day he decided he could take the time off.

He brought the conversation neatly back to the matter in hand, clearing his head of a sudden onslaught of un-customary confusion when he thought of those unused holiday homes, slowly maturing as good investments but never enjoyed, when he thought of his action-packed, high-pressured life that never allowed him time to sit back and take a break. 'Which is why it might work to come here a little more often than I have done in the past.' He strolled towards her, wine bottle in one hand, filling his glass as he walked. He didn't sit down, however. Instead, he chose to stand right next to her, which immediately made her feel as though she was suffocating. 'Of course, it would help if I had someone to show me around...'

'Someone to show you around?'

'I only know my father's house and whatever lies within the radius of about three miles. Even when I used to return here from boarding school, I never bothered to explore the countryside.'

Laura's brain was lagging behind. Who did he have in mind to show him around?

As if she couldn't guess. She felt a frisson of excitement ripple through her. He was so close to her that she had to look up at him and when she dipped her eyes...

Her mouth went dry.

'You should have,' she said faintly. 'It's worth exploring. Maybe we should return to the sitting room.' She pushed back her chair and managed to squirm out of it without coming into contact with his far-too-big, far-too-dominant and far-too-powerful body. 'Roberto has very strict eating times. In a second, my grandmother will fly in here and start fussing over the food.'

'Maybe she could transform it into something edible.'

Alessandro stood aside, allowing her the distracted change of topic, because sooner rather than later he would return to the matter in hand. 'Although that might require a skilled magician.'

They returned to the sitting room to find Edith and Roberto poring over an illustrated gardening book that she had brought back from Glasgow as a present, and there was a jaunty tie resting on the coffee table next to him.

Alessandro looked at the tie, caught his father's eye and was gratified when his father reddened.

'Silly woman insisted on bringing me back this tie,' he muttered while Edith looked at him with open affection. 'Can't imagine where an old man like me is going with a yellow tie with red birds on it!' He picked it up and absently placed it over the navy blue tie he was currently wearing, and Edith beamed.

'And now...' she slapped her thighs briskly '...that everything is sorted and this stubborn father of yours has seen the sense in downsizing, it's time to feed him!'

It was a little after nine-thirty when Alessandro delivered both Laura and Edith back to their house and it had been, for the first time in living memory, a rewarding evening.

At least insofar as the downsizing decision went. Roberto had capitulated to his fate in style. He now knew exactly the sort of place he was looking for and unless the Saunders place filled each and every single requirement, they could damn well go jump.

Alessandro was quietly determined that it would, whatever the cost. Speed was of the essence and he would move quickly. Money talked and he had a lot of it.

'So...' That was his opening word, when Edith had finally retired to bed and Laura was showing him to the door as though she couldn't get there fast enough. 'You never answered my question.' Alessandro leaned against the door frame and looked at her.

Her heart fluttered. 'What question?'

'I'm going to be here for the next few weekends at the very least. I might even split my time until this whole house business has been sorted out. Are you going to be my tour guide while I'm here?'

Laura glanced over her shoulder towards the staircase. Her grandmother had retired with her cup of hot chocolate but there was no telling whether she would reappear without warning and she didn't want Edith's curiosity aroused.

Because there was nothing to be curious about.

Yet...

That treacherous thought slipped into her head without warning and she shivered with forbidden excitement.

'You don't need a tour guide, Alessandro,' she replied, buying time, hating herself for being tempted. 'You've got a car. You can drive yourself around and take in all the sights...'

'But it wouldn't be nearly as much fun, would it?' he said softly.

Their eyes tangled and slow, burning colour crawled into her cheeks.

'What are you so scared of?' he asked. He could see the little pulse beating in the side of her neck, an indication that the cool, composed voice did not reflect what was going on inside her. But he knew what was going on inside...he had felt it in that sizzling, shared kiss.

'I'm not scared!'

'And you keep glancing up the stairs. Do you think your grandmother is pressed to the floor of the bedroom with a glass so that she can eavesdrop on whatever we might be saying?'

'Of course not,' she said uncomfortably. But who knew when it came to her grandmother?

'I'm attracted to you.' Alessandro didn't move an inch closer to her but it *felt* as though he had. It *felt* as though he had caressed her and left a scorching trail behind on her skin. 'And you're attracted to me...'

Laura opened her mouth to protest but she remained silent because to deny it would be to deny the obvious.

'That doesn't mean anything.' She risked a quick look at his dark, handsome, serious face. 'It would be stupid to do anything about that.' She was aiming for dismissive. Instead, she ended up with a nervous squeak. 'Life is about choices,' she continued, clearing her throat. 'I chose the wrong guy when I was in London and I'm not going to repeat my mistake.'

'You will only climb into bed with a man who promises to put a ring on your finger? What if he never comes along?'

'Then I guess I'll end up on my own.'

Alessandro didn't say anything. He had never been rebuffed by any woman and her refusal fired him up like a challenge he now knew he had no intention of resisting.

'My father's possessions will need to be packed up.'

'Huh?' Was that it? She felt unjustly deflated. Her body was still throbbing, as though he had physically touched her. So what was wrong with being careful? Why wasn't she more relieved that he wasn't going to pursue an attraction neither of them had asked for? And how was it that he had somehow managed to make her feel like an unadventurous bore?

'I intend to get the ball rolling on this one first thing in the morning.' Alessandro straightened and opened the front door, letting in some freezing wintry air. 'I'll have to have a look at the place before I make a decision but

I'm hoping that there won't be any gaping construction black holes.'

'Of course.' Her mind was still in a whirl, thinking about the way he had told her that he was attracted to her, as if sexual attraction was the most natural thing in the world, as if acting upon it was a no-brainer.

'Once that's sorted, I can arrange for work to begin on reconfiguring it to my father's exacting standards. In the meanwhile, you probably know more than I do about what personal items will need boxing and what can be left for the removal men.'

'It's moving a bit fast, isn't it?'

'I've never seen the point of delaying the inevitable. And while this is going on, I intend to stay put, make sure that there are no unfortunate hitches.' He paused and looked down at her upturned face. He itched to smooth his hand over her cheek, cup her face, pull her so close that she would be able to feel exactly what she did to his body. 'Would your school be able to release you for a couple of days so that you can help with the packing of my father's things? I have no idea where he keeps anything and even less interest in finding out. I will also have to work while I'm here...'

'I can't just take time off! They need me there.'

'And I need you here.'

The way he said that, in a slow, lazy drawl, imbued the remark with all sorts of delicious, dark innuendo.

'I can't trust outsiders to handle my father's personal possessions, whatever they might be, and he hasn't got the energy to do it himself.'

'Perhaps you ought to see whether the house is going to be available or not first,' Laura said, transfixed by the little smile playing at the corners of his mouth.

'If I want it to be available, then it will be available.

And I want it to be available. When can you let me know about taking time off?'

'I… Okay, I'll talk to Evelyn, see what she says, whether they can spare me for a day or so. I can't promise anything.'

'If you like, I can talk to her. I'm sure I could convince her to release you from your chains for a few days.'

'A few days?'

Alessandro shrugged nonchalantly. 'Who can tell? I have no idea how much my father owns and how much needs packing up. It could be a handful or a vanload.'

Laura thought that if he spoke to Evelyn she would probably let her have the rest of the term off. The man was too charming, too persuasive, too damned sexy for his own good. He was the personification of danger, but instead of backing away from him she stayed where she was, rooted to the spot, mesmerised against her will.

He fancied her, found her attractive…

It felt as though he was something exciting, exotic, unbearably tempting…blown in on distant winds, turning her protected world on its head and making her wonder how long she would hide away in this small village with her grandmother, making her wonder if all this self-protection was really worth it.

She had fled London and had welcomed the soothing balm of being back in Scotland. Her grandmother's temporary frailty had been a distraction and then she had busied herself applying for the teaching job and familiarising herself with the school and the pupils. She had congratulated herself on having a new life and leaving behind a miserable situation. She had told herself that it was better to lead a quiet, contented, uneventful life than one in which she ended up being hurt. She would never be hurt again. She would never *allow* herself to be hurt again.

But had she been *living*?

Alessandro made her question her resolutions. Going to London in the first place had been a huge adventure for her, then Colin had appeared on the scene and everything had gone pear-shaped. She had obeyed her first instinct to run away, back to safety.

Anyone else might have just seen that as an obstacle to be surmounted. She was only twenty-six and he hadn't been the great love of her life, as time had revealed! Anyone else would have carried on, trusting that the next adventure would turn out a bit better.

Instead, she had retreated and she now wondered whether that hadn't become part of her make-up over time. Had the loss of her parents made her fearful? So careful that it had become a handicap? And was that fearfulness going to follow her for the rest of her life?

Alessandro, with his dark, sinful temptation, made her question the choices she had made.

What would happen if she accepted the gauntlet he had flung at her feet? Would she go up in flames? Would the world stop turning?

Of course not!

But maybe she would be able to re-enter the world without wearing so much protective garb around her that she could barely move, never mind live. She couldn't let one poor experience blind her to what life had to offer, could she?

And Alessandro, in a weird way, might pose a danger because she was physically attracted to him, but physical attraction was like a virus that struck hard and then blew over—in another way, he couldn't have been a safer bet. He wasn't luring her on with the pretence of a relationship, as Colin had. And she was never going to fall for him. The guy for her really would be someone who shared her beliefs and values and wasn't motivated by money and power.

'Are you going to carry on staring at me? Or shall we move the conversation along?'

Laura started and reddened. 'I'll get the time off, although I'm not sure myself where his possessions are kept. I mean the ones he wouldn't want a team of removal men to manhandle, and I'm sure he'll insist on doing it himself. He's very proud. Doesn't like accepting help.'

'You knew where to find a scrapbook.' Alessandro clenched his jaw and shoved his hands into his trouser pockets. For a second his formidable self-control seemed to desert him but it was only a fleeting sensation, then he met her green eyes squarely. 'I expect,' he told her drily, 'the rest of his stuff might be in the same cubbyhole. People are nothing if not predictable.'

'It wasn't in a cubbyhole. It was in his bedside drawer. I went to fetch some tablets for him shortly after his operation. It fell out. Maybe he'd been looking through it.'

Alessandro didn't want to feel any softening towards his father. The time for that had come and gone years and years ago. He knew Roberto Falcone for what he was, an unforgiving man who had probably never wanted a child in the first place, a man who kept his past a secret, even though, as a kid, Alessandro could remember asking him for details of his mother until eventually he'd given up. They had retreated into their own worlds and it was a relationship that worked for both of them. There was no room for any sudden curiosity about a scrapbook his father had kept over the years.

'You're quite the Good Samaritan, aren't you?' he murmured softly.

This was where he felt comfortable. He could relax when he was playing a game of seduction and he was certainly relaxed when he noticed the shell-pink colour that rose to her cheeks at his change of tone.

He reached out and delicately brushed a tendril of hair from her face and then he left his finger there, tracing her soft cheek until he was trailing it along her mouth.

This was where he was supposed to be.

Not thinking crazy thoughts that weren't going to get anyone anywhere…

But right here, touching her and putting an end to the will-they, won't-they game. Those sorts of games were tiresome. Reduced to its barest bones, the chemistry between them was as powerful as a live current and there was no way that a three-act tragedy about why she shouldn't sleep with him should get in the way.

Caught in a balancing act of wondering what she should or shouldn't do, Laura allowed her body to sink into that feathery touch. Her mouth trembled and she half closed her eyes, released a small sigh. She wasn't even aware of raising her hands so that she could curl her fingers into the lapels of his coat, or of reaching up on her toes, her whole body leaning towards him and demanding more than just the touch of his finger on her skin.

Her mind went blank when she felt the coolness of his mouth hit hers. She couldn't get enough. She returned the kiss urgently, fiercely seeking out his tongue. Her breasts were pushed against the rock-hard wall of his chest and she nearly collapsed when he shifted his big hands underneath her jumper and cradled them.

Her nipples itched and strained against her bra. She wanted to reach behind and rip it off because the need to have him touch her without the barrier of itchy, starchy fabric was overwhelming.

Somehow he had managed to manoeuvre her against the wall without breaking the contact of their kiss.

Nothing, but nothing, had ever felt like this before. So

this was what it felt like to be submerged in a tidal wave of passion.

He cupped her bottom, shifted her so that she could feel the hot steel of his erection, and she squirmed against it.

'I don't care,' she broke away to whisper, and he looked at her. 'I'm not going to be careful. I want you. You were right. I want you so badly…'

Alessandro was so turned on that he feared the unthinkable might happen, especially as the chances of them ending up in a bed somewhere were remote, not while Edith was asleep upstairs.

When he took her, he wanted to do it slowly, without having to listen out just in case her grandmother came flying out of a bedroom somewhere.

It shouldn't matter but somehow it did. For once, he wasn't operating in his usual vacuum, where he had no one to whom he had to refer and no one whose opinion mattered.

'We can't…here…' He was breathing heavily and his hands were shaking ever so slightly as he set her apart from him. 'Trust me, I would sling you over my shoulder and take those stairs two at a time to the nearest bed, but…'

'But Gran's upstairs. I know.' She straightened her jumper and did something with her hair.

'Dream of me tonight,' he said roughly. 'When we make love, I want to take my time.' He sifted his fingers through her hair, marvelling at its sexy, silky length. 'Trust me, Laura, it'll be worth the wait…'

CHAPTER SEVEN

FROM ALWAYS MAINTAINING a polite distance, Alessandro found, over the next week or so, that his father now seemed to be around constantly.

The sale of the house, as he had confidently predicted, was all progressing nicely. It just went to show that anyone could be bought, because the Saunders children, having initially made noises about their sentimental attachment to the place, jettisoned all that the second there was a concrete and very inflated offer on the table. In fact, they couldn't hurry things on fast enough.

Builders were on standby, ready to begin work on renovations, and his father wanted a say on every single detail of those renovations.

'Not being shoved out of my own house to find myself in a dump!' he had bellowed the evening before as they had sat at the kitchen table, poring over plans.

'I'll get Edith along to back you up when you say that you're being *shoved out*, shall I?' Alessandro had countered. 'I'm thinking she might have a different take on the matter.'

Frankly, he was finding it almost impossible to concentrate on anything, never mind where a greenhouse was going to go, because Roberto Falcone was going nowhere unless there was a greenhouse of a specific size that could house specific plants, flowers and vegetables. Alessandro was making the occasional trip back down to the city, but for the most part he was working from his makeshift office, and for the first time in his life focus was proving a problem.

Laura had somehow eroded his perfectly ordered life and he had quickly worked out that that was because they still hadn't slept together. He saw a lot of her…every evening she came to the house, where they would go through rooms, working out what could go, what could stay and what needed to be packed by them. And every evening, the brush of his fingers against hers as he reached for something, the slightest physical contact, sent his blood pressure soaring. It was a form of protracted foreplay that was driving him crazy. There were a thousand times when he would have taken her in whatever part of whatever room they'd happened to be in, but for his ever-present father.

Never had it taken him so long to get nowhere with any woman. And the longer it took, the more he wanted her. He couldn't get her out of his head. Returning to London full-time and shifting the overseeing of this project to any one of the many, many capable people he could call upon was out of the question.

Now, at a little after six, he pushed himself away from his desk, stretched and sauntered to the window to stare out at a pitch-black nightscape.

There would be no Laura this evening. Parents meeting at the school, apparently. He couldn't remember his father ever being interested in something as mundane as attending a parents' meeting. He had always been abroad, away on business. A suitable replacement had always been sent, usually a nanny.

Realising that it would be a pointless exercise to continue trying to work, he began sorting through the lower reaches of the bookcase that stood against the wall. He'd never noticed them before but since every nook and cranny in the house seemed to contain something, he felt he wouldn't be disappointed.

Alessandro heard the bustle of his father in the kitchen before he entered. The door was ajar and he could make him out, yet again neatly attired in formal clothes, as though the Queen might take it into her head to pay him an unexpected visit for which he had to be ready. They had dumped the formal dining room a while back for the informality of the kitchen. At least in a smaller arena the silences weren't quite so resounding.

He inhaled deeply and glanced down at the wad of envelopes in his hand. They were sepia with age.

'Found one or two things,' he said, walking in, knowing that this was something that had to be confronted. He watched as his father turned around and then he strolled towards the kitchen table and dumped the envelopes down. 'Why didn't you tell me?'

'Tell you what?' Roberto adjusted his tie and cast a baleful look at his son.

'You know what. Why didn't you tell me about my past?'

An hour and a half later, Alessandro was on his way to see Laura. For once, he had no desire to be on his own. He and his father could have continued talking into the night but they were too accustomed to their silences for that. They had stopped talking when both had felt that everything that had been said needed to be digested.

He killed the engine of his car and sat in the darkness for a few seconds, before swinging out and heading to the front door. He half expected Edith to get it but she didn't. Seeing him there, Laura's eyes opened wide, then she stepped aside so that he could brush past her.

'I've only just got back from the parents' meeting,' she said, eyeing him nervously as he prowled into the sitting room and, once there, remained standing by the window, having divested himself of his coat.

'Where's your grandmother?'

'What are you doing here? She's having dinner with friends in the village…why?' Her heart fluttered and she wanted to ask him if he just couldn't stand it any longer, if he had had to come because days of being in the same space, clearing out Roberto's stuff while he'd watched like a relentless chaperone, had been as difficult for him as it had been for her.

Alessandro saw the blaze of unbidden desire in her eyes and smiled slowly. 'Fortuitous.' He put down his coat and walked towards her. 'Been thinking of me?'

'I've seen quite a bit of you recently so why would I…?' Laura went bright red. Yes, she had made her mind up that this was what she was going to do. She wasn't going to fight lust. There were so many reasons for just giving in but there was a limit to what she was ever going to admit. She certainly wasn't going to admit that she had been thinking of him…something about that sentiment would have made her feel uneasy, although she didn't know why because he had said it lightly, jokingly.

'Do you know, I have never…' he was right up close to her now and he hooked his fingers into the waistband of her jogging bottoms and began slowly tugging them down '…spent so long…' he propelled her backwards, in small steps, until she had her back to the wall '…in the company of a woman I've wanted…' the jogging bottoms were halfway down her legs, but instead of removing her panties he slipped his finger under the silky fabric, unerringly finding the wet slit between her thighs '...and been forced to practise such self-restraint...'

He began stroking her, rubbing her clitoris, losing himself in the sensation, letting it flood his mind and overwhelm the raging confusion of his thoughts.

This was exactly what he needed.

Right here. Right now. His chaotic mind was silenced. He felt her wetness and his mind went completely blank, allowing pure sensation to flood through.

'I have wanted this for so long...' he muttered, as she squirmed against his exploring finger, barely capable of breathing. 'I don't want to make love to you here, standing by the front door, with you pushed up against the wall...'

'We can go up to my bedroom...'

'And I don't want your grandmother walking in on us...'

'She won't. She's having dinner with friends and then they're going to the town hall fifteen miles away to hear a lecture on orchids. There'll be a lot of questions...'

'Where's your bedroom?' He drew back, his dark eyes giving her the opportunity to back off, but he didn't know what he would do if she did. He was so tightly wound that he could scarcely think straight.

Laura trembled, linked her fingers through his, and they took the stairs quietly and quickly up to her room.

He had caught her unawares. She hadn't had time to anticipate or for her nerves to build, but her heart was beating fast and when they reached her bedroom she paused as the enormity of what she was about to do sank in.

Was this *her*? *Really?* What had happened to the dream of finding Mr Right? What had happened to her resolution never to have any sort of relationship with any guy who wasn't going to be there for her as a life partner?

When she had made that resolution, she hadn't known about Alessandro, she thought ruefully. She hadn't yet discovered that there would be someone out there capable of driving all those careful plans out of her head. It just hadn't seemed possible at the time, not when she had felt bitter and wounded.

When it came to women, Alessandro Falcone was a taker. Those lazy, dark eyes saw, desired, conquered and then, shortly after, when his appetite had been sated, he dismissed.

He had no sense of anything aside from himself. He had no sense of family, no sense of wanting to start a family of his own, no belief in love, no ability to give commitment. He represented everything she abhorred and yet...

Here I am now...

She didn't switch on the overhead light. Instead, she turned on her bedside lamp, which sent a dull, mellow glow through the room.

'You seem to have a thing for dogs...' For a few seconds Alessandro took time out to glance at the room, which was small and cosy. There was a rocking chair by the window in which sat an assortment of stuffed dogs.

'I should have got rid of them a long time ago.' Laura laughed a little self-consciously. 'I always wanted a dog but Gran put her foot down at that and decided that stuffed dogs would do the trick. I've never been able to bring myself to dump them. They're too much a part of my past.'

Alessandro strolled towards her. 'We have something in common. I wanted a dog as well but, of course, in a boarding school pets were not permitted. I don't want to talk. I want to touch. Take off all those clothes. Let me see you naked.'

After the briefest of hesitations, during which some small voice urged caution, she began doing as he asked. She ignored the small voice. This was her choice, to live in the present, to enjoy this man with no strings attached.

If there were no strings attached, she wouldn't be disappointed. She knew what she was getting into and she was going into it with her eyes wide open.

And it was now or never. Her grandmother wouldn't be back for at least a couple of hours. There was no opportunity to do anything at the big house as Roberto was always around. He seemed to think that unless he was supervising things, valuable possessions would end up in the bin.

This was a golden opportunity and then she knew that he would walk away. They would both leave this behind but right now her want and her need poured through her like a deadly virus and the only way she could clear her system of it was to do what she was going to do, to sleep with this beautiful, arrogant, clever and utterly inappropriate man.

The jumper was on the floor and she unclasped her bra. She could feel his eyes on her and it was a little thrilling, if she was honest. The cool air hit her hot, naked breasts like soothing balm. The sort of women he dated didn't have breasts and she feverishly wondered what he thought of hers. Bigger than he had expected? Not neat and small enough?

Her breath was coming and going in painful gasps as he moved towards her and she fell into his arms, enjoying the way his jumper eased some of the pain of her sensitive nipples. She rubbed herself against him and he lifted her ear and whispered,

'You have the most amazing breasts...'

'They're far too big.'

'Amazing breasts and even more amazing nipples.'

'Too big as well.'

'That's not possible.' He propelled her gently towards the bed, which was unfortunately not king-sized, and Laura fell back onto the pillows with a heated sigh.

In the semi-darkness of the bedroom, Alessandro took a few seconds to just look at her. His erection was a shaft of steel, almost painful, but he had to regain some of his self-control or lose it completely.

Her arms were folded behind her head so that her breasts were pushed up, offering themselves to him like ripe, succulent fruit. She had removed her jogging bottoms but her panties were still on and he knew that if he felt them, they would be soaked through.

He got rid of his jumper and the T-shirt underneath. His hand loose on the button of his trousers, he took a few deep breaths and then pulled down the zipper, very slowly, taking his time. He didn't want to rush this but, God, he was close to coming just looking at her and at the drowsy smile tugging the corners of her mouth as she watched him.

'Enjoying the striptease?' he murmured roughly, and her smile broadened. She wriggled a little on the bed, parted her legs, and Alessandro emitted a low, unsteady groan.

'I've never been treated to one before,' she told him truthfully.

She was so turned on that she could barely get the words out. Even in the dim light she could see the proud bulge of his erection and she cupped her mound, then slid her hand under the panties because she was hurting down there, aching to be touched.

Alessandro stepped out of his trousers, then the boxers, retrieving a condom from his wallet, although he wasn't even conscious of doing so.

He flicked it onto the bedside table and remained standing next to the bed, completely naked.

He was bigger than big, Laura thought. Big all over. A broad-shouldered, powerfully built man and his erection was beyond impressive. She propped herself up on one hand and took him into her mouth, feeling him shudder with a kick of heady satisfaction.

He arched his back and his hand pressed to the back of her head, urging her to suck him, to taste him.

She licked and teased and played with him and his deep groans were impossibly sexy.

When he could take it no more he tugged himself free of her eager mouth and remained perfectly still, controlling his breathing with difficulty.

Finally, he looked down at her. 'I have never wanted any woman the way I want you now.'

Laura wasn't going to analyse that. She fell back onto the pillows, legs parted, and moaned softly when he joined her.

He kissed her slowly, taking his time, his tongue exploring her mouth, then he moved to trail kisses along her jawline. She arched up and then sighed, eyes fluttering shut as he took one nipple into his mouth and began suckling on it, lazy and thorough.

She was drowning in sensation and it was nothing like anything she had felt before.

This must be what it felt like to lose control utterly and completely, knowing that what you were enjoying was a one-off experience that had to be appreciated to the absolute utmost because it wasn't going anywhere and would probably not be repeated.

She was filled with a feeling of liberation. When he slipped his hand underneath her panties, she spread her legs a little wider and gasped as he began stroking her clitoris.

He rubbed his finger insistently over the throbbing nub until she was pleading with him to stop. She didn't want to come like this...

Alessandro straddled her. Opening her eyes to gaze at

him, Laura didn't think that she had ever seen anyone quite so beautiful and she felt that she probably never would again.

She held him in her hands but he gently disengaged her with a smile.

'This isn't just about my satisfaction,' he murmured huskily. 'This is about you as well…' He leaned down to lick her stomach, which was salty with perspiration, then he moved lower until his mouth was on her panties, and without removing them he teased her until she squirmed, until she could barely stand the intense excitement building inside her, an explosion that was on the brink of detonating.

Only then did he ever so slowly pull down her underwear, where it joined the heap of clothes on the floor.

He liked the way she wasn't all skin and bone. The soft roundness of her hips was an exquisite turn-on. Her breasts were abundant, succulent, and he could have stayed buried in them for far, far longer.

He breathed in the musky, honeyed scent between her legs and then gently slid his tongue into her, finding her clitoris once more, but this time the delicate thrust of his moist tongue was a mind-blowing experience for her. She instinctively reached down, curling her fingers into his dark hair, raising her legs slightly so that he could sink his tongue deeper into her.

She knew that she was groaning but the sounds she was making seemed to be coming from someone else, far away.

He teased her until she was going mad with wanting him, until the only satisfaction she needed was to have him in her, and in between the groans she knew that she was pleading with him to stop, to come inside her, that she *needed* him…*right now*…

'Demanding hussy.' Alessandro reached for the condom

and applied it with shaky fingers, resenting that brief interruption, that momentary parting of their bodies.

But he needed to come inside her, too, as much as she needed it.

Foreplay was all well and good but the tipping point had come far too close and far too often for his liking.

He thrust long and deep into her, loving her tight wetness and the way her legs slid up and around his waist so that he could reach and cup her buttocks in his big hands.

He would have liked to have exercised control. And he did, but he was driven to move faster, harder, and he knew that she had come when he felt her body stiffen and heard the rhythm of her breathing faster and faster, more and more breathless, until she was crying out and gasping at the same time.

Only then, and thankfully not a second too soon, did he allow himself the ultimate release. He reared back and reached an unbelievable orgasm on one deep thrust.

Caught in the grip of the physical, he had managed to set aside the ground-shaking conversation he had had with his father. Now, as he lay down next to her and felt the curve of her rounded body lean against him, Alessandro frowned, reliving that conversation.

The room felt too small and he swung his legs over the side of the bed and walked restlessly towards the window.

Laura felt a chill run through her and she sat up, pulling the quilt over her and clutching it under her breasts.

She had enjoyed her no-strings-attached experience and this was what the comedown felt like. Horrible. They had made love and now he couldn't even stand the thought of staying next to her in the bed for five seconds.

Hit-and-run was the expression that sprang to mind, but there was no way she was going to start raising objections or asking for more than he was prepared to give.

She had no idea what to say in a situation like this. She could feel a hollow emptiness clawing at her throat and she shot him a brave smile.

Alessandro noted that brave smile and raked his fingers through his hair. He'd sated his physical needs and he knew he should walk away. He also knew that he wasn't going to do that. Not yet. He'd had her and he wanted more.

He also needed…for the first time in his life after sex… to do more than glance at his watch and bring proceedings to an end.

'Has my father ever confided in you?' he asked abruptly, and she was so startled at his question that she stared at him in round-eyed silence. 'And please don't try lying to me.'

'Alessandro, I have no idea what you're talking about.'

'You and he seem to enjoy a close relationship and then throw your grandmother into the mix and we have a little circle of who knows what kind of touchy-feely confidence-sharing…' He remained by the window, propped against the ledge, arms folded, still completely and gloriously naked.

'Are you going to start accusing me of being a gold-digger all over again?' she asked tersely. 'Are you going to try insinuating that my grandmother and I are involved in some kind of seedy plot to take your father for everything he's got?' She felt tears sting the backs of her eyes. It was one thing to have a one-night stand with someone who was allergic to relationships, but it was something else to have a one-night stand and then be shoved into the firing line.

'I thought you'd got past all of that.'

Alessandro shook his head and pushed himself away from the window ledge to begin scooping up his clothes, his movements oddly lacking their usual grace.

'You found a scrapbook,' he said roughly. Jeans on, shirt

on, though with the buttons undone, he moved to stand by the bed, looking down at her with brooding intensity.

'Oh, yes. That. Alessandro, I don't know what you're talking about and you're making me nervous, standing there and glowering down at me.'

'What else might you have found that you failed to deliver to me?'

'*Deliver to you?* Is that what you think I should be doing? Sorting through your father's stuff and then handing over anything I think you might want to see? Even if it would be up to Roberto to do the handing over himself? Do you think I should be using this opportunity to *spy* on your father? See if he's been investing in anything dodgy? Or maybe sending money abroad because he's been scammed by some crooks somewhere? Or maybe he's just been hiding something you think you should know about! Because you should know *everything*, shouldn't you?'

'Should I?' He walked away and sat at the little chair by her dressing table, dwarfing it with his big, muscular frame. 'Well, it would appear not. I mean, I never knew, for starters, that my mother died giving birth to me.'

Laura gasped and sat forward. *'What?'*

'My father didn't share that with you?' He raked his fingers through his hair. He hadn't meant to say anything. He had needed to lose himself in her, had thought that sex would have been enough to still the turmoil in his head. Obviously not.

'No. He didn't. I…I don't understand. How is it that you're only now finding out about…about your mother?' She reached down to the side of the bed and yanked at her jumper, sticking it on and then wriggling into her underwear.

She couldn't remain lying down while he sat there…

She realised now how utterly self-controlled he was

now that that self-control had slipped. His expression was bleak and she just needed to hold him, touch him, but not in a sexual manner. She felt driven *to be there for him*, although that need barely registered as conscious thought.

There was a little rocking chair by the window, another legacy from her childhood, and she dragged it over so that she could sit right next to him. He didn't object when she laced her fingers through his.

'What else…?'

'What other revelations were aired? Now, let's see. Oh, yes, I had a sister. She died when she was twelve. Fell from a tree, of all things.'

'Alessandro…'

'That's when they decided that having another child might be a good idea. Or rather, reading between the lines, my mother thought it… Do you know something? I have no idea why I'm telling you this.'

'Because everyone needs to vent now and again.'

'I feel you might be confusing me with a loser.'

'Are you upset with him? Angry?' She ignored his dry dismissal of having feelings, of being vulnerable. She would have done anything to wipe the haunted expression from his face because it just didn't belong there.

'Both.' Alessandro shot her a crooked smile. Upset. Angry. Yes, he was both those things but in time those feelings would disappear and he knew that he would be grateful for the conversation he and his father had had, the revelations that had been made.

He was finally understanding why his father had been the remote figure in his life, how his grief over the loss of his much younger wife had somehow transferred into distance from the son he had held responsible.

'I was an old fool,' Roberto had growled, as uncomfortable with sharing his feelings as his son was, 'but the longer time went by, the more impossible it became to remedy the damage, and in the end there was just the silence between us. Should have opened up, explained everything. Got pictures of your mother. Loved that woman more than anything in the world. Would have died for her. When you're ready to forgive the old fool, you're welcome to see the pictures.'

'You know,' Laura said thoughtfully, 'he never talked about where he lived before he came here. There was always a part of himself that he kept hidden away from all of us.' Her fingers were still linked through his. This felt like a moment in time she wanted to bottle and keep for ever and it confused her because what they had meant nothing. They were like two ships passing in the night. They didn't have any sort of *relationship*. So why did she feel as though her heart was breaking when she imagined his life, growing up, when she saw the bleakness in his eyes? Why did she want to make it *all better*?

Alessandro shrugged. She could feel him begin to withdraw from her and she panicked at the thought that he might resent the fact that he had confided, that she had seen him with his guard down, as vulnerable as he was ever likely to be. He was a proud man, the lion accustomed to standing alone.

Now she knew why and she felt for him.

'Did you...come here...to make love to me...because...?'

Alessandro flushed darkly. 'I wanted you,' he said gruffly. 'I don't analyse things before that. And I should go now, before your grandmother returns home and catches me in a compromising situation with her granddaughter.' He began buttoning up his shirt but he didn't take his eyes from her.

He'd never confided in anyone before but he wasn't sorry he'd done so.

'I think,' he drawled, back to his usual self, 'that the

next time we should consider somewhere with a slightly less restricted bed.'

Her heart soared. *So there was going to be a next time...*

'When my grandmother bought me this bed...' she stuck on her jogging bottoms, feeling lighter now because he wasn't going to waltz off into the sunset and leave her behind just yet '...I was twelve. I never imagined I'd need a bigger one because I would one day find myself here with a guy...'

They walked back down the stairs but before they reached the door she rested her small hand on his arm.

'Are you going to be all right?'

Alessandro looked down into her clear, concerned, green eyes and smiled lazily.

'Are you feeling sorry for me?'

She immediately removed her hand. 'I'm sorry for both of you,' she answered honestly. 'For all the time you've lost.'

'I'll go,' Alessandro said, in that same tone of voice that told her that the confidences were over and would not be returning, 'before you decide that you need to give me a hug. I've never been one who saw the point of hugs when it came to women. So many more exciting things to do and, unfortunately for us, not quite enough time at the moment.'

But something about the sincere sympathy in her open, honest, clear-eyed gaze got to him.

She hadn't been gushy in her sympathy. She hadn't tried to plead with him to stay so that she could try to take advantage of his once-in-a-lifetime lapse in self-control. She hadn't plied him with concerned questions and then offered some repeat sex to take the pain away or any such nonsense.

But, then, she was in a league of her own. She wasn't part of his London life, wasn't dating him, wasn't looking for anything more than what they had, which was a brief and highly enjoyable fling, the result of circumstances more than anything else. She knew his father. In many ways their lives were entwined, which was certainly a situation he had never catered for.

And she was a fantastic lover.

As he drove away, he felt himself harden at the memory of their lovemaking. She was responsive, eager, not trying to impress him with gymnastic skill and not making noises about meeting up soon for an encore.

In receipt of his father's confidences, she had been just what he had needed.

And he knew that he wanted more of her.

His father was asleep by the time he got home. Tomorrow they would talk again. Laura had been right when she had said that she felt sorry for both of them and the time they had wasted, the years that had raced by during which he had been ignorant of the jigsaw-puzzle pieces of his past.

He had assumed that his father had been as remote with his wife as he had been with his son. He had been wrong. His father had been giddy with love and when he had lost her he had lost the will to carry on. Certainly, he had lost all desire to bond with the son who was a painful reminder of the woman he had loved and lost. He had buried himself in his work to the exclusion of everything else, using it as a crutch to get him through the loneliness.

For once Alessandro went to bed without first checking his emails, making sure that everything that should be happening in his company was happening.

His father was already up and about by the time he hit the kitchen the next morning, and there were two black leather boxes on his side of the table.

'More where those came from,' Roberto said gruffly. 'And don't just stand there staring at them, my boy! Open them up! Should have given them to you a long time ago.'

Alessandro looked at his father, who was busying himself with the kettle and a mug, fetching stuff from one of the kitchen cupboards. 'Well…' Roberto turned around, studiously keeping his eyes averted, and waved an impatient hand '…what are you waiting for? Be dead by the time you make your mind up! Want you to get to know your mother. Should have done it a long time ago. Would have, but…'

'Time runs away,' Alessandro finished succinctly. 'Don't worry. I intend to look at all those photos.'

'Forgive me, boy?'

Alessandro had never thought he would be having this conversation with his father or hearing those words, and something deep in the core of him shifted. 'Depends…' he drawled.

'On what, eh?'

'On how cooperative you are about moving into the cottage before the greenhouse has been built to your absolute specifications…because that's proving a little trickier than you'd expect…'

Roberto relaxed, shot him a gruff smile. 'I'm an old man. Not sure I can make compromises with my tomatoes and orchids. I'll give it my best shot, though.'

CHAPTER EIGHT

LAURA DIDN'T KNOW what to expect when she came to the house the following morning.

A bitter wind had got up and light flurries of snow speckled a yellow-grey sky. Winter had been strangely polite for the past few weeks but now she could feel it getting ready to make up for lost ground. It was always the way in this part of the world. No civilised, rainy, fairly temperate winters but brutal, freezing-cold ones punctuated by blizzards and dense snowfalls.

She had left her grandmother sorting out the log pile with the radio on full blast and she was relieved that she was on her own. She needed time to get her thoughts in order.

The night before had shaken her. She hadn't expected Alessandro to show up at the house. The way they had spent so much time circling around one another…sharing the odd thrilling touch when Roberto's attention had happened to be elsewhere… It had turned into an almost surreal situation. The reality of their one kiss had become imbued with a dreamlike quality and sometimes she had questioned whether it had really happened or not.

She had wondered if they would ever make love. Or was this just a game they would play, almost getting there but not quite, until the time came when he disappeared over the horizon, never to be seen again or else to be seen only in passing?

She had known that if he disappeared over that horizon, then that would be it. He would fall back into his London life and she would become an almost-there non-experience that he would look back upon with…

She didn't know. Mild regret? Relief? Amusement?

The longer they had circled one another, sharing fleeting glances, the more she felt that they would never make love, even though it was what she had wanted more than anything else.

So when he had turned up unannounced, she had been thrilled, apprehensive, seized with soaring excitement.

And if she'd had any doubts about her decision, they had evaporated the second he had touched her. Sooner. The second she had answered the door to him.

Driving through the snow flurries, she was oblivious to the gathering white around her because she was so immersed in her thoughts.

She had thought he had come to her because he hadn't been able to bear the edge-of-the-cliff suspense that had developed between them, the agonising feeling of wanting something that was just beyond reach. She had thought that he had reached the end of his tether and had found the situation as frustrating as she had.

Yes, he had wanted her but he had come to her because he had wanted physical release and she couldn't help but feel that any willing body might have done at a pinch. He had been dealt a bolt from the blue, had been given an overload of information, and the only way he had been able to process that had been through making love. He was an intensely physical man and it would have made complete sense to him to subdue whatever upset he had been feeling by sleeping with a woman, by losing himself in the act of sex.

It was painful for her to accept that if she hadn't been there, he might have just had one of his many devoted fans flown up to sate his passing need.

And yet he had said that he still wanted her.

Laura knew that she should have killed that at source but she had cravenly succumbed to the pleasurable notion that their weird, fragile relationship might carry on for a little longer.

Now, as she neared the big house, she wondered whether that hadn't just been pie in the sky, something he had said on the spur of the moment because he hadn't been himself. People said all sorts of things when they weren't themselves. He had let his guard slip with her and she knew instinctively that he hadn't planned on that happening. He was a guy who liked complete and absolute control. His formidable control had been dealt a near lethal blow and he had, against all his better judgement, opened up to her. Partially. Enough for her to think that the best thing she could do now would be to pretend that everything was fine, that nothing had changed.

She wasn't going to make noises about wanting him. She wasn't going to let him think that he had to worry about her trying to manoeuvre him into a cubbyhole somewhere because he had made a mistake and said stuff he hadn't meant to say.

She certainly wasn't going to try to encourage him to open up to her, to really express what he felt about what he had been told by his father, the secrets that had been revealed, even though that was something she wanted more than anything.

And that, she thought, pulling to a stop in the courtyard, scared her.

She stared out at the falling snow and frowned. Of course she would be empathetic to anyone whose life had been blighted in the way Alessandro's had been, but what she felt was more than detached empathy and that frightened her. The emotions running through her felt complicated and involved, and with a sigh of frustration she headed towards the house, knowing that the only way to deal with the situation was to ignore it.

So when she rang the doorbell and Alessandro opened the door, she smiled politely and informed him, in a bouncy voice, that she had come to help, if more help was needed, with some of the packing.

She was wrapped up in several layers but she made sure not to begin removing any of them just in case he told her that her help wouldn't be needed.

'I probably wouldn't have come if I'd realised how fast the snow was falling,' she chirruped, 'but by the time my windscreen wipers were on full blast I was practically turning into your drive...' It was an effort to meet those dark, penetrating eyes. He hadn't shaved and he didn't look as though he had run a comb through his hair, but instead of looking untidy he looked dangerously, heart-stoppingly sexy. She wanted to stare and stare. She felt the pulse beating frantically in her neck and her mouth was dry, so dry that she was finding it difficult to swallow.

He was in a pair of faded, low-slung jeans and an old rugby sweater, with just a pair of loafers on his feet. No socks. He couldn't have looked more casual and yet more sophisticated.

Alessandro stared down at her, frowning because this was just the sort of unenthusiastic greeting he didn't want. Not when he had spent most of the night consumed by her, thoughts of her, her smell, her taste, the feel of her under his hands, under his mouth, under his body. He had wanted, *needed*, to drown out his thoughts in her glorious body and he had, so what was wrong with expecting a little more of the teasing temptress when he wanted a repeat performance? Naturally, it would have been too much to maybe expect her to turn up wearing a fur coat with nothing underneath because that would have been utterly impractical and, besides, it wasn't her style. But she *could* have made some attempt to collar him by the front door and drag him off to the nearest vacant room…

After a night of beyond-fantastic sex, safe in the knowledge that he hadn't yet lost interest, there wasn't a single woman he could think of who wouldn't have been planning just how to hold and maintain his interest. Any woman would have shown up in her sexiest house-clearing clothes, feather duster in hand and a very good idea of what she was going to do with it.

A quick glance was enough to tell him that underneath her layers and layers and yet more layers of clothes Laura was probably fully kitted out in her most sensible underwear. He didn't imagine she even owned a feather duster, and if she had it would have been used strictly for dusting.

So they weren't going to get wrapped up in any sort of happy-ever-after scenario, but nevertheless…

He leaned nonchalantly against the door frame and folded his arms. 'There's always time to back up and leave the way you came,' he said coolly. 'Wouldn't want you to be trapped here by falling snow. Happens in this part of the world. I've been told often enough by my father.'

Laura's eyes skittered away and she felt a lump form at the back of her throat.

'You don't want me here, in other words,' she said flatly.

'Come in.' He stepped aside, allowing her to brush past him. Was she going to pretend that they hadn't made love?

he wondered. The mere thought that she might go down that road staggered him.

'Where's Roberto? I'd love to go and have a chat with him. I haven't seen him properly to talk to for a while.' She glanced beyond his shoulder because it gave her eyes time to take a rest from their compulsive staring.

'He's in his greenhouse, having a quick chat to his plants to make sure they're up for the upheaval of moving.' Roberto? *Roberto?* She shouldn't be *asking* about his father! She should be taking advantage of their brief window of privacy to source the nearest empty room!

Women chased Alessandro. He had never really had any need to try. He had the looks, he had the money and he had that all-important invisible aphrodisiac called *power*. He had always been able to enjoy his position of strength from the top of his ivory tower, safe in the expectation that people would come to him and never, ever the other way around.

He had trained himself to enjoy his formidable independence, had liked the fact that he had never had to adjust any part of his life to accommodate anyone else.

His boarding-school experience, pleasant though it had been, had turned him into someone who needed no one and sought no one's approval. The one thing to be said for an absolute lack of family life was that it gave you strength of character, and as far as Alessandro was concerned, that was more important than anything else.

So it was as frustrating as hell to now find himself on the back foot while she continued to frown and scour the hallway as if he had deliberately hidden his father from her.

'Perhaps I could go see him, take him a cup of tea before we get down to the business of clearing...'

There was nothing she had just said that Alessandro was interested in hearing.

'How is he dealing with…? How are you *both* dealing with everything that's happened? I hope you don't mind but I've told my grandmother some of what you said to me, and it seems that she *did* know bits and pieces…'

Alessandro relaxed. This was more like it. Sympathy… tears glistening in eyes…a trembling hand gently laid on his arm…

Under *any* other circumstances he would have been repelled at having his private life regurgitated for the purposes of speculation. It had to be said, though, that he would never have confided in anyone else and the only reason he had felt the need to confide in Laura was because of her connection to his father. And the fact that she was raising the subject now…well, he wasn't going to shoot her down in flames, even though he wasn't about to oblige her by launching into some long, tear-jerking, over-sentimental nonsense. In fact…

'He's fine. We're both fine. It's been…an eye-opener, hearing what my father has had to say.' He jerked his head in the direction of the kitchen. 'I always wondered why the kitchen was so full of old furniture. It seems that when my father moved from the cottage where he and my mother lived, the kitchen furniture, along with the oven, were the only reminders he took of the life he left behind.' He frowned, not sure whether he had intended saying so much.

'I always wondered where he had lived before and how it was he never, ever spoke about it…'

'Cup of coffee?'

'Huh?'

'I'll make you a cup of coffee before we kick-start the day.'

'Right. Sure.' Message received loud and clear. He wasn't going to take her into his confidence again. Why should he? She was a fling and flings didn't qualify for that kind of depth. 'Maybe I could pop out...see your dad...'

'He'll be in shortly,' Alessandro said irritably, spinning on his heel and making for the kitchen. 'You don't need to fuss around him like a mother hen, Laura. When he goes to his greenhouse it's because he needs downtime on his own, not because he wants a queue of people lining up to bring him cups of tea and bracing chats.'

'You're so sarcastic,' she muttered, following him and divesting herself of some of her clothes on the way. By the time she made it to the kitchen door she was down to her fleece. How was it that her *casual* managed to look so charity shop? The jeans were okay but it was really cold out and she had worn her thermal knee-high socks, pulled up over the skinny jeans, both of which were tucked into her fur-lined boots. She knew she looked a sight. She had bunched her hair up into a woolly hat and now it was released into all its crazy glory.

Was he looking at her and wondering how on earth he had been idiotic enough to have ever found her attractive?

He'd made absolutely no mention of renewing any kind of relationship and that, she told herself, was probably for the best.

So why did she feel sick and hollow inside?

He had his back to her as he made them both a cup of coffee and when he turned around she made sure to school her features into the polite smile of someone whose thoughts were far removed from sex.

'Come again?' Alessandro sauntered towards her. Her fleece was an unappealing shade of green but the jeans were nicely tight and even the strange socks halfway up her calves did nothing to detract from the bolt of pure lust that ripped through him.

In his head, he had a perfectly good image of what she

looked like underneath the layers. He could recreate the taste of her and the feel of her with no trouble at all.

'Nothing,' she muttered, taking the mug from him and sidling across to the table, where she sat, blowing on the hot coffee and keeping her eyes pointedly averted.

'Tell me what game we're playing,' Alessandro drawled, moving to perch on the table right next to where she was sitting so that she was forced to look up at him.

'Game?' Laura parroted feebly.

'Because if it's the game of playing hard to get, you can scrap it before it begins.'

'I have no idea what you're talking about!'

'I'm talking about the polite semi-stranger act you're busy trying to perfect.'

'I'm not about to start chasing you, Alessandro.' Laura abandoned the tactic of pretending to misunderstand what he was saying. 'And I'm not playing hard to get. I don't play games!' She glared at him.

'So are we going to both make-believe that last night didn't happen? Shall we enter a conspiracy of silence?'

'I know what you're like and I'm not going to be one of those women who gets clingy in the aftermath of sex.'

'What am I like?'

'You run away from forming relationships faster than a speeding bullet,' she told him bluntly. 'I bet the second a woman starts making plans, you start wondering where the nearest exit is.'

Alessandro laughed, his dark eyes roving over her flushed face appreciatively. 'I like your sense of humour,' he murmured in a voice that was the equivalent of oozing, liquid chocolate, the sort of voice that made her knees feel like jelly and turned her brains into instant mush.

'And I happen to be very good at forming relationships, although, admittedly, they're not of the lasting kind. But that's not relevant with us, is it? You know the measure of me, and after your mistake with a married man you're hardly on the lookout for someone who's not talking long-term. Did you…?' A sudden thought flashed through his head, leaving a sour taste in its wake. 'Did you love the guy?'

'Colin?' She was disconcerted by the question because she didn't think that Alessandro was the sort of man prone to showing much interest in what women had to say about their past relationships. In keeping with someone who planned nothing in advance, because who knew when someone better looking might come along and steal the limelight, she took him for a guy who lived totally for the present. At least in the arena of relationships.

'I thought I did,' she confessed, when the silence threatened to become uncomfortable. 'But I was just swept away by someone cute who knew how to play me. I think I fell in love with the feeling of being in love.' And, in fact, she hardly thought about him and now, sitting here, she could barely remember what he had looked like. 'I suppose you're going to tell me that that's the problem with love. It doesn't exist so it's best to avoid it altogether and just hop in the sack with people you fancy.'

Alessandro smiled slowly and watched as hectic colour invaded her cheeks.

'Would you follow my advice if I told you that?'

'You might not believe in love, but I do.'

'Yet you hopped in the sack with me.'

'You don't have to look so smug about it.'

'I like the thought of you just not being able to help yourself…' He calmly set his mug down on the table and traced the contour of her jaw with a finger.

'That's so arrogant,' Laura told him unevenly.

'I know. I'm arrogant. I want to kiss you and I'm arrogant enough to think that you'd probably like to kiss me back. Am I right? Or are you going to stand up and slap me across my face?'

'Has anyone ever done that?'

'No.' He was smiling at her in a way that made her whole body feel as though it had been plugged into a light socket.

'I don't know why I'm attracted to you,' she said with devastating honesty.

'That's a line of introspection you shouldn't bother wasting time with. There's no mileage in it. Go with the flow.' He tugged her hair gently and she stood up on shaky legs.

She wasn't just *attracted* to him, she thought, she was mesmerised by him. Was it because he was so out of her league? Or because the circumstances that had brought them together were so surreal? Or was he just so sinfully, unfairly good-looking that he just went around mesmerising women?

She linked her arms loosely around his neck and stepped between his legs. His body heat flooded her and she hiccuped a sigh of guilty pleasure.

They kissed slowly, taking their time. She pulled away briefly and glanced over her shoulder.

'What if your father walks in?'

'He won't.'

'How do you know?'

'I know his habits. He heads out to his greenhouse and stays there for a couple of hours. I only just ventured inside the place a few days ago and found that he's set it up like a room. The only thing it lacks is a bed. He's got a chair there, a table with books. It's life in a jungle without having to pay the airfare...'

Laura giggled. She didn't want to talk about Roberto.

She wanted to feel his lips on hers again and she moved closer, rubbing herself against his chest and kissing him as slowly as he had kissed her. His tongue inside her mouth was driving her half-crazy because she could recall what it had felt like to have it on her breasts, teasing her nipples and then sliding into her, flicking against her clitoris until she had been so close to coming she could have screamed.

She wished she hadn't covered up so well that for him to slide his hand onto her breast would have been a mission. She wished she hadn't worn a bra in the expectation that their episode of lovemaking was something he might have wanted to put behind him. She wanted her whole body to be accessible. She didn't want to be confined in tight jeans. She wanted baggy, loose-fitting jogging bottoms so that she could have parted her legs and his fingers would have easily found her wetness and eased the ache down there.

But in the absence of suitable clothing she kissed him, not even bothering to come up for air because she didn't want to break the physical contact.

Alessandro had never tasted anything so sweet. He absently thought that she had a unique smell, light, clean, radiating the coldness from outside. It filled his nostrils and was as powerful on his senses as a drug.

Her breasts, pushing against his chest, were soft, abundant, begging to be touched. If they'd had guaranteed privacy, he wouldn't have hesitated to rip off her clothes, because he ached to feel her naked skin against his.

She had a body a man could get lost in and the beauty of it was that she wasn't even aware of her powerful sex appeal. The catwalk models he had always dated knew the power of their physical appeal and utilised it. No one was ever allowed to bypass them or to forget that they were stunning. They maximised their assets.

Laura Reid downplayed hers. She did her utmost to

blend into the background. She hid her bountiful breasts and camouflaged the lush sexiness of her hips and legs.

He curved his hand over her bottom and massaged its fullness, then he swept the same hand between her legs and pressed hard so that his knuckles were kneading her, seeking to find that throbbing little bud underneath the thick denim.

It took them both a couple of seconds before they recognised the sharp rap of a walking stick on the floor, and as if one sharp rap wasn't enough Roberto kept on rapping until they snapped apart and turned to look at him.

Laura felt the hot burn of embarrassment flood her. She was twelve years old again and her grandmother was ticking her off because she had sneaked downstairs to snitch a bar of chocolate in the middle of the night. She ran her trembling fingers through her hair but she couldn't say anything because her vocal cords seemed to have seized up.

Roberto looked absolutely furious.

'This will never do!' His attention was not on her. It was on Alessandro, who, likewise, was temporarily lost for words as his father angrily tapped his way into the kitchen and stood in front of them like a judge about to sentence a couple of criminals.

'What are you talking about?'

'I know what you're like with the women, my boy, and Laura isn't one of those strumpets you take to bed and then discard like a pair of old shoes!'

Alessandro raked his fingers through his hair and glared at his father. 'I don't know what you're talking about.'

'You know exactly what I'm talking about!' He slumped into one of the kitchen chairs and glared balefully at his son. 'I really thought we were beginning to go somewhere with our relationship, son. But straight away I see that I'm never going to understand you.' He fluttered his hand and looked defeated.

'You've got it all wrong,' Alessandro said, and Roberto eyed his son with a glimmer of doubt.

'I come in here and you're making a pass at this young girl!'

'I'm here, Roberto.' Laura finally found her voice and interrupted him before he could resume his attack on Alessandro. 'And it…er…takes two to…er…tango…'

'Nonsense!' Roberto swept aside the interruption while keeping his eyes firmly fixed on his son. 'You don't know Alessandro like I do,' he declared, his voice rising along with his colour.

'Please, Roberto…' She rested her hand anxiously on his shoulder and looked at Alessandro. 'Have you forgotten that you've recently had a stroke?'

'Not likely to when I'm packing up to move because I'm too infirm to stay anywhere that has more than three bedrooms!' He was still staring at Alessandro and he finally said, 'What do you mean when you tell me that *I've got it all wrong*? Fancy explaining yourself, lad?'

'You think you know me,' Alessandro said quietly, defusing the heated atmosphere in a way that Laura could only admire because she had a feeling that giving way like this was just not his style. His physical stillness permeated the room, calming the situation. 'And I admit that my behaviour with women might have seemed a little on the cavalier side…'

Roberto snorted and raised his eyebrows with open cynicism. 'Seemed? *Seemed?*'

'But I realise that Laura isn't—'

'One of those fly-by-night trollops you have one-night stands with? Might be old, son, but I ain't stupid!'

'I never thought you were. What I'm saying…' He had

managed to get himself back in order while, standing to one side, Laura felt as dishevelled as she had fifteen minutes earlier when Roberto had walked in on them.

Alessandro sighed heavily and threw her a very quick look before focusing on his father once more. 'What I'm saying is that this is…different…'

Laura's mouth fell open.

'Laura and I have a very special connection. She's not one of my fly-by-night trollops.' Alessandro thought wryly that some of the catwalk models he'd dated, whose faces adorned high-end fashion magazines, would have been appalled to have been described as *fly-by-night trollops*.

'Special connection?' He humphed and looked between them.

'This is serious,' Alessandro said gravely, and Laura made an effort to rescue her jaw from where it had fully dropped to the floor. Her feet remained nailed down as he moved smoothly to where she was standing and linked his fingers through hers in a gesture that was oddly chaste.

'How serious?' Roberto asked, eyes narrowed, his voice still bearing the traces of lingering scepticism, and Laura, frankly, couldn't blame him. She only hoped that he didn't turn to her for confirmation of what Alessandro had said, because she had no idea where this was going.

Although she did know where it had come from.

He and his father had arrived at a fragile truce after more than two decades of a civilised but frosty relationship. A door, formerly closed, had opened between them. Not fully but enough, and she guessed that Alessandro wasn't about to jeopardise that now. Throw into the mix the fact that Roberto's health was not as robust as it might have been, and she could understand why Alessandro might have found himself in an impossible situation.

'Very serious,' Alessandro said seriously.

'In that case, I'm prepared to give you the benefit of the doubt!' He eyed Laura. 'Edith know about this?'

'No,' Laura said truthfully. As far as she was aware, her grandmother didn't even know that she and Alessandro had anything going on between them but a purely working relationship, but who knew?

'Then if you lovebirds will excuse me…might just go and fill her in.' He waved his hand between them and headed out of the kitchen, leaving in his wake utter and complete silence, which Laura was the first to break.

'What the heck did you just go and do?' she cried, pulling away from him to stand by the table, arms tightly clasped around herself.

Alessandro took his time answering. 'I salvaged your reputation,' he drawled, with such barefaced arrogance that she was momentarily stunned.

'You salvaged *my* reputation by pretending that we have some sort of serious relationship that's actually going somewhere?' She laughed shortly, although her heart did a treacherous little flip inside her. She didn't want a serious relationship with him…*did she*? A fine film of perspiration broke out on her skin. This wasn't what this was about. This was about lust. Lust was simple. Anything more than that was a dangerous minefield.

'Did you really want my father to think that you were the sort of girl who would jump into bed with a guy just for the hell of it? You don't have to be a genius to see that my father's placed you on some sort of pedestal. I might have known that a lot sooner if we'd had the sort of father-son relationship where meaningful conversation played a part, but we didn't, so I never even knew of your existence until I came here. But as soon as I saw the interaction between the two of you, I knew that he…maybe looks on you as the daughter he once had.' Alessandro's voice was gruff and he began to prowl restlessly through the kitchen, pausing only to lean heavily on the counter by the kitchen sink, where he stared out of the window for a while at the acres of open fields and cultivated gardens outside, barely visible in the thickening snow.

'Did you…' he turned to face her '…really want me to shatter those illusions?'

'Maybe not, but to lead him on like that…'

'It's not a complete lie. We do have a relationship.'

'Of sorts, Alessandro. We have a relationship *of sorts*.' And she wasn't going to make the mistake of turning that into anything else. 'We have the sort of relationship that's going to fizzle out the minute you leave here and return to London. That's something we both knew from the very beginning.' She was proud of the way her voice was low but calm, urgent but composed.

'Let's get past the moral high ground,' he drawled with infuriating arrogance. 'There was also the issue of my father's health. He hasn't been a well man. I had several conversations with his consultant when he had his stroke a few months ago, and I was told that lack of stress was the safest route to ensuring that his health continued to improve.'

'That's rich, considering you came here to yank him away from everything he was accustomed to.'

Alessandro flushed darkly. 'When I decided to move him down to London, I wasn't aware of the extent of the ties he had built up in the community.'

Laura reddened because she knew that. Everything had been straightforward when he had made the decision to move Roberto. He could never have foreseen the way events would unfold.

'It's bad enough that your father thinks that we're involved but it's only going to be worse when he tells my grandmother. She spent so long clucking around me when

I returned to Scotland that she's going to think you're a knight in shining armour who's come swooping in to rescue me. I can't think of anyone less like a knight in shining armour,' she finished glumly, for good measure, missing the irritated frown that darkened his face.

'Well, here we are,' he said silkily. 'For better or for worse.'

'And where do we go from here?'

'Like I said to you earlier, let's just go with the flow.' He shot her a wicked smile, which she did her best to ignore, and walked slowly towards her. 'We may not end up walking up the aisle in happily married bliss but we're good together. Let's not think beyond that.' To prove his point, he touched her cheek and, with satisfaction, watched the way her eyelids fluttered. 'When the time comes, we break up and there will be no fuss. Relationships end, even those that begin with high hopes...so, until that happens, let's take this golden opportunity to enjoy one another.'

No strings attached...and no hiding... He made it sound so simple. So why, Laura wondered, did it feel so dangerous?

CHAPTER NINE

A PROPER HOLIDAY!

Roberto and Edith had confronted them an hour later and announced that that was what they should do. Despite the snow, *the serious relationship* had been compelling enough for Roberto to get in touch with his occasional driver, who had brought Edith to the manor house posthaste.

Laura had been horrified.

She was still reeling from the shock of Alessandro's deception and the ease with which he had accepted their fling as something that would now carry on until, presumably, he got fed up and decided to call it a day. He just went right ahead and assumed that the ball was in his court, that he called the shots, and now the way had been paved for the whole thing to cost him a lot less effort.

For Alessandro, fabricating a so-called serious relationship to appease his father made perfect sense. Indeed, it was an improvement on trying to figure out the details of how they could conduct a sexual liaison behind Roberto's back.

The situation had moved so swiftly that Laura felt as though she had inadvertently stepped onto a roller coaster and was now being swung in sickening circles hundreds of metres above the ground.

Her life had been so orderly before he had crash-landed

into it. She had been contentedly doing her teaching job and getting over her awful experience in London. The peace of Scotland had been a soothing balm for her fraught nerves and if she hadn't asked herself any questions about how long she could continue leading a life of relative contentment before restlessness began to set in, it was because she had chosen not to.

And then suddenly there he was, the missing son whom she had never seen, bringing with him just the sort of dark excitement she had sworn to stay well away from.

Worse—bringing the sort of dark excitement she had never dreamed possible. It overshadowed everything Colin had represented. He had turned those dark, lazy, arrogant eyes on her and her peaceful world had been shattered into smithereens.

It was so simple for him. He took what he wanted. Just the sort of guy she should have run from and kept on running from until she ran out of breath and found herself a nice little hole to hide in.

But what had she done instead? She had let those eyes settle on her, mesmerise her, get her thinking all sorts of things about the perfectly adequate life she had been content to lead.

Wasn't it better to live a little? To take a chance? Why fight the overwhelming attraction she felt for him? Why store up regret for missed opportunities? Why not get out of her comfort zone?

He had infected her with his cavalier way of thinking and she had yielded mindlessly.

She could control physical attraction, she had argued. If anything, it would do her good not to pigeonhole herself.

She'd never expected that she would become so entangled in his narrative to the extent that she lost track of her own.

And here she was now. Involved in a charade of a relationship for the benefit of her grandmother and his father. He might be able to take that in his stride but she wasn't fashioned from such stern stuff.

Guilt nagged at the edges of her consciousness and she surfaced to find that a long weekend was being planned around her. A cup of tea had found itself in her hand and she sipped some hurriedly as she tried to gather herself and focus.

'That house of yours!' Roberto was booming with authority. 'Made a big deal of it in the newspapers a few years ago! Bought with some of the petty cash from that oil-refinery deal of yours! Somewhere hot…escapes me where…'

'The Caribbean,' Alessandro filled in succinctly, amused and still startled at just how much information his father had gathered about him over the years. He looked at Laura, who was gulping down her tea as though her life depended on it.

'Bet you've never stepped foot in the place!' His father looked at him shrewdly and Alessandro decided on the spot that that was precisely where he would take her. Why not?

He didn't like the way he couldn't stop thinking of her. He'd had enough upheavals of late without his work life suffering further because it was constantly being interrupted with visions of her in his arms, naked and spreading her legs, begging for him. He needed to get her out of his system, and once he'd done that he would allow a decent interval before letting slip that things, sadly, had not worked out. Life. What could you do?

In the meanwhile, a few days of uninterrupted sex should do the trick.

If she didn't decide to throw obstacles in the way, and from the look of her stubborn little mouth, he wasn't sure.

He banked down a spurt of irritation. 'It's been hard to find the time,' he murmured. 'Of course, it hasn't been entirely unused. I reward top employees with the occasional holiday there. But you know what? I think a few days' relaxation in the sun wouldn't be a bad idea…'

'But what about the house? The move? All the packing left to do?' Belatedly, she remembered that she was supposed to have found the love of her life, and she tempered her borderline refusal with a smile. 'Just saying…'

'Taking those objections in order,' Alessandro informed her comfortably, 'the house is progressing smoothly, the move is scheduled to take place within the next three weeks and as for the packing…well, we've covered the better part of anything too valuable for the removal men. Why don't we let my father and Edith take it from here? They may want to spend some time together without having us around as chaperones…'

'I'm not sure about clothes…stuff for warm weather…'

Alessandro shrugged his shoulders as though that particular objection wasn't worth answering. 'Don't tell me you only have a wardrobe of winter gear. I won't believe you.' He slanted her a smile of amused, indulgent warmth. 'It may rain and snow a lot in Scotland but summer still occurs once a year. Correct me if I'm wrong. Shorts and T-shirt weather? Anyway, there are one or two shops on the island, if memory serves me. I may not have been there for a couple of years but I distinctly remember them catering lavishly for the tourists. Leave tomorrow morning, return Sunday evening. What could be more relaxing?'

Laura thought that it might have been very relaxing if they weren't going to be labouring under a cloud of deception. As it stood, she could think of a million more relaxing ways of spending a weekend.

'Seems an awfully long way to go for just a few days…' She smiled weakly because Roberto and her grandmother were both staring at her as though she had taken leave of her senses. 'Jet lag, you know…'

'You're young!' Roberto barked, dismissing this half-hearted objection with a wave of his walking stick. 'Leave the complaints about jet lag to old fogies like Edith and myself! *We're* the ones who would suffer from jet lag after a long flight! Suffer from jet lag when I go to Edinburgh! Take yourself out there, my girl, and see a bit of the world! *You…*' he looked at Laura from under his bushy brows '…need to get out of here for a little while before you start fossilising…remember that you're still young! And *you…*' he looked at Alessandro '…need a break from that computer of yours! Not to mention that I could do without having you under my feet all the time! Everywhere I look you're there, nagging, nagging, nagging…'

Over the next twenty-four hours, Laura felt her panic level rise.

She no longer knew where she stood. Her grandmother had cornered her the second they were back at their house and had started making noises about engagements, marriage and babies. She had turned misty-eyed at the thought of a little great-granddaughter. Laura had been frankly appalled but had had to smile through the conversation while making sure to reveal as little as possible.

Yes, she could understand why Alessandro had said what he had said on the spur of the moment, but she still simmered with resentment because it was an added complication to a situation that had already been threatening to become complicated.

Involvement.

That was the dreaded word that hovered at the back of her mind like a nasty little thorn.

She had stupidly signed up for a bit of fun. She had conveniently overlooked the fact that she wasn't a *fun girl*. She was a serious girl who wanted love, security and commitment. And while she had enjoyed every second of Alessandro's raw physicality, she had also strayed into more dangerous territory, had allowed herself to become involved with him. She had done that because that was just *who she was*. Fighting her own nature would have been like trying to plug a leaking hole in a dam with sticky tape.

Which was why, now, waiting for him to collect her and take her to the airport, she just didn't know what she had got herself into.

Her grandmother had been fussing since dawn and had made her a little packed breakfast to take with her in the car. Or on the plane. She had been repeatedly given strict instructions about sunblock, even though Laura couldn't see how much damage could be done to her skin in the space of a couple of days. She had been warned several times about mosquitoes.

She heard the sharp ring of the doorbell and there was a flurry of goodbyes and then she was in the car with him. The snow had diminished overnight, but the fields were still thinly covered and the temperature was bitingly cold.

'It's not going to be a very enjoyable long weekend if you decide to give me the silent treatment,' Alessandro drawled, casting a sideways look at her. He startled her by pulling over to the side of the isolated road and killing the engine.

'What are you doing?'

'Getting our relaxing break off to a good start.'

Laura's eyes skittered over his potent, masculine body,

idly leaning against the car door as he looked at her. She felt a rush of pure sexual craving and wondered why on earth she couldn't just relax and enjoy the situation for what it was. After all, there wasn't anything she could do to change it.

And it wasn't as if they hadn't already made love. They had. He knew her body as intimately as she knew his.

'You're overanalysing. You're letting your mind run away with all sorts of erroneous detail because my father knows about us. So he knows. So he thinks that what we have is more than it actually is. That's an unalterable fact, but,' he said drily, 'let me make this very simple for you. I want you. You want me. And we're about to go abroad for three days of very hot sex.'

'You're very black and white.'

'I'm a pragmatist.' His lean face wore a wolfish expression. In one easy movement he leaned towards her and slowly raised her thick jumper, then the thermal long-sleeved vest underneath, until both were gathered above her breasts.

He was proving how simple sex was. She knew that and while her head was jammed with conflicting thoughts, she still couldn't resist the warm pressure of his hands as he reached behind to unclasp the bra so that her breasts spilled out, her nipples tightening at the drop in temperature.

He looked at them, dark eyes hot and appreciative.

'We…we should be going to the airport… We can't… Not here…'

'I'm not going to make love in this car,' Alessandro said, his eyes flicking to her heated face. 'Too small for a big man like me. No, I'm just going to do a little touching…' He leaned over to lick her nipples and she sank lower in the car seat. To watch his dark head suckling at her breasts with the bleak open fields stretching on either side was unbelievably erotic. Wetness seeped through her underwear but in the confined space she couldn't rub her legs together to relieve the ache there and he wasn't going to put her out of her torment by going any further than her breasts.

It was sweet torture and she was as helpless as a kitten as he continued to suck and tease her nipples. The only sounds were the sounds of his mouth on her, and then he stopped and neatly pulled down her bra, her vest and the jumper, and sat back.

'Enjoy what we have,' he said, starting the car and slowly pulling away from the grass verge to continue their journey. 'We are where we are. No need to get tense about it.'

Laura was busy doing up her bra, tidying herself and wondering how he could manage to prove a point with such consummate ease. How could she explain to him that she wasn't as black and white as he was, when she had gaily launched herself into a no-strings-attached affair, cheerfully accepting that it was going nowhere? What right did she have to suddenly start pulling moral scruples out of the bag? How hypocritical was that?

They were going by private jet. For such a short holiday, she was told that it worked. She listened and contributed to the conversation. She knew that she was asking all sorts of interested questions about a private jet—when he used it, didn't he think it was environmentally destructive?

'You'll have to get rid of all those thick clothes,' he drawled, as they boarded the sleek, black jet that was waiting for them on a private airstrip she had never known existed. For a while, Laura forgot every qualm and doubt.

This was what it felt like to step into something that reeked of money. It was travel without the hassle of an airport and the discomfort of crowds of people. He was amused as he stood back and watched her poke and pry, scarcely hearing him when he told her that he had made sure that a selection of light clothes be brought to the plane. He guided her into a separate, private room with a relaxing sofa and indicated the neat stacks of clothes. He stood by the door, glanced at his watch, eventually told her to get a move on because they would be taking off shortly.

'I brought my own clothes.' Laura looked down at the bright collection in front of her. Tropical colours. Colours she would never have dreamed of wearing.

'So now you have more than you need. Isn't that every woman's dream?'

'I've told you already that I'm not like every woman so, no, that's never been a dream of mine.' She held up one strappy, frothy little number and twirled it in front of her with a frown.

'Try it, Laura,' Alessandro encouraged softly. 'Dare to live a little… And I'll meet you outside in five minutes. I need to make some urgent calls.'

Laura glared at his departing back. *Dare to live a little?* It felt as though she had been doing nothing but *daring to live a little*, for weeks and weeks and weeks. If she hadn't been so *daring to live a little*, she wouldn't be here now, with her thoughts in a dizzy whirl and an orange-and-pink sundress in her hand!

She would be…safe.

And she didn't want to be safe. She wasn't sure whether she would ever *want* to be *safe* again.

Because there was no excitement in a safe world. No thrills, no lurching stomach, no heightened senses, no edge-of-cliff feelings.

No Alessandro.

She sat down heavily on the sofa, her breath coming and going in fast little pants. She stared, glassy-eyed, at the dress in her hand and tried to arrange her thoughts in a way that wouldn't point her in a direction she didn't want to follow, but she felt sick.

When had he become an integral part of her life? When had he stopped being someone she disapproved of and turned into someone who filled all the spaces in her head?

When had she fallen in love with him? How on earth could something as big as love happen so fast?

It was nothing like what she had felt for Colin. That had been a silly crush, born from her own insecurities and his persistent flattery.

Alessandro had seduced her with more than flattery. He had seduced her with his intelligence, his wit, his depth. She had lost her head and her heart to the way he looked at her, the way he smiled, the way he sometimes laughed. The way he had dealt with the upheaval in his life when his father had finally broken the ice and told him about his past. He hadn't played to her insecurities and taken advantage of them. He had dispelled them and shown her what it was to feel beautiful and sexy.

Was that why she had slept with him? Had her heart driven her to do what came naturally, even though her head had not yet had time to play catch-up? She had fooled herself into thinking that she was filling a physical need and hadn't looked deeper.

And this was why she felt so panicked and scared now. Because it was so much more than a fling, so much more than two people enjoying sex before it fizzled out.

She wasn't comfortable, not at all, with the idea of deception, with thinking that her grandmother and Roberto were harbouring the illusion that this was some kind of serious relationship, and she was downright terrified at the murky waters into which she had waded.

'Fallen asleep? Do you need your knight in shining

armour to come and administer some mouth-to-mouth resuscitation?'

Laura heard that deep, sexy drawl and changed out of her winter clothes into the sundress faster than the speed of light. There was a pale, silky cardigan amongst the bundle of clothes and she stuck that on.

'Shame.' Alessandro had spent the past couple of hours with an extremely painful erection and seeing her in a dress that could have been personally made to outline her curvaceous little body didn't help matters. 'I was looking forward to the mouth-to-mouth revival scenario…'

Laura smiled weakly. Now that she had recognised her feelings for what they were, everything about him seemed to affect her all the more powerfully. Draped in the doorway, he was so staggeringly beautiful that she could barely speak. He had stripped down to a T-shirt and his low-slung jeans, and he oozed shameful sexuality. When her eyes drifted south, she went bright red at the glaring proof of how she affected him.

His jeans bulged where a rampant erection sent her senses into a giddy tailspin.

'I know.' Alessandro followed the direction of her gaze and read her reaction with no trouble at all. 'But, sadly, we haven't got time. Although…I *could* tell the crew to—'

'No!' Laura yelped, as he made a move towards her. She remembered the way he had suckled her breasts at the side of the road, not at all fazed at the thought that someone might drive past them and figure out what was going on.

He was in charge of this situation because he wasn't emotionally involved.

She nipped past him and smoothed down the dress with shaky hands. 'It's not really my style at all.'

'You're a knockout in it, though…' He grinned because she might be as hot as a naked flame between the sheets, but out of them she was as skittish as a colt and still blushed like a teenager. 'And you'll be glad for it when we get to the other end. Baking hot.'

They were in their seats and he solicitously strapped her in, shooting her a wicked little look as his arm brushed against her breast.

'What do you think your crew thinks of *this*…of *us*…?'

'Don't know. Don't care.'

'Is there *anything* you really care about, Alessandro?' The sharpness of her tone was muffled by the roar of engines as the jet began taxiing to take off.

'There's a certain deal hanging by a thread.' His voice was amused but his night-dark eyes were cool. '*That's* getting my attention at the moment. I certainly care about *that.*'

'But there must be more to life than deals.'

'Are you about to start delivering a lecture on my life choices?' Alessandro asked smoothly, angling his big body to look at her. 'I immerse myself in what I know. Work. Business. Money. And when it comes to emotions, because I take it that's what you're talking about, I control them.' He raised both eyebrows and tilted his head to one side.

'By control, you mean you never allow yourself to really feel anything for anyone…'

'Since when have you had this interest in what I feel or don't feel and why?'

Laura blushed.

Since she had finally admitted to herself just how deeply she had fallen for him.

She shrugged. 'We all try to find out what makes other people tick. It's human nature.'

'Really? I have yet to want to find out how any woman ticks.' Except that wasn't quite true, was it? He closed his mind to a line of querulous introspection he had no use for.

Laura pasted a smile on her face. No big surprise there. He slept with women, just as he was sleeping with her, but that was the extent of his involvement. As he'd said, he exercised control over his emotions and the things in life that didn't require emotion were the things that garnered his dispassionate interest. Those were the things he wanted to pick apart and examine in detail.

That hurt and she hated that it hurt. When she was with him, she could feel all one hundred per cent of his fabulous interest focused on her and it stung to recognise that he would be the same in the company of any woman he wanted to bed.

She had fallen in love with a guy who had no interest in a future with her or with any woman. She was deceiving her grandmother and an old man she cared deeply for. On both scores she was behaving in a way that was completely against her nature. And now she was on a posh private jet off for a few days of complete seclusion with someone who was happy enough to promote a charade because it made life simpler all round for him. From every angle, she was vulnerable and she would have to at the very least try to curtail the fallout, and step one would be to make sure he didn't get wind of just how deeply he affected her.

She thought about his reaction if he were to discover that this was so much more than just a fling for her.

He would be appalled, horrified, aghast. Or maybe… amused, comfortable with the thought that he could call all the shots, knowing that she would oblige. He wouldn't see it as taking advantage of her. He would simply accept that she had fallen for him so that made her an easier conquest. He would exercise the instincts of the born predator. She wondered how many women had fallen in love with him in his chequered past.

'You've never been tempted to have something more than a superficial relationship with anyone?'

'Whoever said that my relationships were superficial?' Alessandro asked, not liking the way that somehow made him appear shallow. Which he wasn't. Simply practical, careful and controlled. 'I'm a red-blooded man. I enjoy women and when I'm with a woman I'm with her and no one else. Unlike, might I add, the creep you went out with. What sort of man would you prefer? A man who was up-front and honest or a man who was willing to say what-ever he thought would get you between the sheets, even if he had no intention of fulfilling any of the promises he made? And I'm presuming the creep you dated was full of promises.'

Laura flushed because, yes, Colin had had the big ges-tures down pat along with the flowery words and the over-blown promises. But, between the two, surely there was a happy medium, the place that most people occupied? Ex-cept that wouldn't be a place Alessandro would ever have occupied or even been tempted to explore.

She yawned and half closed her eyes because their con-versation was going nowhere.

She didn't think she would be able to sleep at all, not when she was travelling in a private jet with a man she was in love with and a wasp's nest of uncomfortable thoughts buzzing around in her head, but, in fact, she slept soundly and only awoke when Alessandro nudged her and she opened her eyes to find him looking at her with amusement.

'It's unusual to have women fall asleep in my company,' he quipped, still smiling as the plane began its descent.

'I suppose they're too busy trying to impress you.' She struggled into a sitting position and transferred her eager eyes to the bright blue skies outside. Holiday excitement unfurled inside her and she shut the door on all the doubts that had been eating her up for the past few hours.

'They would have spent the better part of the trip trying to get me into the bed in the private room.'

'Idiots,' Laura said tersely. 'Would they be hoping that you might be interested enough with their antics to prolong the relationship?'

Alessandro was still smiling that smile that made her go all shivery and adolescent inside. 'Not a one-way street,' he countered smoothly. 'I'd like to think they'd get as much pleasure as they might be desperate to give. Angling for a committed relationship wouldn't have entered the equation.'

Laura didn't say anything. What was there to say? She directed her attention to the stunning vista now sprawling into view and gasped. She'd had no idea what to expect at the other end of the flight she had largely slept through. Her life had hardly been littered with holidays abroad. Growing up, she and her grandmother had been to France a couple of times and she had been to Spain with girlfriends a few years previously. While she had been working in London her holidays had consisted of returning to Scotland. She certainly had no experience of anywhere outside Europe and her stunned amazement at island life continued to keep her entranced as she followed in Alessandro's imperious wake until finally, with the sun beginning to set, they were heading off to his villa.

It was hot. She had to dispose of the thin cardigan as soon as she stepped foot out of the plane. And the sounds… The sounds of insects all around her, noisy but out of sight. She could smell the faint, salty tanginess of the sea. She began peppering him with all the questions she would have asked on the plane had she managed to keep her eyes open. It seemed that the island was very small, tiny, a little jewel in the sea where the rich and famous had houses that were nestled in lush, tropical grounds, far, far away from the prying eyes of the paparazzi. Tourism accounted for most of the income of the locals and the businesses that had sprung up on the island were there as a response to the millionaires and billionaires who had houses there, some of them permanently occupied rather than used now and again.

There was someone to meet them, a smiling, dark-skinned guy who chatted for the duration of the short trip, at the end of which the four-wheel-drive car bumped away from the main road and ascended an incline. On either side of the narrow road, trees and bushes vied to gain control. Tall coconut palms swayed above dense shrubs, and wildly colourful flowers dotted the undergrowth.

Laura feasted her eyes until the road gave way to a small courtyard in which stood a low, ranch-like house. Simply put, it was spectacular. A wooden porch spanned the length of it. She barely noticed the driver melting into the darkness, and inside the house she paused and looked around her, open-mouthed.

'How can you never come here?' she wondered aloud, and Alessandro shrugged.

'Time constraints. It's late. The place is fully stocked with food. I could have arranged with someone to come and cook while we're here, but I didn't see much point, considering we're only going to be here for a short while...' Her hair had fallen into wild ringlets. He had never set eyes on anything quite so disingenuously tempting. 'But shall we postpone the food until we've freshened up?' he murmured encouragingly, strolling towards her, wanting her to feast her eyes on *him* and not on her surroundings.

He hadn't been to this house for quite a while, but he could still recall its layout, and if memory served him right the bathroom adjoining the main bedroom was big enough and lavish enough to host a party. He looped his arms around her, turned her so that she was looking at him and lowered his head to kiss her.

'I want to explore the house first,' Laura breathed, and Alessandro groaned.

'It's a house. Some bedrooms, a few other rooms, a pool, some lawns. What's to explore? The only room I want you to explore is the bedroom.'

'It's not all about sex!' But the hot urgency of his voice filled her with a fierce longing that craved satisfaction. He occupied so much space in her head that just seeing the way his dark eyes were fastened on her made her want his hands and his mouth on her body. As easy as that, he could ignite all her senses.

It took all her willpower not to blindly let him lead her into the bedroom. Instead, they explored the house, which was beyond amazing.

There was, apparently, air conditioning throughout, but right now the house had been aired and as he flung open doors and shutters, balmy breezes blew in. The smell of the sea was even stronger here and he told her that it was a short walk down to a private cove. 'But not now,' he said drily, noticing the way she gazed wistfully through to the garden.

'It's just the most beautiful house.' She ran her eyes over the exquisite wooden flooring, gleaming through lack of use, and the light bamboo furniture and fine muslin drapes. 'Like from a magazine.'

'And I've saved the best for last,' Alessandro murmured, drawing her away from the living area towards the bedrooms, although he'd already made his mind up, and individual see-and-touch exploring sessions within the seven guest ones wasn't going to happen. At least not right now, when his libido was making walking a challenge.

The master bedroom, reserved for his exclusive use, was at the far end of the house and opened out, through French doors, to a view of the ocean. It had its own private veranda and he watched as she took it all in with open awe. He had flung open the French doors and she stepped outside to breathe in the clean, warm tropical air. Then she admired the giant bed with its gauze curtains, which would have seemed feminine were it not for the dark-coloured bedding and the starkness of the furnishings.

Without even noticing, she only realised that she had been led by the hand into the biggest bathroom she had ever seen when he began tugging the strap of her sundress.

Laura gazed up at him helplessly. It mystified her that she couldn't create some distance between them when she knew that this was a situation that was going to leave her stranded and hurt. There was not one single part of her that could resist when he touched her, even when he glanced at her. She burned for him and made absolutely no attempt to stop him from undressing her. The sundress was tugged down, pooling at her feet, and she obediently stepped out of it, then off came the bra and the knickers so that she was standing naked in the vast bathroom while he was still fully clothed.

It was unreasonably erotic but when she reached to strip him of his shirt, he stilled her hand with a half-smile.

'I need to go slowly,' he breathed huskily. 'Watching you sleep on the plane tested me to the outer limits. If we have sex right now, I won't be able to do justice to the act.'

Pink tinged her cheeks and she reached up as he began kissing her, very slowly and very thoroughly, and as he kissed her he played with her breasts, murmured into her ear, told her things that made her face burn and turned her on so much she could barely contain the feverish excitement coursing through her body.

He eased himself lower until he was kneeling before her. Laura could scarcely stand. Her legs felt like jelly because she was so turned on, and the hand that gently slipped between her thighs to part her legs elicited a moan in response.

Legs apart, she flung back her head and savoured the exquisite sensation of his tongue probing the wet slit, slipping between the folds of her femininity to tickle the roused bud of her clitoris. Of their own accord, her fingers curled into his hair. She widened her stance, created more space for his lazy exploration, sank into the caress of his wet mouth between her legs.

Her orgasm came fast and furious, building quickly and carrying her away with a whoosh.

A sultry breeze blew through the open window. So alien from what she was used to. Even the loud, shuddering groan that escaped her lips didn't seem to come from her. Neither, she thought, opening drowsing eyes and catching sight of herself in the mirrored wall opposite, did this woman resemble the one she thought she was and always had been.

She was in a parallel universe and all she could do was wait for the bump when she returned to earth to happen...

That...and protect herself the best she could...

CHAPTER TEN

SITTING BY THE infinity pool, slowly being toasted by the sun, which was still hot even though it was after five in the afternoon, Laura reflected that time had stood still and now the hands of the clock were once more on the move.

First thing the following morning the private jet that had whisked them to his island paradise would be whisking them away from it and back to reality. Harsh, inescapable reality.

They hadn't spoken once about the so-called relationship they were supposed to have, concocted for the sake of his father and her grandmother. They were supposed to be madly in love. They were supposed to be thinking about a series of *tomorrows* and not just the here and now, but that was just a technicality that suited Alessandro. He'd told her to forget about Roberto and her grandmother and to see the long weekend as an opportunity for hot sex, and such was his hold over her heart that she had pushed her anxieties and misgivings to one side and, yes, coward that she was, she had enjoyed him. Enjoyed him, being with him and the glorious tropical paradise into which she had landed. A little sparrow thrown into an exotic world far beyond her reach.

She couldn't have been further out of her comfort zone. The little island was the playground of the fabulously wealthy. Vast plantation-style houses were screened behind sweeping, palm-tree-lined drives. Exquisite beaches were nestled into the mountains, although they had actually been to only one of those because they had their own beach, a beach with sand as fine and as white as icing sugar with placid, turquoise water to swim in. The town centre was picturesque, with several top-rated restaurants, a few very expensive shops and then all the other businesses that were needed to support the economy of the island and keep the locals employed.

She had felt as though she had inadvertently stepped onto a movie set. Everything was so picture-perfect that there was an air of unreality about the experience.

It was as unreal as their relationship and she knew that being on this island was like being in a bubble, where it was easy to forget about things that would need to be dealt with.

She sighed and shut her eyes. When she opened them, it was to see Alessandro standing by the sun lounger, looking at her through sunglasses.

'You're not the picture of joy and rapture,' he said without preamble.

Laura shielded her eyes against the glare of the sun and propped herself up on her elbow. Would she ever tire of the sight of him? He took her breath away. When he was near, her heart beat faster and her pulse raced. There was no bit of her, emotionally, physically, intellectually, into which he didn't intrude. He had managed to take over her entire being and when she thought about him no longer being around she felt as though she was staring into a black, bottomless void that filled her with tearing emptiness and despair.

She knew that she had only herself to blame. He hadn't asked her to fall in love with him. In fact, he had made it clear from the start that love was a four-letter word that didn't exist in his vocabulary. If her heart had broken free of its leash, that had had nothing to do with him.

'I'm going to miss all this when we leave…' She forced a smile as he settled into the sun lounger next to her.

His first thought was that the house wasn't going anywhere. Who was to say that she wouldn't be back? Then he frowned because that was just the sort of forward planning he always avoided with a woman.

'Holidays in the sun aren't out of reach just because you live in Scotland.' He shrugged and Laura kept on smiling because that was just the sort of response she didn't want. Of course he couldn't guess that a *holiday in the sun*, any old *holiday in the sun*, wasn't what she was talking about.

'I'll have to start saving,' she said lightly. 'Believe it or not, teachers don't earn all that much…'

Alessandro slanted a killer smile and leaned on his side, feathering a light touch on her arm and feeling the soft shudder of her body with a familiar, mounting arousal. She was so responsive and that never failed to turn him on. He couldn't get enough of her. 'I admit this particular resort is probably out of reach for the average teacher,' he murmured, 'unless, of course, the average teacher happens to be the lover of the above-average tycoon… I'm glad you enjoyed it here. It's good for the place to get a little use.'

'Why do you have places like this if you never use them?'

'As investments,' Alessandro said lazily. 'It's not exactly killing me. This house has appreciated substantially in value since it was bought and right now I'm glad I was never tempted to sell it.'

'So you've never brought anyone here?'

'When you say *anyone*…'

'Women. Those lucky women who you happened to be dating…'

'I've tended to stick closer to home.'

'Why's that?'

'I really want you right now...'

'When you don't want to talk, you resort to the physical. I've noticed that.'

Alessandro flung himself back and stared up at the bright blue sky. He'd never known a woman more disrespectful of his boundaries. He pointed them out, she saw them and then she proceeded to trample all over them as though they didn't exist.

'I happen to enjoy the physical,' he said, turning to her, and she looked at him with something approaching pity. 'It beats,' he was pressed to continue irritably, 'having long, meaningful conversations about things that don't matter.'

Laura's soft mouth tightened. 'Well...I hate to burst your bubble but sometimes people do have to have long, meaningful conversations, even if you find them boring and irrelevant.'

She hadn't meant to have this conversation. It cast a stormy cloud over what remained of the little paradise she had spent the past few days occupying, but how could she carry on pretending? Knowing that the more time she spent with him, the deeper in love she fell and the more painful it would eventually be to extricate herself?

What a mess.

Alessandro stilled. Did he want to hear this? He sat up and removed his sunglasses to look at her.

Laura's heart was racing. Her mouth was dry. Did she really want to ruin what was left of their stay here? She could laugh and change the subject. She could just accept that it wasn't an ideal situation but why rock the boat, why not just enjoy what was on offer until the offer was rescinded? Why not play the game, as he suggested, and when things ended, just explain to Roberto and her grandmother that it hadn't worked out in the end? Why not enjoy the hedonistic pleasure they got from one another and enjoy it without an agonising guilty conscience?

But how much enjoyment would she honestly get, knowing that it was just a matter of time before everything came crashing down around her and she was left to pick up the pieces? Every time he touched her, she would think that it might be the last. Every time she gazed at him, she would have to try not to let her feelings show, knowing that if he suspected the depth of what she felt, he would run a mile.

It would be like walking in a field of flowers knowing that underneath the perfect ground a series of landmines was waiting to be detonated.

'I never said that I found them boring or irrelevant,' Alessandro said carefully.

'I can't play this game. I can't just have a mindless affair with you. I can't take advantage of what my grandmother and Roberto mistakenly assume to have no-strings-attached sex. That's just not the way I'm made.' Her eyes shot away from his lean, beautiful face. 'I know you think it's a straightforward situation, I know you think that it makes it easier for us to…well, have this fling and then, when it comes to an end, we just break the news and walk away, but I…I can't do that.'

'Why not?' Alessandro demanded.

He knew. He raked restless fingers through his dark hair and stood up abruptly. The open space around him felt too small, pressing down on him. For the first time in his life the job of ridding himself of a woman who had made the terminal mistake of falling in love with him felt like an anchor dragging him down. And she did love him. He'd managed to shove that into his blind spot but she loved him.

He had his rules. He always made them clear. It had always been easy to bid farewell to someone who hadn't taken them on board. But then again, his boredom threshold was low. He had never felt the need to pursue any woman who wanted more than he was prepared to give. On the few occasions when this situation had presented itself, he had already been on the way to finding the whole thing pretty tedious anyway. Ending it had never been a hardship.

Not so now. He wasn't ready.

'Aside from the fact that I don't feel comfortable deceiving Roberto and Gran—'

'How are we being deceptive?' He spread his hands in a gesture of frustration. 'We have a relationship!'

'We don't have the sort of relationship they imagine we do.'

'We're not hurting anyone,' Alessandro persisted, bemused by his own inability to start the process of disentanglement and not wanting to voice the reality lying like a leaden weight between them. Their eyes tangled and he flushed darkly.

'Why don't you just say what you have to say and get it over and done with?' he rasped.

Laura hesitated, torn between a desperate need to try to patch things over and a driving urge to just tell him how she felt. She knew there was still a part of her that half hoped an admission of love wouldn't drive him away, and feeling like that, hoping against reason, annoyed and dismayed her.

She drew in a deep breath and held his gaze levelly, even though she was quaking inside.

'I'm too involved with you emotionally to do this, Alessandro,' she said, choosing her words carefully. 'It's not a game for me and if I carry on with…with *this*, I'm going to end up horribly hurt, and I don't want to be hurt.'

'I warned you not to…get involved. I told you I don't do love.'

'Sorry if I disobeyed orders!' Laura's voice had risen angrily. How could he just stand there and look at her as though she had suddenly turned into a stranger? His dark eyes were guarded and cool. 'Some of us actually have emotions!'

'I have emotions. I just know how to control them!'

'I can't do this.' She stood up and stormed off.

Alessandro watched her go but he had to force himself not to follow her. He waited until she was out of sight, unnerved by his indecision, and finally he swung round angrily and headed for the beach.

The sound of the sea would soothe him. He needed perspective but for the first time in his life perspective eluded him. She loved him and he had known and he hadn't walked away. Shouldn't that have been his first instinctive response?

He barely saw the picture-perfect-postcard beauty of the little cove, the clear water lapping at the shore, the backdrop of rocks and coconut palms. He barely felt the warmth pressing against him. He sat down, his back against one of the rocks, oblivious to everything but the swirling confusion of his thoughts.

She had breached his boundaries and no one could accuse him of not making those boundaries perfectly clear. She had strayed into no man's land.

And he had known. Deep down, he had known and he had basked in what she was giving him. And now that she had done the unthinkable and confirmed his suspicions, now that she had exposed the heart she had been wearing on her sleeve...

He raked his fingers through his hair, stood up, sat back down, glared at the perfect scenery.

How could he still want her? Why did the thought of her walking away fill him with fear and panic? Everything in his life had been so clear-cut before...*especially relationships*...

Why was the way forward so hard to see now? When he thought of her vanishing from his life, he felt...*empty*. It was as if a wilderness of trees had dropped down, obscuring the clear, open horizons of his life, and he just didn't know how to get past them. He could turn a full circle, and he still wouldn't be able to see past them to the life he'd had before.

With a low growl of bewilderment, frustration and inner turmoil, he strode out to the sea, dropping clothes en route, and took to the water.

Laura wanted him to follow her so badly that it was a physical ache in the pit of her stomach. Pride compelled her not to look round. She packed furiously, chucking her clothes into her bag while listening for the sound of his footsteps, and the longer the house remained silent, the more she held back the tears.

By eight, after a light snack, she resigned herself to the fact that he just wasn't going to follow her. There was no more talking to be done. In fact, she had no idea where he had gone and she refused point-blank to go out searching for him.

Even though worry clenched at her stomach when nine o'clock rolled round and there was still no sign of him.

For the first time since they had arrived, she fell asleep in the bed alone. At some point during the night she half heard him return and her whole body stiffened at the thought of him sliding into bed with her.

She longed for him but she knew that she had had no option but to be open and truthful.

Even though the consequences were beyond endurance.

He didn't sleep next to her. She heard the soft sound of him rustling and then he left the room.

The silence between them the following day was oppressive. When he addressed her it was with the politeness of a complete stranger and she heard herself responding in the same frozen voice, making sure to avoid eye contact, making sure to keep her distance. On the plane, she buried herself in her book while he sat in front of his computer, working.

They had nothing more to say and she was miserable.

They landed back in wintry weather and grey skies. Snow blanketed the ground and reflected her mood. The bright blue, tropical skies were gone for good. Next to her, Alessandro had spent most of the drive on the telephone. One call after another, catching up on work. After wearing nothing but the bright summer wear he had provided for her, she felt weighed down in her thick clothes.

'You don't have to deliver me back home.' She broke the silence to glance across at him.

'How do you suggest you get back?' Alessandro enquired. 'Do you plan on walking from my house back to your grandmother's with your suitcase on your back?'

'I don't want us to finish like this,' she said shakily. 'We could still…you know…remain friends…'

'That's not my style.' He'd been dumped. For the best because the last thing he needed was the complication of someone falling in love with him, someone expecting him to be the kind of man who was willing or, for that matter, *capable* of sharing himself. But he couldn't rid himself of the bitter, sour taste in his mouth. He'd spent hours the evening before walking on the beach, sitting and staring out at the black ocean in a foul mood, and things had not got better since.

Even more infuriating was the fact that he still wanted her. She had sat on the plane, absorbed in some book, oblivious to him, having dropped her little bombshell, and he had *still wanted her*.

He wasn't used to being dumped and he wasn't used to being ignored.

And now she talked about *being friends*?

'Fine,' Laura said stiffly. 'Don't say that I'm not trying to make peace between us.'

Alessandro's mood worsened. 'I take it your grandmother's expecting you?' he said curtly.

'I texted when I'd be back. Look, it's going to be very awkward if we walk in like enemies…'

'Well, now, maybe you should have considered that before…' He slid his eyes sideways. 'And how do you intend to break the news?'

'I'll just say that spending a long weekend together demonstrated that we didn't get along.'

'Which is a bald lie, isn't it?'

'I'm not prepared to keep something going for the sake of other people, not when it's a lie.' She sighed and looked at his harsh, averted profile. 'If I'd known… I…well, I never meant to get so wrapped up…'

He could never fall in love. He had built his entire life ruling out something he saw as a weakness. It was all she could do to stop herself from crying.

It was beginning to sleet by the time they made it to her grandmother's house. 'You don't have to see me in.' She turned to him as he killed the engine and sprawled back in the seat to look at her. 'It'll be easier if I go in alone and sit her down, break the news. You can…fill your dad in…'

'And then when we next meet we…what, exactly? Pretend we haven't been lovers? Going to be hard when you're in love with me and would like nothing better than to find the nearest bed, wouldn't you say?'

'Then I'll make sure to stay away until you're gone,' Laura said sharply. She opened the car door, bracing herself for the freezing cold, and was alarmed when he stormed out of his side, reaching to take her case to the front door.

He rang the doorbell, ignoring her as she scrambled to catch up to him. What the heck was he up to?

'You don't get to disappear,' he growled. They stared at one another. Unfair as it was, she couldn't tear her eyes away from his beautiful face.

She knew he was going to kiss her. She could read the intent in his dark eyes, but she was nailed to the spot and when his mouth met hers she whimpered and clutched the lapels of his coat. Oh, God, he tasted so sweet. *What was she doing?* Drowning. She was drowning and she hated herself for it but she couldn't seem to surface for life-giving air.

She was hardly aware of the door opening but when she was, she sprang back, her whole body trembling as she met her grandmother's eyes.

'This isn't what it looks like!' She looked at Alessandro, who was staring at her, not saying a word, making her wonder whether he had manoeuvred this situation just to make things difficult for her…because he still wanted her and wasn't ready to let her go.

Would he do that?

She could have slapped him.

'Roberto's here!' Edith chirruped, ushering them in, and so he was, along with another man whom Laura recognised, with a sickening jolt, as the local vicar. What on earth was he doing here? Somewhere between entering the house and finding themselves standing in the sitting room, Alessandro had taken her hand, linking her fingers through his.

Words tumbled over her head. The vicar just happened to be passing by...dropped in for a cup of coffee...was keen to meet the lovebirds...there was nothing more fulfilling than marriage...so many young people choosing to live together...but what a sight for sore eyes they both made...not meaning to presume but he would be honoured should they decide...

Laura tried and failed to meet Alessandro's eyes. Was he as shocked as she was? He seemed to be carrying the conversation, laughing and chatting and being horribly, horribly friendly, while she remained in mute silence, barely taking anything in until, after half an hour, she and Alessandro somehow found themselves alone in the sitting room.

'What just happened there?' Laura whispered. Alessandro had moved to stand by the fireplace and she looked at him, still reeling from the shock of having a future arranged on their behalves while Roberto and her grandmother had looked on contentedly.

'What did you expect me to do?' he asked fiercely. 'I was as surprised as you were.'

'Why didn't you say anything?'

'Why didn't you?'

'I was too dazed. I barely knew what was going on. Gran never mentioned a word... I can't believe Father Frank just happened to be passing by. What do we do now?' she half wailed and was taken aback when he continued to look at her without saying anything. He always knew what to say! Why was he just staring?

'It's not such a bad thing,' he muttered, and Laura's mouth fell open.

'Is that *all* you have to say? What the heck does that mean anyway?'

Alessandro raked unsteady fingers through his hair and

circled the room, finally coming to rest directly in front of her, a towering, brooding alpha male who, for once, was not his usual composed self. 'I'm not ready to...end what we have...'

'You're not ready to end what we have?' She laughed shortly. 'You don't give a damn about anyone but yourself, do you?' she demanded. 'You don't care how messed up I am, being an idiot to fall for you. You don't care that you've put me in an impossible situation. Just so long as you get what you want.' Tears pricked the backs of her eyes and she couldn't look at him. When she stared down, her fingers were restively curling and uncurling on her lap.

'You don't understand,' he muttered.

'Then why don't you explain? Tell me what it is I don't understand.'

'You make my world feel alive. When I'm with you, I feel as though my life makes sense.'

Laura's eyes fluttered. She didn't want to hope. Was this some kind of trick? Was she dreaming? Disoriented, she watched as he dragged a chair to sit next to her and for a few moments hung his head in a gesture that was so unlike him that she was worried. She tentatively laid her hand on his arm and without looking at her he blindly clutched it and held it tightly.

'You told me that you didn't expect to fall in love with me,' he said so quietly that she had to strain to hear. He raised his eyes and held hers. 'I rejected that. It was an automatic reaction. I always had my rules. No love, no commitment. No getting any ideas of permanence, but I hated the thought of not having you around. I hated it when we stopped talking to one another.'

'You hated not being able to carry on having sex with me because I haven't got past my sell-by date yet,' Laura persisted stubbornly.

'This is about more than just sex.'

'Strange you never mentioned that before, when I laid my soul bare. Strange all you did was disappear for hours and then sleep in a separate room! Where did you go anyway?'

'Are you jealous?'

'Oh, forget it!'

'I sat on the beach and looked at the sky and did some thinking.'

'And that's when you decided that you'd keep me on at all costs because you weren't sick of me quite yet?'

'I told myself that it was a good thing to finish it because I couldn't handle the expectations of any woman being in love with me.' He sighed heavily and pressed his thumbs over his eyes, then he looked at her. 'It never occurred to me that I only started asking myself why I didn't want what other people seemed to want when I met you. You made me question my pattern of behaviour. I grew up alone. I always saw that as a strength. To become emotionally involved with a woman would be to lose that strength and I never wanted to do that. But...'

'But...?' Laura pressed, her heart beating so hard she felt it might just burst out of her chest.

'But...I began to find out about my father, about myself. I began sharing myself with you in a thousand small ways and I didn't even realise I was doing it. I thought it was all about sex because that was how I had programmed myself to think, but it wasn't and today, driving back here...'

Laura held her breath, afraid to hope because it was impossible to second-guess this wonderful, complex, utterly fascinating man.

'I was scared,' he admitted, his amazing cheekbones tinged with a dark flush.

Something inside her melted. *He was scared*. That was

the most telling thing he had ever said to her and, looking at him, she believed him.

'Are you telling the truth?' she was still forced to ask, and he smiled crookedly at her.

'Lies are something I don't do as well. I'm telling the truth. I couldn't see a future unless you were in it and I knew that that must be love. What else? I'd never felt this way before. I barely recognised the signs and it was only now that it all made sense. I love you. I don't just want you. I need you and I love you and I can't stand the thought of you not being next to me every day for the rest of my life. Are you going to say anything? Or are you going to let me ramble on?'

'I'm keen to let you ramble on,' Laura whispered, and he grinned.

'I wasn't shaken by seeing the vicar here,' he said simply. 'I was glad. I was overjoyed because I want to do precisely what he and my father and your grandmother want us to do. I want to marry you. So…will you, Laura Reid, be my wife?'

And she smiled. *He loved her!* She wanted to fling her arms around him and shout from the rooftops at the same time.

'I love you so much, Alessandro,' she said instead, tracing the fabulous contours of his face with trembling fingers. 'You're my whole world and, yes, I'll marry you. You may have spent your life avoiding commitment but I'm warning you, you'll have a life sentence with me…'

'I can't think of anything I'd rather have more…'

'You see, there we have the crunch of the matter.'

* * * * *

SEDUCTION ON
HIS TERMS

SARAH M. ANDERSON

To the Quincy Public Library and the lovely librarians and staff, especially Katie, Farrah and Jeraca, who feed my book addiction! Thank you for helping make my son a reader and for making literature a part of so many lives!

One

"Good evening, Dr. Wyatt," Jeannie Kaufman said as the man slid into his usual seat at the end of the bar. It was a busy Friday night, and he sat as far away as he could get from the other patrons at Trenton's.

"Jeannie," he said in his usual brusque tone.

But this time she heard something tight in his voice.

Dr. Robert Wyatt was an unusual man, to say the least. His family owned Wyatt Medical Industries, and Dr. Wyatt had been named to the "Top Five Chicago Billionaire Bachelors" list last year, which probably had just as much to do with his family fortune as it did with the fact that he was a solid six feet tall, broad chested and sporting a luxurious mane of inky black hair that made the ice-cold blue of his eyes more striking.

And as if being richer than sin and even better looking wasn't tempting enough, the man had to be a pediatric surgeon, as well. He performed delicate heart surgeries on babies and kids. He single-handedly saved lives—and she'd read that for some families who couldn't afford the astro-nomical costs, he'd quietly covered their bills.

Really, the man was too good to be true.

She kept waiting for a sign that, underneath all that per-fection, he was a villain. She'd had plenty of rich, hand-some and talented customers who were complete assholes.

Dr. Wyatt…wasn't.

Yes, he was distant, precise and, as far as she could tell, completely fearless. All qualities that made him a great sur-geon. But if he had an ego, she'd never seen it. He came into the bar five nights a week at precisely eight, sat in the same spot, ordered the same drink and left her the same tip—a hundred dollars on a twenty-dollar tab. In cash. He never made a pass at anyone, staff or guest, and bluntly rebuffed any flirtation from women or men.

He was her favorite customer.

Before he'd had the chance to straighten his cuffs—something he did almost obsessively—Jeannie set his Man-hattan down in front of him.

She'd been making his drink for almost three years now. His Manhattan contained the second-most expensive rye bourbon on the market, because Dr. Wyatt preferred the taste over the most expensive one; a vermouth that she or-dered from Italy exclusively for him; and bitters that cost over a hundred bucks a bottle. It was all precisely blended and aged in an American white oak cask for sixty days and served in a chilled martini glass with a lemon twist. It'd taken almost eight months of experimenting with brands and blends and aging to get the drink right.

But it'd been worth it.

Every time he lifted the glass to his lips, like he was doing now, Jeannie held her breath. Watching this man drink was practically an orgasmic experience. As he swal-lowed, she watched in fascination as the muscles in his throat moved. He didn't show emotion, didn't pretend to be nice. But when he lowered the glass back to the bar?

He *smiled*.

It barely qualified as one, and a casual observer would've missed it entirely. His mouth hardly even moved. But she knew him well enough to know that the slight curve of his lips and the warming of his icy gaze was the same as anyone else shouting for joy.

He held her gaze and murmured, "Perfect."

It was the only compliment she'd ever heard him give.

Her body tightened as desire licked down her back and spread throughout her midsection. As a rule, Jeannie did not serve up sex along with drinks. But if she were ever going to break that rule, it'd be for him.

Sadly, he was only here for the drink.

Jeannie loved a good romance novel and for three years, she'd imagined Robert as some duke thrust into the role that didn't fit him, nobility that hated the crush of ballrooms and cut directs and doing the pretty around the ton and all those dukely things when all he really wanted to do was practice medicine and tend to his estates and generally be left alone. In those stories, there was always a housekeeper or pickpocket or even a tavern wench who thawed his heart and taught him to love.

Jeannie shook off her fantasies. She topped off the scotch for the salesman at the other end of the bar and poured the wine for table eleven, but her attention was focused on Wyatt. She had to break the bad news to him—she'd be gone next week to help her sister, Nicole, with the baby girl that was due any minute.

This baby was the key to Jeannie and her sister being a family again. Any family Jeannie had ever had, she'd lost. She'd never met her father—he'd left before she'd been born. Mom had died when Jeannie had been ten and Nicole...

It didn't matter what had gone wrong between the sisters in the past. What mattered was that they were going to grab this chance to be a family again now. Melissa—that was what they were going to call the baby—would be the tie that bound them together. Jeannie would do her part by being there for her sister, just like Nicole had been there for Jeannie when Mom had died and left the sisters all alone in the world.

In an attempt to demonstrate her commitment, Jeannie had even offered to move back into their childhood home with Nicole. It would've been a disaster but Jeannie had still offered because that was what family did—they made sacrifices and stuck together through the rough times. Only now that she was twenty-six was Jeannie aware how much Nicole had sacrificed for her. The least Jeannie could do was return the favor.

Nicole had told Jeannie that, while a thoughtful offer, it was absolutely *not* necessary for them to share a house again. Thank God, because living together probably would've destroyed their still-fragile peace. Instead, Jeannie would keep working nights at Trenton's—and taking care of Dr. Wyatt—and then she'd get to the house around ten every morning to help Nicole with the cooking or cleaning or playing with the baby.

Jeannie might not be the best sister in the world but by God, she was going to be the best aunt.

That was the plan, anyway.

The only hiccup was sitting in front of her.

Wyatt didn't do well with change, as she'd learned maybe six months into their *partnership*, as Jeannie thought of it. She'd gotten a cold and stayed home. He'd been more than a little upset that someone else had made him a subpar Manhattan that night. Julian, the owner of Trenton's, said Tony, the bartender who'd subbed for her that night, had gotten a job elsewhere right after that. Jeannie knew that wasn't a coincidence.

Maybe half the time Dr. Wyatt sat at her bar, he didn't say anything. Which was fine. But when he did talk? It wasn't inane chitchat or stale pickup lines. When he spoke, every single word either made her fall further in love with him or broke her heart.

"So," he started and Jeannie knew he was about to break her heart again.

She waited patiently, rearranging the stemware that hung below the bar in front of him. He'd talk when he wanted and not a moment before.

Had he lost a patient? That she knew of, he'd only had two or three kids die and those times had been…awful. All he'd ever said was that he'd failed. That was it. But the way he'd sipped his drink…

The last time it'd happened, she'd sobbed in the ladies' room after he'd left. Below his icy surface, a sea of emotion churned. And when he lost a patient, that sea raged.

After three years of listening to Dr. Wyatt pour out his heart in cold, clipped tones, Jeannie knew all too well how things could go wrong with babies. That was what made Jeannie nervous about Nicole and Melissa.

"I heard something today," he went on after long moments that had her on pins and needles.

She studied him as she finished the lemons and moved on to the limes. He straightened his cuffs and then took a drink.

She fought the urge to check her phone again. Nicole would text if anything happened and there'd been no buzzing at her hip. But tonight was the night. Jeannie could feel it.

Wyatt cleared his throat. "I was informed that my father is considering a run for governor."

Jeannie froze, the knife buried inside a lime. Had she ever heard Dr. Wyatt talk about his parents? She might've assumed that they'd died and left the bulk of the Wyatt Medical fortune to their son.

And who the heck had *informed* him of this? What an odd way to phrase it. "Is that so?"

"Yes," Dr. Wyatt replied quickly. That, coupled with the unmistakable bitterness in his voice, meant only one thing.

This was extremely *bad* news.

Jeannie had been working in a bar since the day she'd turned eighteen, three whole years before she was legally allowed to serve alcohol. She'd been desperate to get away from Nicole, who hadn't wanted Jeannie to get a job and certainly not as a bartender. She'd wanted Jeannie to go to college, become a teacher, like Nicole. Wanting to own her own bar was out of the question. Nicole wouldn't allow it.

After *that* fight, Jeannie had moved out, lied about her age and learned on the job. While pouring wine, countless men and women poured their hearts out to her. In the years she'd been at this high-priced chophouse, she'd learned a hell of a lot about how the one percent lived.

But she'd never had a customer like Robert Wyatt before.

Wyatt finished his drink in two long swallows. "The thing is," he said, setting his glass down with enough force that Jeannie was surprised the delicate stem didn't shatter, "if he runs, he'll expect us to stand next to him as if we're one big happy family."

Wiping her hands, she gave up the pretense of working and leaned against the bar. "Sounds like that's a problem."

"You have no idea," he muttered, which was even more disturbing because when did precise, careful Dr. Robert Wyatt *mutter*?

His charcoal-gray three-piece suit fit him perfectly, as did the shirt with cuff links that tonight looked like sapphires—he favored blues when he dressed. The blue-and-orange-striped tie matched the square artfully arranged in his pocket. It was September and Chicago still clung to the last of the summer's heat, but the way Dr. Robert Wyatt dressed announced that he'd never stoop to *sweating*.

She could see where the tie had been loosened slightly as if he'd yanked on it in frustration. His hair wasn't carefully brushed back, but rumpled. He made it look good because everything looked good on him, but still. His shoulders drooped and instead of his usual ramrod-straight posture, his head hung forward, just a bit. When he glanced up at her, she saw the worry lines cut deep across his forehead. He looked like the weight of the world was about to crush him flat.

It hurt to see him like this.

If it were any other man, any other customer, she'd honestly offer him a hug because Lord, he looked like he needed one. But she'd seen how Wyatt flinched when someone touched him.

"So don't do it," she said, keeping her voice low and calm.

"I have to." Unsurprisingly, he straightened his cuffs. "I won't have a choice."

At that, she gave him a look. "Why not?" He glared but she kept going. "For God's sake, you have nothing *but* choices. If you wanted to buy half of Chicago to raise wildebeests, you could. If you opened your own hospital and told everyone they had to wear blue wigs to enter the building, there'd be a run on clown hair. You can go anywhere, do anything, be *anyone* you want because you're Dr. Robert *freaking* Wyatt."

All because he had looks, money and power.

All things Jeannie would never have.

His mouth opened but unexpectedly, he slammed it shut. Then he was pushing away from the bar, glaring at her as he threw some bills down and turned to go.

"Dr. Wyatt? Wait!" When he kept going, she yelled, "Robert!"

That got his attention.

When he spun, she flinched because he was *furious*. It

wasn't buried under layers of icy calm—it was right there on the surface, plain as day.

Was he mad she'd used his given name? Or that she'd questioned his judgment? It didn't matter. She wasn't going to buckle in the face of his fury.

She squared her shoulders and said, "I have a family thing next week and I'm taking some vacation time."

Confusion replaced his anger and he was back at the bar in seconds, staring down at her with something that looked like worry clouding his eyes. "How long?"

She swallowed. She was taller than average, but looking up into his eyes, only a few inches away… He made her feel small at the same time she felt like the only person in his universe.

He'd always leave her unsettled, wouldn't he?

"Just the week. I'll be back Monday after next. Promise."

The look on his face—like he wouldn't be able to function if she wasn't there to serve the perfect Manhattan to the perfect man—was the kind of look that made her fall a little bit more in love with him while it broke her heart at the same time.

"Will you be okay?" she asked.

Something warm brushed over the top of her hand, sending a jolt of electricity up her arm. Had he *touched* her? By the time she looked down, Robert was straightening his cuffs. "Of course," he said dismissively, as if it was impossible for him to be anything *but* perfectly fine. "I'm a Wyatt."

Then he was gone.

Jeannie stared after him. This was bad. Before she could decide how worried about him she was going to be, her phone buzzed.

It's time! read Nicole's message.

"It's time!" Jeannie shouted. The waiters cheered.

Dr. Wyatt would have to wait. Jeannie's new niece came first.

Two

Jeannie was back tonight.

Robert hadn't gone to Trenton's, knowing she wouldn't be there, and he felt the loss of their routine deeply. Instead, he'd spent a lot more time in the office, reviewing cases and getting caught up on paperwork and not thinking about Landon Wyatt or political campaigns.

But finally, it was Monday and Jeannie would be waiting for him. On some level he found his desire to see her again worrisome. She was just a bartender who'd perfected a Manhattan. Anyone could mix a drink.

But that was a lie and he knew it.

He never should have touched her. But she'd stood there staring at him with her huge brown eyes, asking if he was going to be okay, like she cared. Not because he was the billionaire Dr. Robert Wyatt, but because he was Robert.

That was what he'd missed this week. Just being… Robert.

Lost in thought, he didn't look at the screen of his phone before he answered it. "This is Wyatt."

"Bobby?"

Robert froze, his hand on the elevator buttons. It couldn't be...

But no one else called him Bobby. *"Mom?"*

"Hi, honey." Cybil Wyatt's voice sounded weak. It hit him like a punch to the solar plexus. "How have you been?"

Almost three years had passed since he'd talked to his mother.

He quickly retreated to his office. "Can you talk? Are you on speakerphone?"

"Honey," she went on, an extra waver in her voice. "You heard from Alexander, right?"

That was a *no*, she couldn't talk freely.

Alexander was Landon's assistant, always happy to do the older man's bidding. "Yes. He said Landon wanted to run for governor." A terrible idea on both a state level and a personal level.

Robert knew the only reason Landon Wyatt wanted to be governor was because he'd discovered a way to personally enrich himself. He wasn't content having politicians and lobbyists in his pocket. He always wanted more.

"Your father wants you by his side." The way she cleared her throat made Robert want to throw something. "*We* want you by *our* sides," she corrected because the fiction that they were all one big happy family was a lie that had to be maintained at all costs, no matter what.

"Are you on speaker?"

She laughed lightly, a fake sound. "Of course not. All is forgiven, honey. We both know you didn't mean it."

Hmm. If she wasn't on speaker, she was probably sitting in Landon's opulent office, where he was watching her through those cold, slitted eyes of his—the same eyes Robert saw in the mirror every damn morning—making sure

Mom stuck to the script. "Let me help you, Mom. I can get you away from him."

"We're having a gala to launch his campaign in two weeks." Her voice cracked but she didn't stop. "It's at the Winston art gallery, right off the Magnificent Mile."

"I know it."

"It'd mean a lot to your father and me to see you there."

Robert didn't doubt that his mother wanted to see him. But to Landon, this was nothing more than another way to exert control over Robert and he'd vowed never to give Landon that much power again—even if it cost him his relationship with his mother.

"Tell me what I can do to help you, Mom."

There was a brief pause. "We've missed you, too."

Dammit. He didn't want to pretend to be a happy family, not in private and most certainly not in public. But he knew Landon well enough to know that if he didn't show, Mom would pay the price.

Just like she always did.

Robert couldn't let that happen. Of all the things Landon Wyatt had done and would continue to do, dangling Cybil as bait to ensure Robert cooperated was one of the meanest.

He had to fix this. "Think about what I said, okay? We'll talk at the gallery."

She exhaled. "That's wonderful, dear. It starts at seven but we'd like you to get there earlier. Your father wants to make sure we're all on the same page."

Robert almost growled. *Getting on the same page* meant threats. Lots of them. "I'll try. I have to make my rounds. But if I can get you away, will you come with me?" Because after what had happened last time...

"Thank you, Bobby," she said and he hoped like hell that was a *yes*. "I—*we* can't wait to see you again."

"Me, too, Mom. Love you."

She didn't say it back. The line went dead.

Robert stared at nothing for a long time.

This was exactly what he'd been afraid of. Landon was going to force Robert to do this—be this…this *lie*. He was going to make Robert stand next to him before crowds and cameras. He was going to expect Robert to give speeches of his own, no doubt full of bold-faced lies about Landon's character and compassion. And if Robert didn't…

Would he ever see his mother again?

Landon would do whatever he wanted, if Robert didn't stop him. There had to be a way.

You can do anything you want because you're Dr. Robert freaking *Wyatt*, he heard Jeannie say.

Maybe she was right.

Now more than ever, he needed a drink.

"Well?" he said in that silky voice of his.

Once, Cybil had thought Landon Wyatt's voice was the most seductive voice she'd ever heard.

That had been a long time ago. So long ago that all she could remember was the pain of realizing she'd been seduced, all right. She could barely remember the time when she'd been a naive coed right out of college, swept away by the charming billionaire fifteen years her senior.

She'd been paying for that mistake ever since. "He's coming."

Landon notched an eyebrow—a warning.

Cybil smiled graciously. "He'll try to get there early, but he has rounds," she went on, hoping Landon would dismiss her. Hearing Bobby's voice again, the anger when he'd promised he could get her away from her husband of thirty-five years…

God, she'd missed her son. Maybe this time would be different. Bobby had grown into a fine man, a brilliant surgeon. Landon hated that both because Bobby worked for a living and, Cybil suspected, because Landon knew Bobby was far smarter.

If anyone could outthink Landon Wyatt, it'd be his own son.

Something warm and light bloomed in her chest. With a start, she realized it was hope.

What if there really was a way?

But Landon would never let her go.

A fact he reinforced when he stood and stroked a hand over her hair. Years of practice kept her from flinching at his touch. "I know you've missed him," he murmured as if he hadn't been the one keeping her from her son. His hand settled on the back of her neck and he began to squeeze. "So I know you'll make sure he does what's expected. Otherwise…"

"Of course," Cybil agreed, struggling as his grip tightened.

Like she did every day, she thanked God Bobby had gotten away. If he were still trapped in this hell with her, she didn't know how she'd bear it. But the knowledge that he was out there, saving children and living far from *this*— that kept her going. As long as her son was safe, she could endure.

She looked up at the man she'd married and smiled because he expected her to act as if she enjoyed being with him. Maybe… Maybe she wouldn't have to endure much longer.

"Mr. Wyatt?" The sound of Alexander's reedy voice cut through the office. "My apologies, but the campaign chairman is on line one."

"Now what?" he growled, abruptly letting her go.

Cybil did not exhale in relief because he'd already forgotten she was here. She merely escaped while she could.

She didn't want Bobby to be drawn back into his father's world, and the fact that Landon was using her to get their son to fall into line sickened her. But Bobby's anger, his willingness to stand up to his father...

No, maybe she wouldn't have to endure this marriage much longer at all.

She needed to be ready.

Would Robert convince his mother to leave Landon?

The last time, it'd gone...poorly.

He needed a better plan this time.

More than just hiding Cybil Wyatt, Robert needed to make sure Landon wouldn't ever be in a position to track her down.

His heart beat at a highly irregular pace. Last time he'd merely tried to hide his mother, in his own home, no less. He hadn't had a contingency plan in place and without that plan, the whole rescue had been doomed to fail.

This time would be different.

Wyatts didn't fail. They succeeded.

He entered Trenton's at five past eight. Thank God Jeannie was back tonight. She might not be able to offer assistance but she could at least tell him if New Zealand was a good idea or not. She might be the only person he knew who'd tell him the truth. Now all he had to do was find a way to ask.

A soft, feminine voice purred, "Good evening, Dr. Wyatt. What can I get you?"

His head snapped up at the unfamiliar voice, the hair on the back of his neck standing up. The bar at Trenton's was dimly lit, so it took a few moments for Robert to identify the speaker.

The woman behind the bar was *not* Jeannie. This woman was shorter, with long light-colored hair piled on top of her head. Jeannie was almost tall enough that she could look Robert in the eye, with dark hair cropped close.

"Where's Jeannie?" he growled.

It was Monday. She was supposed to be *here*.

The woman behind the bar batted her eyes. "I'm Miranda. Jeannie's on vacation. I'm more than happy to take care of you while she's gone…"

Robert glared at her. Dammit, Jeannie had said one week. She'd *promised*. And now he needed her and she wasn't here.

The pressure in his head was almost blinding. If he didn't see Jeannie tonight—right *now*—he might do something they'd all regret.

"Dr. Wyatt?"

The world began to lose color at the edges, a numb gray washing everything flat.

He needed to leave before he lost control.

But he couldn't because his mother had called him and there had to be a way to save her and he *needed* to see Jeannie.

She was the only one who could bring color back to his world.

"She's not on vacation. Tell me where she is." He leaned forward, struggling to keep his voice level. *"Or else."*

Miranda's teasing pout fell away as she straightened and stepped back. "She's not here," she said, the purr gone from her voice.

He wasn't going to lash out. A Wyatt never lost control.

So instead of giving in to the gray numbness and doing what Landon would do, Robert forced himself to adjust the cuffs on his bespoke suit, which gave him enough time to breathe and attempt to speak calmly.

He studied Miranda. She held his gaze, but he could see her pulse beating at her throat. She was probably telling the truth.

"I'd like to speak with the owner. Please."

The buzzing in his head became two discordant sounds. He could hear Landon snarling, *Wyatts don't ask*, at the same time as he heard Jeannie say, in that husky voice of hers, *There, was that so hard?*

When was the first time Jeannie had said that to him? He didn't remember. All he remembered was that she was the first person who'd ever dared tease him.

When he was sure he had himself back under control, he looked up. Miranda the substitute bartender wasn't moving.

"Now," Robert snarled.

With a jolt, she turned and fled.

It felt wrong to sit in his seat if Jeannie wasn't on the other side of the bar. Like this place wasn't home anymore.

Which was ridiculous because this was a bar where he spent maybe half an hour every night. It wasn't his sprawling Gold Coast townhouse with million-dollar views of Lake Michigan. It wasn't even the monstrosity of a mansion where he'd been raised by a succession of nannies. This was not home. This was just where Jeannie had been when he'd walked into this restaurant two years and ten months ago and sat down at this bar because he'd felt...lost.

It had been thirty-four months since Jeannie had stood in front of him, listening while he struggled to get his thoughts in order because his mother had refused to stay with him and Landon had come for her. Everything in Robert's carefully constructed world had gone gray, which had been good because then Robert didn't have to feel anything. Anything but the overpowering need for the perfect drink.

Sometimes, when Robert allowed himself to look back at that moment, he wondered if maybe Jeannie had been waiting patiently for him.

Where the hell *was* she?

Then it hit him. She'd said she had a family thing. She wasn't here now.

Something had gone wrong.

The realization gave him an odd feeling, one he did not

SARAH M. ANDERSON

like. He liked it even less when Miranda the substitute bartender returned with a man that looked vaguely familiar.

"Dr. Wyatt, it's so good to see you, as always," the man said, smiling in a way Robert didn't trust. "I'm sorry there's a problem. How can I correct things?"

Robert was running out of patience. "Who are you?"

"Julian Simmons." He said it in a way that made it clear Robert was supposed to remember who he was. "I own Trenton's. You're one of our most valued customers, so if there's a problem, I'm sure we can—"

Robert cut the man off. "Where's Jeannie?"

Robert couldn't tell in the dim light, but he thought Simmons might have gone a shade whiter. "Jeannie is taking some personal time."

Only a fool would think personal time and vacation time were the same thing. Robert was many things, but foolish wasn't one of them. "Is she all right?"

Simmons didn't answer for another long beat.

Something *had* happened; Robert knew it. Helplessness collided with an ever-increasing anger. He was not going to stand by while another woman was hurt. Not when he had the power to stop it.

"Jeannie is fine," Simmons finally said. "We're hopeful that she will rejoin us in a few weeks. I know she's your personal favorite, but Miranda is more than happy to serve you."

Both Miranda the substitute bartender and Simmons the restaurant owner recoiled before Robert realized he was snarling at them. "Tell me where she is. Now."

"Dr. Wyatt, I'm sorry but—"

Before he was aware of what he was doing, Robert had reached across the bar and took hold of Simmons's tie.

Robert could hear Landon Wyatt shouting, *No one says no to a Wyatt*, in his mind.

Or maybe he hadn't heard the words. Maybe he'd said them out loud because Miranda squeaked in alarm.

"You," he said to the woman, "can *go*."

He didn't have to tell her twice.

"Dr. Wyatt," Simmons said. "This is all a misunderstanding."

Belatedly, he realized he was probably not making the best argument. Abruptly, he released Simmons's tie. Robert realized he had overlooked the path of least resistance. Instead of allowing his temper to get the better of him, he should've started from a different negotiating position.

"How much?"

"What?" Simmons winced.

"How much?" Robert repeated. "I have frightened you and your employees, which wasn't my intent. I like coming here. I would like to return, once Jeannie is back in her position. I would like to…to make amends."

Which was as close as possible to apologizing without actually apologizing because Wyatts did *not* apologize.

Ever.

Simmons stared at him, mouth agape.

"Shall we say…" Robert picked a number out of thin air. "Ten thousand?"

"Dollars?" Simmons gasped.

"Twenty thousand. Dollars," he added for clarity's sake. Everyone had a price, after all.

Jeannie was in trouble and he had to help her. But to do that, he had to know where she was. If Simmons refused to take the bribe, Robert had other ways of tracking her down, but those would take more time. Time was one commodity he couldn't buy.

The buzzing in his head was so loud that it drowned out the hum of the restaurant. He gritted his teeth and blocked it out.

Simmons pulled his pocket square out and dabbed at

his forehead. "Do you realize how many laws you're asking me to break?"

"Do you realize how little I care?" Wyatt shot back.

When it came to things like abuse or murder, Wyatt knew and respected the law. When it came to things like this? Well, he was a Wyatt. Money talked.

Simmons knew it, too. "Do I have your word that you won't hurt her?"

"I won't even touch her." *Not unless she wants me to.*

The thought crossed his mind before he was aware it was there, but he shook it away.

Simmons seemed to deflate. "There was a family emergency."

The longer this man stood around hemming and hawing, the worse things could be for Jeannie. Belatedly, Robert realized he did not have twenty thousand dollars in cash on him. He placed a credit card on the bar. "Run it for whatever you want."

After only a moment's hesitation, Simmons took the card. "Let me get you the address, Dr. Wyatt."

About damn time.

Three

Jeannie all but collapsed onto the concrete step in front of Nicole's house, too numb to even weep.

No, that was wrong. This was her house now.

Nicole was dead.

And since there were no other living family members, Jeannie had inherited what Nicole had owned. Including their childhood home.

Everything left was hers now. The sensible used family sedan. The huge past-due bills to fertility clinics. The cost of burying her sister.

The baby.

It was too much.

Death was bad enough because it had taken Nicole, leaving Jeannie with nothing but wispy memories of a happy family. But who knew dying was so complicated? And expensive? Who knew unraveling a life would involve so much damned *paperwork*?

That didn't even account for Melissa. That baby girl was

days old. It wasn't right that she would never know her mother. It wasn't right that the family Nicole had wanted for so long...

Jeannie scrubbed at her face. It wasn't Melissa's fault that delivery had been complicated or that Nicole had developed a blood clot that had gone undiagnosed until it was too late. Dimly, Jeannie knew she needed to sue the hospital. This wasn't the 1800s. Women weren't supposed to die giving birth. But Jeannie couldn't face the prospect of more paperwork, of more responsibilities. She could barely face the next ten minutes.

She looked up at the sky, hoping to find a star to guide her. One little twinkling bit of hope. But this was Chicago. The city's light pollution was brighter than any star, and all that was left was a blank sky with a reddish haze coloring everything. Including her world.

She was supposed to be at work. She was supposed to be fixing the perfect Manhattan for the perfect Dr. Robert Wyatt, the man whose tipping habits had made her feel financially secure for the first time in her life. A hundred bucks a night, five nights a week, for almost three years—Dr. Robert Wyatt had single-handedly given Jeannie the room to breathe. To dream of her own place, her own rules...

Of course, now that she had an infant to care for and a mortgage and bills to settle, she couldn't breathe. She'd be lucky if her job at Trenton's was still there when she was able to go back. *If* she would be able to go back. Julian might hold her job for another week or so, but Jeannie knew he wouldn't hold it for two months. Because after an initial search of newborn childcare in Chicago, she knew that was what she'd need. Jeannie had found only day care that accepted six-week-old babies, but the price was so far out of reach that all she'd been able to do was laugh and close the browser. If she wanted childcare before Melissa was two months old, she needed a *lot* of money. And that was something she simply didn't have. Even if she sued the hospital, put the house on the market, sold the family sedan—it still wouldn't be enough fast enough.

Even though there were no stars to see, she stared hard at that red sky. This time she caught a flicker of light high overhead. It was probably just an airplane, but she couldn't risk it. She closed her eyes and whispered to herself, "Star light, star bright, grant me the wish I wish tonight."

She couldn't wish Nicole back. She couldn't undo any of the loss or the pain that had marked Jeannie's life so far. Looking back was a trap, one she couldn't get stuck in. She had no choice but to keep moving forward.

"I need help," she whispered.

Financial assistance, baby help, emotional support—you name it, she needed it.

There was a moment of blissful silence—no horns honking in the distance, no neighbors shouting, not even the roar of an airplane overhead.

But if Jeannie was hoping for an answer to her prayers, she didn't get it because that was when the small sound of Melissa starting to cry broke the quiet.

Sucking in a ragged breath, Jeannie dropped her head into her hands. She needed just a few more seconds to think but…

The baby didn't sleep.

Was that because Jeannie wasn't Nicole? Or was Melissa sick? Could Jeannie risk the cost of taking Melissa to the emergency room? Or…there was a pediatrician who'd stopped at the hospital before Melissa was discharged. But it was almost ten at night. If anyone answered the phone, they'd probably tell her to head to the ER.

The only person she knew who knew anything at all about small children was Dr. Wyatt, but it wasn't like she could ask him for advice about a fussy newborn. He was a surgeon, not a baby whisperer.

Jeannie had helped organize a shower for Nicole with some of Nicole's teacher friends and she had picked out some cute onesies. That was the sum total of Jeannie's knowledge about newborns. She wasn't sure she was even doing diapers right.

"Please," she whispered as Melissa's cries grew more agitated, although she knew there would be no salvation. All she could do was what she had always done—one foot in front of the other.

Jeannie couldn't fail that baby girl or her sister. But more than that, she couldn't give up on this family. She and Nicole had just started again. It felt particularly cruel to have that stolen so soon.

A car door slammed close enough that Jeannie glanced up. And looked again. A long black limo was blocking traffic in the middle of the street directly in front of the house. A short man wearing a uniform, complete with a matching hat, was opening the back door. He stood to the side and a man emerged from the back seat.

Not just any man.

Oh, God, Dr. Robert Wyatt was here. Her best, favorite customer. All she could do was gape as his long legs closed the distance between them.

"Are you all right?" he demanded, coming to a halt in front of her.

She had to lean so far back to stare at him that she almost lost her balance. He blocked out the night sky and her whole world narrowed to just him.

Yeah, she was a little unbalanced right now. "What are you doing here?"

Because he couldn't be here. She looked like hell warmed over twice, and the shirt she was wearing had stains that she didn't want to think about and she was a wreck.

He *couldn't* be here.

He was.

He stared at her with an intensity that had taken her months to get used to. "Are you *all right*?"

It wasn't a question. It was an order.

Jeannie scrambled to her feet. Even looking him in the eye, it still felt like he loomed over her. "I'm fine," she lied because what was she supposed to say?

She liked him as a customer. He was a gorgeous man, a great tipper—and he had never made her feel uncomfortable or objectified. Aside from that phantom touch of his hand brushing against hers—which could've been entirely accidental—they'd never done anything together beyond devise the perfect Manhattan. That was *it*.

And now he'd followed her to Nicole's house.

The man standing in front of her looked like he would take on the world if she asked him to.

His brow furrowed. "If everything's fine, why aren't you at work?"

"Is that why you're here?"

"You promised you'd be back today and you weren't. Tell me what's wrong so I can fix it."

She blinked. Had she actually wished upon a star? One with magical wish-granting powers?

"You can't fix this." It didn't matter how brilliant a surgeon he was, he couldn't help Nicole. No one could.

"Yes, I can," he growled.

He growled! At her! Then he climbed the first step. "I need you to be there, Jeannie." He took another step up, another step closer to her. "I need..."

"Robert." Without thinking, she put her hand on his chest because she couldn't let him get any closer.

She felt his muscles tense under her palm. It was a mistake, touching him. That phantom contact a week ago in the bar? The little sparks she'd felt then were nothing compared to the electricity that arced between them now. He was hot to the touch and everything had gone to hell, but he was here.

He'd come for her.

He looked down to where she was touching him and she followed his gaze. He wasn't wearing a tie, which was odd. He always wore one. She stared at the little triangle of skin revealed by his unbuttoned collar.

Then his fingertips were against her cheek and she gasped, a shiver racing down her back. "Jeannie," he whispered, lifting her chin until she had no choice but to look him in the eye. His eyes, normally so icy, were warm and promised wonderful things. His head began to dip. "I need…"

He was going to kiss her. He was going to press his perfect mouth against hers and she was going to let him because she could get lost in this man.

Just as she felt his warmth against her lips, Melissa's cries intruded into the silence that surrounded them.

"Oh! The baby!" Jeannie hurried into the house.

"The *baby*?" he called after her.

How much time had passed since Robert had emerged from the back of that sleek limo? Could have been seconds but it could've just as easily been minutes. Minutes where she'd left Melissa alone.

By the time she got back to the baby's room, Melissa was red in the face, her little body rigid, her arms waving. Was that normal? Or was Melissa in pain? Or…

"I'm sorry, I'm sorry," Jeannie said as she nervously picked the baby up, trying to support her head like the nurse had shown her. She was pretty sure she wasn't doing it right because Melissa cried harder. "Oh, honey, I'm so sorry." Sorry Nicole wasn't here, sorry Jeannie couldn't figure out the problem, much less how to fix it. "What's wrong, sweetie?" As if the baby could tell her.

Melissa howled and Jeannie couldn't stop her own tears. She couldn't bear the thought of losing this last part of her family.

"Here," a deep voice said as the baby was plucked out of Jeannie's arms. "Let me."

She blinked a few times, but in her current state of exhaustion what she saw didn't make a lot of sense.

Dr. Robert Wyatt, one of the Top Five Billionaire Bachelors of Chicago, a man so remote and icy it'd taken Jeannie years to get comfortable with his intense silences—*that* man was laying Melissa out on the changing pad, saying, "What seems to be the problem?" as if the baby could tell him.

"What…" Jeannie blinked again but the image didn't change. "What are you doing?"

Instead of answering, Robert pulled out his cell. "Reginald? Bring my kit in."

"Your kit?"

He didn't explain. "How old is this infant? Eight days?"

She wasn't even surprised he hadn't answered her question, much less come within a day of guessing Melissa's age. "Nine. Nicole, my sister, went into labor right after I last saw you." She tried to say the rest of it but suddenly she couldn't breathe.

Robert made a gentle humming noise. The baby blinked up at him in confusion, a momentary break in her crying. "What was her Apgar score?"

"Her *what*?"

Who the hell was this man? The Dr. Wyatt she knew didn't make gentle humming noises that calmed babies. There was nothing gentle about him!

Robert had Melissa down to her diaper. The poor baby began to wail again. He made a *tsking* noise. "Where is the mother?"

Jeannie choked on a sob. "She's…" No, that wasn't right. Present tense no longer applied to Nicole. "She developed blood clots and…"

Robert's back stiffened. "The father?"

"Sperm donor."

He made that humming noise again. Just then the door-bell rang and Melissa howled all the louder and Jeannie wanted to burrow into Robert's arms and pretend the last week had been a horrible dream. But she didn't get the chance because he said, "My kit—can you bring it to me, please?"

"Sure?" When Jeannie opened the door, the man from the car was there. "Reginald?"

"Miss." He tipped his hat with one hand. With the other, he hefted an absolutely enormous duffel bag. "Shall I bring this to Dr. Wyatt?"

"I'll take it. Thank you."

"Babies cry, miss," he said gently as he handed over the bag. "The good doctor will make sure nothing's wrong. Don't worry—it gets easier."

The kind words from an older man who looked like he might have dealt with crying babies a few times in his life felt like a balm on her soul.

"Thank you," Jeannie said and she meant it.

Reginald tipped his hat.

It took both hands, but she managed to lug the kit back to the baby's room. Melissa was still screaming. Probably because Robert was pinching the skin on her arms. "What are you doing?" Jeannie demanded.

"She's got good skin elasticity and her lungs are in great shape." He sounded calm and reasonable. "Ah, the kit. Come," he said, motioning right next to him. "Tell me everything."

Jeannie did as she was told, putting her hand on Melissa's little belly as Robert dug into the duffel. "She hasn't stopped crying since I brought her home two days ago. Nicole never even left the hospital. I don't know anything about babies."

"Clearly." She couldn't even be insulted by that. "Which hospital? Who were the doctors?" He came up with a stetho-scope and one of those tiny little lights.

Oh. His kit must be an emergency medical bag. "Uh, Covenant. Her OB was some old guy named Preston, I think? I don't remember who the pediatrician is." She realized that, at some point, Robert had shed his suit jacket and had rolled up his sleeves. He still had on his vest but there was something so undone about him right now...

He'd almost kissed her. And she'd almost let him. The man who didn't like to be touched, didn't show emotion—she'd touched him and he'd come within a breath of kissing her.

Even stranger, he was now touching—gently—Melissa.

This just didn't make sense. Robert didn't like touching people. Simple as that.

What exactly had she wished upon? No ordinary star had this kind of power behind it.

Robert listened to Melissa's chest and then peered into her mouth and ears before pressing on her stomach.

With a heartbreaking scream, the baby tooted.

"Oh, my gosh. I'm so sorry," Jeannie blurted out.

"As I expected," Robert said, seemingly unbothered by the small mess left in the diaper that was thankfully still under Melissa's bottom. He listened to her stomach. "Hmm."

"What does that mean?" Dimly, Jeannie was aware that this was the longest conversation she'd ever had with him.

"When was the last time you fed her?"

"Uh, about forty-five minutes ago. She drank about two ounces." That, at least, she could measure. She'd watched a few YouTube videos on how to feed a baby. Thank God for the internet.

Wait—when had she started thinking of him as Robert? Except for that one time, she hadn't allowed herself to use his given name at Trenton's because that implied a level of familiarity they didn't have.

Or at least, a level they hadn't had before he'd shown up

on her doorstep to make an accidental house call. Or before she'd touched his chest and he'd caressed her cheek and who could forget that near-kiss?

Robert it was, apparently.

"What are you feeding her?"

"The hospital sent home some formula…" She couldn't even remember the brand right now.

"Get it."

She hurried to the kitchen and grabbed the can and the bottle she hadn't had the chance to empty and clean yet. By the time she got back to the baby's room, Robert had apparently diapered and dressed the baby and was wrapping her in a blanket so that only her head was visible.

"This is called swaddling," he explained as, almost by magic, Melissa stopped screaming. "Newborns are used to being in the womb—not a lot of room to move, it's warm and they can hear their mother's heartbeat."

Embarrassment swamped her. "I thought… I didn't want her to get too hot."

"You can swaddle her in just a diaper—but keep her wrapped up. She'll be happier." He scooped the baby burrito into his arms and turned to Jeannie, casting a critical eye over her.

"Where did you learn how to do that?"

"Do what?"

She waved in his general direction. "Change a diaper. Swaddle a baby. Where did you learn how to take care of a baby?"

He notched an eyebrow at her and, in response, her cheeks got hot. "It's not complicated. Now, some babies have what we call a fourth trimester—they need another three months of that closeness and warmth before they're comfortable. Hold her on your chest as much as you can right now. She doesn't need to cry it out." His lips curved into that barely there smile. "No matter what the internet says."

She blushed. Hard.

He tucked Melissa against his chest as if it was the easiest thing in the world. He didn't seem the least bit concerned about how to support her head or that he might accidentally drop her or any of the worries that haunted Jeannie. Nor did he seem worried in the slightest about holding a baby in the vicinity of a suit that probably cost a few thousand dollars. He made the whole thing look effortless. Because it wasn't that complicated, apparently.

She wanted to be insulted—and she was—but the sight of Dr. Robert Wyatt *cuddling* a newborn, for lack of a better word, hit Jeannie in the chest so hard she almost stumbled.

"Here," she managed to say, holding the formula out for him.

With a critical eye, he glanced at the brand. Then, without taking it, he pulled out his cell again. "Reginald? Find the closest grocery store and pick up the following items…"

He rattled off a list of baby products that left Jeannie dizzy. When he ended the call, he nodded to the formula. "That brand has soy in it. Her symptoms are in line with a soy sensitivity."

"Crying is a symptom?"

He gave her a look that was almost kind. But not quite. "Her stomach is upset and she's not supposed to be that red. Both are signs she's not tolerating something well. Reginald will bring us several alternatives."

"So…there's nothing wrong with her?"

"No. Of course it could be colic and something more serious…"

All the blood drained from Jeannie's face so fast that she felt ill. *More* serious?

Robert cleared his throat. "I'm reasonably confident it's the formula."

"Oh. Okay. That's…" She managed to make it to the rocker that Nicole's fellow teachers had all pooled their money to buy. The baby just had a sensitive stomach. It wasn't anything Jeannie was doing wrong—the hospital had given her the formula, after all. "That's good." Her voice cracked on the words.

Robert stared at her. "Are you all right?"

Only *this* man would ask that question. She began to giggle and then she was laughing so hard she was sobbing and the words poured out of her. "Of *course* I'm not okay. I buried my sister and there was so much we didn't say and I'm responsible for a newborn but I have no idea what I'm doing and I don't have the money to do any of it and you're here, which is good, but *why* are you here, Robert?"

He stared at her. It would've been intimidating if he hadn't been rubbing tiny circles on the back of a tiny baby, who was making noises that were definitely quieter than all-out wailing. "You weren't at the bar."

"This," she said, waving her hand to encompass everything, "qualifies as an emergency."

"Yes," he agreed, still staring at her with those icy eyes. "When will you be back?"

If it were anyone else in the world, she'd have thrown him out.

Jeannie had made sure Miranda at work knew exactly how Robert liked his drink. Because Jeannie aged it in a cask, Miranda didn't even have to mix it. She just had to pour and serve. Even someone with standards as impossibly high as Robert's could be content with that for a few damn nights while Jeannie tried to keep her life from completely crumbling.

But for all that, she couldn't toss him onto the curb. He'd examined Melissa and calmed the baby down. He had a good, nonterrifying reason for why she kept crying and he had sent Reginald to get different formula. For the first time in a week, Jeannie felt like the situation was almost—*almost*—under control.

But not quite.

"Why do I need to go back to work?" she asked carefully because this was Dr. Robert Wyatt, after all—a man of few words and suspiciously deep emotions.

He looked confused by her question. "Because."

A hell of a lousy answer. "Because *why*?"

His mouth opened, then shut, then opened again. "Because I… I had a bad day." He seemed completely befuddled by this.

"I'm sorry to hear that. I'm currently having a bad life." He didn't smile at her joke. "Look, I don't know what to tell you. I have to put the baby first—you know, the baby you're currently holding? She's the most important thing in my life now and I'm all she's got. So I can't go back to work until I figure out how to take care of an infant, pay for childcare, possibly sue a hospital for negligence, settle my sister's outstanding debts and get a grip on my life. You'll have to find someone else to serve you a Manhattan!"

If he was insulted by her shouting, he didn't show it. "All right."

"All right?" That was almost too easy. "Good. Miranda at the bar knows how to pour… What are you doing?"

He had his cell again. "I don't like Miranda." Before Jeannie could reply to that out-of-the-blue statement, he went on, "Len? Wyatt. I've got a case for you—malpractice. Postpartum mortality. I want your best people on it. Yes. I'll forward the information to you as I get it."

"Robert?" Admittedly, she was having an awful day. But…had he just hired a lawyer for her?

"One moment." He punched up another number, all while still holding Melissa, which was more than Jeannie had been able to accomplish in the past two days. "Kelly? I'm going to need a full-time nanny to care for a newborn. Yes. Have a list for me by eleven tomorrow morning. I'll want to conduct interviews after I'm out of surgery."

Jeannie stared at him. "Wait—what are you doing?"

"My lawyer will handle your lawsuit. It won't get that far—the hospital *will* want to settle, but he'll make sure you get enough to take care of the child."

She heard the threat, loud and clear. His tone was the same as one time when he'd threatened a woman who'd groped him once. This was Robert Wyatt, a powerful, important man. He might be Jeannie's best customer and she might be infatuated with him but he also had the power to bend lawyers and whole hospitals to his will.

This was what she couldn't forget.

If he really wanted to, he'd bend *her* to his will.

She had to keep this from spinning out of control. "Melissa."

"What?"

"Her name is Melissa."

"Fine." But even as he dismissed that observation, he leaned his chin against the top of the baby's head and—there was no mistaking what she was seeing.

Dr. Robert Wyatt *nuzzled* Melissa's downy little head.

Then it only got worse because he did something she absolutely wasn't ready for.

He smiled.

Not a big smile. No, this was his normal smile, the one so subtle that most everyone else wouldn't even notice it. But she did. And it simply devastated her.

She had to be dreaming this whole thing. In no way, shape or form should Dr. Robert Wyatt be standing in what was, essentially, Jeannie's childhood bedroom, soothing a baby and somehow making everything better. Or at least bearable.

"Now," he went on, "I'll have a nanny over here by two tomorrow." He made as if he wanted to adjust his cuffs, then appeared to realize that he'd not only rolled his sleeves up to his elbows but was also still holding an infant who wasn't crying at all. He settled for looking at his watch. "You should be back at work on Wednesday."

Her mouth flopped open. *"What?"*

"You don't know how to care for an infant. I need you to be back at work. I'm hiring a nanny to help you." He glanced around the room. "And a maid."

He was already reaching for his phone when she snapped, "I don't know whether to be offended or grateful."

"Grateful."

Oh, she'd show him grateful, all right. "I'm not going back to work on Wednesday."

He paused with the phone already at his ear. Something hard passed over his eyes, but he said, "I'll also need a maid. Three days a week. Thanks." Then he ended the call. "What do you mean, you won't go back?"

She pushed herself to her feet. Thankfully, her knees held. "Dr. Wyatt—"

He made a noise deep in his throat.

"Robert," she said, trying to keep her voice calm and level because if she didn't at least try, she might start throwing things. "I'm sorry you're having a bad day and I appreciate that you're willing to throw a bunch of money at my problems, but I'm not going back to work this week. Maybe not next week."

"Why not?" His voice was so cold she shivered. "What else could you possibly need?"

She'd been wrong all these years because it turned out that Dr. Robert Wyatt really didn't have a heart. "To grieve for my sister!"

Four

Jeannie was yelling at him. Well. That was…interesting.

As was Robert's response. Very few people shouted at him and from an empirical standpoint, it was curious to note that his body tensed, his spine straightened and his face went completely blank because betraying any response was a provocation.

Rationally, he knew Jeannie was upset because of the circumstances. And he also understood that she wasn't about to attack him.

But damn, his response was hardwired.

He forced himself to relax, to exhale the air he was holding in. There was no need to let his fight-or-flight instincts rule him.

Jeannie was not his father. This was not a dangerous situation.

He would make this better.

In his office, when there was bad news, he had a basic script he followed. He offered general condolences, promised to do his best to make things better and focused on quantitative outcomes—heart valves, ccs of blood pumped, reasonable expectations postsurgery. And on those rare occasions when he lost a patient, either on the table or, more frequently, to a post-op infection, he kept things brief. *I'm sorry for your loss.* No one wanted to talk to him when he'd failed them, anyway.

Then there was the baby—*Melissa*, as Jeannie had insisted. Robert didn't often think of his patients in terms of their names because children were entirely too easy to love, and he couldn't risk loving someone who might not survive the day or the week or even the year.

But Melissa wasn't a patient, was she? Her heart and lung sounds had been clear and strong, with no telltale murmur or stutter to the beat. This was a perfectly healthy infant who simply needed different formula.

Robert couldn't remember the last time he'd held a healthy baby. By the time patients were referred to him at the hospital, they'd already undergone a barrage of tests and examinations by other doctors. The closest he got was seeing patients for their annual postoperation checkup. Most of them did well but there was always an undercurrent of fear to those visits, parents praying that everything was still within the bounds of medically normal.

Aside from general condolences, though, none of his scripts applied here. He'd already done everything obvious to fix the situation and somehow that had upset Jeannie. If he wasn't so concerned about her reaction, he'd be interested in understanding where the disconnect had happened.

But he was concerned. Jeannie wasn't the parent of a patient. She was… Well, he couldn't say she was a friend, either. She existed outside of work or personal relationships. She was simply…

The woman he'd almost kissed.

Because when the car had pulled up in front of her house, it had felt as if she'd been sitting out there, waiting for him.

Thankfully, he hadn't kissed her. Because she didn't look like she'd appreciate any overtures right now. She was a mess, her short hair sticking up in all directions, dark circles under her eyes, her stained, threadbare T-shirt hanging off one shoulder, revealing a blue bra strap.

He tore his gaze away from that bra strap. He normally didn't respond to the exposure of skin but knowing what color her bra was made him…uncomfortable.

Which was not the correct reaction, not when she was sitting there, quietly crying. It hurt him to see her like this, to know that she was in pain and there was a hard limit on what he could do to fix the situation. And, more than anything, he felt like a bastard of the highest order because he wasn't really doing anything for *her*. The lawyers, the nanny, the maid—that was all for his benefit. The sooner he took care of Jeannie, the sooner she could be there for him.

She swiped her hand across her cheeks and looked up at him. The pain in her eyes almost knocked him back a step.

"I'm sorry," she mumbled.

"Excuse me?"

She sniffed and it hurt Robert worse than a punch to the kidneys. How odd. "I didn't mean to yell at you. It's not your fault everything's gone to hell in a handbasket and you're just trying to help." She blinked up at him. "Aren't you?"

Wasn't he?

Say something. Something kind and thoughtful and appropriate. Something that would make things right. Or at least better.

The doorbell rang.

"That'll be Reginald." Although it certainly wasn't the brave thing to do, Robert hurried to the door.

"They had everything but that one brand—Enfamil," his driver said, straining under the weight of the bags.

"Make a note—have some sent over tomorrow." Robert stepped to the side as Reginald nodded and carried the bags into the house. The smell of something delicious hit Robert's nose. Chicken, maybe? "What did you get?"

"I thought the young lady might enjoy dinner," Reginald said, nodding at Jeannie, who was standing in the hallway, a look of utter confusion on her face. "It's hard to cook with a newborn."

"I… That's very kind of you. I'm not sure I've eaten today," she said, her voice shaky.

Robert experienced a flash of irrational jealousy because Reginald was the kind of man who didn't need a script to recite the appropriate platitudes at the appropriate times. He had a wife of almost forty years, four children and had recently become a grandfather. If anyone could help Robert find the right way to express condolences, it'd be Reginald.

But then Landon's voice slithered into Robert's mind, making him cringe. *Wyatts never ask for help.*

Right. Reginald was an employee. Robert paid him well to fill in the gaps, which was all he was doing here. It simply hadn't occurred to Robert that Jeannie might not have eaten recently.

Reginald smiled gently at Jeannie. "Where would you like the groceries?"

"Oh. The kitchen's right through there." She stepped past Robert and Melissa, her gaze averted. "Thank you so much for this."

Robert glanced down. The baby had fallen asleep, which was a good sign. Robert went to the nursery and laid the child on her back in the crib. She startled and then relaxed back into sleep.

He frowned. A blanket and two stuffed animals littered the mattress, both suffocation risks. He pulled them out. Jeannie really didn't know what she was doing, did she?

If he didn't want the chance to personally interview prospective nannies, he'd have one over here tonight. Maybe he should stay instead…

But he shut down that line of thinking. He had surgery tomorrow, which meant he needed to be at the hospital at four in the morning. He'd never needed a lot of sleep but he always made sure to get at least four hours before surgery days. He never took risks when lives were on the line.

He studied Melissa. The sound of murmuring from the kitchen filled the room with a gentle noise and the baby sighed in her sleep. Robert had handled so many babies and children over the course of his career but this infant girl was…different. He wasn't sure why.

"Sleep for her," he whispered to the baby.

By the time he made it back to the living room—really, this house was little more than a shoebox—Reginald was at the front door as Jeannie said, "Thank you so much again. How much do I owe you?"

Reginald shot Robert a slightly alarmed look over Jeannie's shoulder.

"That's all, Reginald."

"Miss, it's been a pleasure." With a tip of his hat, Reginald was out the door before Jeannie could protest.

A moment of tense silence settled over the house. No babies crying, no helpful drivers filling the gaps of conversation. Just Robert and Jeannie and the terrible feeling that instead of making everything better for her, he'd made things worse.

"Robert," Jeannie began and for some reason, she sounded…sad? Or just tired?

He couldn't tell and that bothered him. This was *Jeannie*. He was able to read her better than he could read anyone. "I'd recommend starting the baby—I mean, Melissa—on this formula," he said, picking the organic one. "No soy."

In response, she dropped her head into her hands.

"It'll take a day or two before the other formula is completely out of her system," he went on in a rush, "but if she gets worse at any time, call me."

Her head was still in her hands. "Robert."

"The nanny should be here by two tomorrow at the absolute latest," he went on, because he was afraid of what she might say—or what she might not say. "She'll teach you everything you need to know. Don't put blankets or stuffed animals in the crib."

She raised her head and stared at him as if she'd never seen him before. *"Robert."*

Inexplicably, his heart began to race. And was he sweating? He was. How strange. "Do you need any other financial assistance? Until Len is able to negotiate a settlement with the hospital, that is? Just let me know. I can—"

"Stop." She didn't so much as raise her voice—it certainly wasn't a shout—but he felt her power all the same.

He swallowed. Unfortunately, he was fairly certain it was a nervous swallow. Which was ridiculous because he was not nervous. He was a Wyatt, dammit. Nerves weren't allowed. Ever.

Still, he stopped talking. Which left them standing in another awkward silence.

Jeannie ran her hands through her hair, making it stand straight up as if she'd touched a live wire. She looked at him, then turned on her heel and walked the three steps into the kitchen.

What was happening here? He took a step after her but before his foot hit the ground she was back, hands on her hips. He stumbled as she strode to him.

"Robert," she said softly.

"I put Melissa in her crib," he said as she advanced on him. "She was asleep."

Relief fluttered across Jeannie's face but she didn't slow down. Unbelievably, Robert backed up. He'd learned the hard way that Wyatts didn't retreat and never, ever cowered.

But before her, he retreated. Just a step. Then all his training kicked in and he held his ground. But he felt himself swallow again and damn it all, he knew it was nervously.

Her mouth opened but then it closed and he saw her chest rise with a deep breath. "Why are you doing this, Robert?"

Doing what? But he bit down on those words because they were a useless distraction from the issue.

He knew what *this* was. So did she.

How could he put it into words? He wasn't entirely sure what those words were, other than he needed her. She was having problems that prevented her from being where he needed her to be so he was solving the problems.

But none of that was what came out. Instead, he heard himself say, "You need the help."

Her eyes fluttered closed and she did that long exhale again. "So that's it? You're not going to tell me why you tracked down my address, performed a medical examination on my niece, ordered your staff to hop to it and are now standing in my living room, condescendingly refusing to answer a simple question?"

"I'm not condescending," he shot back before he could think better of it.

"Of course you're not." Was that...sarcasm? "If you can't tell me why, then I have to ask you to leave." Her throat worked. "And not to come back."

A raw kind of panic gripped him. "I need you. At the bar."

She leaned away from him. "Miranda is perfectly capable of making your drink. I showed her how and there's enough blend in the cask to last a few months. Worst case, I can always go mix up more."

"But she's not you."

Jeannie's brow furrowed. "And that's a problem?"

She was too close. He could smell the sour tang of old formula on her shirt and see how very bloodshot her eyes were. But, in this light, he could also see things that he'd missed in the dim bar at Trenton's. Her dark hair had red undertones to it and her eyes were brown but with flecks of both green and gold. If anyone else had him in this position, Robert would either get around them or force the issue. It was always better to go on the offensive than be left in a weakened position.

But that's where he was now. Weakened.

"I…" To admit weakness was to admit failure and failure was not an option. "I can't talk to her. Not like I can to you."

"Robert, we barely talk," she said, her exasperation obvious. He was doing a terrible job of this. "I mean, I get the feeling you just don't talk to anyone. That's how you are."

"But you're different."

She stilled under his touch, which was when he realized he was, in fact, touching her. His hand had somehow come to rest on her cheek, just like it had earlier. Her skin was warm and soft and just felt…right.

"I can't afford to pay you back," she whispered, her hand covering his. But instead of flinging his fingers away from her face, she pressed harder so that his palm cradled her cheek.

Finally, he found the damned words. "That—that right there is why you're different. Anyone else, they'd look at me and you know what they'd say?" She shook her head, but carefully, like she was afraid she might break that singular point of contact. "They'd be calculating how much they could get out of me, what they'd have to do to get it. Your Miranda—"

"She flirts with everyone, Robert," Jeannie said softly. "Bigger compliments mean bigger tips. That's how things work. Everyone does it."

The thought of Jeannie acting like Miranda for money wasn't right. "You don't. Not with me."

She leaned into his touch. "What happened?"

What *hadn't* happened? Without conscious effort, he wrapped his arm around her waist and pulled her into his chest. "I might have made some threats. There may have been bribes exchanged."

She gasped but didn't pull away. She should have. For years now, he'd kept that part of himself on lockdown, refusing to let Landon win. But tonight he'd been a Wyatt through and through. Thank God she hadn't been there to see it.

"Oh, Robert," she said, his name a sigh on her lips. "Just because I wasn't there?"

No. The denial broke free but somehow, he kept it in because it was a damned lie and he'd come this far. Lying to her would be worse than what he'd done at the bar. "Yes."

"Hmm." Her body came flush with his, soft and warm. She felt right in his arms, her breasts pressed against his chest.

How long had he been waiting for this moment?

"You're touching me," she murmured, tucking her chin against his neck.

"That is correct." He felt her lips move against his skin. Was she smiling? He hoped she was smiling.

"You don't like to be touched."

Of course she knew. That was why he'd needed to see her tonight, needed to do whatever it took to get her back behind the bar. Because she understood him. "No."

Of course, if she were back behind the bar, he wouldn't have this moment with her. She sighed into him, her arms around his waist, her chest flush with his and it should've been too much, too close, too dangerous but...

It wasn't.

He gathered her closer in what he belatedly realized was a hug. How strange.

"I'm sorry for your loss." The words felt right so he kept going. "You must've loved her very much."

"I didn't love her nearly enough. It's...it's complicated.

We had a pretty messed up family and we'd gone almost five years without speaking. We were just..." She sniffed. "We were just figuring out how to be a family again," she went on, her voice tight. "And now we'll never get that back. It's gone forever."

An odd sensation built in his chest. "I'm sorry to hear that."

Was it possible to start a family over like that? Obviously, Landon Wyatt would never be a part of a do-over. But if Robert could get his mother away... Could they figure out how to be a family again?

"So I can't come back to work right now. You understand? I have to protect Melissa and make things right and... and honor my sister, imperfect as she was and as I am. I have to honor our family."

Moisture dampened his skin. He leaned back and tilted her chin up. Tears tracked down her cheeks. He wiped those away with his thumbs. "Anything I can do to help, I'll do."

Her smile was shaky at best. "You mean, besides the lawyer, nanny, maid and your chauffeur making grocery runs for me?"

"Yes."

"Can you tell me why you're here?" It wasn't an ultimatum this time, merely a question.

He opened his mouth to tell her because talking to her was the whole reason he was here, wasn't it?

But she'd had the worst day of her life. And although things were not particularly wonderful for him right now, he simply couldn't bear to add his burden to hers. "No. I won't make things harder for you."

Was that disappointment in her eyes? Or just relief? "You understand that I might not be able to go back to work, right? Julian will hold my job for a few weeks but—"

"Your job will be there," Robert interrupted. "If I have to

buy the restaurant from him at triple what it's worth, you'll have a job there."

Her eyes got very wide but she didn't pull away. "You would do that for me?"

"If that's what you need, I'll make it happen." His gaze dropped to her lips, which were parted in surprise or shock or, hell, *horror*, at his autocratic ways for all he knew.

"Why?"

"I told you," he said, his voice gruff. He dragged his gaze away from her mouth and saw what had to be confusion on her face. She was closer than she'd been outside on the front steps, closer than she'd been during that hug.

"Tell me again," she said, her voice barely a breath on his lips.

Close enough to kiss.

"Because I need you," he whispered against her and then he took her mouth with his.

Five

Fact: Robert was kissing her.

Fact: He didn't like to be touched. But seeing as his mouth slanted over hers, his hands cupped her face and angled her head so he could deepen the kiss, it seemed he was okay with this type of touching. But that just led her back to…

Fact: Dr. Robert Wyatt, heir to the Wyatt Medicals fortune, one of the Top Five Billionaire Bachelors in Chicago, was providing her with a lawyer, a nanny, a maid and was also apparently willing to buy a restaurant just so she could serve him a Manhattan.

And, unavoidably, it came back to this fact: *He was kissing her.*

Heat cascaded from where he touched her, shivering sparks of white-hot need that burned through her with a pain that was the sweetest pleasure she'd ever felt.

When was the last time she'd showered?

That thought pushed her into breaking the kiss, which

was really a shame because for all his overbearing, condescending, threatening behaviors, he was a hell of a kisser.

Right man, wrong time.

That was the thought that ran through her mind as she stared at him, her chest heaving. She crossed her arms in front of her to fight off a shiver. Why now?

"That was…" He seemed to shake back to himself. He started to straighten his cuffs and then realized they were still rolled to his elbows so instead he fixed his sleeves. "That was not what I intended."

"Oh, for Pete's sake, Robert." Okay, so she'd kissed *the* Robert Wyatt. Her favorite customer. The man who had fueled more than a few years' worth of hot dreams and needy fantasies. But even if that kiss would keep her going for a few more years, it didn't change anything.

This was still Robert. Small talk was beyond him.

His brow furrowed as he got one cuff fixed. "What?"

"That's not what you say after you kiss a woman."

He paused and then, amazingly, straightened the sleeve he'd just fixed. "It's not?"

"No." She took a deep breath, but that was a bad idea because without the bar to separate them and the tang of wine and whiskey in the air to overpower her senses, she inhaled his scent, a rich cologne that was spicy and warm and still subtle.

So. There was one aspect of him that wasn't designed to dominate. One and counting.

She headed toward the kitchen where the scent of chicken was stronger. Her stomach growled and she knew she needed to eat. The chauffeur hadn't been wrong. She wasn't sure she'd eaten today and if Melissa would just sleep for another few minutes, Jeannie might be able to get both a meal and a shower out of the deal.

That was a huge *if.* That baby hadn't gotten more than thirty minutes of sleep at a time since… Well, in her whole life. Frankly, Jeannie was probably lucky she'd made it through one of the most perfect kisses she'd ever had without interruption.

"What am I supposed to say?"

She almost smiled because the man had *no* clue. "Something that doesn't make it sound like you wish you hadn't just kissed me." She waved this away. "It's not important."

A rumbling noise caught her attention and she spun to realize that not only was Robert growling, he was moving fast, too. With both cuffs fastened. "You're important," he said and if anyone else had said that in that tone of voice, it would've been a threat but for him? His voice was possessive and demanding and needy all at the same time and it wasn't a threat.

It was a promise.

Oh, how she wanted him to keep that promise.

"The kiss was important," he went on, his ice-blue eyes fierce and surprisingly warm. "But I don't want to make you feel like you *owe* me a kiss or your body. That's not what this is. I'm *not* like that."

"Then what is it?" She managed to swallow. "What are you like?"

His mouth opened and then snapped shut and he stepped back. Damned if he didn't adjust his cuffs again.

"Will you be all right tonight? I can have a nanny here for the night."

Part of her was so, *so* thankful that he wasn't going to suggest he should stay because…she might take him up on that.

So yeah, the other part of her was disappointed that Robert had suddenly become Dr. Wyatt again. Super disappointed. Because if that kiss was any indication, *man*. All that precision and control combined with the heat she felt every single time their bodies touched?

He would be *amazing*.

"We'll be okay." She rested her hand on his arm. Even through the fine cotton of his shirt, she could feel the rock-hard muscles in his arm.

Focus, Jeannie.

"Are you sure?"

Frankly, Robert Wyatt was kind of adorable when he was concerned. Perhaps because the look did not come naturally to him. "Positive. I had this kind man teach me about swaddling, get me different formulas and generally be amazing." She squeezed his arm.

He lifted her hand away from his arm and her heart dropped a ridiculous amount because he was back to being Dr. Wyatt and she shouldn't be touching him. But again, he surprised her because he didn't drop her hand. Instead, he brought it to his lips and, with that hint of a smile tugging at the corners of his mouth, kissed her knuckles.

It was an old-fashioned move right out of a romance novel but damn if it didn't work all the same.

He would be *so* amazing.

She had always managed to keep her lustful thoughts about this man safely contained, but nothing was contained right now, not with his lips warming her body.

His eyes shifted to the side. "Ah," he said, finally releasing her and moving to where Nicole had a message board hung up by the coat hooks. He picked up the marker. "This is my personal number. Call or text anytime. I have surgery in the morning so this," he added, writing a second number, "is my assistant."

She started to protest that she could handle things for another twenty-four hours, but that was when Robert added, "I'll stop by tomorrow night, see how the nanny is settling in."

Oh. He was coming back. The thought sent a little thrill through her, even though she knew it shouldn't. She would definitely make sure she'd showered by then. "That's not necessary."

"I disagree."

Of course he did.

"It should be fine."

"I'll expect the pleasure of your company, then."

The air rushed out of her lungs because that was not only a good line, but coming out of Robert's mouth?

A pleasure, indeed.

"Will you tell me what's bothering you, then?"

A shadow crossed over his eyes. She could feel him retreating—emotionally and physically, because he opened the door and walked out of Nicole's house. "No."

"Why not?" she asked his back.

He was halfway down the steps when he turned, with that confused look on his face. "Because."

She rolled her eyes. "That continues to be a terrible answer, you know."

"Because I won't put you in danger," he said.

Then he walked off to where Reginald was waiting, with the car door open.

The chauffeur tipped his cap at Jeannie and then they were gone.

What the ever-loving *hell*?

Melissa was crying when the doorbell rang because of course she was.

"One second!" Jeannie yelled.

No matter how many times she watched the video tutorial, she couldn't get the baby swaddled. At least, not anything like Robert had done. And while Melissa had definitely slept more after drinking the soy-free formula Robert had recommended, Jeannie was still unshowered and exhausted. Getting ninety minutes of sleep at a time was an improvement over forty-five minutes at a time, but not much of one.

Screw it. She picked Melissa up and settled for tucking the blanket around her little body.

The doorbell rang again at almost the exact same moment her phone buzzed. Jeannie grabbed her phone and looked at the text. Of course it was from Robert.

Maja Kowalczyk
Text me immediately if you don't like her.

This was accompanied by a photo of an older woman, her hair in a bun and her face lined with deep laugh lines.

"Miss Kaufman? Are you able to get the door?" an accented voice yelled—politely—over the sounds of Melissa wailing.

That man was lucky she'd been able to check her phone. That was just like him to expect her to drop everything to respond to him when, in reality, texting back was a pipe dream, one that ranked well below showering.

Jeannie shoved the phone in her pocket and gave up on the blanket. Instead, she wrapped her arms around Melissa and held her tight against her chest, like Robert had been doing last night. It helped, a little.

The doorbell rang and this time, it was accompanied by knocking. Her phone buzzed again but she ignored it and managed to make it to the front door.

"I'm here," she snapped, which was not the most polite start to any conversation but seriously, could everyone just give her a second?

"Ah, good." The woman on the stoop matched the woman in the photo. But Jeannie was surprised to see a rolling suitcase next to her. The older woman smiled warmly and said, "It's all right—she's here. Yes, everything is fine. Thank you, Dr. Wyatt."

Which was the point that Jeannie realized that Maja wasn't talking to her but on her cell phone. To Robert.

And to think, Jeannie had once concluded that Nicole was the biggest control freak in the world.

The nanny ended the call and clasped her hands in front of her generous bosom. She was wearing a floral dress, hideous tan shoes and a cardigan, for Pete's sake. It was at least eighty degrees today! "Hello, Miss Kaufman, I'm Maja Kowalczyk."

"Hi. I'm Jeannie."

Maja's eyes crinkled as she went on, "Dr. Wyatt said you needed..." Her voice trailed off as she took a good look at Melissa and Jeannie. Melissa chose that moment to let out a pitiful little wail. "Oh, you poor dears," she clucked. "May I come in?"

"I guess?" Jeannie didn't have much choice. She needed help and, if Robert was still planning on stopping by at some point in the near future, she needed a shower.

Frankly, she wasn't sure she hadn't hallucinated last night. She'd wished upon something that probably wasn't a star and then Robert had shown up, kissed her, thrown a whole bunch of money at her problems and...driven off into the night.

It was the stuff of dreams. And also possibly nightmares. She wasn't sure which.

Because there was definitely something unreal about watching Maja wheel her little suitcase into the house. Jeannie peeked out the front door, but no long black car blocked traffic and no gorgeous billionaire climbed her stairs, hellbent on upending her world.

Maja gasped at the mess and Jeannie figured if it was a dream, the house would be a whole lot cleaner. It wasn't like she hadn't tried because she *had*. But Melissa was still super fussy and a splotchy red color. Jeannie had not somehow acquired the power to swaddle anything, much less an agitated infant, and housekeeping had never been a priority for her in the first place, which had always driven Nicole nuts.

So yeah, everything was still a disaster.

"Sorry about this," Jeannie began, but Maja just shook her head.

"That nice Dr. Wyatt, he told me what to expect. I am so sorry about your sister."

And that was when Jeannie found herself folded into a hug against Maja's impressive bosom. Tears pricked her eyes but she didn't know this woman and could only hope that Robert knew what he was doing in hiring her.

"There now," Maja said, taking a step back and looking completely unruffled. "I think I will take this *babisui* and get her dressed and you, my dear, will take a shower and lie down, yes?"

If Jeannie stood here much longer, she was going to start crying because a shower and a nap sounded like the best things ever. "Yeah, okay." Maja reached out for Melissa but Jeannie interrupted. "Um, just so we're clear, what are your qualifications?"

Any qualifications were better than what Jeannie had. But if she was going to hand Melissa off to a complete stranger and then fall asleep with said stranger in the house, she wanted reassurances.

Jeannie had full faith that Robert wouldn't just hire some random woman but she needed to be a part of this decision. Robert might be paying the bills because… Well, she was still really unclear on his reasons at this point.

"Ah, yes." Maja nodded firmly as if she approved of Jeannie's caution. "My husband died and there wasn't much left for me in Poland, so I came here twenty-seven years ago, when my son married a nice American girl. I was a nurse in a hospital nursery in Poland and here I cared for my grandchildren when they were small. When they went to school, my daughter-in-law had a friend who was starting the nanny business and she took me on. I speak fluent Polish, English and Russian, as well as some German and

French. Not much French, actually," she said with a rueful smile.

"I, uh, speak English. And some bad Spanish," Jeannie blurted out, feeling woefully outclassed by this woman. Five languages plus she'd been a nurse? No wonder Robert had hired her.

Maja nodded. "I have cared for small babies my entire life. I have copies of my medical certifications and background checks for you. Dr. Wyatt also has copies. He has instructed me to stay for a week, including overnights, with your approval until you feel more confidence. Then I am to come every day from noon until midnight, unless you have a different schedule in mind?"

Yeah, noon to midnight was Robert gaming the system so she could be back at Trenton's, serving his drink.

Maja was a former nurse. Someone who'd spent a lifetime with babies. Someone who would know if something was really wrong and would teach Jeannie how to handle the basics and…and…

Relief hit her so hard her legs began to shake. This was going to work out. Things were going to get better. They *had* to.

She almost smiled to herself. Robert simply wouldn't allow them to get worse, would he?

Melissa fussed and that was when the blanket and diaper fell off. "Uh, sorry about this," Jeannie muttered as Maja gave her a sympathetic smile. "You're hired and I would *love* a shower."

"And a nap, dear." She took the naked, fussing baby from Jeannie's arms. "Go on. The *babisui* and I will get to know each other, won't we?" she cooed at Melissa, who responded by straightening her legs and arms and farting loudly.

Without a diaper.

"Ah, good," Maja said, not horrified in the least even as Jeannie's face shot hot with mortification. If only Melissa could stop doing *that* when someone walked into the house! "The bad milk is working its way out. Better, my little angel? Let's get you cleaned up. Oh, yes, it's very hard to be a *babisui*, isn't it?" Murmuring softly, she carried Melissa back to the nursery as if she'd spent more than ten minutes in this house.

"Nicole," Jeannie whispered, looking up at the ceiling, "I'm doing the best I can. I hope this is okay."

Her phone buzzed. It was, unsurprisingly, Robert. What was surprising was that he was actually calling her. "Yes?"

"Does Maja meet with your approval?"

"And hello to you, too."

He made that noise that was almost a growl again and although Jeannie was exhausted in ways she'd never even imagined possible, a thrill of desire raced through her. "Is she acceptable or do I need to find a replacement?"

"She's lovely, Robert," Jeannie sighed. "Thank you for sending her over."

"Good. I'll be by later." Before she could get any details about that—like a specific time—he ended the call.

That man.

He was only coming to make sure Maja would be able to get Jeannie back to work as soon as possible. His visit likely had nothing to do with the way he'd held her last night and less than nothing to do with the kiss.

She glanced at the clock. It was two-thirty. If she knew Robert…

That man would walk into this house at exactly eight tonight.

She all but ran to the shower. The clock was ticking.

Six

Last night he'd held Jeannie in his arms. She was right; he didn't like to be touched but with her...

"Sir?"

When he'd felt the light movement against the skin of his neck—she'd been smiling, he was just sure of it. Smiling in his arms and it hadn't been wrong. He hadn't had his guard up like normal. But that'd been the problem, hadn't it? If he'd been operating with his usual amount of caution, he wouldn't have kissed her.

Or ruined it by apologizing. Would she have kissed him again if he'd kept his mouth shut?

"Dr. Wyatt?"

Robert dragged his thoughts away from Jeannie and looked at Thomas Kelly, his assistant.

"Will there be anything else, sir?"

"You have the maid lined up?" Jeannie's house was such a disaster it was veering close to being a health hazard for the child.

Melissa, he corrected.

"Yes, sir," the young man said eagerly.

Everything Kelly did was eager. Only twenty-three, he'd been working for Robert since he'd graduated from Loyola, on the recommendation of a professor whose grandson had come through open-heart surgery with flying colors. Thomas Kelly was someone who existed outside the spheres of influence of Landon Wyatt, which made him valuable.

Kelly checked his tablet. "Rona will arrive at the house tomorrow at ten a.m. She's Darna's sister and the background check was clean."

"Ah." Darna was Robert's maid and had, over the past few years, proven to be trustworthy. He would've preferred Darna handling Jeannie's house herself but Darna's sister was the next best option.

If Landon Wyatt knew that Robert had developed a soft spot for a bartender...

Dammit. What was he supposed to do? He couldn't abandon Jeannie to the winds of fate. Nor could he turn a blind eye to that baby girl. Yes, her allergic reaction had been mild and not life-threatening and yes, Robert could turn the case over to a pediatrician but...

Jeannie had kept him going after what had happened the last time he'd seen his parents. God willing, she'd never know how much he owed her, but he wasn't about to let her twist in the wind. Jeannie needed that infant to be well. Robert needed Jeannie.

What was the point of being one of the most powerful men in the country if he didn't use that power to get what he needed?

"Rona signed the nondisclosure agreement?"

"Yes. Copies are on file."

"Good."

Everyone who worked for Robert signed NDAs. Unlike

Landon, who used NDAs to hide his monstrous behavior, Robert used them to keep his employees from talking. To the press, to Landon, to the board of Wyatt Medicals.

Not that NDAs stopped the talk completely. Robert had still been named to that ridiculous list of billionaire bachelors, which had the same effect as painting a big target on his back. And he didn't make his patients sign NDAs, although after the last time a family had gone to the newspapers to tell everyone how Robert had quietly covered their hospital bills, he'd considered it. Sadly, the hospital lawyers had informed him that making patients sign NDAs was not allowed.

Funny how it'd never even occurred to him to have Jeannie sign one. But then again, she existed on a different level. Besides, she wouldn't tell anyone anything. He trusted her.

He eyed Kelly. "You enjoy working for me, don't you?"

"Yes, sir." The young man didn't even hesitate.

"You feel you're adequately compensated for your work?" Kelly was on call twenty-four hours a day.

Kelly smirked. "If I say yes, have I talked myself out of a raise?"

Robert would give anything to discuss this plan with Jeannie. She'd see things from a different angle, spot any holes in his plan. But she had so much to worry about right now that Robert couldn't add to her burdens.

Kelly was his assistant, not his friend. As much as he liked the young man, Robert couldn't risk weakening his position by confiding uncertainty to an employee.

Which meant Robert was on his own here. "I need a plane."

"I can have your jet ready to take off inside of forty-five minutes," Kelly said, already tapping on his tablet.

"No." Robert must've said it more forcefully than he intended because Kelly's head snapped up. "I need a hired plane and an independent flight crew on standby. They're not to know who's paying them and they can't ask questions."

A look crossed Kelly's face. Confusion? Or concern? It didn't matter. "When?"

"Saturday after next." He straightened his cuffs as Reginald turned onto Jeannie's street.

"That's the night of…" Kelly trailed off and Robert realized he was glaring at the man.

"Yes." This idea felt risky, with a high probability of failure. If he got Mom away, Landon would do everything in his prodigious power to punish his wife and Robert.

If Mom didn't agree… Could Robert really leave her to Landon? Could he abandon his own mother a second time?

It wasn't even a question.

"The destination will be Los Angeles," he went on. "From there, I'll need two first-class tickets to Auckland."

"New Zealand?" Kelly's voice jumped an octave.

"Yes. And it goes without saying that, if you mention these arrangements to anyone, I will be *upset*."

"Completely understood, sir." Kelly cleared his throat. "I'll need names for the commercial tickets."

"Cybil Wyatt."

Kelly inhaled sharply. How much did he know about Robert's family? Kelly had to interact with Landon's assistant, Alexander, from time to time. Surely, he at least suspected…

"I cannot guarantee we'll be able to use her passport, so make arrangements for travel documents."

Kelly nodded. "And the second ticket?"

Robert considered adding his name to that second ticket but someone had to stay in Chicago and throw Landon off the trail.

The possible outcomes played out in his mind. If Robert did this right, not only would he get his mother to safety, but he'd also expose Landon's behavior during the aftermath of

Mom's disappearance and single-handedly knock Landon out of politics. Hopefully, for good.

The car stopped in front of Jeannie's house. Robert's heart did an odd little skip at the sight of the small box of a house. It was squat, with a distinctive air of disrepair. He should hire contractors to fix the siding. That roof looked like it was on its last legs. Plus, the yard was a mess...

Jeannie needed help and he couldn't help her from a different hemisphere, could he?

Plus, you can't kiss her from Auckland, a voice whispered in his mind.

Right. Well. It had been a perfect kiss. But it'd be best for all parties if he didn't kiss her again.

"Make sure there's a nurse on board—that's the second ticket," he said. He wanted to be there for his mother because he missed her in ways that it hurt to think about but if she wasn't around Landon, he could talk to her whenever he wanted. "All expenses paid, with generous bonuses. Be sure to run every check on whoever you hire. This situation requires complete secrecy and discretion. They may be required to prevent Cybil from contacting Landon or returning to Chicago before..." *Before it was safe.* "Before it's appropriate."

Because if he got his mother to Los Angeles but she gave in to fear and tried to back out of the plan like she had three years ago, Robert knew Landon wouldn't stop at just cutting off all contact like he had before. No, the man would salt the earth behind him.

Robert dealt in life and death every day. This was another situation where he couldn't risk a loss.

"Arrange housing in New Zealand," he directed Kelly. "Someplace secluded and safe, with an open-ended lease. Make sure it's staffed appropriately. And hire a guard for this house," he added, motioning to Jeannie's house. It didn't even have a fence to slow someone from approaching the front door. Jeannie had been just sitting on the stoop last night, with the door open behind her. "I don't want anyone to realize the house is under surveillance." Just in case Landon started digging and came across Jeannie.

No, Robert couldn't risk losing anything.

It might not be enough to just get his mother away. If Robert left Landon with the means of tracking her down, the bastard would.

Which meant only one thing.

His stomach turned.

"Yes, sir. Anything else?"

"Schedule a meeting tomorrow morning at six a.m. with Len at my office in the hospital. Who do we know in the prosecutor's office? And a private investigator—someone we trust. Oh, I'll expect you to be there, as well."

Robert had to go on rounds at seven and then see patients. But he could get a lot of strategic planning laid out before that. Kelly could make a great many things happen, but if Robert wanted to take on Landon, he'd need more than just an escape plan.

He'd need to be the one to salt the earth behind him.

Kelly didn't even blink at the early hour. "Of course."

Reginald opened Robert's car door at precisely 7:58 p.m. "That will be all for now."

"Yes, sir," Kelly said as Robert climbed out of the car. He called out, "Have a good evening, sir."

Robert didn't bother to respond as Reginald snapped the car door behind him. "See Mr. Kelly home," he told Reginald. "I won't need you for at least an hour."

It would take that long to get a report from Maja and check Melissa over and make sure that everything he'd ordered had been delivered and...

And see Jeannie.

But just to find out how she was doing. Not because he needed her or anything. He was Robert Wyatt. He didn't need anyone, most especially not a bartender. Last night had just been…

One of those things.

"Very good, Dr. Wyatt."

He strode up the stairs to Jeannie's house but before he could knock, the door opened and suddenly all the air rushed out of his lungs because there she was.

"Robert," she said, her voice soft. "You're on time. As usual."

She'd been waiting for him. Again, he had that sense that she'd always been waiting for him.

"Jeannie." She looked better, he realized. She had on a pair of loose-fitting denim shorts and an old-looking Cubs T-shirt and her feet were bare.

She looked good. She'd showered and the dark circles under her eyes were less prominent and she was smiling.

It hit him like a kick to the chest.

He must have been staring because she asked, "Is there something on my shirt?" as color washed her cheeks. "I just put it on…" She held it out from her chest, which made the deep vee of the neck gape even lower.

Her bra was white today. And moments ago she hadn't been wearing that shirt.

He was here to check the baby and make sure Jeannie had the support she needed for the optimum outcome. He was here to confirm that the people he'd hired were doing a satisfactory job. Jeannie was his bartender and he wanted everything to get back to normal. Because the longer he stepped outside of his routine and the more attention he drew to Jeannie, the more dangerous things were for all of them.

None of that careful logic prevented what happened next.

Knowing he was putting her at risk didn't stop him from stepping into her. Understanding that she'd suffered a painful loss didn't prevent him from pulling her hands away from the shirt and settling them around his neck.

"Oh," she breathed, her eyes wide as she stared up at him.

And God help him, he captured her small noise with his lips and then drank deep.

Today she smelled of…oranges, bright and tart and incredibly sweet.

So he was kissing her. Which was not what he'd planned. But it just felt right, her body flush against his, her arms tightening around his neck, her whispering, "Oh, Robert, *yes*," against his mouth.

He went hard at that. How he wanted her hands on him. His name on her lips, her body moving over his…

"Jeannie," he all but groaned.

"Yes," she whispered back. His hands went to her waist and then he was walking her backward and kicking the door shut and—

Bang.

The sound of the door slamming jolted them apart. And not a moment too soon because the nanny emerged from the baby's room, a perfectly swaddled Melissa in her arms. "Ah, Dr. Wyatt," Maja said, smiling broadly. "We are doing well."

Robert straightened his cuffs to give himself a moment to get his body back under control but then he made the mistake of glancing over at Jeannie. She was bright red and staring at her toes but he thought he saw a smile tugging at the corners of her lips.

Lips swollen with his kiss.

That made him feel oddly proud of himself, as if he'd done something noteworthy instead of making a messy situation even messier.

Damn it all, he'd lost control and that wasn't allowed.

When he was sure he had his responses locked down, he said, "Yes, Mrs. Kowalczyk. What is your report?"

"The organic formula is helping and lovely little Melissa is already less fussy. Miss Jeannie is an excellent student and has already learned how to properly swaddle a *babisui* and change a diaper." She cast a maternal look at Jeannie. "I think, however, it would be good for Miss Jeannie to get out of the house. She has been under a great deal of stress and we all need a break, don't we?"

"Excellent idea."

He already had his phone out to call Reginald back as soon as he'd dropped Kelly off at home when Jeannie made a noise of surprise. "Not tonight, Robert! For Pete's sake!"

"What?" That was how she'd sounded last night after he'd ruined the kiss. Like there was an expected code of conduct in situations like this and he wasn't following it.

"I'm not going anywhere tonight," she said, her tone gentler. "Just because I had a nap and a shower doesn't mean I'm operating on all cylinders today." Her gaze dropped to his lips and, as he watched, the tip of her tongue darted out and swiped over her lower lip.

Hmm. That was interesting. Did that mean she was having second thoughts about that second kiss? All he knew was that he could still catch the scent of oranges in the air.

Cautiously, Robert looked at Maja. She nodded in agreement. "Perhaps for lunch tomorrow?" she suggested.

"Lunch." He didn't eat lunch on a regular basis. He was always at the hospital, making rounds or seeing patients.

"It's a meal? Most people eat it around the noon hour?" Jeannie was definitely smiling now. Something in his chest loosened.

She was teasing him, he realized. No one else would dare, but she did. "Yes, I'm familiar with the concept." Her smile got even bigger. "I have appointments tomorrow but we could do lunch on Saturday." He already knew Maja would be here. He was paying her an exorbitant rate to live in the first week, but it was worth it to see Jeannie without that haunted look in her eyes.

Maja was doing her job. Robert had made it clear that the nanny was responsible for making sure both people in this house were cared for.

Maja gave him that approving nod again as Jeannie said, "Okay, but nothing too fancy. And not Trenton's."

"Of course not." He wasn't entirely sure that he was welcome back. Better to wait until Jeannie could return.

Jeannie eyed him warily. "You do eat, don't you? You never order anything but the Manhattan at the bar."

"Of course I eat." Darna made sure there were fresh-cooked meals for him at home. She cooked to his specifications and that was all he needed. He didn't need to try the latest food craze or go out to be seen. He liked his corner at Jeannie's bar and then he liked his peace and quiet.

For a second, he considered just bringing Jeannie to his town house and serving her the cuisine Darna left for him. If he called Darna right now, she'd probably have time to put together something special. Her roast pork was amazing and those little rice cakes wrapped in banana leaves—Jeannie would like them. He could show her his home and…

And…

That was a terrible idea. Yes, he'd kissed Jeannie twice now—but taking her to his home felt dangerous.

So Kelly would find a restaurant. Someplace quiet, but not romantic. Someplace where Jeannie could relax. Someplace where gossip would not reach Landon Wyatt.

Someplace where she could smile at Robert but a table would keep them from touching.

It was safer that way.

"I know the perfect place," he hedged. He would know it by noon tomorrow, anyway. Kelly did good work. "Now," he went on, because Reginald would be back soon enough and Robert had a role to fulfill. He held out his hands and Maja placed the baby in his arms without hesitation. Melissa squirmed at the change in elevation but when he cradled her, she blinked up at him with her bright baby-blue eyes. "Let's see how we're doing."

Forty minutes later Jeannie had demonstrated everything she'd learned today—how to properly change a diaper, how to swaddle an infant securely, even how to hold the bottle so Melissa didn't have to work as hard to drink.

The whole time Robert had watched her with those icy eyes, doing little more than nodding when she apparently passed inspection. Because that was what it felt like. An inspection. One she'd definitely failed yesterday. Today?

He'd kissed her.

He'd walked right up to her and kissed her and she'd kissed him back and everything felt so much better and that much worse at the same time because he was here and that was great but nothing made sense.

Because he'd kissed her.

And now he was standing there, judging her as she burped a baby.

A baby who thankfully fell asleep.

"Maja," Robert said after Jeannie had laid Melissa down in the completely empty crib and they'd all returned to the living room, "you've done well today."

Jeannie glared at him. Maja was a good teacher who obviously knew what she was doing but *come on, Robert.* Jeannie was the one learning everything from scratch on a few hours of sleep. But the man wasn't even looking at her!

"Thank you, Dr. Wyatt," Maja said, her eyes twinkling. "Jeannie is a most capable student."

"Hmm," he murmured as if he wasn't sure he agreed with that assessment. Which made Jeannie glare harder.

But before she could tell him where to shove his humming noises, he said to the nanny, "Take an hour and get dinner."

Wait. Jeannie cut a glance at Maja, who looked mildly surprised at this…well, this *order*. Which was pretty much how Jeannie felt, as well, considering they'd eaten dinner around six. But Maja was obviously used to taking odd orders from her clients, because all she said was, "Of course, Dr. Wyatt. I need to pick up more formula."

"What…" Jeannie started to say as Maja grabbed her purse and was out the door in seconds. She moved awfully quick for a woman easily in her sixties.

"Reginald?" Robert said before the front door had closed behind Maja. Because of course Robert was on the phone. Probably ordering a butler or something. "An hour from now. Yes."

She stared at him as he ended the call. What was Robert even doing here? Besides continuing to completely take over her life.

"I'm not going to work tomorrow," she said. Unfortunately, it came out sounding petulant and immature. "I don't want to and I'm not ready."

"Of course you're not," he said, sounding almost agreeable about it.

"O…kay. So if you're not going to convince me to get back to work, why are you here?"

He adjusted his cuffs. He still had on his jacket today, although she noted he had foregone a vest. Probably because it'd been close to ninety danged degrees today. To the average person, it might not look like he was stalling but she knew this was how Robert played for time.

He cleared his throat. Yeah, totally stalling. "Are you better?"

"I am." God, this felt six kinds of awkward. She wanted… to go back to where they'd been when he'd walked up her front steps like a man on a mission.

Where he'd come because he wanted to see her.

"Will you sit with me?" she asked, holding out her hand.

He looked at her hand like he didn't trust it. Or maybe he didn't trust himself?

"Are you sure?" he asked and she heard the strain in his voice.

He didn't trust himself. At least, not around her. The realization set her back on her heels.

"Yes," she said because she knew he could be terrifying but he'd never once made her feel unsafe. "Are you?"

He hesitated.

"I only want to sit with you," she said. "Come here." It was as close to an order as she'd ever given him.

An emotion rippled across his face, one she couldn't quite identify. She had to wonder—had anyone ever tried to tell him what to do before? Surely, at medical school?

"*Please*, Robert."

Why didn't he trust himself around her?

She didn't think he was going to bridge the divide between them but then he laced his fingers with hers. They moved to the couch, and he sat. Stiffly at first, but when Jeannie sat next to him and tucked her head against his shoulder, she felt a tremor pass through his body and then, bit by bit, he relaxed.

She didn't let go of his hand. Instead, she covered it with her other hand and stroked along the side of his thumb with her own. His hands were strong, with long fingers and impeccably groomed nails.

"Maja was what I needed," she told him, but what she really wanted to say was that *he* was what she needed. "Thank you."

"Good," was all he said, because of course.

Her mind raced even as her body calmed. Like last night when she'd needed a hug, tonight she needed to lay her head on his shoulder and let his warmth seep into her body. If Robert was here, then things were okay. He wouldn't allow it to be otherwise.

She thought of the nanny, the maid that would probably show up in the next few days, the lawyers, the insistence that she go back to work as soon as was humanly possible, hell, even lunch on Saturday—it all pointed back to something big in his life.

To the bad day he'd mentioned when he first showed up.

"Robert?"

"Yes?"

"Are you okay?"

She had the distinct feeling that, if she hadn't been holding on to his hand with both of hers, he would've straightened his damned cuffs. "I won't let any harm come to you. Or Melissa."

She tensed. "Are we in danger?"

"No," he answered too quickly and then, "No," again, but softer.

"You're touching me." He smelled faintly antiseptic today. *Surgery*, she remembered.

"I…don't mind." He swallowed. Was he nervous? Because they were discussing feelings or because they were touching? "Because it's you."

The man might not spout romantic poetry or random compliments but… "That was probably the nicest thing you've ever said to me."

"What a low bar to meet." Was that humor in his voice? He cleared his throat again. "You did well today. I'm impressed at how quickly you picked things up." Her breath caught in her throat and she tilted her head back to find his face less than four inches from hers. "There," he said, sounding almost cocky about it. "How was that?"

"Better," she told him breathlessly. "Much better."

He smiled. Just the corners of his mouth moving upward but it took everything warm and comfortable about him and kicked it right on over to pure, simmering heat.

"Good," he said again.

That did it. Before she could talk herself out of it, she slid into his lap, straddling his powerful legs and bringing her pelvis flush against his. He inhaled sharply and she felt him tense underneath her.

"What are you doing?" he asked in a strangled voice. His arms stretched along the back of the couch, as far from touching her as he could get.

"Listen to me, you silly man," she said, motioning in the narrow space between them. "I'm not afraid of you, Robert. I trust you."

"You shouldn't," he ground out, digging his fingers into the couch cushions.

"Well, it's too late because I do." She cupped his face in her hands and made him look at her. "I've known you for years and *I trust you* so get used to it. I don't understand you, but for the love of everything holy, stop acting like you're a villain in this story."

"Do you have any idea what I'm capable of?" he demanded, glaring.

Now she was getting somewhere. He couldn't hide behind his shirt cuffs or the bar or the Manhattan. He couldn't hide from *her* anymore.

"Yes," she said, touching her forehead to his. "You're capable of single-handedly saving incredibly sick children, you're rescuing me and Melissa and you're the most obnoxious perfectionist I've ever met. By, like, *a lot*."

His chest heaved. "You don't know." As he spoke, his hands came to rest on the curve of her waist. "You just don't understand."

"No, I don't." She wrapped her arms around his neck and buried her face in his shoulder and hugged the man for all he was worth. "But I will because you'll tell me when you're ready," she murmured against his skin.

After a heart-dropping pause, his arms curled around her. "Jeannie."

She knew what he was going to say and she cut him off with a growl. He really was the most infuriating man. "This is not an obligation, dammit."

"But—"

She leaned back. "Robert—did you ever think that I *wanted* to kiss you? That I'd want to do it again?"

Seven

She was sitting in his lap.

His *lap*.

Worse, she wanted to kiss him. *Just* kiss? Perhaps not, what with the way she straddled him, her breasts flush against his chest.

It should be wrong, the way her weight pressed him against the couch cushions. She shouldn't be like this, definitely shouldn't trust him. Not if she knew what was good for her.

"You want to kiss me."

"I do." She sighed, her warm breath stroking over his neck. "I've wanted to kiss you for years. *Years*. You never realized it, did you?"

He opened his mouth to point out the flaw in her logic, realized he had no idea what that flaw might be and snapped it shut again.

"I'll take that for a *no*," she said. Smugly.

People didn't touch him. Yes, he'd shake hands with worried parents and examine their children, but outside of the office? *Never*.

Except for her, apparently. Because not only had he kissed her, but he also...*liked* her touch.

Jeannie molded herself to him. Her body was warm and light against his and it reached inside him, drawing an answering pulse from his blood. Her thighs felt strong and sure as they bracketed his legs and although he most certainly did not want an erection right now, all that pounding blood began to pound in his dick, as well.

Oh, yes—he liked it.

The heat of her core settled against his groin and he almost groaned at the delicious tension because she was sitting *in his lap* and he couldn't remember wanting to be this close to a woman.

Much to his surprise, he realized he was stroking her back and he'd turned his face into her hair so he could inhale her scent.

It was good.

Because it was her.

She was a temptation he couldn't resist.

She really had no idea what he was capable of, did she?

A tremor raced through his body. It wasn't fear. Because Wyatts weren't afraid of anything. He was merely holding himself back.

For her sake. Not his.

She wanted him...but not for his money or his power?

She was right. He didn't understand a damn thing.

"Stop thinking, Robert," she murmured against his neck. "Just *be*. We've both had crappy weeks and this is nice." She sighed into him. "You're a good hugger."

He highly doubted that. When was the last time he'd been hugged?

Suddenly, he was talking without being entirely sure what was coming out of his mouth. "I'm *not* taking you out to lunch. You're coming to my home. We'll have a quiet meal on the terrace and…" He swallowed, trying not to sound desperate because desperation wasn't allowed. "I… I can just *be* there. With you."

What if she said no or demanded a fancy meal at a trendy spot, like he'd promised? The sort of thing that Dr. Robert Wyatt, a Top Five Billionaire Bachelor, should do?

The thought was almost physically painful. Because, he realized with alarm, that wasn't who he was with her.

Say yes, he thought and dammit, there was desperation in those unspoken words.

Say yes to me.

Her lips moved against his skin. His body responded accordingly. He'd made her smile. It felt like a victory.

"Of course," she agreed. She pushed back to look at him, her weight bearing down on him. God, she was perfect. "No obligations, no expectations. Just two people who can *be* together."

All those colors in her eyes played with the light, making her look soft and otherworldly, like a princess who'd disguised herself as a commoner to test the prince.

He might have failed his mother but by God, he wasn't going to fail Jeannie. She didn't know what he was capable of. He prayed she never would.

"I'll pick you up at twelve," he told her, stroking his thumb over her cheek.

She leaned into his touch. "I'll be waiting."

"Are you sure this is okay?" Jeannie asked for the fourth time. Or maybe it was the fortieth.

Her sleeveless sundress was bright yellow, with a happy print of little pink and blue flowers all over it. Rona, the maid who'd arrived promptly at ten this morning, had even ironed the dang thing.

Jeannie had bought the dress for a date some years ago

and then repurposed it with a shawl to attend Easter services with Nicole, who'd been a church regular. It'd been part of their reconciliation.

It was the fanciest dress Jeannie owned. Hopefully, paired with the shawl and her platform brown sandals, it would be nice enough for a private meal with Robert. He always cut such a dashing figure in his custom three-piece suits and gemstone cuff links and she had…a cotton sundress she'd gotten on clearance four years ago.

But what else did one wear to a private meal with the billionaire bachelor next door? Cutoffs seemed like the wrong answer.

This was ridiculous.

She couldn't go to lunch with him. She shouldn't be alone with him. If she was smart, she'd change into her jean shorts, curl up on the couch and let Maja boss her around in a highly educational way.

"Yes, yes," Maja said again, patting Melissa's back. "You look lovely. Very sweet. Rona, doesn't she look lovely?"

"Oh, yes," the tiny Filipino woman called from the kitchen, where the smells of something delicious wafted throughout the house. "Very pretty."

Upon arrival, Rona had promptly taken over everything Maja hadn't. Dishes had been washed, laundry laundered, the bathroom was already immaculate and who could forget the cooking? It was a little bit like living in a hotel.

Jeannie had no idea who would appear next but she had a feeling Robert wasn't done hiring a staff of potentially dozens to take care of her. She was going to draw the line at a butler, though.

The baby let out a tiny little belch—without crying. Seriously, Maja was magic. Jeannie didn't know how much Robert was paying her, but it was worth it.

"Caregivers need breaks," Maja went on, shifting from side to side. Jeannie was sure the older woman didn't even know she was doing it. Would Jeannie ever get that level of comfort handling Melissa? "The *babisui* and I will be fine together—she will sleep, I will help Rona and you will enjoy a break with your handsome doctor."

Jeannie's cheeks heated so she quickly turned back to her room to rifle through her meager jewelry collection. "He's not *my* doctor." No disputing the handsome part, though.

"Mmm," Maja replied. Or maybe she was just talking to the baby.

Trenton's didn't let employees wear more than simple stud earrings, and most of Jeannie's jewelry was like her sundress—cheaply made, purchased on clearance and several years old. And most of it felt…juvenile. From a period of her life that had passed.

She wasn't the same girl who could ironically wear neon-pink plastic hoops, not anymore. She was something very like a mother now. Besides, the neon hoops definitely didn't match this dress. So in the end, she went with her basic fake diamond studs that she wore at the bar every night.

"He's *not* my doctor," Jeannie reminded her reflection.

This was just lunch. With her favorite customer. While wearing her best dress.

And the cutest pair of matching panties and bralette she owned. The set she'd ordered online in a pink that was more dusty than neon and was very lacy.

Very lacy.

She'd tossed and turned all night long, drifting in and out of lust-fueled dreams that left her hot and bothered. She hadn't stopped with just straddling Robert or holding him. She hadn't stopped at all.

The doorbell rang. "He's here," Maja sang.

Although it wasn't ladylike, Jeannie sprinted out of the bedroom, yelling, "I'll get it!"

Which turned out to be pointless because Maja had already opened the door. Jeannie stumbled over her sandals and nearly took a header at the sight of the man waiting for her.

He wasn't wearing a suit.

Had she thought Robert looked undone days ago when he hadn't been wearing a tie? Because the man standing before her was so far from a suit and tie that she barely recognized him.

Except for his eyes. She would never forget the burning intensity of Robert's eyes for as long as she lived.

Especially when they darkened. "You look lovely," he said. A shiver raced down her back at the sound of his voice, deep and raw and—this wasn't about lunch, was it?

"So do you." Instead of that suit, he was wearing a dark blue button-up shirt that had short sleeves and maybe some little pattern on it, all paired with light khaki shorts.

Shorts. That revealed his well-muscled legs. Her pulse began to stutter as she stared at those defined legs. When had calves gotten so damn sexy? Lord.

"I didn't think you owned anything but suits."

"I didn't know you wore anything other than vests before this week," he returned with a smile that melted her.

"Dr. Wyatt," Maja interrupted. Jeannie startled. She'd forgotten the older woman was in the room. "Would you like a report?"

"The thirty-second version," he replied, not taking his eyes off Jeannie. Dear God, she could practically smell the sexual desire coming off him in waves.

"Little Melissa continues to improve, Rona has made an excellent start and Jeannie—"

"Is late for lunch," he said, coming forward to take her by the arm.

When he touched her, electricity raced over her skin, taking everything that had started to melt and tightening it to the point of delicious pain. She fought to keep from gasping as his hand slid down until his fingers laced with hers.

She threw a glance back at Maja, whose expression clearly stated, *your handsome doctor.*

"We'll be back later," Robert announced in that way of his.

"Enjoy yourselves," Maja said with a conspiratorial wink, shooing them out. "We'll be fine here."

Oh, Jeannie would. If she got the chance, she was going to enjoy this with every fiber of her being.

Reginald was waiting at the car for them. "Miss," he said, tipping his hat to her as she approached.

"Hello again." Reginald's expression was remarkably similar to Maja's, like there was a conspiracy to make her and Robert…

Well, not fall in love or anything because that simply wasn't possible. He was a billionaire surgeon whose family owned a huge medical company and his father was maybe going to be the next governor. She was a bartender who'd never finished college and whose grand dream to own her own bar had been completely derailed by becoming the legal guardian to an infant. Their paths could only ever cross at a place like Trenton's.

She would never fit into his world and he would never understand hers.

Jeannie didn't know what to do with her legs. The hem of the sundress was well above her knees and Robert sat across from her. His gaze roamed over her. Was that hunger in his eyes? Or was he noting the shabby dress, the worn leather straps on her sandals, the hundred other little things that marked her as a different class?

She tucked the hem of her dress around her thighs and stared right back. Of course he looked completely at ease sitting there. In shorts. Shorts! She still couldn't get over it, or the way the sight of the dark hair on his legs stirred something deep inside her.

The man was sin in a suit but there was something so

casually masculine about him right now that her clothes felt too tight.

He, at least, had no problem crossing his legs. "So," she began because several quiet moments had passed and Robert showed no sign of breaking the silence. "What's for lunch?"

"Darna—that's Rona's sister—is preparing a traditional Filipino meal of chicken satay, tinola soup and suman for dessert."

She stared. "Did you hire Darna just for today?"

"No, she's worked for me for almost six years. I trust her," he added as an afterthought.

For some reason that made Jeannie happy. He needed people he could trust. She just wished he counted himself on that list.

He didn't say anything else. They were driving toward downtown and, for once, traffic was light. "What else are we doing today?"

She heard him inhale sharply and felt an answering tug in her chest. "Nothing."

She met his gaze. "Pity."

The tension between them sharpened. "Jeannie…"

"Robert," she replied. If he didn't want to sleep with her, that was fine. But she wanted him to say it. She didn't want any misunderstandings. "Aren't we on a date?"

His mouth opened and snapped shut and Jeannie got to appreciate that rare, wonderful thing where Dr. Robert Wyatt was flummoxed.

"Because this seems like a date," she went on. "I'm wearing a dress, you picked me up in a limo and we're going to eat a meal. Pretty standard date stuff, really."

He was doing that fish thing, his mouth opening and closing and opening again. "I don't date."

"You mean, you're not currently seeing anyone? That's good. I'm not involved, either. Which," she added, "is good for the status of our date. I'm not into being anyone's side piece."

"Side... Never mind." He shook his head. "No. I mean, I don't date. Ever."

"Ever?" Because that sounded ominous. She knew he wasn't married—kind of went with the territory when he was named a top bachelor—but...

He had kissed her. Twice now. And he had definitely started it the second time.

"No," he said sharply. Ominously, even.

"Just going out on a limb here, but you're not going to tell me why?"

That got her a hard look.

"Right." She looked out the window again. They were making great time. "So sex is off the table, then?"

He made a choking noise. "Do you have a filter?"

"Yes. In case you've never noticed, I use it all the time—at work. But we're not at Trenton's. I don't know what's going on with you or what's going on between us but..." His face was completely unreadable, so she went on with a sigh. "This is who I am, Robert. I'm a bartender who hasn't completed a college degree and barely passed high school. My big dream is to open my own bar. I left home when I was eighteen and didn't talk to my sister for almost six years. I can be mean and bitter and a huge pain in the ass when I put my mind to it and I am *not* a shy, retiring virgin. I like sex and I'd like to have sex with you." It was hard to tell in the darkened interior of the limo, but she would've bet large sums of his money that he was blushing. "But I'm not going to push you into anything that makes you uncomfortable."

"Well, there's that," he said under his breath. She detected sarcasm.

"But," she went on, "beyond that, I'm a hot mess. I am singularly unqualified to raise a child, not to mention I have no way to pay for what a baby needs." Robert opened his mouth, no doubt to find another way to spend his money on her. "No, I'm not going to take more of your money. She's not your daughter and we're not your responsibility. I'm in this car with you because I like you. I know what I want from you, you confounding, infuriating man. Not your money, not your name—I want you, Robert. I have for a long time. And I know I may not get it and that's okay, too." She leaned forward and put her hand on his knee. "But the question is, do you know what you want from me?"

He stared at her hand, resting on his knee. She could feel him practically vibrating with nervous energy.

But he didn't say anything.

The car came to a stop.

Eight

If there was one thing Robert had learned growing up in Landon Wyatt's house, it was how to control his physical reactions, because showing joy or sorrow or, worst of all, fear, was the quickest way to pain.

Over the years Robert had gotten so good at controlling those giveaways—the increased heart rate, the stomach-wrenching nausea, the shallow, fast breathing—that, for the most part, he'd simply stopped feeling distress. Even when a surgery went wrong, he was able to keep his emotional reactions on lockdown and he'd lost count of the number of times his cool head had prevented disaster or, worse, death.

Which was good. Great, even. No one wanted to go through life afraid. He certainly didn't.

So why did he feel like he was going to vomit as he led Jeannie up the stairs to his house?

He didn't know. Jeannie was many things—including, apparently, a self-described "hot mess"—but one thing she wasn't was a threat.

At least, not the kind Robert was used to.

"This is…*wow*," she marveled as the front door swung open.

"Welcome home, Dr. Wyatt. Miss Kaufman." Darna beamed at Jeannie. She had a crisp white apron over her uniform and a welcoming smile.

Odd. Darna was efficient and did exceptional work for him. But had he ever seen her smile?

"Darna, is it? I was just getting to know Rona. She's your sister, right?" Jeannie took Darna's hand in hers and half shook it, half just held it. "It's such a pleasure to meet you. I hope you didn't go to too much trouble for this."

Darna's eyes danced with what was probably amusement. "No, no—no trouble at all. I hope you enjoy the meal." She retrieved her hand and turned to Robert. "Everything is set up on the terrace, sir. Will there be anything else?"

"No." Jeannie slanted him a hard look. "No…thank you?"

Jeannie beamed at him. For her part, Darna looked as if Robert had just declared his undying love. "My," she all but giggled. "My, my. Yes." She patted Jeannie on the arm and giggled. "Yes," she repeated.

Robert could feel his pulse beginning to speed up, beating wildly out of time. Which was ridiculous because this was not a risky situation.

This was, as Jeannie had pointed out, lunch. Between two people who…liked each other?

All right, fine. He *liked* Jeannie. He needed to see her on a near-daily basis to function, it seemed. And he was doing everything in his power to help her through a difficult time. True, he'd done that for some of his patients, the ones where the bills would've bankrupted the families.

But he hadn't ever wanted to see those people again. And he certainly hadn't ever wanted to kiss any of them. Like he'd kissed Jeannie. Twice.

Kissed her and held her close—so, so close.

His pulse jumped to a new level of erratic.

With a nod, Darna disappeared into the house and Robert was left standing in the foyer with Jeannie. He needed to move but he wasn't sure he could. Every system he'd spent years mastering was in open revolt right now and that was when Jeannie turned to him, a knowing smile on her lips. "I take it you don't bring a lot of people home?"

"No," he replied. There. At least his voice was still under his control. He sounded exactly normal, even if he felt anything but.

A few nights ago she'd straddled him. Today—mere moments ago—she'd boldly announced that she not only liked sex, but she'd also like to have sex with him.

He would not lose control. He would not hurt her and he would not risk destroying this…liking.

She took a few steps away from him, staring at the ornate ceilings. "This place is huge."

"Yes."

She looked back over her shoulder at him. "Is it just you?"

He began to shake. "Yes. I value my privacy."

"I must say," she went on, running her fingers lightly over the hand-painted wall coverings, "this is more…floral than I would've guessed."

"Oh?" His voice cracked a little as she moved into the parlor. Had she always had that sway to her hips?

"I pictured you in a modern, stark condo—all harsh lines, lots of stainless steel and black. This?" She made a little turn in the parlor. "This is *extravagant*. Obnoxiously so."

No one else would tell him his house was obnoxious, but it was true. And Jeannie saw it. The dress swung around her legs, exposing more of the bare skin of her thighs, and Robert had to brace himself against the door frame. "It came like this."

She stopped twirling, the dress falling back around her

legs. "You…bought the house like this and didn't change anything?"

He shook his head because he wasn't sure he could speak, not with her making her way back toward him, that sway in her hips, that smile on her face. Like she'd been waiting for him.

It wasn't alarm knotting up his tongue and making him feel light-headed and dizzy. It wasn't panic sending his pulse screaming in his veins. It wasn't fear that had given him a rock-hard erection, the one he'd been fighting to contain ever since this woman had slid onto his lap. No, that wasn't right. He'd been fighting this ever since she'd opened the front door and announced she'd been waiting for him. Since she'd been waiting on her stoop.

This was desire. Raw, pure, dangerous desire.

Oh, hell.

Somewhere below, he heard the faint sound of the alarm system being engaged and then a door shut. The noise echoed through the house—the sound of Darna leaving. They were well and truly alone, and Jeannie wanted to have sex with him and he was starting to think it'd be a good idea but how could he let her strip him bare without his control snapping?

"Hey," she said softly, coming toward him. He almost flinched when she put her hand on his cheek. "Just *be*, Robert. Nothing has to happen." She notched an eyebrow and instead of sympathy or worse, pity, he saw nothing but a challenge. "Although I reserve the right to make fun of this wallpaper because who wallpapers a ceiling?"

Odd. He was sure he was glaring at her, which normally sent people running for the closest exit. But instead, this woman smiled and absorbed it. Understood it.

Understood him.

"I don't want to hurt you," he got out and dammit, his

voice shook with the force of emotions that tumbled through him. Desire. Fear. Need. Pain. Want.

An emotion shimmered in her eyes and was gone before he could identify it. "Oh, I don't know about that. Those floral drapes are borderline painful," she said with a mischievous grin and oddly, he was able to draw in a breath. "Why haven't you changed them?"

"It was done by someone famous back in the thirties, and my mother…"

Against his will, his eyes shut. But that was a mistake because he could see his mother delicately arranged on the cushioned chair by the fireplace, a blanket tucked around her legs to help hold the ice packs in place. She'd gazed at the obnoxious wallpaper and frenetic drapes and the gold leaf and said, *I love this room. The riot of colors…it's wild but free.* Then she'd smiled at him, her eyes unfocused from the pain or the meds or both, and had said, *Silly, isn't it?*

He wanted Cybil Wyatt to enjoy riotous colors and silliness and freedom. He had to get her away from Landon. The alternatives were unthinkable.

He heard himself say, "My mother liked it."

"Ah," Jeannie said, her tone softening with what he hoped was understanding and not pity. "So you keep it this way for her?"

He nodded. Darna dusted this room—all the rooms done in this overblown style—twice a week. They were kept in a permanent state of readiness, just in case.

But three years ago it hadn't been enough to keep his mother here. *He* hadn't been enough to keep her here.

"Does she visit often?"

Twice. His mother had been in his home exactly twice. The second time he'd had to carry her in because she couldn't climb the steps. She'd stayed only long enough to be able to walk back down on her own power. Robert had stood in the window, watching her get into Landon's black limousine.

Cybil Wyatt hadn't looked back.

Robert had found himself at Trenton's that night. "No," he said shortly, remembering to answer the question.

"I see."

He was afraid she did.

Suddenly, her touch was gone and Robert stumbled forward, his eyes popping open to find Jeannie moving through the room, her happy yellow dress both clashing with the greens and reds and blues of the formal parlor and, somehow, blending in perfectly.

"So if this is for your mom," she said, running a hand over the hand-carved marble fireplace mantel, "where *do* you live?"

This was a mistake. He didn't bring people here for a good reason. He kept to himself because it was better that way—safer, easier. He preferred being alone.

But Jeannie…

He held out his hand to her and she didn't even hesitate. Her fingers wrapped around his and, on impulse, he lifted her hand and let his lips trail over her knuckles. The contact pushed him that much closer to the edge.

She inhaled sharply. Did she feel the same connection he did? Or was she just looking to get lucky?

Did the answer even matter?

It did. God help him, it did.

"Come with me."

Jeannie did the math as Robert led her up one garish flight of stairs—really, this wallpaper was *something*—to another.

She'd spent about an hour with him five nights a week, approximately fifty-one weeks out of the year, for almost three years. That meant…uh…somewhere around eight thousand hours with this man.

She'd never imagined him living like this. High-rent, yes. Opulent? Sure. But…

It was like she'd entered Opposites Land, where up was down, quiet was loud and Robert was surrounded by hideous decorating. The man was so incredibly particular about everything—the precise formulation of his Manhattan, the cuffs on his sleeves, hell, even where his bartender was. How did he live *here*?

Even accounting for the fact that his mother liked it… it just didn't make sense. If she woke up to these walls and marble and what was probably real gold leaf, she'd have a headache every day of the week and two on Sunday. Jeannie had never pegged Robert for being a momma's boy.

Except he'd sounded so raw when he'd said his mother liked it. Like he had the first time he'd ever walked through Trenton's doors.

Was Mrs. Wyatt a good person or not? Jeannie had a feeling that, if she knew where the woman fell on the spectrum between Sainted Angel and Worst Mother in The World, she'd understand Robert's choices better.

But she also understood that he wasn't going to tell her. In that eight thousand some-odd hours she'd spent with him, she'd barely heard mention of his parents until a few weeks ago. The man knew how to hold his cards close.

When they reached the landing on the third floor, things changed. The landing opened up onto a short, wide hallway and at the end, she could see two French doors thrown open. On either side of that hallway was a door.

That wasn't what caught her attention. Instead of gaudy wallpaper, the walls changed to a soft peach color. She wouldn't have chosen this color for Robert but at least it didn't make her eyeballs bleed. Compared to the explosion of pattern downstairs, this was downright calming—and that was including the fact that Robert had art hung on these walls. It looked old and expensive.

She tore her gaze away from the priceless paintings. Robert unlocked the door on the right side of the stairs and stood at the threshold. Jeannie studied the tension in his shoulders, the way he practically vibrated with nervous energy. She was just about to suggest they go straight to the terrace, where their meal had been set up, because it was clear that Robert wasn't exactly jumping at the chance to show her around.

But the moment she opened her mouth, he turned and held his hand out. She couldn't pass up this opportunity to understand a little bit more about what made the man tick.

Not to mention the way he'd kissed the back of her hand earlier.

So she put her trust in him and let him lead her into a…

"This is my study," he said, softly shutting the door behind him.

Jeannie gasped. *Books.* Shelves and shelves of books and not the kind that had been tastefully arranged to look good. Oh, no. These were paperbacks with broken spines that had been crammed into every square inch of available space—which went all the way up to ceilings that had to be at least twelve feet high. The walls were lined with shelves, and the long room appeared to run the entire width of the house. She turned to the closest one and saw at least twenty Tom Clancy books wedged together. The next shelf had John Grisham and after that, Janet Evanovich. And it just went on and on. Was that an entire bookcase of Nora Roberts?

Thousands and thousands of books in this room. So many he even had one of those little ladders to get to the top shelves.

The rest of the room had an almost cozy feel. Skylights kept the room bathed in a warm glow. The exterior wall housed a fireplace, which, unlike the one down in the formal room, looked like it had actually seen a fire in the past year. It was also only one of two places that didn't have shelves. But even that mantel was crowded with books underneath what was probably another priceless work of art. Before that was a leather chair with matching footstool, next to a side table with a lamp and paper, pens—book clutter, basically—next to it. Behind that was a long desk, piled high with even more books and a computer holding on to a corner of the desk.

She spun, breathing in the smell of paper and leather and trying to grasp the sheer number of books here. "You read," was the brilliant observation she came up with.

"Yes." He sounded embarrassed by this admission. "I don't watch much television."

"This is your room?"

"My study, yes. Darna only comes in here once a quarter to dust."

In other words, this was his private sanctuary. And he'd invited Jeannie inside.

Oh, Robert.

Light streamed in from the French doors that led outside. Robert unlocked them and then wrapped his strong fingers around hers and led her outside to the terrace.

Jeannie gasped, "Oh, my *God*." She was sure the space itself was impressive. She was dimly aware of the sweet smell of flowers, of green and orange and space. A lot of space. But beyond that, she couldn't have described the terrace at all.

Because somehow, despite the fact that they were three blocks away from the shore and surrounded by high-rise condos, she had an uninterrupted view of Lake Michigan. The afternoon sun glinted off the water, marking the only difference between the water and the sky. A breeze blew off the lake, bathing them in cool, fresh air.

"You have a view of the lake." She turned to him. "*How* do you have a view of the lake?"

He wasn't looking at the water. He was staring at her with the kind of intensity she should be used to. But that was in the dim interior of Trenton's, with a bar between them. Here, under the bright sunlight, his gaze felt entirely different.

Entirely possessive and demanding and maybe just a little bit needy.

"I bought the buildings blocking my view and had them razed," he said in the same way he might've said *I got whole milk instead of skim*. "They're parks now. I had playground equipment installed. One has a community garden. The kids plant things, I'm told."

Jeannie's mouth dropped open. "You did *what*?"

He shrugged. "I wanted this house, but with a view."

Jeannie looked back out at the water. The buildings surrounding the view were four or five stories tall, prime Gold Coast real estate that had probably housed condos and apartments that sold for a few million dollars. *Each.*

It made her nightly hundred-dollar tip look like a handful of pennies, didn't it? She knew he was rich. Billionaire bachelor and all that crap. But…

In this real estate market, Robert had single-handedly erased maybe a hundred million dollars of potential profits. So he could sit on his terrace and see the lake.

Sweet Jesus.

Really, why was she here? This man could have any woman he wanted. He could have a wife and mistresses and private jets and his own art museum and nannies and chefs and limos and…anything. He could have it all with just a snap of his fingers.

She was just a bartender. Working-class at best, nowhere near owning her own place. She could never exist in his world. She shouldn't have accepted his help, shouldn't have come to lunch and most definitely shouldn't have told this man she would like to have sex with him.

But she had.

She couldn't have him. Not forever. But she could hold him for just a little bit and then let him go. It was definitely a mistake and just might break her heart, but it was better to have loved and lost…or something like that.

He might just be the best mistake she was ever going to make.

"Do you like it?" he asked, his voice deep and riveting. She felt it all the way down to her toes, that voice.

She nodded. Out on the lake, a sailboat drifted by. It was so perfect it was almost unreal. Much like Robert.

She asked, "Can you see the stars from here?" Because Chicago's light pollution blotted out everything for her. But for him?

Only Robert Wyatt could make the stars shine.

His lips moved in that small way that meant he was smiling and her heart began to pound. "On clear nights, if you look right there…" He stepped in behind her and pointed toward a distant section of the horizon.

His body was warm and solid against her back and the lake breeze teased at the hem of her dress. Jeannie didn't know if this was a seduction or not, because this was Robert and who the heck could tell, but she had to admit, she was being seduced. Perfect, rich, gorgeous Dr. Robert Wyatt, who had his own personal section of the night sky.

"I'd love to see that," she said quietly.

One of his hands came to rest on her waist. Then the other followed suit. "I can show them to you," he said right against her ear.

Oh, thank God. Her nipples went hard as his lips brushed ever so lightly over her earlobe. That lightest of touches sent little bursts of electricity racing over her skin. She had to clench her legs together to keep her knees from buckling, but even that small movement spiked the pressure on her sex to almost unbearable levels of need.

Moving slowly, she lifted his hands off her waist and wrapped them around her stomach so she could lean back into him.

All she felt and heard was Robert.

How he'd turned his head and his breath cascaded over her ear as if he'd buried his face in her hair. Of the rise and fall of his chest as he inhaled her scent. Of the way his arms tightened around her, so slowly as to be almost imperceptible, until he had her locked in his grip. Of how he slowly lowered his chin until it came to rest on her shoulder.

Of the way his entire body seemed to surround her as if he was afraid of startling her or worse, driving her away.

Of how she felt safe in his arms because this was a man who would never let anything hurt her. Hadn't he spent the past few days showing her just that, over and over again?

"You're touching me," she said softly as she ran her hands over his exposed forearms. The hair there was dark and soft and intensely male. Her blood pounded harder, demanding satisfaction as it coursed through her body.

She felt him swallow, then felt his lips move against her neck. "I am."

She turned her head toward him, her mouth only centimeters away from his cheek. She could press her lips against his skin if she wanted, but she waited. More than anyone she'd ever been with, she needed to make sure he wanted her to move, to touch, to *take*.

"Do you like touching me?"

He shifted his arms, grabbing her hands and holding them flat against her stomach so she couldn't pet him. "Yes," he growled.

She shivered, wanting to pull him down into her, wanting to unbutton his shirt and strip off his shorts and leave him well and truly bare to her. Just her and no one else. "Then touch me," she breathed against his skin.

"I don't want to hurt you." He sounded like a man begging for salvation.

She rested her head against his shoulder and he automatically supported her weight. "You won't. But if something's not right, I'll say—" she cast about for a word "—*sailboat*," she said as another boat came into view. "If I say that, you'll stop."

He didn't reply for the longest of seconds—so long, in fact, that she began to think he wasn't going to agree, either to the safe word or the sex. *"Sailboat?"* he finally asked, shifting his grip so that he held both her wrists in one hand. The other hand he set low against her stomach.

She arched her back, pushing her torso into his arms. "It's not a word I shout during sex a lot," she said with a smile.

He jolted as if she'd jabbed him with a needle, his grip tightening. She couldn't touch him, couldn't turn into him. All she could do was stand there, watching Lake Michigan shimmer in the summer heat.

"Jeannie." Her name on his lips was like a call to arms because this wasn't going to be some soft-focus, romantic intimacy marked by sweet words and tender touches. Oh, no.

Sex with Robert was going to be a battle.

She'd always loved a good fight.

Then he kissed her like it was a challenge and for the life of her, she couldn't figure out if he was throwing down the gauntlet for her or for himself. Either way, she met him as an equal on the field, kissing him back just as fiercely as he was kissing her. Their mouths met with a savageness that made her legs shake with need.

She nipped at his lower lip and felt the responding tension ripple through his body. Something hard and long and so, *so* hot began to push against her hip.

She began to pant as the tension spiraled in her body. He didn't loosen his grip on her, didn't give her anywhere else to go. And damn him, he didn't touch her anywhere else. He was holding himself back too carefully, so she bit him again. This time he growled and pulled away, burying his face against her neck. She felt his teeth skim over her skin so she angled her head to give him more.

"Yes," she whispered, hoping encouragement would help him get over this whole *don't want to hurt you* hang-up.

He bit her—gently—right at the spot where her shoulder met her neck. *"Yes,"* she hissed again. When was the last time she'd been this turned on? Every part of her body practically begged for his touch. "Oh, yes. Just like that."

"Don't," he growled against her neck. "Don't talk."

Even through the haze of desire, she laughed at the sheer ridiculousness of that order. "Seriously? Come on, Robert. Have you *met* me?"

"Please," he said. "I…need it to be different."

Different from what? She pulled away from him and he let her go. "But I thought you said you didn't…" He didn't have girlfriends or dates or people he brought back here. But he'd made it clear—he wasn't a virgin. He was breathing hard, panting almost, looking like he was being torn in two.

Oh, God—he really was going to break her heart, wasn't he?

"Okay," she told him. "Those are your rules? No touching, no talking?"

"I… Yes. Those are my rules."

Talking was almost half the fun and touching was definitely the other half. But she was getting a clearer picture of Robert all the time and she was beginning to think he hadn't had a normal, happy childhood. Neither had she, but she had to wonder—how much of what was happening here was Robert letting his scars finally show?

"Fine. My rule is that either one of us says *sailboat*, the other person stops immediately."

"That's it?"

"That's it." She nodded toward the other set of glass doors. This pair was behind a table and chairs set for two. "Is that your bedroom?"

"Yes." But he didn't move.

This man. Honestly, what was she going to do with him? "Can we use your bed?"

"Oh. Yes. Of course." This time he didn't hold out his hand and she didn't reach for him.

He unlocked the glass doors and led her into a masculine bedroom. The walls were a deep navy blue paper with a subtle blue-on-blue pattern. A fireplace with another marble mantel stood in the same spot where the one in the study had been, another impressive piece of art hanging over it.

But what really drew her eye was the massive four-poster bed. Truly, it was huge. She'd heard of California king beds but she'd never seen one in person and the bed probably took up more space than Melissa's whole room back home. Which would've been overwhelming enough but that didn't take into consideration the drapes. Around each of the four posts, airy white drapes were overlaid with pale blue damask that made it look almost like a fairy bed.

"I hope this is all right," Robert said, jamming his hands into his pockets.

"It's amazing and you're cute when you're nervous."

"I'm not nervous," he shot back in a way that was 100 percent nervous.

"That's good, because you're not cute, either." She took a step toward him. He didn't move back, but he inhaled sharply. Not nervous, her fanny. Besides the fireplace, she saw one of those wooden butler things men used to set out their suits. Over the shoulder of a royal blue jacket was a red silk tie. "Here," she said, stepping around him. She snatched up the tie, trying not to wince at the label—Armani, of course. She was about to permanently mangle a tie that probably cost a few hundred dollars.

But then again, this was Robert, who'd knocked down some of the most expensive real estate in the world so he could have a lake view. To hell with the tie.

She looped a quick slipknot around one wrist and turned back to him, her arms outstretched. "How about this? You can tie my wrists to make sure I don't grab you."

His mouth dropped open as color rushed to his cheeks and Jeannie took a perverse sort of pleasure in shocking him. He was barely hanging on to his control and after so many thousands of hours of watching him lock down every emotion, practically every response and expression, she was demolishing those walls.

"You— I—" He snapped his mouth shut and tried to straighten cuffs he wasn't wearing. *"No."*

"No?" She loosely wrapped the other end around her wrist and then lifted the tie to her mouth, letting the silk play over her lips. "Not even to keep me quiet?"

He had to grab one of the bedposts to keep upright. She smiled but didn't get any closer to him. Instead, she circled around him, kicking off her sandals. "Unless you wanted me to leave the shoes on?"

He managed to shake his head.

The bed was so damn big there was a little step stool at the foot of it. She climbed up onto the bed and walked to the center of it.

Robert's eyes never left hers. At this angle, he probably had a decent view of her legs and, if she twirled, maybe even her panties. She knelt on the bed and held out her hands. *"Robert.* Come to me."

"No," he said again, more forcefully. "I could hurt—"

"I don't believe that for a second," she interrupted. "You're not a damned monster, Robert, so stop acting like one. You're a man. And not even a cute one. You're the most gorgeous, complicated, outright *kind* man I've ever met and you're learning how to be a good hugger and you take care of babies and kids and I've spent literal actual years dreaming about you, about this moment. Besides, I'm not that breakable. I trust you."

"I don't trust myself," he ground out, clinging to the bedpost. "Don't you see? I…" He set his jaw. "You shouldn't trust me, either."

Oh, Robert. She let the tie drop away from her wrist and undid the slipknot as she pushed back to her feet.

"Fine," she told him. "Give me your hands."

He shot her a look of disbelief. "What?"

"Your hands. Don't talk. Just do it." For a second she didn't think he was going to do it. "You don't trust yourself? *Fine.* I'll tie you to the bedpost and then you won't be able to do anything."

Nine

Robert sucked in air as Jeannie got closer to him. "I'll tie you down and ride you hard. I won't talk and I won't touch you and you won't be able to do anything about it."

"Wyatts don't submit," he got out, sounding like she'd rabbit-punched him.

That sounded like…like something that had been said to him, but she couldn't think about what it meant right now. The look he gave her would've turned a lesser mortal to stone but she knew him far too well to let a well-placed glare put her off.

"Don't make me wait," she pleaded. Because if he said no…

"Would you really wait for me?" His voice was ragged.

She wasn't supposed to touch him—that was the rule. But she couldn't *not* touch him, not when he looked so desperately devastated. She touched the tips of her fingers to his forehead and, when he didn't pull away, she skimmed them down the sides of his face.

"Always," she whispered against his forehead. "I'll always wait for you. But trust me. Trust yourself."

He made a choked noise and pushed her away. She stumbled a little because this bed was so danged plush and yeah, she'd broken the rules and that was that. But when she got her balance back, she saw he'd held out his hands.

He didn't look at her. He kept his eyes down, shoulders back and yep, this was war. But she knew now—he wasn't fighting her.

He was fighting himself.

Oh, Robert.

She looped the silk tie around his wrists and then around the bedpost. Nothing was tight—if he wanted, he could twist his way free. But this wasn't about restraining him for safety, no matter how he tried to frame it like that.

This was about proving he could trust himself. Because he needed that. She was afraid to ask why.

The knot secured—sort of—she scooted off the edge of the bed so she could stand next to him. "Just to help you on the bed," she said softly as she put her hands on his shoulders.

The man was shaking as she turned him around and undid his belt and the fly of his shorts. For all his defensiveness, there was no mistaking that erection. Dear God, even contained behind his boxer briefs, Robert swelled upward, long and rock-hard. There was so much she wanted to say—that he was as impressive as hell, all the ways she'd dreamed of having him, asking him what he liked, telling him how to touch her—if only to break the oppressive silence of the room.

But she didn't because those were the rules. Instead, she focused on the harsh panting sound of his breathing, the way he tensed when her hand brushed along that impressive ridge. But she didn't palm him, didn't slip her hand inside his briefs. Hell, she didn't even push his briefs down. She could do that when she was on the bed.

She could explore quite a bit before he could get free. She could rip open his shirt and finally take what she wanted from him.

She didn't. He'd given her so much—his money, his time, peace of mind when it came to Melissa. But this? Robert was giving her the most precious gift of all.

His trust.

No way in hell was she going to abuse it.

So she guided him down onto the bed and then swung his legs up. "Scoot down," she said, keeping her voice low and calm. "Just—yeah, like that."

She was trembling, too, she realized. This man was broken in ways she was afraid to understand and definitely couldn't fix, but that wasn't the sum total of who he was. He was still Robert—thoughtful in his demands, overbearing in his caring, seductive in his intensity.

She arranged him so his legs pointed to the center of the bed—which left her plenty of room to work with.

"Okay?" she asked, watching him closely as she slid her panties off.

He nodded.

Okay, she thought, climbing back onto the bed and standing over him.

Even tied to the post, his pants undone and his color high, there was something so ethereal, almost otherworldly, about the way his pale eyes stared at her.

"Dress on or off?" she asked, lifting the hem.

His gaze snapped to where she'd exposed her sex and he inhaled sharply. "On."

Yeah, that didn't surprise her. She stepped over him, still holding on to the hem, letting him get a brief glimpse of her body. Heat flooded her sex as he stared at her hungrily, his hands trapped over his head. He made no move to get free.

She had one of the most formidable men in the city,

maybe even the whole country, at her mercy. The power was intoxicating.

She let her hem drop. Robert made a noise of need, in the back of his throat, but she didn't let him look again. Instead, she lowered herself to her knees, sitting on his thighs. "Okay?"

"Yes." His voice was deeper now as he stared at her breasts, and underneath his briefs, his erection jumped.

She pulled his briefs down, gasping as he sprung free. His length was proud, long and ruddy and curving slightly to the right. She wanted to wrap her hand around it and feel the hot skin sliding over his hardness, wanted to suck him deep into her mouth and let her tongue drive him wild until he broke.

But she'd promised, damn it all. So instead of exploring, she just said, "Condoms?"

He jerked his chin to the bedside table. "The drawer." Somehow, his voice was even deeper now. She felt it rumble throughout her body.

Oh, he was going to be so good.

She slid off him and, half sprawled across the massive mattress, got the box of condoms out of the drawer. The box was unopened, but the expiration date was several years off. Had he bought these just for her?

She got one out and opened the packet, then made her way back to Robert. As efficiently as she could, she rolled the condom on—although he kept twitching, which made it a bit of a challenge, she thought with a smile.

Then she scooted forward so his erection was right beneath her. She could feel him pulsing, sending little sparks of desire throughout her sex. She wanted to touch him so badly but because she couldn't, all her attention was focused on where their bodies met.

"Okay?"

He didn't hesitate. "Yes." If anything, he sounded a little surprised by that.

"Good." She began to rock her hips, letting his erection drag over her sensitive flesh without taking him inside. Her whole world narrowed to the way she moved, how she had to be careful with her balance. To the ragged sound of his breathing mingling with hers. To the splash of red around his wrists that stood out in the sea of blue. To the way he couldn't take his eyes off her.

This was the most erotic moment of her life.

She cupped her breasts through her dress, lifting them and tugging on the nipples. The sensation was dulled by the fabric and her bralette, but she didn't care. She tugged harder, her legs clenching around his hips, her weight bearing down on his erection. Robert groaned as she teased herself, his hips thrusting faster, his movements wilder.

Unexpectedly, an orgasm broke over her, showering her with stars. Moaning, her head dropped back. She would've toppled right off him if he hadn't shifted, bringing his knees up and catching her.

The sound of their panting filled the room. He pulsed against her swollen sex, hot and needy and unable to do a damn thing about it. When she could sit up again, she stared down at him with a dreamy smile on her face. "That was wonderful," she said. What she wouldn't give to lower herself to his chest and kiss him because orgasms like that didn't exactly grow on trees.

He growled. Because of course he did.

She *tsked* him as she lifted herself up and felt his erection rise to meet her. Slowly, she took him inside.

There was nothing else in the world but this. The slash of red above his head. The intense pale blue of his eyes. The cords of his neck straining as he filled her, inch by agonizingly wonderful inch. She bit back a cry of need because *oh, God* she'd never felt anything as wonderful as Robert inside her.

She sucked two of her fingers into her mouth and then lifted the hem of her dress just enough so she could press her slick digits against herself. Robert groaned again, trying to roll his hips, trying to thrust up into her, but she used all her weight to pin him to the mattress.

"Wait," she said, letting her fingers move in slow circles, brushing against where he was joined with her, adjusting to the fullness of him. "Just *be*, Robert. Be with me."

He nodded, a small movement. Maybe it was all he was capable of.

She kept her word. She didn't touch him, except where he was buried deep inside, except where her hips rested on his. She didn't moan or scream his name, didn't tell him what she wanted. She waited until his breathing had started to even out, just a little—until she was sure he had himself back under control and could focus on this intimacy between them.

She tightened her inner muscles around him, pleasure spiking hard and fast as he inhaled sharply. Even that small movement from him—she felt it travel up his length, felt her own body responding. She rubbed herself as she began to shift her hips, rising and falling on him at a languorous pace.

With her free hand, she went back to her breast. She pulled the neckline of the dress down, shoved the pink lace of the bralette aside and, after licking her thumb, began to tease her own nipple.

Robert's eyes were almost black now and he shifted underneath her, using his feet so he could thrust. But that wasn't it. As Jeannie stared down at him, she saw that he reached for the tie.

She froze, just managing to keep her balance. But instead of jerking at the knots, Robert gripped the loose ends of the tie and held on tighter. "Don't…stop, Jeannie." He swallowed. "Please."

Relief broke over her almost as potent as another climax. "There," she said, tugging at her nipple, pulling the hard tip until the most pleasurable pain rocketed through her. "Was that so hard?"

She felt him jolt deep inside her. Then, miracle of miracles, he smiled. Just that small movement of his lips, so tiny no one else would notice it. Just for her.

He was just for her.

This time, when he thrust up into her, she met him as his equal, taking his thrusts and setting her own slow rhythm. She kept rubbing herself, pulling at her nipple, feeling him straining for his release, refusing to make it easy for him. If she wanted to, she knew she could get him off in a matter of minutes. Seconds.

She had no idea if she'd ever get to have him like this again and she wasn't going to waste a single moment of their time together. This moment might have to last her the rest of her life.

She moved over him, fighting for control when all she wanted to do was fall upon him. The noises of sex filled their room, the slap of her flesh against his, their mingled breathing, the squeaking of the mattress.

The red of the tie, the dark desire of his eyes, the pressure on her sex, the way he moved inside her—perfect and strong and right. So, so right.

Oh, God. She gave first, pitching forward. She managed not to plant her hands on his chest, but it was a close thing. Instead, she braced her hands on the mattress and drove her hips down onto him faster and faster.

"Robert," she got out, her climax spiraling but not breaking—building, pushing her faster, slamming onto him harder and harder. "Oh, God."

"Jeannie."

She came apart at the need in his voice and then she kissed him as her orgasm robbed her of thought, of the ability to hold herself apart from him. She kissed him in victory and in defeat, for love and for loss.

She kissed *him*.

He groaned into her mouth, a noise of satisfaction, of completion. He groaned and pistoned his hips up into her before holding and straining and she took him in, all of him. Everything he had, she took—and it all pushed her orgasm even higher. She couldn't help it when she tore herself away from him, throwing back her head as she peaked.

Then she collapsed onto his chest, struggling to get enough air. She barely had the energy to pull herself free of him. "Oh, Robert," she sighed, snuggling down into his chest.

She felt the sharp intake of his breath, felt his hands on her arms as he moved her off his body. He didn't follow her, didn't cover her with his weight.

All she saw was Robert's back as the door slammed shut.

He was gone.

Ten

Robert stood at the top of the stairs. He needed to go to Jeannie. Maybe apologize. Maybe wrap his arms around her and kiss her again.

Probably both.

He couldn't move.

He saw a shadow cross the terrace. Ah. She'd gone outside. Pulled by the lake, no doubt. He was glad she liked his view. He hoped she approved of him buying the land and donating the cleared spaces to the city.

Would she be here long enough to see the stars?

He slipped into his room and grabbed new clothes. Aside from the faint scent of oranges, there was no trace of her in the room. The tie had been returned to its starting place. The bed sheets had been straightened; the condom wrapper gone. Even her shoes had been removed.

Strangely, he found himself longing for her to leave her mark.

Silently, he got cleaned up and changed and then stood, watching her through the open doors.

She'd opened the wine. Hadn't needed his help at all. Of course she didn't—she was a bartender. And she'd found the kitchenette, where Darna had undoubtedly had all the food arranged in containers that kept it warm.

Robert wasn't sure how long he stood there, watching Jeannie through the doorway. She looked…the same. Beautiful, but the same.

He envied her that.

It wasn't until she went to refill her wineglass that he moved. He stepped out onto the terrace. "Here," he said, his voice gruff but unable to do anything about it.

She didn't seem surprised when he appeared, nor when he pulled the bottle out of her hand. "I know how to pour wine," she scolded, but at least there was no acid in her voice. He dared to hope she sounded amused.

"You've served me for years," he replied, pleased to see that his hands weren't shaking. Surgeon's hands should always be steady. "It's my turn to serve you."

He saw her smile, but she didn't look at him. Instead, she kept her gaze fixed on the lake.

Robert topped up her glass and then poured a healthy glass for himself because he could use a drink, he realized. Then he put a little chicken on a dish. He wasn't hungry. He rarely ate lunch. But moving around the terrace gave him something to do.

Normally, Robert was fine with silence. He worked in silence. He read at night with nothing but the faint sounds of the city wafting through his terrace doors. He was old friends with quiet.

But at this exact moment, the fact that Jeannie wasn't talking bothered him.

He pushed his food around his plate. She ate silently. They both drank their wine.

"You can talk now," he finally blurted out, feeling ridiculous.

"No," she said slowly, "I've already said my piece. It's your turn."

He forced himself to breathe slowly, to keep his pulse from running away. He was just…overwhelmed by the new sensations, that was all. He'd never dined with company on the terrace. Never shared his view with anyone. Never brought someone to his bed. Never let his arms be tied.

It was a lot to take in. That was all.

Then he was talking. Words flowed out of his mouth as easily as wine flowed from the bottle. "Something changed when I was fourteen," he was horrified to hear himself say. But it was too late. The bottle had been smashed and he couldn't contain the spill. Not around her. Not anymore. "I grew, I guess. *He* called me into his office. It was never good, being called down. Always bad."

Out of the corner of his eye, he saw her grip tighten on her glass. But all she said was, "Oh?" And strangely, that made it easier to keep going because that was what she would've said if they'd been at the bar, shielded by the dim lights.

It was bright out, but the small table stood between them.

"This time there was a woman there. She…" He swallowed, but kept going. "She wasn't wearing much. She was pretty."

Shame burned through him as he remembered his confusion. He'd been braced for threats, for pain. But not for a woman in a slip and nothing else.

"He said—" Robert drained his glass "—I was a man now. I needed to know how to treat a woman, how to dominate."

Jeannie inhaled sharply. She didn't say anything, though. And for once, Robert hated the silence.

"He made me touch her. Kiss her. He wanted me to…"

He took a breath, trying to find the words without remembering all the terrible details. "And when I couldn't…"

Unexpectedly, Jeannie stood. Before Robert could process what she was doing, she'd plucked his plate and glass from his hand. Wine dripped from his fingertips. He hadn't realized his hands were shaking.

She sat sideways in his lap, burying her face against his neck, and it should've been awful because he didn't like to be touched and *never* talked about why but she was touching him and he was talking.

He couldn't stop.

"He pulled me off the woman and told me to watch. Then he showed me what he wanted me to do."

Jeannie's arms tightened around his neck and he realized he was gathering her closer, holding her like he was afraid she would rip herself away from him.

He didn't allow himself to think of that day. He was very good at controlling his reactions, and those memories weren't allowed.

But now?

He remembered everything. The woman's muffled screams. The way his father had smiled. The familiar guilt that, if he'd only done what Landon had wanted, he might've protected her. The realization that he couldn't protect any woman.

Only the knowledge that he would've been beaten senseless for displaying weakness had kept him from leaving the room.

"Breathe," Jeannie whispered against his skin. "It's okay. I'm here. Just breathe."

He wasn't sure his lungs would ever properly draw in air again. "I told my mother what'd happened. I shouldn't have because it wasn't safe. If you were too happy, too sad, too angry—he didn't like it. But I couldn't keep it inside.

I *couldn't*…and she was so mad that she marched into his office, screaming and throwing things and…"

And Landon had exacted his revenge in a thousand small cuts. He'd been exacting that revenge with interest over the past three years, no doubt.

"Did it ever happen again?" Jeannie asked softly.

Out on the lake, a speedboat raced through his view and was gone. "Not right away." His mother's anger had somehow bought Robert a few months of grace.

"Oh, Robert." Something wet and warm ran over his skin as she held him. She didn't push him aside, didn't look at him with disgust. "What did your mom do after the next time?"

"I didn't tell her." Robert hadn't been willing to risk his mother. So he'd buried his disgust and horror and tried to be the man Landon wanted.

He almost laughed. If Landon could've seen him a few short minutes ago, tied to the bed and helpless while Jeannie gave him the gift of her tenderness, her touch—the gift of herself—the old man might just have had a stroke.

Even more so if he heard what Robert was going to say next. "I was overwhelmed when you kissed me. Earlier. I…"

That kiss had been perfect and terrifying. He'd wanted to never let go of her and he hadn't been able to leave fast enough and it had not been his finest moment.

"It's okay," she said softly. "I'm fine. I broke the rule. I'm sorry."

He pulled her in closer because he liked her there. "Me, too."

Oh, how Landon Wyatt would mock him for that apology, even if it barely qualified as such.

He didn't know how long they sat there. The sun glittered off his own personal view of the lake. Finally, he heard himself say, "I haven't seen her in almost three years. My mother, that is."

He had no reason to tell Jeannie any of this. What had happened in his bed earlier…that hadn't come with the obligation that he owed her the truth.

But he couldn't stop himself.

"What happened?" Jeannie asked softly.

The sun began to dip behind the buildings, casting the sky in deeper shades of gold. No matter what happened—who lived, who died or who walked the fine line between the two states—the sun rose and set every day. It kept going. Just like he did.

"She wouldn't stay with me. He'd beaten her badly and I brought her here. But she didn't trust me to keep her safe. She went back to him and…" He swallowed around the rock lodged in his throat.

"When was this?"

"The day I walked into Trenton's."

The day he'd been utterly lost had been the day he'd found Jeannie. It hadn't been an accident. It couldn't have been something as random as a coincidence.

She'd been waiting for him.

She gasped, drawing air across his throat like a caress.

"Will you get to see her again?" Her voice wavered and Robert prayed she wouldn't cry. There was no point to tears. Never had been.

"That's why I have to go to the campaign kickoff. He's using her as bait so I will pretend we're this perfect happy family."

"To lie for him, the asshole." This time she sounded mad. Strangely, her anger made Robert feel better. "What are you going to do?"

"If she'll come, I'll take her away. Send her where he can't get to her."

Jeannie leaned back. He could tell she was staring up at him, but he couldn't look at her, couldn't risk drowning in her brown eyes. He kept staring at the water. "You're not going to bring her *here*, are you? You can't hope that this time she'll walk away just because she has a weak spot for tacky wallpaper."

He almost smiled because he hadn't just spilled his deepest, most shameful secrets. He'd told Jeannie. Somehow, that made things better. "Of course not. I'm sending her to New Zealand." Now he did look down at her. The impact of her watery eyes hit him square in the chest. "That was why I needed to talk to you, the night you weren't there. I had to see you. I needed…" He brushed her short hair away from her eyes. "I needed to know I was doing the right thing."

Because he was technically going to be kidnapping his mother and he didn't doubt that she might hate him, at least a little. Not to mention Landon might punish him and get Cybil back.

The man would try.

But Robert wasn't a kid anymore. Lawyers, accountants, reporters—all were eager to be a part of what had the potential to be the biggest scandal in Chicago since Al Capone had run this town. And Robert was pulling all the strings.

It was time Landon knew what Wyatts were truly capable of.

"You are," Jeannie said simply. "You're absolutely doing the right thing, Robert." She cupped his face in her hands. "What happened before—that was *never* your fault. And you're not like him. He didn't break you, do you understand? You're stronger than he is. You always were. He knows it, too, I think."

Robert's eyes stung, so he closed them. He wanted desperately to believe what Jeannie said. Wanted to feel the truth of it in his bones.

But if he was really that strong, he would've been able to keep Mom safe all these years. And he hadn't.

Jeannie pushed off his lap, pulling him to his feet. Silently, she led him back into his bedroom. For some reason, she stripped him down to his boxers and then pulled her dress over her head. But instead of removing the pretty lingerie she wore, she turned down the sheet and pushed him into bed. He didn't resist. He couldn't. Whatever she was doing, he needed it. He needed her. So he made space for her and she climbed in after him, pulling the sheet over them both.

Then she curled into his side. "I can't stay to see the stars. Not tonight," she murmured, her breath warm against his chest. "I have to get back to Melissa."

His arms tightened around her even as he forced himself to say, "Of course," even though he wanted to argue.

How very odd. He *wanted* her to stay. All the more so when she threw a bare leg over his, tangling their limbs together. It felt…right. Good, even.

"But Robert?"

"Yes?"

Something warm and soft pressed against his chest. A kiss. One of forgiveness, he hoped. "I won't let you face him alone." Before he could process what she could be talking about—because she couldn't *possibly* be suggesting that she would voluntarily place herself anywhere near Landon Wyatt—she leaned up on one elbow and stared down at him with a look he couldn't identify. "I'm coming with you to the kickoff."

Eleven

Jeannie hadn't seen Robert since he'd walked her to her door three nights ago, kissed the back of her hand like an old-fashioned prince and then been driven off by an absolutely beaming Reginald.

She knew he was talking to Maja or Rona or both. Like when Maja said, "Dr. Wyatt wants you to make sure you're getting fresh air, so let me show you how to use this stroller."

Or when Rona said, "Dr. Wyatt asked me to make sure you're enjoying the meals? I can cook other things, as well," as if anyone would turn down real Filipino cooking, which Rona prepared every other day when she came to tidy the already spotless house and do the laundry. Even the next-day leftovers were fabulous. If Jeannie had been on her own, she would've been living on frozen pizza and beer.

But Robert didn't ask *her* how she enjoyed the meals or the walks or the time with Melissa. He didn't talk to her at all and her texts thanking him for a nice time went unanswered. Which was unnerving. Jeannie knew he was busy—

with his practice or Wyatt Medical or making plans for his mother. She refused to think that he was avoiding her because she'd tied him up or kissed him or listened to his secrets. He wasn't a chatty man to begin with. She could see that he simply wouldn't know how to strike up a conversation after what they'd shared.

But after another day of silence passed, she began to wonder if he was trying to keep her from going to the kickoff. And she had no intention of letting him do that.

So instead of small talk, she went to war over text. And it turned out, he was downright chatty.

What time on Saturday?

No.

Yes. I'm coming with you.

You are not. It's not safe for you.

It's not safe for you, either.
Why should you face him alone?
You need backup.

Absolutely not. I won't risk you like that.

Jeannie smiled at that one, pausing to rub Melissa's back. They were snuggled up on the couch and the house was silent. Maja wasn't here. Rona would be back tomorrow. It was just Jeannie and a drowsy infant.

A week ago this situation would've inspired sheer panic, but now? Jeannie let the baby's warmth sink into her chest as Melissa dozed. She still had no idea how she would handle raising a child when Robert stopped paying a small army of people to help her but she was at least no longer panicking at the thought of holding her niece. As long as Melissa got the right formula and stayed swaddled while she slept, things were better.

I won't risk you, either.

I'm not taking you.
End of discussion.

Then I'll just crash the party.

No, Jeannie.

She chuckled softly to herself. She could hear his exasperated tone, see him glowering at his phone. He could get anyone to do anything he wanted with a snap of his fingers and money—anyone but her.

Yes, she'd talked to Miranda at Trenton's. Robert had handed over a credit card and rumor had it that Julian had run that sucker for thirty thousand dollars and Robert hadn't disputed the charge.

Robert hadn't been back since. Which was fine by Miranda. She didn't care how hot and rich Robert was, she wasn't dealing with him ever again, she'd said. Miranda had related the whole thing in breathless, disbelieving tones but Jeannie believed it all. Thirty thousand was nothing to Robert.

"He's freaking *terrifying*," Miranda had said.

Jeannie had just laughed. As far as she could tell, no one at work had any idea that Robert had appointed himself her guardian angel—or that they'd shared a wonderful, messy evening together.

I *will* crash.
I've been sneaking into parties and clubs since I was 14.

I'll show up in my yellow dress and be loud and obnoxious. Trust me I'm good at it.

No.

You can't keep me away so just accept that you're taking me.
If you take me, you can keep an eye on me.
Who knows what kind of trouble I'll get into otherwise? Might step on a candidate's toes or splash red wine on his face.

Jesus.

Whoopsie.

Robert didn't answer that salvo right away but Jeannie let the space build between them. Melissa grunted in her sleep, warm and perfect and okay. She was seventeen days old today. It'd been ten days since Nicole had died, nine days since Jeannie had brought this baby home and eight days since Robert had turned out to be the star she'd wished upon. Today was the first day Maja wasn't living in the house full-time.

The next time Jeannie was at Robert's house—assuming he invited her back—she wasn't leaving until she'd seen the night horizon over the lake.

She could almost see Nicole walking into the small living room, trying her best not to roll her eyes or let fly with a cutting comment about how this was exactly what Jeannie always did—rushing into something *way* over her head without thinking.

"You're trouble," Nicole had always said. "And like follows like."

When Jeannie had been a little girl, Nicole had hissed it

at Jeannie with pure venom, usually seconds before she got Jeannie in trouble. Maybe there'd been a time when Nicole had set Jeannie up—shoving a ruined sweater under Jeannie's bed and then blaming it on Jeannie.

All Jeannie could really remember was deciding that if she was going to get into trouble, she was going to *earn* it.

After their mom had died and it was just Nicole, still only seventeen, and Jeannie, barely ten, Nicole had kept on saying it. But the hatred had changed, deepened. Now Jeannie could look back and see the pure fear Nicole must have been living with, an unwelcome guest who refused to leave. The same fear Jeannie had been stuck in when she'd wished upon a star.

Jeannie had kept right on getting into trouble. Parties, boys, alcohol—driving her sister to the breaking point. They'd both been relieved when Jeannie had packed a bag and left.

Then, when the two of them had finally reconciled, after Nicole had decided she was having a family come hell or high water, Nicole had still said that. Jeannie was still trouble. But now Nicole had said it with almost fondness, and instead of hearing it as an attack, Jeannie heard what Nicole was really saying.

I'm sorry. I'm glad you're here. I love you.

That was how Jeannie chose to remember Nicole. Someone who was complicated, who did the best she could with what she had—a missing dad, a dead mom, a hellion for a sister.

I'm sorry, Jeannie thought. Hopefully, wherever Nicole was, she would know the truth. *I'm glad you were here. I'm doing the best I can. I love you.*

Jeannie's phone chimed again.

I can't allow this.

Oh, wasn't that just like the man? If he were in front of her, she'd be hard-pressed to pick between strangling and hugging him. Hell, maybe she'd just tie him to the bed again and work through some of the frustration he inspired.

He was a very inspiring man.

It'd been three days since their lunch date. Three days since the unreachable, untouchable Dr. Robert Wyatt had let himself be touched. Since he'd held out his hands for her and she'd ridden him in silence. Since he'd shared his darkest secret.

He'd done so much for her and Melissa and all Jeannie had ever done for him was serve him the perfect Manhattan. She might not be able to provide material comfort for the man but by God, she could help him face his demons.

Specifically, one demon.

Like followed like, after all. But this time she promised herself it would be good trouble. The plan was simple. Back up Robert. Help his mom. Hell, protect the good people of Illinois from a damn monster.

Really, it was going to be one hell of a party.

She shifted Melissa so she could text faster.

Robert. I am not your employee.
You don't ALLOW me to do anything.
Let me be there for you.
It's not weakness to accept help.

I can't ask this of you.

You're not asking.

This is not an obligation.

I'm coming. Let me come with you.

Melissa stirred, pushing against her blanket. The little noises she made—Maja had said those were hungry noises. Jeannie glanced at the clock—right on schedule. Who knew babies had schedules? But this baby did, thanks to a stand-in grandmother and by God, Jeannie wasn't going to screw that up. Which meant she couldn't lie around texting much longer.

Robert. Let me come with you. Please.

You can't wear the yellow dress.
This is a formal event.

I don't have anything more formal.
Unless you want me to wear my vest and bow tie?

Lord.
I will send some things over.
If we're going to do this, we're going to do it right.
He can't know who you really are.

I can blend. Promise.

The typing bubble showed for a long time but Jeannie knew she'd won. She absolutely could blend. She'd been serving the upper crust drinks for years now. She knew the mannerisms, the topics the one percent discussed. She could be just as obnoxious and ostentatious as Robert's wallpapered ceilings or as cold and aloof as Robert himself. She could absolutely fake it until she made it, whatever form *it* took.

It couldn't be a small lie because those were obvious and easy to disprove. To pull one over on someone like Landon Wyatt, it'd have to be a grand lie, so bold and ostentatious that no one would dare question her or her place on Robert's arm. She'd have to not just belong there—she'd also have to own the room.

She glanced at the book on her coffee table. *To Dare a Duke*. Hmm.

Of course, it all depended on what she'd be wearing. Heaven only knew what Robert would be sending this time.

Finally, the typing bubble disappeared but instead of a long paragraph of text, all that popped up were two little words that made her grin wildly.

Thank you.

There. Was that so hard?

Saturday at six.

I'll be waiting.

He didn't reply, but then, he didn't need to. He'd said *thank you*. For Robert, that was the equivalent of a regular dude standing outside her bedroom window with a boom box blaring '80s love songs.

Melissa fussed more insistently and Jeannie struggled to her feet. She had to feed the baby and check her diaper and then?

Then she had to get ready for Saturday night.

She had a date with the hottest bachelor in Chicago and she had a feeling that, before it was all over, she was going to see stars.

Twelve

Robert was not nervous because he was a Wyatt and Wyatts didn't get nervous. Anxiety was a symptom of uncertainty, and Wyatts were confident and sure at all times.

So the sense of unease, the sweaty palms, the unsettled stomach—absolutely not nerves. He wasn't concerned about how tonight would go. He had no worries about the traps he'd laid and how it'd all unfold in the public eye. He was confident he could get his mother away and handle Landon.

Robert was positive he could handle himself. Which was why he wasn't nervous at all.

He was excited to see what the stylists had done with Jeannie, that was all. Kelly had sent over a team of three people—hair, makeup and clothes. He anticipated seeing her dressed for his world.

God, he *missed* her.

It'd been a week since he'd brought her into his home. Seven days since he'd allowed her to touch him. Allowed himself to take comfort in another person. All he'd focused on in that time was laying the groundwork to remove the threat that was Landon Wyatt.

Missing her was more familiar now, a sensation he recognized. It was the same feeling that had thrown him off the night she hadn't appeared at the bar. The same longing that had gripped him after he'd brought her home after their date.

Date. Ha. As if that word got anywhere close to accurately describing their afternoon together. Something as simple as lunch didn't leave him a changed man.

And she had changed him, damn her.

The strange thing was...well, he'd missed her. Not just the way she talked to—or texted—him, although he did miss that because no one else dared argue with him. But then, no one else listened like she did, either.

Because of what she'd done—what he'd *let* her do—he had achieved something he'd always assumed to be beyond him.

Sex with Jeannie had been different. So very different, in fact, that he'd been able to keep it separate from his previous experiences. He'd stayed in the moment. Did she have any idea how unusual that was? Of course not. But he'd been lost to the way the silk had bitten into his skin, the way she'd ground down onto him, her weight warm and slick and silent. Perhaps too silent but after all those times marked by fake moans and real screams, it'd been a gift.

She'd given him the gift of something new, something real. He'd watched her take her pleasure, her body drawing his in, tightening around him, and she'd been raw and honest and even now, after a week, it still left him wanting more.

Which was bad.

Wasn't tonight proof? She'd left him in a weakened position, one where he allowed her to convince him to bring her to meet his parents, of all the damn things.

He wasn't entirely sure he wasn't losing his grip. Because Robert Wyatt would've never agreed to this. Introducing her to Landon was not just a bad idea—it carried real risks for Jeannie. For them both.

Reginald parked in front of Jeannie's little house and some of what was definitely not nervousness eased. Well. It was too late to turn back now. The plans had been set into motion. The newspaper photographer and guards were already in place. Kelly, Robert's assistant, had a plane on standby.

And Robert had personally interviewed the nurse, a young single woman with impressive grades, exceptional references, a valid passport and a desire to see the world, in addition to numerous outstanding student loans and a sister who had no means of affording higher education. She had been more than willing to relocate to a foreign country for six to twelve months at the salary and signing bonus Robert was offering.

Perhaps tonight would go well. He would get his mother to leave with him and, ideally, they'd show the world who Landon Wyatt really was.

They'd just need a distraction.

Would Jeannie really throw a glass of wine into Landon's face? Oh, who was he kidding? Of course she would. The better question was, what else would she do?

This was madness.

Reginald opened Robert's door and he stood, surveying the scene before him. Good. The yard had been trimmed and he was fairly certain there were new shrubs around the foundation. The housepainters were due to start after the roofers had finished, which was scheduled for next week.

He almost smiled as he strode up the sidewalk. Jeannie's little house was small and cramped and no one would ever accuse it of conveying wealth or power or even taste but... there was something he liked about climbing those three simple steps, about the way her door swung open before he could ring the bell, about seeing her...

Everything came to a sudden halt. His breathing, his heart, his forward movement—all stopped.

"Robert." She smiled, this goddess, blessing him with her benevolent kindness. "I've been waiting for you."

Oh, dear God. He had to catch himself on the railing to keep from stumbling back. *"Jeannie?"*

The goddess's eyebrow notched up as she grinned at him and then it all snapped back into place and he could see Jeannie underneath the dramatic makeup, the big hair and that *dress*.

"Well?" she said with what sounded like a knowing smirk. He couldn't tell for sure because he was too busy staring at *that dress*. She did a little turn. "What do you think?"

Robert lurched forward, grabbing on to the door frame. A wave of lust, pure and intense, nearly brought him to his knees. He'd seen her body dressed in nothing but those lacy pink underthings. Seen the trimmed swath of dark hair that covered her sex, watched in fascination as her fingers had stroked over it while he strained to be deeper inside her, more a part of her.

But he'd never seen her like *this*.

His bartender was nowhere to be seen. Instead, Jeannie had been completely transformed. Her short hair had been blown out so that it crowned her head, a far cry from the sleek style she normally wore. Her eyes were dark and mysterious, lips two shades darker than the red dress. Diamonds dripped off her ears and an enormous diamond teardrop pendant hung nestled between her breasts, which were barely contained by the vee of her dress that went almost to her waist. The rest of the dress clung to her hips and legs in a way that could only be described as *indecent*.

She was bold and scandalous and, most important, completely unrecognizable.

She was perfect.

"Hmm," she mused, her lips forming a little pout. He noticed, which meant he'd apparently stopped staring at her body. "I do believe I've stunned you speechless. It's quite different from your normal silence." She touched the tip of her tongue to her top lip. Robert had to bite back a groan. "Yes," she practically hummed and he realized he barely recognized her voice. She bit off her vowels differently, held herself taller. Although maybe it was the dress? "*Quite* different."

Maja appeared from the baby's room. "See?" she clucked in that grandmotherly way. "I told you it'd work."

Jeannie beamed and there she was again, *his* Jeannie. "I was afraid the dress was too much—to say nothing of the danged diamonds, Robert," she explained, as if Robert had asked a question when all his brain wanted to do was peel that dress off her and get lost in her body again. And again. And again, until nothing else mattered. "The stylists brought a black one but—"

"But with her coloring—" Maja added. Dimly, Robert realized she was holding the baby "—red was the obvious color," she concluded, sounding triumphant. "The color of luck."

"Yes," he managed to agree. Somehow.

Jeannie turned back to him and she was different again. He couldn't say how, but she was. "And you," she said, her hips swaying indecently as she moved toward him. "That's quite a tuxedo you're filling out there, Robert." She reached out and straightened his tie.

He nodded, which was probably not the correct reaction but it was all he had. What had she texted him?

She could blend. She'd promised.

By God, this was not blending. And he couldn't care less.

"Go on now," Maja said, scooping something off the coffee table and handing it to Jeannie. A handbag, small and black and sparkling. "Enjoy your night. I'll be here the whole time so…"

Her words trailed off and Robert realized the nanny was giving them both permission not to come home.

Well. He did pay her for going above and beyond, didn't he?

He nodded again, this time managing to find his usual imperiousness. Jeannie smoothed his lapels, sending licks of fire over his chest. But then she notched an eyebrow at him again and he saw the challenge in her eyes.

"Thank you," he added. Maja inclined her head in acknowledgment.

Jeannie beamed up at him and it took every last bit of self-restraint he had not to pull her into his arms and mess up her lipstick. This time he wanted to touch her, to see her body bared completely. By candlelight. He wanted to feel her hands on him. He wanted to taste her, every single part, his lips on her skin, inside her body.

To hell with the perfect Manhattan. He would be forever drunk on her.

"We should go," she said softly in that strange voice of hers, giving his lapels a pat.

"Yes," he said, barely recognizing his own voice.

She turned and walked—swayed—back to Maja. "Be good tonight, sweetie," she said, brushing her fingertips over Melissa's head. "Love you."

Robert had to grip the door frame again because this was something new and real and he didn't know how to make sense of it, this display of maternal affection. There was something so right about Jeannie looking down at the baby with such tenderness.

Then she turned back to him, a sultry smile playing across her lips. "Shall we?"

"Yes," he repeated again.

"Have fun!" Maja called out after them.

* * *

Working in silence, Cybil applied the thick foundation liberally, blending it all the way down her neck. Lupe, her maid, spread it over Cybil's back and shoulders, covering the bruises. They hadn't faded yet and if Landon saw any trace of his violence…

It'd be so much easier if she could wear a dress with a jacket, but Landon had chosen a deep blue gown for her to wear tonight and of course it was off the shoulder, with an attached capelet. Elegant and sophisticated—and it left her décolletage and shoulders bare.

Lupe finished with the makeup and began to fix Cybil's hair into an upswept French twist. They worked in silence. In theory, Lupe's English was not very good, which made conversation difficult. In practice, Cybil had learned long ago not to trust a single person on staff.

Tonight she was going to see Bobby again. He was coming, his assistant had assured Landon's assistant, Alexander. He *would* be there. She would see her son with her own eyes, see that he was healthy and whole and, she dared to hope, happy, even. That she'd kept him safe by staying, by keeping Landon away from Bobby.

She dared to hope that Bobby had forgiven her for leaving. That he understood she'd done so to protect him.

She dared to hope…

But she did not allow any of this hope to show. No excitement danced in her eyes as she watched Lupe work in the mirror. She was resigned to her role as hostess for the gala, a role she could perform effortlessly. She was prepared to act the politician's wife, smiling widely as her husband lied through his teeth about how he cared for this state, this city, the millions of people whose lives he could improve—or ruin. She'd had years of practice, after all.

And if Bobby offered her shelter again…

She couldn't go to his home. She couldn't risk him like

that again. But surely, he knew that. Surely, he wouldn't make the same mistake again.

Dear Lord, Cybil prayed, *please don't let me make the same mistake again, either.*

There had to be a way.

"Are you breathing?" Jeannie asked as the car crawled through downtown traffic.

She stroked her thumb over Robert's knuckles. He had a hell of a grip on her hand. She'd explained the persona she was adopting tonight and she could tell he wasn't 100 percent on board. Not that she could blame him.

This was, hands down, the craziest thing she'd ever done.

"Yes," he said after a long moment in which she was pretty sure he hadn't breathed. "I'm fine."

"I doubt it." She saw a quick flash of teeth. "Is there a plan? Because I can wing it but this sort of feels like one of those situations where a plan would be a good idea." After another few seconds, she added, "Sharing it would be an even better idea."

His grip tightened on her hand and she had to work hard not to gasp. "Reginald will be parked by the service entrance in the basement, engine running. There's a service elevator in the back, next to the restrooms. It's down a short hallway." He cleared his throat, sounding painfully nervous. "If I can get her to come with me, we'll leave without a look back."

She thought on that for a moment as she fiddled with the heavy diamond pendant. The rock alone was probably worth more than she made in a year, not to mention the earrings or the dress. A Valentino dress, for God's sake! She was easily wearing thirty, forty thousand dollars' worth of fabric and diamonds. Which was not a huge deal to Robert but, if she let herself think about it too much, it would easily freak her the heck out.

But tonight she wouldn't fret about cost or Robert's

world. Tonight she was going to waltz into that gala party on his arm like she owned the damn room and if it took three stylists, diamonds and a Valentino to do it, so be it. "So I'm to…what, distract your father while you two make a run for the airport?"

"God, no—you stick with me." He pulled his hand free and—shockingly—adjusted his cuffs. "You are not to be alone with him under any circumstances. Ever."

She almost rolled her eyes at his tone. "I can handle myself, Robert. I've been fending off drunks and avoiding wandering hands since I was a teenager. Don't worry."

His head swung around and even in the dark interior of the car, she shivered at his intensity. "You are *not* to be alone with him, Jeannie." His voice was dangerously quiet, all the more menacing for it. *"Ever."*

"O…kay. So how do we know he won't follow us?"

"He won't want to make a scene. The whole point of tonight is to put on a public performance."

She mulled over the options. "What if—and I'm just throwing this out there—what if I can get your mom alone? Like, we go to the ladies' room together. You can stay behind to keep an eye on your father and I can get her to the car." Assuming Mrs. Wyatt would go with Jeannie. A complete stranger.

But it would be easy to get her alone. She needed a drink. One that stained would be best.

Robert's expression reflected doubt. "Reginald knows where to go. Everything else is ready. Take her and leave." He leaned over, his fingertips barely brushing over her cheek. "Just be safe. I… I can't bear the thought of anything happening to you."

Oh, Robert. "Listen to me, you stubborn man. I will be fine. It's you I'm worried about." He was already a mess. The average person wouldn't be able to tell, but she knew. His voice was rough and he was straightening his cuffs *again*. Worst of all, his leg had begun to jump. "If you can get an opening, promise me you'll take it. Send me two texts in a row—so I know you're gone and I'll get away. Trust me, Robert. Don't worry."

"I'm a Wyatt," he said sternly as the car pulled up in front of a building right off the Magnificent Mile, as if that was the cure for the world's ills. "We never worry." But then the hard lines of his face softened and the very corners of his lips curved up in a faint smile. "Ready to crash a party?"

She grinned. "Hell, yes."

Reginald opened the door for them, his normally jovial face a blank mask. Robert handed her out of the car and then tucked her fingers into the crook of his arm. Then he murmured, "Be ready," as they passed and Reginald nodded smartly before closing the door behind them.

A crush of people waited to get through security. The crowd was a sea of black—black tuxedos, black gowns— Jeannie was suddenly glad she'd gone with the red. Her role was to be a distraction and in this dress, she stood out like a siren. Seriously, her boobs in this dress were practically works of art. For how much this dress cost, they damn well better be.

Jeannie squared her shoulders, lifted her chin and tried to look bored as Robert cut through the crowd. A weaselly-looking man with thinning hair stood at the front of the line.

Robert leaned down to whisper in her ear, "Alexander, Landon's loyal assistant."

She nodded, sticking close to Robert's side. Loyal? In other words, this was not a person to be trusted. It was easy to look all icy and disapproving when that was exactly how she felt.

When the weasel caught sight of Robert, he waved them past security, calling, "Dr. Wyatt? This way." Someone in line started to protest, but Robert swung around, daring anyone to complain with a cold glare. Jeannie tried to match his look.

The crowd fell oddly silent in the face of Robert's displeasure. Somewhere nearby, a camera flashed.

Which was good because Jeannie needed to remember that she wasn't here with Robert, a complicated and conflicted man who cared for sick children and infants and who had literally been the answer to her prayers. No, she was here with Dr. Robert Wyatt, of the Chicago Wyatts, a billionaire bachelor and one of the most powerful, dangerous men in the state.

Time to own this room.

She let her gaze slide over the people she passed as if she couldn't be bothered to see them. Alexander led them through the crowd, up a spiral staircase. She was barely able to keep up with Robert's long strides in the strappy black sandals the stylist had put her in to go with this dress.

But even if she didn't acknowledge the other party-goers, she could feel their reactions as she and Robert moved effortlessly through their ranks. People stopped and stared as they passed, but the moment they'd gone by, the loud whispers started.

Hadn't there been rumors of a falling-out between the elder Wyatt and the younger?

How gauche that Wyatt dirtied his hands practicing medicine.

And who was *she*?

Dear God, was Jeannie really doing this? This was more than just crashing a gala. This was pulling a fast one over on the person who could put the fear of God into Robert.

She stiffened her spine. Go big or go home.

"This way," Alexander said. He glanced at Jeannie and she stared down her nose at him, daring him to make a comment about Robert bringing a date.

He didn't. Instead, he led them to where a handsome

man, almost as tall and almost as broad as Robert, was holding court. Landon Wyatt, billionaire gubernatorial candidate and total asshole. Not that anyone else would know it.
All the tuxedoed men and glamorous women around him
laughed heartily at his jokes, champagne flutes in hand,
gems glittering at their necks and wrists and ears.

They sounded like jackals. Maybe they were. Thank God
she didn't recognize any of them as customers from Trenton's.

Next to Landon stood an elegant older woman, smiling
brightly and occasionally touching her husband on the arm
or shoulder as he talked, as if she had to let him know where
she was at all times. As Alexander wormed his way through
to the inner circle, Robert's mother caught sight of them.

Although the crowd was too loud to hear Cybil Wyatt,
Jeannie physically *felt* the woman's sharp inhalation, saw
the overwhelming longing in her eyes.

Alexander tugged on Landon Wyatt's sleeve and motioned to Robert with his chin. By the time Landon turned
to his wife, her face was carefully blank.

Wyatt's face was how Jeannie might've imagined kings
of old looking when a foreign dignitary dared grace his
throne room. "Ah, here he is. Robert, my boy, how have
you been?"

Jeannie felt the tension in Robert's arm. *Say something*,
she mentally ordered him.

"Father," he managed. Then he looked to Cybil. "Mother."
He cleared his throat and his arm moved and Jeannie knew
that if she hadn't had a hold of him, he would've been
straightening his cuffs.

This was exactly why she'd insisted on coming tonight.
Robert could be intense and scary—boy, could he—but
when faced with his father in front of a crowd, he froze up.

Landon's gaze flicked over her. "What do we have here?
I didn't realize you were bringing a date, *son*."

She gave Robert a whole two seconds to respond but when he didn't she stepped into the gap. "How do you do," she said in her snootiest British accent. She released Robert's arm and extended her hand to Landon, palm down. "Lady Daphne FitzRoy. Charmed."

"*Lady* FitzRoy?" Landon said, his lip curling as if he instinctively knew she was an imposter.

"Of the London FitzRoys?" She sighed heavily and let her gaze narrow dismissively. She hadn't been reading historical romances for the last fifteen years or so for nothing. All those ballroom scenes, with cuts direct and dukes and duchesses—an informal education in the British aristocracy was about to pay off *big time*. "But of course. I forget how you Americans are. Perhaps you've heard of my brother? The Duke of Grafton?"

Because nothing caught the attention of a bully like a good old-fashioned reminder of where he really stood in the food chain.

And it worked like a freaking charm. Landon Wyatt inhaled, his nostrils flaring as his pupils darkened and for a fleeting second, Jeannie understood exactly why Robert was terrified of this man. She felt like a little rabbit who'd just realized the wolf was pouncing.

But she was no meek bunny. She cleared her throat and shot a disdainful look at her extended hand.

Wyatt got the hint. He pressed cold lips to the back of her hand. Jeannie refused to allow her skin to prickle. "I'm not familiar with the FitzRoys of London," he admitted, putting humor into his voice. "But welcome! Any sister of nobility is a friend of mine. And, apparently," he added, cutting a glance to Robert, "a friend of my son's. Well done, Robert."

Had she thought a wolf? That was wrong. He was a snake, one with hypnotizing eyes.

She wouldn't let him charm her. She tugged her hand free and turned to Robert's mother. "You must be Cybil.

Delighted, I'm sure." Jeannie kept her voice bored, determined not to give away her interest in Robert's mother.

"I didn't realize Bobby—Robert—was bringing a guest," Cybil said, her gaze darting between her son and Jeannie. "How…nice to make your acquaintance."

Years of observing customers kicked in and Jeannie noticed Cybil Wyatt wore her makeup too thick and that it went all the way down her neck and across her chest. Hiding bruises, maybe? She held her left shoulder higher than her right and her smile only used half her mouth, as if her jaw on the right side pained her.

Jeannie caught sight of a waiter and impatiently snapped her fingers, mentally apologizing to the dude. People who snapped for attention at the bar got either too much ice in their glasses or a small pour.

He hurried over, looking not the least bit bothered by her rudeness. Jeannie took two glasses from his tray and handed one to Robert. "Is this champagne or that American knockoff you all seem so proud of?" she asked in a voice too loud to be a whisper.

She physically felt people pull back. Good. She'd shocked them—which meant they wouldn't be able to stop looking at her.

With a light laugh, Cybil said, "The champagne is French, I assure you. Sparkling white wine just isn't the same, is it?" Her gaze darted to her husband and then she stepped around him. "It's so good to see you," she said, gripping Robert by the biceps. Jeannie could hear the truth of it in her voice. "I'm so glad you came."

"So am I," he said, staring down at his mother, his concern obvious. Then he seemed to snap out of it. "Daphne was curious how politics work in America."

Right. This was her role. She waved this comment away, slugging back half her glass. She'd need to look drunk in relatively short order. "He exaggerates, of course. Politics and politicians are a complete and utter bore."

The hangers-on actually gasped out loud at this brazen insult but Jeannie refused to cower. She would not cede a bit of her pretend high ground. She was counting on keeping Wyatt's attention by pretending to be beyond his spheres of influence. Instead, she rolled her shoulder in a not-apology.

After a beat too long, Wyatt burst out laughing and quickly, everyone around them joined in. "Ah, that dry British humor," he said out loud, his hand closing around her wrist like a manacle and drawing her by his side. Which was not a safe place to be, but it had the advantage of pushing Cybil and Robert a little farther away. "Tell me about yourself, *Duchess*." This last was said in an openly mocking tone.

"Oh, I'm not a duchess. That's my sister-in-law. You may address me as Lady FitzRoy." She said it pointedly because a true lady would demand respect.

"My lady," Wyatt said, his mouth moving in what might have been a grin. Oh, he was playing along but Jeannie knew he hadn't decided if she was legit or not. "Do tell."

"What is there to say?" She finished her champagne and snapped at the waiter, who hurried to exchange her glass for a full one. "Grafton—my brother—does his part in the House of Lords but he's dreadfully dull, as I said. So responsible." She let her lip curl in distaste but at the same time, she brushed an invisible piece of lint off Wyatt's shoulder and let her fingers linger. "Tell me, why would anyone want to run for office? Especially someone of your *considerable* stature? Public service is just so public. I'd think it'd be beneath a man of your obvious…talents." She cut a dismissive glance at Robert. "Like working. In a hospital, for God's sake," she added in a stage whisper that everyone heard.

Oh, that did the trick. Wyatt threw back his head with a brutal laugh—real humor at the expense of his son. A shiver of terror went down her back, but she smiled and notched an eyebrow at him, playing along. She saw the answer in Wyatt's eyes when he looked at her—he was drunk on power and like any addict, he needed more.

But like a good politician, he said, "As you know, we Wyatts are quite well-off."

She rolled her shoulder in that dismissive shrug again as if being billionaires was just so much dross.

His pupils dilated. He was enjoying himself. Good. "I don't seek the office of the governor for myself, you understand. I have everything I could ever want." Wyatt's gaze dipped to her breasts. She repressed a shudder. "It's time to give back to the good people of Illinois. They deserve more and, having managed my company for so long, I alone have the skills to set things right and steer this great state into the future!"

The fawning jackals broke out in applause. Flashbulbs flashed.

Jeannie snapped for the poor waiter again because Lady Daphne FitzRoy was a bitch—and an alcoholic at that. She exchanged her half-empty glass for a full one and drank deeply. She needed to look sloppy drunk.

She could feel Robert's gaze on her.

She refused to look.

Thirteen

"Come with me."

Robert kept his voice low, using the laughter of the crowd to hide his words. He didn't look at Cybil Wyatt as he spoke. Instead, his gaze was locked on to Jeannie—or, rather, Lady FitzRoy. He couldn't believe people were buying this line of BS, but even Landon seemed smitten with her. Or at least smitten with her breasts.

"…in a hospital, for God's sake," she said, wobbling to-ward Landon as she said it. How much had she drunk? Aside from the wine at lunch last weekend, he'd never actually seen her drink before.

Everyone laughed at his expense, Landon loudest of all.

"I can keep you safe," he added as Landon's predatory gaze zeroed in on Jeannie. Jeannie had sworn she could handle herself. And he had to admit, she was one hell of a distraction.

His mother's grip on his arm tightened before she re-moved her hand entirely. "It's not safe," she said, smiling that smile he hated because it was a mask, a lie. "He'll come after you. He'll find me."

Like last time. She didn't say it, but she didn't need to.

Mom looked awful. The way she held her body—didn't anyone else here see the lines of pain around her eyes? The way her shoulders weren't even? Had that bastard broken her ribs again?

Landon Wyatt was going to pay for everything he'd done.

The world went a little red at the edges, narrowing to Landon and Jeannie. She had another champagne flute in her hand and was waving it around. Champagne sloshed everywhere and people stepped back to make sure they didn't get hit. Then she took another long drink and all but dropped the flute. A beleaguered waiter caught it before it hit the ground and then Jeannie had a fresh glass.

Landon slid a taunting glance his way and then slid his arm around Jeannie's waist, pulling her closer so he could whisper in her ear.

Robert's stomach rolled. Hard. Because he was supposed to be protecting the women he cared about. He wasn't a kid anymore, forced to stand by and watch helplessly as Landon hurt women in the name of a teachable moment.

This wasn't happening. Jeannie wasn't a paid escort. And she knew who she was dealing with.

Trust me, she'd said.

Did he have a choice?

She looked at Robert, a mean smile on her lips. But then her glance bounced to his mother and back to him, her eyes widening just a little, and Robert got the distinct feeling she was telling him something.

"He won't find you," Robert told his mother, hiding his mouth behind his glass as he spoke. His plan had been set into motion tonight and he couldn't stop it if he wanted to— and he didn't want to. He just needed to be sure Cybil was nowhere near Landon when the chips began to fall. Robert couldn't bear to think of that bastard blaming Mom when things all fell apart. "He can't win. But I need you to come with me."

For what felt like a century, she didn't answer, didn't look at him. She laughed politely at something rude Jeannie had said—about Robert, probably. He wasn't paying attention.

"When?"

Relief hit him so hard he almost cried. "My car is waiting. Jeannie or I will take you there."

That got her attention. She turned to fully face him, which was a rare mistake. It was never a good idea to give Landon Wyatt your back. "Who?"

"My date."

Color deepened on Mom's cheeks as if she was embarrassed that someone else knew their private shame. But all she said was, "Ah," and turned back to face Landon just as Jeannie pulled away from his grip.

She took another deep drink of her champagne and then held the glass at such an angle that nearly half the contents poured directly onto the floor. "But I'm ignoring our hostess!" she cried in what was truly a terrible British accent.

Robert couldn't *believe* people were buying this act. How was he even looking at the same person who blended behind the bar at Trenton's, ready with the perfect Manhattan and a sympathetic ear? How was this the same woman who'd wrapped a silk tie around his wrists and then wrapped her nearly nude body around his?

She was so much more than just the sum of those moments.

And she was heading straight for him and his mother, pausing only long enough to get another glass of champagne. Landon's friends—men who had power and wealth, although never as much of either as Landon had—sniggered at the sight of this supposed *lady* making a complete ass of herself.

"Do you know," Jeannie began, her words now notice-ably slurred, "that I do think this is very good champ—*whoopsie!*"

She stumbled forward, splashing Mom right in the chest and somehow managing to get a good part of the champagne onto Robert's sleeve and face, as well.

He nearly burst out laughing. *Whoopsie.* She'd had this planned from the moment she'd informed him she was com-ing with him, hadn't she? By God, he'd never known a woman like Jeannie before.

She wobbled dangerously on her heels, her dress nearly falling off her shoulders and exposing her breasts as she stumbled into Mom. "Oh, dear," Jeannie said, a hysterical laugh in her voice that made her accent even more awful. "Oh, I've made a mess of your lovely dress. Oh, what a pity, it was so pretty. Grafton will be *so* displeased. Oh," she said, clutching Mom by the arm and looking properly terrified, "you won't tell him, will you?"

Mom looked around wildly, wine dripping off her chin and running down her chest. Her makeup gave up its hold on her skin as flesh-colored rivulets ran onto the bodice of her dress.

An uneasy hush had fallen over the crowd. People weren't sure if they should laugh or offer assistance or what. An-other round of flashbulbs went off, reminding everyone that this series of unfortunate events was on the record.

Landon Wyatt shot Robert a look that promised pure pain. Robert didn't allow himself to shy away. He met Land-on's stare head-on and then wiped alcohol from his chin. Really, Jeannie had done an excellent job making as big a mess as humanly possible.

"No, no," Mom said, finding her voice and grabbing Jeannie's hand before she could start smearing the body makeup. "But why don't you and I go to the ladies' room? I bet you'll feel better after we both freshen up." She looked to her husband—for permission. The pause made Robert's teeth grind.

This, he vowed, would be the very last time Cybil Wyatt asked her husband for permission to do anything.

Landon nodded. "Perhaps we should cut the duchess off." He turned back to the crowd. "I suppose the Brits can't hold their liquor."

"I'd like to hold *her*," someone muttered. Robert didn't see who'd spoken but he refused to allow himself to react.

Leaning heavily on Mom, Jeannie allowed herself to be led toward the ladies' room, babbling about how Grafton would be *most* upset…

She'd missed her calling as an actress; that much was clear. Robert felt an odd sort of pride at her performance. But that was immediately followed by an even odder sort of fear as he caught Landon looking after the women. Robert recognized that look. It seemed benign, that level gaze, that slight quirk to the lips. Friendly, almost.

A shiver raced down Robert's back and he had to dig his nails into his palm to keep from letting it out. Because the times he'd seen Landon Wyatt look like that—especially if he made it to a full smile—those were some of the worst moments of Robert's life.

Like a nightmare come to life, Landon's smile widened.

It didn't matter that Jeannie hadn't looked or acted like herself. She was in danger for embarrassing Landon in front of his friends and donors and cameras. Jeannie might as well have painted a big red target on her back, and Robert? He would be in just as much trouble for bringing the notorious Lady FitzRoy to the party in the first place.

That was bad enough. When Landon discovered Jeannie had actually absconded with his wife…

Robert's lungs wouldn't move, wouldn't inflate. It only got worse when Landon turned back to the crowd. His gaze snagged on Robert and the man smirked.

Smirked.

This was Robert's doing, all of it. He'd agreed to let her come, agreed to let her act the part of a noble drunk. It was Robert's job to keep Jeannie safe. A deadening hole opened up in his stomach as he realized what that meant.

He had to stay as far away from her as possible. No more lunch dates, no more evening drinks at Trenton's. It didn't matter if she went back to work or not; Robert couldn't risk her by ever darkening the restaurant's doors again.

Well, that was being a little melodramatic. But as long as Landon Wyatt had power and a means to wield it, he was a threat. Robert had always known that. That was why he was sending his mother halfway around the world. Landon was a threat to Robert, to Mom and now to Jeannie.

Tonight would be it, then.

Robert fought the urge to look at his phone. God willing, in less than two minutes, Reginald would be on his way to the private airfield north of the city, where the plane and flight crew were on standby.

Landon's smile shifted subtly into a more genial look as Robert felt another trickle of champagne drip off his chin. "She got you, too, eh, son?" he said to chuckles, as if he was a sympathetic father.

"I shouldn't have let her drink," Robert replied, because that was a sentiment Landon would approve. "I'm sorry for the mess."

How many seconds had passed? Had it been a minute? Were they in the elevator yet?

Landon stared at him, his eyes flinty, before his whole face changed into one of good humor. "Go get cleaned up— but I expect to see you back here. I'm giving my big speech in a few minutes and the cameras will be rolling."

"I wouldn't miss it," Robert said, managing to paste some sort of smile on his face. It must have been appropriate because people made noises of sympathy.

He hadn't taken three steps before his phone buzzed. Jeannie. *Thank God.*

In car

Go

Waiting for you

Go, dammit

Thirty seconds

> Jesus, that woman.
> Robert broke into a run.

"Buckle up," the woman in red said, sounding not particularly drunk nor particularly British.

"Who are you?" Cybil asked, impressed that she could speak at all.

This was really happening. She was really in a private car with a complete stranger who had dragged her into an elevator and then shoved her into a car.

And she was going along with it because the alternative to what was potentially a kidnapping was to stay with Landon.

"A friend of your son's," was the reply she got, which was almost comforting. Then the woman in red had her head through the dividing window and was talking to the driver. "Thirty seconds!" the not-lady all but shouted. "Just a few more seconds!"

The driver replied, but Cybil couldn't make out his words over the pounding of her pulse in her ears.

Landon would be so mad if he knew about this. Bobby was putting himself directly into harm's way—the very place Cybil had worked so hard to keep him from—and for what? For her?

"I should get back," she said, fumbling with the seat belt.

"Sorry, Mrs. Wyatt, but that's not happening." The woman in red slid into the seat next to her and put a firm hand on the buckle. "And I apologize for ruining your dress. It was pretty." This strange creature turned her head to the side, appraising Cybil with unnervingly frank eyes.

"He'll come after Bobby," Cybil said, her voice breaking on the end. She scrabbled at the woman's hands, trying to pry them loose of the seat belt. Panic tasted metallic in her mouth. "He'll hurt my son! I have to protect him!"

"He's a grown man," the stranger said, taking hold of Cybil's hands. Her grip was firm but not cruel. "Bobby is capable of protecting himself. And you, if you'll trust him. Just trust him."

The car started to move. "Five more seconds!" the woman yelled at the driver.

"He said to go now!" the driver yelled back.

"What's happening?" Cybil said, hating how the weakness bled into her voice. Hating that this was what she'd been reduced to. Begging a complete stranger for information.

To her surprise, the woman carefully wrapped an arm around Cybil's shoulders. "You're going somewhere safe. Believe me, your husband will never be able to find you."

The car began to roll again just as the passenger door wrenched open and Cybil screamed as the woman in red shielded her because for a second she thought it was Landon there, eyes blazing, chest heaving, and she knew this time, a few broken bones would be child's play. But then it was Bobby, her Bobby, climbing into the car and slamming the door shut behind him. Bobby yelling at the driver to *go, dammit*. Bobby helping the woman into the seat across from Cybil.

Bobby sitting next to her, wrapping his arms around her.

"My son," she said, promptly ruining his tuxedo jacket with her tears and smeared makeup and spilled champagne.

"I've got you, Mom," he said, his voice breaking as he held her—but gently, like he could tell where she was hurting. "You're safe now."

"You're not," she wept because Landon would destroy him. Landon would destroy them all. "*Why*, Bobby? Why would you risk yourself for *me*?"

"He's stronger than you think," the woman said, her voice kind. "Because that's how you raised him to be."

Cybil got herself under control. Years of practice made it practically second nature. "Who are you?" she asked because clearly this was someone her son trusted.

The woman smiled. It looked real and soft, and unfamiliar hope fluttered in Cybil's chest. Had Bobby found someone?

But then the woman spoke and dashed her hopes. "I'm his bartender."

Fourteen

"Are you sure about this?" Mom asked as Robert guided her up the narrow stairs into the plane.

"I'm sure. We'll talk anytime you want and in a few months, I'll fly down and visit you." Robert settled her into her seat. "He won't keep us apart."

Mom was crying softly. "Don't let him hurt you," she said, her voice surprisingly level despite her tears. "I couldn't live with myself if…"

Robert pressed a kiss to her good cheek. "I'm not a little kid anymore, Mom. I promise you, I've got the situation under control. You focus on getting well." He motioned the nurse forward. "Bridget here will be with you the whole time."

Mom nodded, looking panicked. Then she glanced out the window and seemed to calm. Robert followed her gaze and saw Jeannie standing near the limo, wind billowing her skirt. "I hope you know what you're doing," she whispered.

"I do."

Landon Wyatt wouldn't have any idea what'd hit him. The disappearance of his wife was merely the first domino to fall.

Mom turned back to him. She took a deep breath and nodded. "All right. But promise me this, Bobby—if you get the chance at real happiness, grab it. Hold on to it." She gripped his hand with surprising strength. But then, she'd always been so much stronger than she let on. "Be happy, Bobby." She looked at Jeannie again. "Be well and be happy. It's all I've ever wanted for you."

Robert had to swallow a few times before his throat worked right. He'd gotten a little bit of happiness for a short time. It would have to do. "That's what I want for you, too." Mom gave him a scolding look, tinged with a smile, so Robert promised. "I will. I swear."

He kissed her goodbye and checked in with Bridget one last time. Then he was climbing down the stairs and Jeannie was waiting for him. After tonight he wouldn't get the comfort of going to her when he needed her.

How was he supposed to go on without her?

But he didn't have the luxury of loving Jeannie, not until Landon was either behind bars or six feet under and not until Robert could be sure the bastard hadn't left behind instructions that would endanger Jeannie or his mother.

Jeannie slipped her hand in his and a brief moment of hope flared in his chest as the plane door shut and locked. She'd said she'd wait for him, hadn't she? If Robert knew that she'd be there with the perfect Manhattan and that take-no-crap smile—maybe even with a silk tie tangled in her fingers—after this thing with Landon was settled, he'd be content to wait.

But that wasn't fair to her. She had a life—a baby to care for, a job she enjoyed. He was a customer, a benefactor—and a lover, perhaps—but that didn't make her his.

Robert knew what Landon would say. He'd say Jeannie

belonged to Robert. He was a Wyatt and Wyatts took what they wanted. Landon would spout off about how Robert had to demand respect when he meant fear, as if fear was somehow more magical than love or trust.

Yes, that was what Landon Wyatt would do.

Which was exactly why Robert would let Jeannie go.

As the plane began to move, Robert caught a glimpse of his mother's face, tear-streaked and shocked. She lifted a hand and Robert returned the small wave.

Jeannie leaned against him, shoulder to shoulder, almost the same height he was in her heels. They stood together in silence as the plane taxied down the runway and took off.

It was done. Mom was on her way. Everything else was falling into place.

So why couldn't he move?

Because moving would bring him closer to the end of tonight. To the end of his time with Jeannie.

He wasn't sure he was strong enough to do what had to be done.

"Sir?" Kelly came forward. "Do you want the updates?"

Mechanically, Robert nodded. But he turned to Jeannie. "Wait for me?" Because he wasn't strong enough. Not... yet, anyway.

Her fingers tightened around his hand. She was less than a breath away—closer than that when she lifted her other hand and brushed her thumb over his cheek. "Of course."

Then she kissed the spot she'd just stroked, her lips lingering. He could smell champagne on her breath mingling with the orange scent she always wore.

He had to let her go. He *had* to. And if she wouldn't listen—because this was Jeannie, after all—then he'd have to keep her away.

He wrapped his arm around her waist and held her tight, inhaling her scent deeply. Each moment was another memory he tucked away, another glimpse of happiness that he'd hold on to for later.

He'd promised, after all.

"I'll wait in the car," she whispered in his ear.

But he didn't let her go. Not just yet. Another moment, that was all he needed. He couldn't take her home because Landon might show up at any moment, full of rage and hate, and follow them. And Maja was at Jeannie's house, to say nothing of the baby.

"After this," he murmured against her temple, "I'll take you to see the stars."

He felt the tremor of excitement move through her. "From your terrace?" Her body pressed against his, a promise of more than just another moment. She reached up between them and tugged the ends of his bow tie loose and just like that, he went rock-hard for her. "I'd like that. But I couldn't wish for anything more."

He shook his head. "You deserve more than one star. You deserve them all." That would be his parting gift to her. The night sky and all those stars to wish upon.

She pulled the tie from around his neck as she put distance between them. Black silk dangling from her fingertips, her knowing smile in the dim lighting made him want to forget about Landon and revenge and corporate takeovers and everything but Jeannie and him and this wanting that existed between them.

She turned on her heel and, with a come-hither look over her shoulder, strode to the car, where Reginald was waiting to open the door for her. Robert couldn't move as she climbed in, revealing the curve of her leg as she pulled her foot inside. He wasn't even sure he was breathing until the car door closed.

Then Reginald had the nerve to wink. At Robert! Really, this was too much.

But that cheekiness broke the spell Robert was under.

He turned to find Kelly pointedly looking at everything but Robert or the limo and, one presumed, Jeannie.

"Is everything on track?" Robert asked, straightening his cuffs. He felt undressed without his tie. Which was most likely the point.

Well, one of them.

"Yes. The photographer reports that Landon is still at the gallery, although he's delaying the start of his speech and growing more agitated by the second." Kelly held out his phone. "Would you like to see the shots?"

"No." The less space Landon took up in Robert's brain from here on out, the better. "The lawyers have been notified?"

One for the divorce, a few from the District Attorney's office and several for the former employees who'd been subjected to Landon's sexual assaults. In just a few short days they'd found four former maids and six former employees of Wyatt Medical willing to come forward. A few claims were past the statute of limitations, so Robert was funding the civil suits. The others had been turned over to the authorities. The actual number of victims was probably quadruple the ten they'd confirmed, easily.

"Yes. The judge should be approving the emergency search warrant as we speak."

"Excellent. The guards are on standby?" One posted at Jeannie's house, just in case Robert had left a loose thread out there for Landon to pull. The others, including two off-duty police officers—one of whom was extremely grateful that his eldest son had just celebrated his sixth birthday after a successful heart valve repair—were watching his house.

"Yes. The forensic accountant has already found some very large…discrepancies between the Wyatt Medical financials and Landon's campaign fund." Kelly closed his portfolio. "You're sure about this?"

This was completely and methodically destroying his father, piece by piece.

Robert almost smiled. He was a Wyatt, after all, and Wyatts demanded respect. They didn't hesitate or have second thoughts. When someone slighted a Wyatt, they responded by dominating. By destroying, if that was what it took.

It wasn't enough to have Landon publicly humiliated.

He had to be ended. Simple as that.

And Robert was the only person who could do it. Because he was a Wyatt and this was what Landon had made him into. Someone cruel and hard and utterly without mercy.

So he nodded once. Landon Wyatt would get no mercy. Not from his only child.

Kelly let out a breath he apparently had been holding and said, "Then we're doing this."

Kelly was a good kid, not the kind of man who'd been raised to engage in this level of back-channel manipulation. Robert appreciated that his assistant wasn't entirely comfortable with the situation but he also appreciated an employee who did as he was asked.

"I may be…offline for a few hours," Robert told Kelly, fighting the urge to touch his shirt collar, "but keep me informed."

He thought Kelly's cheeks might have darkened but it was hard to tell. "Yes, sir."

Robert nodded again and turned back to the car but then an image of Jeannie notching an eyebrow at him in challenge floated before his mind's eye. He turned back before he could think better of it. "Kelly?"

"Sir?" The young man snapped to attention.

"Thank you. I know this is far outside your normal purview but…" Bordering on criminal, in fact. "But I appreciate everything you've done for me and my mother. So thank you."

There, was that so hard? Jeannie's laugh echoed in his mind.

No, it wasn't. In fact, it was getting easier all the time.

"Oh. Well. Uh, you're welcome?" Kelly sounded just as confused by receiving this compliment as Robert had felt giving it.

"Where to, sir?" Reginald asked and dammit, the man had a twinkle in his eye.

"The beach," Robert said decisively because he was a Wyatt and the time for second-guessing was over. "Take us to see the stars. Please."

Reginald nodded smartly as he opened the door for Robert. It wasn't until the door had closed behind him, leaving him completely alone with Jeannie, that Robert was able to breathe.

Champagne and oranges and Jeannie. The scent surrounded him and he felt his shoulders relax. "Well?" she asked as he settled into his seat. Instantly, she was at his side, curling into him.

Without consciously choosing to do so, his arm went around her shoulder, gathering her tight. He could hold her like this now without hesitation, without flinching. She'd given him that.

"Everything is fine," he said and, at least for the next hour or so, it truly was.

"Good," she replied, her hand sliding under his tux jacket. She undid his vest and then rested her hand on his stomach. That simple touch, muted through the layers of his shirt and undershirt, still pushed his pulse faster. It took so little for her to affect him now.

She pushed herself onto her knees without letting go of him, her breasts brushing against his chest as she shifted. Her scent, warm and inviting, filled his nose. He could get drunk on her, he realized. Maybe he already was. "What are the rules?"

Here in the dark interior of his car, nothing else existed. Just him and her. A woman who had stood by his side through one of the hardest moments of his life and yet still wanted *him*. Not his fortune or his name or any of it. Just him.

It was a hell of a thing.

He wished he could give her so much more. But tonight was all he had. So he said, "Same as last time."

But this time it wasn't because he was worried he would hurt her. He wouldn't. No, this time he needed the restraint to remind himself that she was not his to have and to hold.

Would that she was. But it wasn't safe. Not now. Maybe…

If her lips twisted to the side in disappointment, he couldn't say. "Hold out your hands."

It felt right, letting her do this again. It'd worked the last time. He'd lost himself in her, but he hadn't lost control. Hadn't become the man Landon had demanded he be.

Tonight Robert had come closer to being that man, that *Wyatt*, than he ever had before and it was necessary and important but it was also…unsettling that he had it in him.

He could do bad things, even if for good reasons.

But not to her. Never to her.

He trusted Jeannie, tonight more than ever. He needed her this one last time and then he'd let her go.

Jeannie lifted his arms into the air and then slid onto his lap. Instantly, the warmth of her core rocketed through his body. She wasn't wearing panties, he realized with a jolt. "Jeannie," he groaned as she pulled his arms down so his knotted wrists were looped around her neck. Because this counted as touching and God help him, he needed it. Needed to feel her over him, around him, under him.

One last time, he repeated silently to himself. That was all this was.

"Hush." She shifted back, her weight perfect on his lap

as her hands moved to his trousers. She undid his belt and zipper in silence.

He opened his mouth to tell her where the condoms were—inside pocket of his jacket—but that was when she reached over and snagged that tiny purse Maja had handed her. When she opened it, a strip of condoms popped out like a jack-in-the-box without the terrifying clown.

"You're prepared," he said, his breath coming faster as she snapped off one and tore it open.

"Luck favors the prepared. Now quiet." She had to grab at his jacket as they took a corner. In that moment he felt the strength of her thighs' grip on his legs. She was so strong. God, he loved it.

Then she grinned at him as she smoothed out his lapel and added, "Or else."

Desire pounded through him at that challenge. She'd already tied him up. How far would she go?

She rolled on the condom and Robert realized he was holding his breath as her fingers stroked over his length, hard with wanting her.

"Or else what?" he heard himself ask through gritted teeth.

Her grip on him tightened. "Or else," she whispered, leaning forward to let her lips brush over his earlobe, trapping his aching erection between them, "I'll touch you. Slowly."

As if to demonstrate, her fisted hand slid up over his shaft, the lubrication of the condom smoothing the way. His breath caught in his throat as he strained against her. It was too much—far, far too much—and yet not enough.

"Yes, like that," she whispered, her voice nothing but breath that caressed over his skin. "And harder." Her grip tightened as her hand moved back down, inch by agonizing inch.

A groan ripped free because she was touching him and

he was letting her and it was something new, and he'd never been so turned on in his entire life.

"Then," she said, shifting so his length was pressed against her sex, trapped in her embrace, "then I'd touch you here, too."

Her hand slipped down, cupping his balls and pressing up ever so gently as her hips moved, dragging his tip over her.

"Jeannie," he moaned, helpless to stop her, helpless for her.

"And then?" She pushed back, his arms still around her neck, his hands in tight fists as he let go of everything but the way her hand squeezed him, tormented him—made him whole again.

She smiled, wickedness brought to life. "Then I'd stop."

She pulled her hand away.

For all that he'd trained himself to control his emotions, control his reactions, Robert couldn't help it—he whimpered.

Her smile was pure victory. "Will you be quiet?"

He nodded. It was all he could do.

"Thank God," she said, raising herself onto her knees and positioning him at her entrance.

Then she sank down on him, taking him in completely until Robert was on the verge of losing control.

"Just be," she said, her breathing faster now. "Just be with me, Robert."

Although it was a risk, he had to let her know. "Always."

She would always be this perfect memory, this utterly wonderful moment in time when he was the man she needed and she was his everything.

One last time.

The car came to a somewhat sudden stop and she scrabbled to grab hold of his jacket to keep from falling right off him. He used his bound hands to pull her back to him, her breasts flush with his chest and in that moment, he wished he hadn't insisted on the clothing because he wanted to see her in her nude glory, feel her body against his.

He didn't just want part of her. He wanted all of her.

One last time. Dammit.

Giggling, she leaned back, but he didn't let her pull away. He kept her against his chest, feeling her nipples harden through the thin fabric of her dress as she rose and fell on him.

He needed to touch her. He'd never needed anything so badly in his life.

Somehow, he got his wrists shifted so he could cup the back of her head and tangle his fingers in her short hair.

"Robert," she sighed softly as he angled her head toward his. "What…"

"Kiss me." He wasn't begging because Wyatts didn't beg, but it wasn't an order, either. "I need you to kiss me while I'm inside you."

He felt the shudder move through her body and then her lips were on his, their tongues touching and retreating and touching again, all while she rode him and he held her, and this was the moment he would never forget. No matter what happened in an hour or tomorrow or next month, no one would ever take this moment from him.

She moved faster and faster, chasing her climax and all he could do was grit it out and hold on until she'd found her release.

When she threw back her head, the lines of her neck taut, he did the only thing he could—he leaned forward and buried his face between her breasts. The diamond pendant hit him in the nose but he didn't care as he kissed her there, thrusting up into her as he let go.

He let go.

How could he ever let her go?

Fifteen

Jeannie could feel the goodbye in the air as Reginald opened the car door after what felt like an unnaturally long pause. Probably giving them time to set their clothing to rights.

Thoughtful man, that Reginald. She hoped Robert gave him a raise.

But he needn't have worried because after the most amazing orgasm of her entire life—which was saying something because the one last week had been pretty damn spectacular—Robert had gently lifted her off him and then buttoned up. In complete silence.

Yep. The goodbye was definitely in the air.

Robert helped her out of the limo and then, with an unbelievable, "Thank you, Reginald," he swept Jeannie right off her feet. Literally.

"Robert!" she shrieked as he tossed her into the air a little, adjusting his hold.

"Your shoes aren't made for sand," he said as if that was all the explanation necessary.

"Honestly," she laughed, but she linked her arms around his neck and let her head rest on his shoulder.

He hummed. He sounded happy. *Please*, she thought, *let him be happy.*

Without another word, he carried her down the beach. She didn't know where they were, but far north of Chicago proper, she guessed. She could see the orange glow of the city to the south but out over the lake, all she could see were…

"Stars," she breathed. Hundreds of them. Millions, maybe.

"Yes," he agreed in that Robert way as if he had personally decreed there would be stars and lo, the universe had made it happen.

He walked on, his pace slow as he ruined his shiny tuxedo shoes in the sand. "Where are we going?"

"Away from the light," he replied, as cryptic as ever.

The night sky stretched out vast and endless before her. The moon was nowhere to be seen, so the only way to differentiate between the water and the sky was the twinkling of light.

"It's beautiful," she sighed. So many stars—if only she had that many wishes.

But she'd already gotten what she'd asked for, hadn't she? More than that. She had a nanny and a maid and a reasonably good grip on how to care for Melissa. She had a lawyer who was working on a settlement from the hospital to make sure Melissa would always be cared for.

And she'd had the most amazing, complicated, messy, perfect man in Chicago at her mercy.

No, she wouldn't wish on another star. If there was one thing she'd learned over the years, it was not to push her luck.

After long, quiet minutes, Robert set her down on her feet. She slid her hand into his and leaned against his shoulder. A breeze flowed off the lake and despite the warm summer temperature, she shivered. It was always cooler by the lake.

"Here," he said gruffly, removing his jacket and draping it over her shoulders.

"Thank you." The superfine wool smelled like him, dark and spicy with just a hint of champagne and orange on top. The smell of them together. He wrapped his arm around her shoulders, holding her tight.

Her knees began to shake. "Robert?" She wanted to ask before she lost her nerve.

"Hmm?"

"Have you ever been in love?"

"No." He didn't even hesitate. The word was out like a gunshot and it made her heart ache for him.

Then he leaned down and pressed his cheek against her hair. "At least…not yet."

Dammit. He was going to make this painful, wasn't he?

"What about you?" he asked when she failed to come up with anything to say.

Oh, how their situations had reversed. "A few times."

"What happened?"

She shrugged. "I was young and foolish. Sometimes…" She had to swallow to get around the rock that had suddenly appeared in her throat. "Sometimes you fall in love with the wrong person at the right time and you don't realize it until times change. And sometimes…"

She blinked against her stinging eyes and focused on the stars. Their light, hopeful and bright against the darkest of times, wavered. Must be the breeze.

"And sometimes," he finished for her, his voice thoughtful, "you fall in love with the right person at the wrong time."

She had to blink some more. Damned wind.

"I don't want this to be the wrong time," she said. *De-*

manded. "This isn't the wrong time. And you're *not* the wrong person."

"No," he finally said.

But she knew him too well, didn't she? She heard the pain and confusion and loss and love in his voice, all blurred together in that one syllable. Two measly letters were all it took to break her heart, apparently.

"Robert, listen," she began, desperate to hold on to him. They'd only just gotten started! There was so much more between them. So much more than a perfect Manhattan and a fake lady. "I'll—"

"No." Another two measly letters. She was really beginning to hate that syllable. He looked down at her, cupping her cheek in his strong hand. "I won't ask it of you."

"Please," she whispered. "We can—"

He just shook his head and then he leaned down and kissed her.

He kissed her goodbye.

"Ask me," she murmured against his ear. "Please, Robert. Just ask."

He stared down at her, his forehead resting against hers. "I have to keep you safe, Jeannie. I won't let any harm come to you or Melissa."

"You won't. I know you won't."

When he didn't reply to that, she snapped. To hell with his rules. She dug her fingers into his hair and dragged her lips across his, biting and sucking and showing him how much more there could be between them, if only he'd trust her.

If only he'd trust himself.

He was breathing hard when he broke the kiss. He pulled her hands away from his head and then swept her back into his arms. The walk back was silent and awful and far, far too short because he'd made up his mind and who was she to try and change it? She was nobody.

She was just his bartender. A pretend lady, a willing accomplice, a sympathetic ear and a shoulder to lean on. Nothing more.

She would not cry. Wind be darned.

Eventually, they made it back to where Reginald and the limo were waiting. This time Robert opened her door for her and handed her inside. But instead of climbing in after her, he shut the door.

"Robert," she almost shouted, feeling frantic. Was he not even going to give her a proper goodbye?

Of course not, because talking was not Dr. Robert Wyatt's strong suit. Instead, he heard the muffled sound of Reginald getting behind the wheel and, even more distant, Robert saying, "Take her home."

"Yes, sir."

The car started and she rolled down the window. "Robert!" she yelled. "I'll wait." The car started to move. "I'll be waiting!" she shouted out the window.

The car turned and the breeze blew so she couldn't be sure but she thought she heard him say, *"Sailboat."*

Damn him.

But then, what had she expected?

"You're back early. How was your evening?" Maja said from the recliner where Melissa was asleep on her chest. The whole place smelled like lemons and every surface shone like the top of the Chrysler Building.

That was because of Robert.

The right man at the wrong time.

"Fine," Jeannie said dully. Because, really, it was the wrong time. He was about to go to war with his father, and Jeannie had to figure out how to be a mother for the rest of her life and she couldn't expect Robert to foot the bill for polished woodwork and overnight nannies forever.

Maja's grandmotherly face wrinkled in concern. "Is everything all right, dear?"

"Fine," Jeannie repeated. She stared down at her sandals and the Valentino dress that had cost God only knew how much, at the heavy diamond pendant that had definitely cost too much.

Robert was the right man and she was hopelessly in love with him.

But Dr. Robert Wyatt, billionaire bachelor and noted surgeon—he was the wrong man. For someone like her. Because she could pretend to fit into his world, but they both knew she didn't belong there.

God, she hated goodbyes.

"Dear?"

Jeannie looked up with a start to see Maja standing in front of her. "I've decided to go back to work. In two weeks. I don't know how long you're going to be able to watch Melissa for me but—" she swallowed "—if you could at least help me line up alternative childcare before you go. Something I could afford."

Because she couldn't afford Maja or Rona or Reginald or any of them.

Maja looked tired in the dim light. "I'm paid for three months, which leaves us quite a bit of time to make plans." She sighed again, disappointment on her face. "I'm sorry things didn't work out with your handsome doctor."

But he'd never been hers, had he? They had been like... this outfit. Like Lady Daphne FitzRoy. An illusion.

"So am I," she said, the tears starting to fall. "So am I."

Sixteen

Robert called for a ride, which was a novel experience. By the time the driver picked him up, Robert had himself under control. He'd done the right thing. Jeannie might be upset now but he was confident that a woman as worldly and intelligent as she was would see how this was for the best by the light of day.

She still had his jacket, but his vest smelled faintly of oranges.

God, he was tired. Tired of dealing with Landon, worrying about his mother, tired of holding himself back, tired of being Robert Wyatt.

Just be with me, Jeannie had said. Of all the things she'd given him, that might've been her greatest gift.

But it didn't matter how tired he was—his night was just beginning.

Kelly texted just as the car hit Lake Shore Drive.

He's at your house.

Status?

Speech was a disaster.
Social media is asking if he was high.
Visibly upset.
Banging on your door.
Hasn't broken anything.

Don't interfere yet.

Yes, sir.

Robert focused on breathing. Slow. Steady. Orange-scented. Everything was going according to plan. Landon had discovered that his wife, son and a random woman who might or might not have been nobility had all disappeared from his grand kickoff campaign gala. As Robert had hoped, Landon had not taken the news well.

Robert was counting on the next part. He didn't have long to wait.

He just put a planter through your front door.
Alarm is blaring.

Wait until he gets in
then have him arrested.

Because that was the fail-safe of his plan. He could fund civil lawsuits and give federal investigators access to financial reports but Landon was a slippery bastard and money talked.

Breaking and entering, however, was harder to disprove. Especially when there were security tapes, off-duty officers as witnesses and a son who refused to drop charges.

The driver turned onto Robert's street. "Here is fine,"

Robert said, fishing a hundred out of his wallet. He didn't know what the tipping protocol was but rare was the person who'd turn down cash.

"Hey—anytime, man! You're going to get a great rating out of this!"

Robert had no idea what the man was talking about but he didn't care. As he got out of the car, he could hear his alarm screaming into the night and, underneath that, sirens in the distance.

"Get your hands off me! Do you know who I am?" Landon Wyatt's screech of rage cut through the noise.

"What's going on here?" Robert said, aiming for concerned innocence. "Father? What are you doing here?"

"Where is she?" Landon screamed, lurching at Robert.

"Easy, buddy," the officer said, hauling Landon back. Robert recognized Officer Hernandez; he'd covered the Hernandezes' outstanding balance for a recent procedure.

Landon's arms were handcuffed behind his back. The sight made Robert almost smile because it was something he could definitely get used to seeing. "Where is who?"

"You know damned well, you useless bastard. Where is *she*?"

Robert made a big show of looking up at his dark house. "No one's home. I just got here." Kelly sidled up the sidewalk and Robert spotted the reporters, cameras flashing and video recording. "My date got sick and I took her home. I don't think we'll be seeing each other anymore," he explained for the audience.

Landon snarled and lunged again. This time the other officer had to use so much force to hold him back that Landon wound up on his knees in the middle of the sidewalk.

"You'll pay for this," he said, his eyes bugging out. "By the time I get done with you, you all will wish you'd never been born!"

The officers made as if to haul him up but Robert waved

them off. Instead, he crouched down in front of Landon, who was struggling to get to his feet. Robert put a hand on the older man's shoulder and forced him back down because that was what a Wyatt would do. Dominate. Control.

Robert demanded respect, but right now, from this man, he'd settle for fear.

The older man's eyes widened with surprise as his muscles tensed under Robert's hands. "What do you think you're doing?"

Robert leaned close. He didn't want anyone to hear this. "You'll never see her again."

"I'll find her," Landon barked with a truly maniacal laugh. No wonder everyone at the gallery had been asking if he was high. Robert's plan was working perfectly. "You can't keep her safe. You never could. She's mine! And after I find her, I'll find that duchess of yours, whoever she was. And I'll make her pay." He licked his lips and tried to surge to his feet again. "I can't wait. Will she scream your name in the end, do you think?"

Robert didn't allow any emotion to cross his face. But he tightened his grip on the old man's shoulder, feeling the muscles clench and grind under his hand and he made *damn* sure Landon stayed down on his knees.

"Do you have any idea how easy it would be to get you out onto a boat and drop you in the middle of the lake?" It was a struggle to keep his voice level, but given the way Landon went rigid with what Robert hoped was fear, he thought he'd done a good job. "But I'm not going to do that because you deserve so much more than a quick, easy death." He tightened his grip on the old man's shoulder and by God, he bowed under the pressure. "No matter how hard you look, you'll never find either of them."

Robert had lived his entire life in fear of this man but in the end, it wasn't that hard to take control. He was a Wyatt and that was what they did.

"Try me," Landon said but the menace had bled out of his voice and instead, he sounded like a man who was starting to realize he'd made a grave tactical error.

Because he had.

"You're going to be divorced, sued, arrested and tried and, if I have anything to say about it, found guilty on charges of sexual assault, embezzlement, campaign finance fraud, breaking and entering, and God only knows what else my people are uncovering as we speak." Robert forced himself to stare into Landon's eyes because Robert was in charge now. It was Landon's turn to cower because he'd come up against a force he couldn't dominate. "And we haven't even rolled Alexander yet. But we will."

"Sir?" Kelly cleared his throat. Robert was running out of time to say his piece. "Sorry to interrupt but I've just received word that Alexander Trudeau has been picked up on charges of money laundering."

It was hard to tell under the yellow light from the streetlamps, but Robert thought Landon had suddenly gone pale. "See?" he said with a smile. Because now he could smile in front of Landon, just to watch the old man squirm. "Not that hard to roll, after all."

"You son of a bitch," Landon said, starting to struggle again. "I'll get you for this."

"Oh, you'll try, but you'll be busy with the lawsuits and trials. And I do think this marks the end of your career in politics, doesn't it? Everything you ever had or wanted, gone." Robert snapped his fingers. "Just like that. And do you know why, *Dad*?"

Landon glared at him but Robert didn't feel the usual panic churning up his stomach.

He smiled again, this time for real. "Because this is what you raised me to do." He let go of the old man's shoulder and, as he broke that singular point of contact, a sense of finality washed over him. "I hope you're happy with what you created."

This wasn't over, not by a long shot. But they were done.

Freed of Robert's grip, Landon surged up. "I'll kill you!" he screamed, flecks of spittle flying off his lips. "I'll kill that bitch and that whore in front of you and then *I'll end you*!"

Robert got ready to throw a punch but then Officer Hernandez and his partner were there. One drew his gun but Robert said, "No need for that, Officer." Landon straightened and smiled in victory, but then Robert added, "If you have to subdue him, use the Taser."

Landon screamed in rage but Robert just smiled. God, it felt good to smile.

It felt good to *win*.

The cops led a struggling, furious Landon to the police car. As they closed the door on what had, just a few hours ago, been the most powerful man in Chicago, Robert straightened his cuffs and stood tall.

Landon Wyatt's era was over and there would be no redemption tour.

There was a lot of talking after that—Robert gave a statement to the cops and confirmed that, yes, he would like to press charges and yes, his father had a temper but no, he'd never made death threats before and yes, perhaps a restraining order would be a good thing.

He obtained security footage and talked with lawyers and judges and began circulating rumors that Cybil Wyatt had been on the verge of leaving Landon but had been convinced to stay for the campaign but after this…

And even when dawn broke over Lake Michigan and the last star blinked out of sight, Robert didn't stop because there was so much to do. He had to contact members of the board of Wyatt Medical and make sure that his mother had landed safely in LA and taken off again and he had to do rounds at the hospital.

He couldn't stop.

Because if he did, he'd think of Jeannie. And if he thought of her, he might not be able to stay away and it wasn't safe yet. Not yet, damn it all.

Sailboat.

Seventeen

"He's not going to come back just because you're back, is he?" Miranda asked as Jeannie grabbed the crate of clean wineglasses. "If he is, I'm not dealing with him."

"He won't," Jeannie replied. "Can you move? This is heavy." Honestly, could Miranda just give her a little space?

It'd be nice if everyone at Trenton's could give her a little space on her first night back. Sure, there'd been a cake and a few baby presents but did anyone actually ask about Melissa? Nope. It was all Robert, all the time. Had he contacted her after he'd left the bar? Did she know anything about the all-out war being waged in the press and in the courts between the elder Wyatt and his son? Or, worst of all, what did she make of that mysterious "duchess" who'd appeared on Robert's arm at the ill-fated campaign kickoff but had disappeared right before everything had gone to hell and didn't she look familiar?

Maybe Robert had left a bigger mark on her than she'd realized because she had apparently perfected his icy glare.

At least she could blame her mood on the baby. Poor Melissa, taking the fall.

But it was fine. Things were always rough after a breakup and this was kind of one.

She was just about to back through the swinging door that separated the kitchen from the bar when it burst open, knocking into her. She had to juggle the crate of glasses but she managed not to drop the danged thing. "What the—"

"He's here!" Julian said in a panic, moving so fast he ran into her again.

Jeannie managed to get the crate of glass onto a countertop because suddenly, her hands had started to shake.

Miranda asked, "Who?" in a terrified whisper, the blood draining from her face.

"Him! Wyatt!"

"Breathe," Jeannie said. What was he doing here? He'd made it clear they were done and he was protecting her or something by staying away and she wasn't to wait for him. Done, done, *done*.

Or not.

"Should we call the police?" Julian asked, hands clutched in front of his chest.

Jeannie rolled her eyes. "For the love of everything holy, no. I'll handle this."

She took a second to compose herself. Which wasn't easy because not only did she have to deal with Miranda and Julian quaking in fear but also the whole kitchen staff had gone quiet, and even the normal sounds of the restaurant and bar were almost nonexistent.

She pushed through the swinging door to find herself squarely in the sights of Dr. Robert Wyatt, in his normal spot. When he saw her, his eyes narrowed and—big surprise—he adjusted his cuffs.

He'd come for her. And to think, there hadn't been a single star in the sky last night. Not even an airplane she could pretend was a star. But she'd hoped against hope that one day Robert might slide into his seat and order his Manhattan and give her that almost invisible smile and tell her everything was perfect again.

That they could be perfect together, because the time was right.

But Jeannie saw more than that. She saw how he was moving as if his leg was bouncing against the rung of the bar stool. And how, when he wasn't adjusting his cuffs, he was tapping his fingers on the bar.

How about that. Not only had Robert put in a surprise appearance, but the man was nervous about it, too. None of that mattered, though, because he'd come for *her*.

Unless something else had gone wrong? That thought led to a sickening drop in her stomach because what if he wasn't here for her? What if he...just needed a sympathetic ear and a drink?

"Well?" asked Julian from behind the door. "Cops?"

"*No*, for Pete's sake. Just leave us—him—alone." She let the door swing back and heard a muffled yelp. That was what Julian got for peeking. She made her way down the bar. Robert's intense gaze never once left hers.

"Robert." She winced. "Dr. Wyatt. The usual?"

"Jeannie."

For as long as she'd known this man—years now—every word he spoke could either make her fall further in love with him or break her heart.

Dear God, please don't let the sound of her name on his lips be another heartbreak. She couldn't take much more.

Then he smiled. That small movement of his lips curving up just at the corners, where no one else would think to look for it. But she saw it. She saw him. Maybe she always had.

Her hands hadn't stopped trembling but she ignored them as she filled a glass with his Manhattan and added the twist.

She had to use both hands to steady it as she placed the drink on the bar.

"Here for your drink?" she managed to get out, proud of the way her voice stayed level. Not a verbal tremble in sight.

"No." He didn't even look at his drink. "I'm here for you."

Her breath caught in her throat. "Me?" she squeaked. Dammit.

"Us," he corrected. Before she could process those two little letters—that one measly syllable—he dropped his gaze to a tablet she hadn't noticed on the bar next to him. "Here's the thing."

"Oh?" Her heart began to pound wildly out of control but she didn't say anything else. He'd get to it in his own sweet time.

He tapped the screen and called up a picture of a...mansion?

"Robert?" If he'd bought her a huge house out of guilt or something, she was going to have to draw the line. She and Melissa did *not* need a mansion.

"I bought it through a shell company, so there aren't any names on the paperwork, just to be sure," he began, tapping more to bring up additional pictures of a gorgeous house with amazing decorating—clean lines, warm colors and not a single shred of tacky wallpaper. "It overlooks the lake and there's a path down to a small private beach." More pictures whizzed by—was that an indoor pool? "It's got a clear view of the night sky—the light pollution doesn't drown out the stars." A victorious smile spread across his face. "I made sure of that."

"Robert," she said, barely able to get the words out. "What is this?"

He straightened in his chair before straightening his cuffs. "My mother sends her thanks for your help. I put my home in her name so that, when she's able to come back, she can enjoy the wallpapered ceilings to the fullest extent."

Oh, God. "Did you…give up your house?"

He nodded once, a quick and efficient movement. But she could tell that his leg was still jiggling and, when he started to straighten his cuffs for the third time in as many minutes, she reached over the bar and took his hands in hers. Behind her, someone gasped. Probably Miranda.

"Robert," she said again, softly. "Tell me what's happened."

A look of need flashed over his face and was gone, replaced by imperial iciness. "I don't want you to wait for me," he said in a gruff voice.

None of this made sense. There was something going on here, something that would tie the houses and his jumping leg and his very straight cuffs together and she was missing it.

"I will," she told him. "As long as it takes, I will."

He shook his head firmly and said, "No, I mean…wait." He took a deep breath and then, miracle of miracles, laced his fingers with hers. "I was supposed to stay away from you because Landon still has a lot of power and if he knew who you were, you'd be in danger and you…" Jeannie's heart kicked into overdrive. "You're very important to me."

"Oh?" He wasn't the only one who could wield single syllables in a conversation, dammit.

He stared down at their hands. "I've never been in love so I don't know for certain that this is that. But I need you. I need to see you every day so I can talk to you and you can make me laugh and touch me and make me feel…right. I don't feel right without you anymore and I tried. *I tried*," he repeated, sounding mad about that.

No, she couldn't imagine that Dr. Robert Wyatt tried and failed at too many things. Her eyes began to burn and this time there was no lake breeze to blame it on.

"But then I realized that by staying away from you to

keep you safe, I was still letting him win because he still dictated what I did and how I did it and you know what?"

"What?" she said breathlessly. Why was there a stupid bar between them? Why wasn't he in her arms for this— this—this declaration of love? Because that was what it was.

He loved her.

Oh, thank God.

"To hell with him. He can't win," Robert said fiercely and she knew this was a man who would lay down his life to protect her. "I won't allow it. If I want to be with you, I'm going to be with you because you are the right person for me, Jeannie Kaufman, and I will *make* it the right time."

Of course he would. He was a Wyatt. "So you bought a mansion?"

"For you. You and me and Melissa and…us." He looked up at her and she saw love and worry and hope in his eyes. Finally, hope. "For our family, whether it grows or not."

She almost fell over. *"Robert."*

"Marry me," he said and damn if it didn't sound like an order. But before she could call him on it, he quickly added, "Wait. No, let me do that again." He lifted her hands to his lips and kissed her knuckles like he really was a duke of the realm and she was the tavern wench who'd won his heart. "You've shown me what love is, Jeannie. And I want to spend the rest of my life sharing it with you. We can get married or not. I'm not your boss and you're not my employee or even my bartender. You're the woman I need and I hope I can be the man you want."

"Oh, Robert," she said, tears flowing.

"You're crying," he said, alarmed.

"I love you, too, you complicated, messy, wonderful man." But then the past few weeks flashed before her eyes— his reaction after the first time they'd made love, the way his father had treated him and his mother, the fact that the legal mess was going to be the headline for weeks and months to come. "And I do want to marry you—on one condition."

"Name it," he said with a devastatingly gorgeous smile. "Anything. I can buy a different house or…"

"I've never wanted you for your money." Something deepened in his eyes. An answering shiver of desire raced down her back. "But I want you to see a counselor to help you work through your…*issues* because marriage isn't a magical cure-all. You have to work on some things yourself."

He didn't even hesitate, bless the man. "Yes. Of course. I'll work on talking and hugging and…" His cheeks darkened and she had to wonder—was he *blushing*? "What else?"

She began to laugh and cry at the same time and that was when Robert let go of her hands and then vaulted over the bar. *Vaulted!* Then he had her crushed to his chest, his mouth on hers and those were definitely gasps because not only was he kissing her, he was also doing so in public. "Anything else, Jeannie?" he said against her lips. "*Anything* for you. If you want to work a bar, I'll buy you one. I'll buy you this one, if you want."

Behind them, she heard a squeak of alarm and rolled her eyes.

"We can make plans later but—will you adopt Melissa?"

He scoffed at that. "Of course."

"Will you just *be* with me, Robert? Through good times and the not-great times?"

His hands flattened against her back. She couldn't get close enough. "There is nowhere else I'd ever want to be if it's not by your side."

"Then the answer is yes because you're the right man, Robert."

He grinned wolfishly and dear Lord, he was just the most handsome man in the world and he was choosing her.

Epilogue

"**P**ackage for you, Cybil," Bridget said as the physical therapist, Anne, moved Cybil into the last stretch. "It's on your chair. I'll get your water."

"Thank you." Cybil smiled, despite the burning exhaustion that went with a tough PT appointment.

She liked being *just* Cybil. She liked being Bridget's equal. She liked the quiet villa in Kauri Cliffs, at the far north end of New Zealand. She even liked being disconnected from the rest of the world. By and large, she didn't want to know what was happening back home. She had no interest in keeping up-to-date on what her soon-to-be ex-husband was doing. She wasn't available for comment on news stories.

She could focus on herself. It was selfish and something she was still getting used to—but with the help of a psychologist and a physical therapist, she was rediscovering who she'd been before Landon Wyatt and, more important, who she wanted to be after him.

"You're the right woman for me and when it's right, there is no wrong time. Not if I have anything to say about it. After all, I'm a Wyatt." He leaned down but instead of kissing her, he whispered in her ear, "And soon you'll be one, too."

And just like that, she fell more in love with him.

"Perfect," she told him.

Because it was.

But most of all, she was getting used to talking with her son again. Not every day, because he was still a busy man, but at least every other day. At one in the afternoon her time, Bobby would call at what was eight his time. They talked of her progress and his work. They'd avoided discussions of Landon, but after a while, Bobby had begun to mention Jeannie more and more.

She wished she could've been there for the wedding, but someone named Darna had streamed the whole civil ceremony, all fourteen minutes of it, for Cybil to see.

For the first time in decades, she could breathe again.

"There," Anne said, helping Cybil to stand. She wobbled a little—today had been tough. "Make sure to drink plenty of fluids, okay? I'll see you in two days."

Cybil patted the young woman's shoulder and gratefully sank into her chair, the package in her hands.

She'd received mail from Bobby before, legal notices of her divorce proceedings, usually—her son had hired an absolute shark of a lawyer. But this felt different.

Her hands began to shake and it wasn't just from the physical exertion.

Ah, her divorce papers. It was done. She was no longer legally bound to Landon Wyatt and it appeared half of his earnings from throughout their awful marriage were now hers. She was an independently wealthy woman. No longer would she have to beg for money or wear what Landon bought for her. She could do as she saw fit.

The next thing in the envelope was the front page of the *Chicago Tribune*, with a handwritten note that said, "Any deposition can be handled safely and your income will be protected—R." Landon Wyatt was being charged for criminal sexual assault—several maids and employees had come forward to press charges. Represented, she knew, by a lawyer Bobby had chosen. Oh, but this was new— Wyatt Medical had voted him out as CEO and Landon was also being investigated by the SEC for insider trading and campaign fraud? Apparently, Alexander, Landon's assistant, had turned on him. All his friends had abandoned him and his political aspirations were dead in the water. His disgrace was complete and if Bobby had anything to say about it, Landon would spend a good chunk of the rest of his life in jail.

How fitting. She wanted to savor this moment, this permanent freedom.

But then a cream envelope fluttered out of the package and Cybil's breath caught in her throat. She knew she was crying as she read the engraved print, but she simply didn't care.

"Dr. Robert Wyatt and Jeannie Kaufman are pleased to announce their marriage in a private ceremony on October 12. They are also proud to welcome Melissa Nicole Wyatt to the family."

The next thing was a slim hardbound book. Oh, he'd sent her a wedding album! When she opened the cover, a handwritten note slid out. "I took a chance on happiness," the note read in Bobby's scrawled handwriting. "That's because of you."

"Oh, Bobby," she sighed. He'd always been such a thoughtful boy. Thank God Landon had never succeeded in destroying that.

She flipped through the album, greedily taking in the signs of happiness.

The first picture showed Bobby and Jeannie standing side by side. Bobby was smiling down at his bride. Smiling! Dear God, it did her heart good to see her son looking at peace—the same peace she was beginning to feel.

Cybil barely recognized Jeannie as the same woman who had gotten her away from Landon with a well-placed glass of champagne. In real life, Jeannie smiled wider, had kinder eyes and looked downright sweet in her tea-length lace gown in a soft shade of rose pink that was gorgeous on her.

Cybil fondly traced a finger over the picture. Bobby would need someone bold and daring, someone strong enough to withstand his personality—and someone who would understand why he was the way he was but would never pity him. If that was his bartender, then that was the perfect woman for him.

The second picture showed Bobby and his new wife with a small infant. Only a few months old, the little girl was wrapped in a soft blanket, grinning a toothless grin up at Bobby from Jeannie's arms. Bobby's hand cupped the baby's cheek with such tenderness that Cybil's eyes watered again.

A note was paper-clipped to the page. "We'll bring her out soon—R."

"Everything all right?" Bridget said, concern in her voice as she sat the tea tray down. "You're crying!"

"I'm a grandmother," Cybil got out as she showed Bridget the album. "Look at my family!"

"Oh, wow," Bridget said, sounding wistful. "They look so happy!"

Happy. It was a long-cherished dream, one that had gotten Cybil through so many dark times. "You know," Cybil said, dabbing at her tears, "I do believe they are."

* * * * *

LET'S TALK

Romance

For exclusive extracts, competitions
and special offers, find us online:

f facebook.com/millsandboon

🐦 @MillsandBoon

📷 @MillsandBoonUK

Get in touch on 01413 063232

For all the latest titles coming soon, visit
millsandboon.co.uk/nextmonth